Belle Ruin

MARTHA GRIMES

Belle Ruin

VIKING

VIKING
Published by the Penguin Group
Penguin Group (USA) Inc., 375 Hudson Street, New York, New York 10014, U.S.A.
Penguin Group (Canada), 90 Eglinton Avenue East, Suite 700, Toronto, Ontario, Canada M4P 2Y3
(a division of Pearson Penguin Canada Inc.)
Penguin Books Ltd, 80 Strand, London WC2R 0RL, England
Penguin Ireland, 25 St. Stephen's Green, Dublin 2, Ireland (a division of Penguin Books Ltd)
Penguin Books Australia Ltd, 250 Camberwell Road, Camberwell, Victoria 3124, Australia
(a division of Pearson Australia Group Pty Ltd)
Penguin Books India Pvt Ltd, 11 Community Centre, Panchsheel Park, New Delhi – 110 017, India
Penguin Group (NZ), Cnr Airborne and Rosedale Roads, Albany, Auckland 1310, New Zealand
(a division of Pearson New Zealand Ltd)
Penguin Books (South Africa) (Pty) Ltd, 24 Sturdee Avenue, Rosebank, Johannesburg 2196, South Africa

Penguin Books Ltd, Registered Offices:
80 Strand, London WC2R 0RL, England

First published in 2005 by Viking Penguin,
a member of Penguin Group (USA) Inc.

10 9 8 7 6 5 4 3 2 1

Grateful acknowledgment is made for permission to reprint excerpts from the following
copyrighted works:
   "Dust in the Eyes" from *The Poetry of Robert Frost*, edited by Edward Connery Lathem.
Copyright 1928, 1969 by Henry Holt and Company. © 1956 by Robert Frost. Reprinted by
arrangement with Henry Holt and Company, LLC.
   "Cocktails for Two," from the Paramount motion picture *Murder at the Vanities*. Words and music
by Arthur Johnston and Sam Coslow. Copyright © 1934 (renewed 1961) by Famous Music
Corporation. International copyright secured. All rights reserved.
   "Tonight You Belong to Me" by Billy Rose and Lee David. © 1926 (renewed) Chappell & Co. and
C & J David Music Co. © 1926, renewed C & J David Music. All rights reserved. Used by
permission. Warner Bros. Publications U.S. Inc., Miami, Florida.

Publisher's Note
This is a work of fiction. Names, characters, places, and incidents either are the product of the
author's imagination or are used fictitiously, and any resemblance to actual persons, living or dead,
business establishments, events, or locales is entirely coincidental.

LIBRARY OF CONGRESS CATALOGING IN PUBLICATION DATA

Grimes, Martha.
Belle ruin : a novel / Martha Grimes.
      p.   cm.
ISBN 0-670-03461-4
1. Graham, Emma (Fictitious character)—Fiction.   2. Summer resorts—Fiction.
3. Hotels—Fiction.   4. Girls—Fiction.   I. Title.
PS3557.R48998B45 2005
813'.54—dc22   2005042289

Printed in the United States of America
Set in Berkeley
Designed by Daniel Lagin

To little Scott Holland
and his mom, Travis,
and the way home,
Love
(with crinkles on it).

If, as they say, some dust thrown in my eyes
Will keep my talk from getting overwise,
I'm not the one for putting off the proof.
Let it be overwhelming, off a roof
And round a corner, blizzard snow for dust,
And blind me to a standstill if it must.

—Robert Frost, "Dust in the Eyes"

1

"*Fame will not wither her, nor custom stale / Her infinite variety.*"

Dwayne quoted that to me, saying it was by Shakespeare. It's really "age," not "fame," he said, but he changed it to suit my life. "Age" (he said) could hardly be a threat to someone who's twelve years old ("and has been for a long time," I thought he didn't need to add). And my recent fame is the most notable thing that's happened around Spirit Lake since, well, forever. He said Shakespeare was describing Cleopatra, also famous in her time, almost as famous as I was. He was telling me this while he was under Bobby Stuck's old Studebaker. Dwayne is a master mechanic.

I was sitting on a stack of new tires in Abel Slaw's Garage. I was not supposed to be in here with the cars and tools and lifts, so I waited until Abel Slaw got on his office telephone and then came in. I've never seen anyone who could spend as much time on the telephone as him.

Dwayne pushed out from under the Studebaker on one of those flat things with wheels and went back to looking under the hood. The trouble with all this is I can't see his face when he's under the car and can see only half of it when he's bent under the hood, so I can't tell if he's smiling and laughing at me inside. He can kid around a lot and it's nearly impossible to tell if I can't see his face.

I know it must seem like I've been twelve years old for a long time, but that's only because so much has been crammed into a few weeks, and I have to put in all these details, like Dwayne being a "master" mechanic, a detail I'm going to probably drop, which is what I told him.

"Don't I wish."

That's Dwayne with his head down under the hood of the Studebaker.

I want to review what's happened, not the entire story (which you should already know if you've been paying attention at all), but just the very end, where my fame starts to assert itself. (I've picked up some smart words from the newspaper articles about me.) My fame is the "aftermath" of the crime. The crime and its aftermath. The crime was really something, blood and bullets, which happened to me and that's the reason for its aftermath. And sometimes I almost think it's even more important than the crime.

The aftermath had reporters sitting on the porch of the Hotel Paradise, rocking in the dark green porch rockers, drinking coffee or martinis (depending on who's hosting, my mother or Lola Davidow) as if they were hotel guests who'd paid for the privilege, and asking me questions about what happened at the boathouse on Spirit Lake, and wasn't I terrified, and so forth.

This is what I mean: the reporters were there for me. It was hard for my mother and Mrs. Davidow and her unfamous daughter Ree-Jane—*especially* Ree-Jane—to believe. It was hard to believe since I'd spent my whole twelve years without getting serious attention from anyone. To see me the subject of all these newspaper stories, well, it was just too much. My mother was pleased I was famous, Lola Davidow was pleased for an occasion to break out the Gordon's gin and Ree-Jane was not pleased at all.

There we were on the porch, the reporters, my mother, Mrs. Davidow, Ree-Jane and me. My brother Will was not there. He's usually not there. He spends all of his time up in the Big Garage with his best friend and musical genius, Brownmiller (who we called "Mill"), both of them making up songs and scenery for their production. My brother is too busy to care about fame, even his own, which probably says a lot about him. I do not share that attitude. Frankly, I could not be too famous for me.

Details piled upon details, which I have been told is one of the problems about this story. It is drowning in details. Like Mary-Evelyn Devereau drowned in Spirit Lake. Like I almost drowned there, too.

Ree-Jane said that I go on and on, endlessly, that it's boring to bring in every little thing, that I'm boring. I'm endless. She doesn't know the difference between the two things.

Remember, I said this before: it's my story. It's about the Hotel Paradise and Ben Queen and Cold Flat Junction. It could be, like me, endless, me going on endlessly, unwithered and various like Cleopatra. Not that I'm comparing.

"You'd better be careful in those woods. You've got your hunters out there after deer," Dwayne said, his head down almost flush with the engine.

I was inspecting the tread on the pile of tires beneath me. As if I had a car. "It's not deer season."

"It ain't coon season, either, but that doesn't stop some people." He was piercing a can of Sinclair Oil as if it were a beer and now I could see his face. It looked even handsomer in the shadow thrown up by the hood of the car.

"Like you-know-who," I said.

He looked at me. "You been huntin' out of season again?"

"Not me. You."

That's how I met him. It was in another part of the woods, not the deer park, but the woods nearer Lake Noir. It was hard to tell where one wood began and another wood ended. I'd been investigating Brokedown House, if you can call shinnying up a tree "investigating." I'd heard twigs snapping and leaves crisping as if someone were walking my way and I was scared to death. It had turned out to be Dwayne with his shotgun and his sack of dead rabbits. It had been night and one of those black-hole darknesses where it's so dark night just sucks everything into it and you couldn't tell where the tree ended and I began, or the ground ended and he began.

"There's this old hotel," I said, pointing in the direction of the highway beyond the garage. "It burned down one night, all of it, except part of the ground floor is still there. It was a ballroom. This hotel was way bigger than the Hotel Paradise, a lot bigger. It was called the Belle Rouen. That's French." In case he didn't know.

Dwayne watched the oil nozzle and wiped his hands on a greasy rag, the kind all mechanics seem to keep in their back pockets.

"I found out a lot about it from the woman in the historical society. In La Porte."

"Girl, I'd see a deer climb up a tree before I'd ever see you in that museum, studying history."

"What? I know a lot of history."

"You don't even know the history of your *own* hotel, talk about another one." He pushed the oily rag back into his pocket.

I was insulted and jumped off the tires. "I most certainly do! My great-grandfather owned it before my grandfather and my mother (and, I didn't want to remind myself, Lola Davidow). It really belongs to Aurora Paradise and her sister." Aurora Paradise was ninety-one and lived up on the fourth floor.

Dwayne tossed the empty oil can into a big bin and slammed down the hood. "That's not what I mean, precisely. What really went on there?"

I was back sitting on the stack of tires and squinting as if this would better help me see what he meant. "Well, why would I want to know that?" I didn't know what went on anywhere. "Nobody talks about it, I mean, my mother once in a while talks about the awful Paradises—she isn't one, you know, she just married into it. But that's all . . ." My voice kind of faded away. I was getting anxious (thanks to Dwayne), as if I'd been neglecting family history all this time, as if the family's history were my responsibility. I don't know, maybe it was.

Dwayne had raised the hood of another car and fixed the thin rod that held it open. He was looking at me through the triangle of space the hood made. "You look white. What's wrong?"

"Nothing."

Dwayne kept looking at me and I must have gone from white to furious red because he pulled back. I must admit that's one thing he's good about: pulling back if he thinks something's too hard on a person. He said, "So go on about this ballroom."

"Not if you're going to keep on interrupting." I got haughty. I wasn't very good at haughtiness, since no one noticed mine. That's along with sadness, madness and misery.

He smiled slightly. "Sorry," he said, wiping his fingers on the rag he'd once again taken from his pocket. He did this so carefully you'd think the rag had just come fresh from the laundry.

You can imagine how many times I've heard "sorry" from an adult. It was another good thing about him. So I was offhand. "Oh, that's okay. Anyway, the hotel had these balls—more than dances, they were—fancy, with the orchestra in tuxedos and the women wearing dresses embroidered with beads and sequins and the dance floor so glossy with polish it looked on fire. Could have been two hundred people—why're you looking at me like that?" He looked doubtful.

"You sure got a lot of detail there." He tossed the oily rag over his shoulder and bent down to look at the engine.

I continued. "Two hundred people dancing or near that. I guess this was in the thirties" (a time that hardly existed since I wasn't in it) "when the music was like 'Bye Bye Blackbird' and 'When the Swallows Come Back to Capistrano.'" For some reason I started to sing: "No one here can love or understand me—" for a moment I was taken out of myself or out of one self and dropped down in another where my feelings were bottomless.

"Oh, what hard luck sto-ries they all haaaand me."

That was Dwayne singing. He was trying to pull me back, I think from some kind of sadness. It was almost like the way Ben Queen had dragged me back from drowning. I could have cried right then with the relief of someone's trying. I kept my face down, studying my feet. Dwayne went back to clonking with his wrench or whatever tool he used.

"So go on," he said.

I cleared my throat—it isn't frogs you get in your throat; it's memories. "There's a kind of pond that deer drink from. In this one picture it looks like a fawn and probably its dad, you know, with antlers."

"Hmm. Fawn with a buck? Usually, they hang around their mothers."

"Probably it's because you helped kill off all the mother deer." I could be sarcastic, too.

"I hardly ever hunt deer and never would shoot a doe."

"You shouldn't be shooting at anything. They have a right to keep on living just like you and me." Especially me.

"My, but ain't you ever up on your moral high horse today."

He was busy with the wrench under the hood.

Actually, I didn't give the subject of hunting much thought. Truth was, the only time I'd given it any thought at all was when Dwayne came along with his bag of rabbits.

2

What I had told Dwayne was true, for I had found out about the Belle Rouen in the historical society's little museum. It was in what once had been a house belonging to the Porte family, the ones who had practically owned La Porte at one time. It was a nice old redbrick building and what I especially liked about it was that it was small enough that it wouldn't wear me out looking around. Dwayne was right: I didn't give two sticks for history as such, but I liked it a lot if it was a backstory to some mystery. "Backstory"—there was another newspaper word which I liked.

The museum was overseen from 11:00 to 3:00 by Miss Alice Llewelyn, who had drifting white hair like Queen Anne's lace and was always dressed in pastels of pink or blue or green. She had a pastel face, too, a rosy complexion. But, then, only an old person would have a job like this one, being able to appreciate the way the past clung to things like dust.

When I asked her about the old hotel in the deer park, she said, "Ah, the Belle Rouen," easing the R sound out rather than coughing it up as Ree-Jane always did. Miss Llewelyn said that, yes indeed, they certainly did have some "exhibits" of the Belle Rouen, and led me over to one of the display cases covered with glass.

There were a number of photographs of the hotel and several had been done as postcards. There was a postcard of the hotel in sun and a postcard in snow. There was one that showed the deer drinking from the pool in winter, which I really liked. Then another of what I supposed to be an aerial photograph showing the hotel and the grounds—the golf course, the swimming pool, a stable and lots of walks leading into woods. "It was so big," I said.

Miss Llewelyn nodded. "It had well over two hundred and fifty guest rooms and of course the public rooms, including a huge ballroom where there were dances on Saturday night. Not one but two golf courses, if you can believe it."

I didn't try, golf being a pastime I thought almost as boring as a lecture on place settings from our headwaitress, Vera. "Well, they had a lot more guests than the Hotel Paradise." Which wouldn't be hard. The courthouse jail had more guests than the Hotel Paradise.

I peered at one of the photos which showed a group alighting from a large car beneath a porte cochere three times the size of ours. It could accommodate six or seven cars at once. They pulled up and passengers got out, assisted by several bellboys. I should show this to Will as a demonstration of what his life could be like if people weren't as lenient on him. The suitcases and trunks resembled Aurora Paradise's. I thought the women's clothes kind of charming, too. The women passengers wore big floppy hats, or ones that looked like the helmets gladiators wore in movies set in Rome, where Christians were attacked by lions. (I wondered how they kept the movie lions from actually eating the Christians. Since Ree-Jane Davidow also planned to be a famous actress, I thought this would be a good starting place for her.)

"You see," said Miss Llewelyn, who was looking over my shoulder, "from all that luggage they're carrying that they plan to stay the season."

The season. Imagine someone staying "the season" at the Hotel Paradise. Usually, it only takes a weekend for them to see sense. "Did it cost a lot?"

"Yes, I believe it was very expensive. But business seriously fell off after that baby was kidnapped."

Jarred by this news, I stepped back. "A baby? Kidnapped?"

Miss Llewelyn nodded, her eyes shut as if to follow the scene in her head. "It was such a beautiful night with a full moon. It just seemed so romantic, the night and the dance. Well, this baby was their only child, and it was taken right out of its little crib while the parents were down-stairs dancing. The father was from here, you know. Morris Slade, a well-known local playboy."

Now, granted my experience of playboys was limited, I do know they wore nice clothes, chased girls, drank champagne and drove fast in sporty cars. They were handsome and social butterflies. What I couldn't understand was how a playboy could be living in La Porte and even less, how one could have grown up here. What playboy ways could they have learned from their fathers? There were no old play-boys in La Porte that I ever knew about, except maybe Jamie Make-piece, who'd romanced the Devereau sisters. But I wasn't sure Jamie was in the "playboy" category.

Then I remembered my cousin, way older than me, the one who vis-ited from the city now and then. He wore white linen suits and brought presents. I didn't care about the presents, only about him. He was, I guess you could say, "exotic." I always made sure I was the last person, not the first, to greet him. I would watch from my window on the third floor, which looked out over the cocktail garden behind the hotel, looking down as others ran out to tell him hello, except for Will, but it was hard to think of Will running out to greet anybody except Spike Jones or Medea. I would hang back and then go down and stroll up to the cocktail garden and be really casual, as if I were yawning my way through our hellos. Of course, it backfired when he said, "Emma. You finally bothered to come out and see me?" He wasn't making a joke of it. He was really annoyed. But what could I say?

He was the only one I knew who could be a playboy. He'd sit around for aeons drinking martinis with Lola Davidow. But I hardly think she'd be called a playgirl.

All of this ran through my mind as my eyes were fixed on the photo of the Belle Rouen guests, the women in their helmetlike hats and fashionably dressed, right down to their shoes. The men wore summer suits and stiff-looking white collars. But the thing was they all looked happy. They looked almost brilliantly happy. And this made me sadder even than the scarcity of playboys. I have never seen a group of people enter the Hotel Paradise looking that happy unless they were drunk.

It must have been the Belle Rouen itself; it must have held out such a promise of happiness that its guests would pay anything and come from anywhere just to be happy.

I looked at other pictures, ones of the interior. That dining room! It was twice the size of ours. Its tables were crammed with place settings, silver, water goblets, wine goblets around snowy-white napkins and fresh flowers. Maybe I should put a blossom in a bud vase for Miss Bertha. I knew what she was allergic to.

Here was the ballroom, with the band members in tuxedos and the dancers in evening wear. They were swinging and turning as if a wind were sweeping them along. The gowns of the women were so much more sophisticated than Ree-Jane's sweet sixteen dress, it hardly bore mentioning. Perhaps they were more sophisticated than the Waitresses but then the Waitresses had lived on a whole other plane of existence.

Looking at the aerial view of the hotel, I wondered if maybe Miss Llewelyn had a drawing of it, like a diagram. I asked her.

"No. No, we don't. Why would you want one?"

I don't think she was being nebby, just puzzled. "Because I'd like to see it better in my mind. I'd just like to know how the rooms—I mean the ones downstairs that you called the public rooms—were arranged. To get a better picture, I guess."

"I see." She crooked her finger against her chin and appeared to be thinking. "You know, we could probably work it out, between the aerial view and the photos and postcards."

It was a good idea. She went to get a ruler and a sharp pencil, and we set about working it out. She drew little squares and oblongs—lobby, kitchen, reading room, ballroom, solarium (What's that?).

I was getting so caught up in the romance of the Belle Rouen I actually forgot about the kidnapped baby. I wondered about a newspaper account; I didn't see any clippings in the display case.

When I asked Miss Llewelyn if she'd attended the dance that night when the baby was taken she said no, she hadn't, so I couldn't hear her version. That didn't make any difference, though, as the only version I ever cared about of anything was mine.

As she rolled up the diagram and put a rubber band around it for me, she said, "All I was told was that the babysitter left the room for a little while and when the father came upstairs from the dance, he found the baby gone. Can you imagine? How horrible that must have been for the parents?"

It didn't sound too good for the babysitter, either.

"Police thought it just might have been somebody *in* the hotel, too, rather than come from outside."

"And the baby was never found?"

She shook her head and was silent. "Most people couldn't say the name 'Rouen' correctly, so it just became the Belle Ruin. That's what we all came to call it, it seems; it fits, doesn't it?"

I nodded. And then it came to be almost forgotten; it was a place you would have to be reminded of: *"Oh! The Belle Rouen. Yes, I remember that place."* Only you didn't, really. For you had to be reminded of it: the Belle Ruin.

3

Guests, what there are of them at the Hotel Paradise, enjoy what is called the modified American plan, meaning that breakfast and dinner are included in the price of their hotel room. What they do for lunch is their responsibility. This doesn't mean we don't serve lunch, which of course we have to, and this means I have to be around to do the serving. Anyone who wants lunch has to pay extra.

This modified American plan I think would make perfect sense at those resort hotels where there was so much to do outside the hotel grounds, like going antiquing or shopping, or horseback riding, or making the rounds of museums or historical sites. Here there is nothing to do, unless you want to drive ten miles to Lake Noir. Spirit Lake, from which the village took its name, is choked with lilies and although it has a boathouse, no one takes out the rowboats anymore. It's a very small lake about a mile from the hotel. So lunch itself can be an event to fill up the guests' boring day.

We only have two full-time guests, Miss Bertha and her friend, Mrs. Fulbright. Mrs. Fulbright is as sweet as cotton candy—which she somehow resembles, with her long neck and cloud of soft white hair. She was a beauty in her day (which was also the day of Aurora Paradise and there the similarity ends). I can picture Mrs. Fulbright twirling a pink parasol the color of her cheeks and all the men gathering around her.

When I'm in the dining room, dropping cold butter patties from my icy dish onto the bread plates, I think about this. Then I plunk a patty on Miss Bertha's and pink parasols fly right out the window. Imagine a squirrel with its cheeks full of walnuts. That's what Miss Bertha looks like, only not as cute. She's small and has a back that's bent over with a hump that's from some kind of bone trouble (my mother says). Like the Hunchback of Notre Dame? I ask. My mother just gives me one of her looks.

When you have a guest like this who's fussy and completely unreasonable and demanding, it gets to be a challenge to see in what ways you can drive her crazy. I've come up with some really good ones. Miss Bertha wears a big beige hearing aid and you can imagine. My brother Will, though, is even more artful when it comes to Miss Bertha. Will opens his mouth and pretends to be talking to her, and when she can't hear him, she blames the hearing aid (*"Damn fool contraption!"*) and bangs it on the table.

My mother caught him at it one day when she came into the dining room to check the coffeemakers. She said to him, "Sometimes I think you're worse than your sister."

What? Does my mother have the least idea what he's like? No, because Will puts on this smarmy smile for the guests and chats to them about their trip while he carries their bags. He manages to make out like he's doing everyone a favor, when he's actually the bellboy and is supposed to be carrying bags. He gets big tips, which he squanders with his friend Mill over in Greg's on the pinball machine, Orange Crush and MoonPies.

The dining room is large and rarely crowded. Somehow, its emptiness is magnified by having one table taken, which is Miss Bertha and Mrs. Fulbright's, right in the middle of the room.

Today's lunch was to be Spanish omelets (or plain, if you weren't adventurous).

"Spanish? Why is it called that?"

Miss Bertha always asked that when the Spanish omelets were served. "Because it's tomatoey and sp—" I caught myself about to say "spicy" and stopped. Miss Bertha hates anything spicy and is always complaining if any food has too much in it, which it wouldn't if I didn't add things like a few shakes of cayenne pepper or bits of those little green peppers that Will and Mill once got Paul (the part-time dishwasher's son) to eat. Paul ran all around yelling, and they gave him water, which they knew would make it worse.

So instead of "spicy" I said "special."

"What's special about it?" She just wanted to argue.

Mrs. Fulbright sighed. "Bertha, just have a little sauce in a separate dish. You can taste it that way and see if you like it." She turned to me. "You can do that, can't you?"

I chewed my lip. Of course, I could do it; I just didn't want to. The thing is, Miss Bertha could then avoid eating any sauce, so adding the pepper would be a waste of my time. Still, I said I'd be glad to go to the extra trouble. Pointing that out.

Miss Bertha slapped her big-knuckled hand on the table. "I want a toasted cheese with relish and tomato."

"We don't—" But we did have cheese, of course. My thoughts lingered on the relish. "Okay, you can have that." I smiled to let her know the hotel would go to any trouble. Which it wouldn't; guests were lucky if Will was passing through so he could carry their bags. And Lola Davidow had been known to refuse a room to someone she didn't like the look of.

I left the table to push through the swing door and go into the kitchen.

"The old fool—" said my mother, when I told her about the toasted cheese sandwich.

A kind of snorting laugh came from Walter, our dishwasher, from back in the melting shadows of the dishwasher. Walter loved it when my mother called Miss Bertha an old fool.

"—when I'm trying to get out of here early!" She folded the beaten egg yolks slowly into the whites. Even though she was in a hurry, she did this carefully. There was a cast-iron frying pan already heating on the stove.

"Oh, I'll make it," I said, with real enthusiasm. "I can certainly make a toasted cheese sandwich." I certainly could.

"I'll help," called Walter.

My mother was looking dubious as the omelet was rising in the pan.

I said, "Walter helped out a lot when you were in Miami Beach." I watched the omelet being folded over. It was a golden brown on the bottom, now the top. It was a good two inches high. I know this be-cause I measured one once with a ruler.

"Well . . . all right. Good. Just spoon the sauce over this when it's done and it'll be done in another thirty seconds. And take it in right away so that it doesn't fall."

You should see her soufflés.

She untied her butcher's apron and hung it on a nail at the end of the counter. She smoothed her hair, which she wore up on both sides in a roll, and she often tucked wisps of hair up on the sides. Her hair was dark and neat, although she went to no trouble over it. And the high roll matched her high cheekbones.

"Good bones," she often said, *"mean good breeding."* Not beauty, but breeding. My mother's got a thing about good breeding. But when it comes to cheekbones I'm sure she's wrong, as Walter has high ones and I don't think she'd hold out much hope for Walter's breeding. Wal-ter is a little "slow," as they say. But I don't look down on him at all; he does a lot of things for me. Even Aurora Paradise likes Walter, and if that's not a free pass to heaven, I don't know what is.

The moment my mother banged out of the kitchen's screen door, I asked Walter to get the relish out of the refrigerator, slapped cheese on white bread, slid the omelet out of the pan onto a heated plate and put the sandwich into the pan. I slid a slice of tomato from Mrs. Fulbright's salad into the sandwich.

I was busy chopping up hot pepper when Walter set down the jar of relish. He laughed his strange disjointed laughter.

"I guess that's for the old fool."

"Right." The toasted cheese was done on one side and I lifted the other and sprinkled in the hot pepper relish. I poured Spanish sauce over the omelet. The plates went on the tray and I whisked the food into the dining room, served them and then went back to the kitchen and waited.

A shout came from the dining room. Then a chair must've over-turned. I hotfooted it to the kitchen's back entrance, saying, "I'm going into La Porte, Walter. Can you take care of that?" I hitched my thumb over my shoulder.

He snuffled out a laugh. "Sure can," he said as he put down the dish towel and moved in his slow way toward the dining room.

Walter was really good at blame taking.

Axel's Taxis showed up less than twenty minutes later. Over the phone in the back office, I had asked if Axel himself could drive and was told: "Sure, hon, he's right here." The dispatcher—as if they needed one, for they had only two cabs—always said this, and Axel never turned up himself.

So here I was, driving into La Porte with Delbert at the wheel, as usual. If I hadn't seen Axel driving around once in a while, I'd have thought there was no such person and that maybe he'd died and the taxicab business was just keeping it quiet.

Actually, there *was* something peculiar about Axel and his cab— always the maroon-colored Chevy—for whenever I saw him gliding by, if I was walking the highway, for instance, Axel never had a passenger in the backseat. I never could understand this; coming or going, there were no passengers. "You see Axel around often?" I asked Delbert.

"See him ever' day. Why?"

Delbert's eyes were rooting me out in the rearview mirror. I slid way down. "I just wonder why he never drives me. I ask for him every time. No offense." Hoping there would be.

"Axel's just busy is all."

"Well, he could pick me up and still be busy. He's being busy picking up *somebody*, Delbert." But Delbert didn't see the sense in this and shrugged.

"Who does he drive, then?"

"Who? Ever'body."

I rolled my eyes even though Delbert couldn't see them in the mirror. "He doesn't drive everybody. He doesn't drive me. Didn't I just say?"

"If he drove you he'd be goin' between Spirit Lake and La Porte a dozen times a day. I swear you just about worn a rut in the road, all the times you go back and forth." He gave a choked sort of laugh, several of them. He thought he was so funny. I rolled my eyes again, thinking if Delbert couldn't see them, maybe God could. But God never seems to bother Himself over Delbert's dumbness. Axel, however, He might have plans for.

I would have to see Mr. Gumbrel, too. I was writing my own account of what had happened at Spirit Lake for the *Conservative*. I put in everything and even a little more. I admit I exaggerated a little, but that was what I heard a reporter who interviewed me refer to as "artistic license." I told her I hoped she wasn't using artistic license for *my* story and she laughed and made a little note on her pad about my sense of humor, which I appreciated.

The Sheriff had been talking to Maud Chadwick in the Rainbow Café about my first installment of the story. He said that being shot at over and over "like Emma says" (I had been sitting right there) "would be hard, wouldn't it? Listen: 'The bullets rained down all around me, spattering the lake and the rowboat.' That'd be kind of hard, seeing as how the shooter was using a revolver that would have to be reloaded again and again—and quick, too, don't forget—as it's not your machine gun or even your automatic or semiautomatic that can fire one bullet right after the other in quick succession. What?"

Maud just dropped her head in her hands. "Oh, for God's *sakes,* Sam! For a grown *man,* you're acting like a kid!"

The Sheriff shook out the paper and said, "Grown *sheriff,* don't forget, and if I can't tell the difference between a revolver and a machine gun we might all wind up in the middle of Spirit Lake just like Emma, with bullets raining down around us."

Maud just couldn't stand it. "*You're* the twelve-year-old, not Emma!"

Remembering this made me smile.

When Delbert got to the outskirts of La Porte, I told him to drop me off at the Rainbow.

"You mean for a change? You go there like ten times a day, too."

He was trying to catch my eyes in the net of his rearview mirror, so I again slid down on the seat. That really frustrated him; he even rose up a little in his seat. "How come?"

I sighed and paid him the fare but decided against tipping. I figured I wasn't going to reward Delbert for driving me to an early grave (another fond saying of my mother's). "Because I get such a kick out of riding with you." I got out quick.

Delbert is so dumb he thought I meant it. He smiled like a Halloween pumpkin, missing teeth and all.

4

The Rainbow Café was the most popular place in La Porte for breakfast and lunch. Maud Chadwick had worked there for years as a waitress, and I often wondered why, as she was so much smarter than any other woman I knew (except my mother and, I must admit, Lola Davidow). I asked her why she didn't teach at the high school, as she had a college degree. She said she didn't like it; it was too "political."

If there was one thing the Rainbow Café was not, it was "political." Mealtimes there were always the same, with its owner, Shirl, sitting on her tall stool in front of the cash register, surveying the help and the customers, and looking like she didn't think much of either. Her eyes were slightly bulbous (a thyroid condition, said Lola Davidow, whose own eyes were ever so slightly the same, which I put down to a Gordon's gin condition), and they seemed to *ticktock* back and forth around the Rainbow like one of those cat-faced clocks.

Shirl was tough to work for. The breaks she allowed were so short the help hardly had time to turn around. Except for Maud, who got special treatment because Shirl thought she was so valuable. But Shirl was a good pastry cook (even my mother said so and that was a huge compliment); Shirl's doughnuts were near famous, and she was always running out of them.

I was looking at them now on the glass shelves next to where Shirl was sitting. I smiled at the new waitress, Wanda Wayans, and walked toward the back, past the usual customers sitting on their usual stools. The way they sat every day, they could have been painted there. Mayor Sims and Dodge Haines and Bubby Dubois, with his white hair like meringue. He's said to know the Sheriff's wife Florence a little "too well." The idea that any woman could prefer Bubby to the Sheriff just makes me laugh. My mind can't grasp it any more than my fist can grab air.

The Sheriff is Sam DeGheyn. He told me to call him Sam, but I just could never do it; it would be like me calling Gary Cooper "Coop" (as if I had the chance). Before I mostly stopped talking to him (and this was because he questioned the whole business about Ben Queen), we'd walk around La Porte and check the parking meters and discuss various things. It's the kind of person he is; he never lords it over you. Certainly he could have made his weasel of a deputy, Donny Mooma, do the meter checking. Even Donny asked the Sheriff why he didn't get someone who was even lower than Donny (that was hard) to check the meters. (I noticed Donny didn't suggest himself.) The Sheriff had adjusted his dark glasses and looked at Donny for a long moment and said, "Because." Then he went back to chewing his Teaberry gum, and we went back to the meters.

So I was surprised on this day when he said he was going to check the meters and did I want to come along? I nearly answered until I remembered I wasn't speaking to him, that is, not beyond correcting him about my first installment of the Devereau business. His dark glasses were hitched in his shirt pocket, so that meant I was looking right into his blue eyes. They are intense. They can cut like a diamond cuts glass; they can look like pictures I've seen of blue-cast ice floes that burn in the sun without melting. No wonder he wears those black glasses.

When he saw I wasn't going to answer he said okay and Maud, who was sitting on the outside of the booth, got up, and the Sheriff slid out. I watched him walk past the long soda counter, where everyone sitting on a stool there had a word for him or a slap-hand handshake and I felt sunk.

Maud lit up a cigarette and turned the matches over and over on the table. They were from the Silver Pear outside of town and near Lake Noir. It was an expensive restaurant where I'd been when I was investigating the woods out there around White's Bridge, where the murder of Fern Queen happened. The crime scene.

I knew Maud was looking at me hard, so I sipped up what was left of my cherry Coke, mostly melted ice, just to have something to do. She crossed her arms on the table and leaned toward me.

"Emma, I want to tell you something about being right: being right is much harder on a person than being wrong."

That really puzzled me. I was sipping up air now, and I looked at her. But I didn't say anything.

"You don't want to forfeit a friendship with someone like Sam because he was wrong and you were right. He's too good a friend, Emma."

I would have shot straight up except the booth table was holding me down. "But he didn't *believe me*! After all that happened, he thought I was lying—"

Maud shook her head. "No, he didn't."

"—or just"—I flailed my arms around—"just imagining things! After I'd nearly got *killed*! He didn't think I was telling the *truth*." My anger suddenly deflated, for I knew I was on shaky ground. And so did Maud.

"Emma, he did not think you were lying. He thought all along that you weren't telling him all the truth, that you knew things you weren't telling him. That's a lot different from thinking you were lying."

I could feel my face burning, which only got me more angry. It was almost the same thing Dwayne had said when I complained about the Sheriff: *"He's the law, girl. You can't expect him to accept what you say without him looking at it objectively."*

"Well . . . what about him? Why does he have to make fun of my writing?" I held up my copy of this week's *Conservative*, containing the second installment of my story. Mr. Gumbrel, the publisher, wanted it to be a three-part piece. I didn't know how I was going to come up with the third part, for I'd already told about the shooting, and that was pretty much the climax. "Even if there were . . . well, one or two things wrong, like the gun."

Shirl was calling her, but Maud ignored her and sat, turning the book of matches over and over, looking at me. I really hate it when someone seems to think I'm grown up enough and smart enough to reach a conclusion all by myself. I'm not. But, grudgingly, I said, or mumbled would be more like it, "Okay, he wasn't really making fun of me. He was just trying to get a rise out of me." I hated conceding even this much. "Maybe he was even trying to do me a favor. I should have done my research better."

"Thing is," Maud said, smiling, "who would you rather have pointing out mistakes to you—Sam or Regina Jane Davidow?"

That was certainly a good point. At least now I'd have a chance to make up my defense in case Ree-Jane knew anything at all about guns, which I couldn't imagine she did. But a lot of men around here used them, and she might have heard a comment on this "raining bullets" detail. Anyway, she'd be looking for mistakes to throw up to me.

Shirl was marching toward the back. "Maud! Maud!" she cried out as if she were trying to throw a lifeline to her instead of giving her a dressing-down.

"Sorry, Shirl," she called over her shoulder, stopping Shirl in her tracks. It was peculiar the way Maud could just control people sometimes. "Be right there."

As she slipped out of the booth, I asked her, "When were you at the Silver Pear? I thought you didn't like it because it's so—"

"Pretentious? It is."

What I really wanted to know wasn't when but who. Who had she been with? The Silver Pear wasn't a restaurant where you just stopped in and tossed yourself down on a stool, like you did in the Rainbow Café. You'd almost always go *with* somebody. (As if I'd had so many dates there, I'd know.)

"Went with a friend of mine. He's from out of town."

He? Who was *he*?

Then she set her hands on the table and leaned down. "Emma, what I was saying about friendship. I really wish you'd think about it. I wish you'd take it to heart."

She walked away and I had the strangest feeling of something chill washing over me, of something slipping away, the way that rowboat had slid away from the dock, me in it and scared right down to my shoes. Really my shoes, for the boat itself had been shot and the icy water of Spirit Lake was leaking into it. This feeling was almost like that feeling, except this one was caused by something invisible. First, the Sheriff; now, Maud.

I eased down in the booth, wanting no one to see me in case I would start to cry. I turned my spent straw over and over, end to end, and listened to Patsy Cline singing "I Fall to Pieces."

Taking it to heart.

5

When Delbert dropped me off under the porte cochere, there was Ree-Jane in one of her Heather Gay Struther dresses, posing on the front porch railing with a copy of the *Conservative,* just waiting for me to show up. As I got out of the cab, she was already giving me her silent laugh treatment.

"I've just been reading your story."

She stopped to laugh soundlessly some more, and I took the opportunity to get there ahead of her: "Yes, I told Mr. Gumbrel I'd like a correction printed for next week. About the kind of gun. Since it was a revolver it couldn't have rained down bullets." I flopped down in one of the green rockers, congratulating myself for the quick way I had stolen her thunder.

Now there was nothing for her to say. I mean there probably was, but she had been pinning her hopes on the "raining bullets" mistake (someone had likely pointed this out to her). Now, she had to quickly make up something else. And Ree-Jane just wasn't quick. She said, "I'm surprised everybody in town isn't laughing at you."

That was weak. I said, "Well, nobody seems to be. You're the only one who's said anything. But I'm glad I caught it just the same. Reporting has to be accurate."

She slapped the paper down. "Why the *Conservative* would want another story after bigger newspapers and the real reporters wrote it up, I can't imagine. And you writing it? . . . Well, you're only twelve, for God's sakes."

"I guess you don't want to be interviewed, then."

Her milky blue eyes widened. "Interviewed?"

"That's what Mr. Gumbrel thought would make a good install-ment. Interviewing a few people to get their reactions to the whole thing, like to Ben Queen and whether he's been treated fairly, and so forth. To see what people believe. I was thinking of doing maybe three people—the Sheriff for one, then Ben Queen's brother, maybe. And you. But if you don't want to, I could probably get Miss Louise Landis to talk to the paper." I loved referring to myself as "the paper." I could just see Ree-Jane preening on the inside, her ego spreading out like a peacock's tail.

"Well, maybe I'll answer a few questions, but not unless I get to see what you've written before it ever gets printed." Her eyes narrowed. This was Ree-Jane on full alert or as full as she could be.

"Sure. I'll type it up and show it to you."

She flipped a wave of her Veronica Lake–blond hair over her shoulder. "What about pictures? Will there be pictures of the one in-terviewed?"

"Mr. Gumbrel didn't say. But it's a good idea." It was a stupid idea.

"Well." She looked up and down the vast porch, empty of guests except at the far end where Miss Bertha sat still as stone. Maybe she was dead; a person could always hope. Ree-Jane arranged her blue linen skirt, crossed her legs and leaned her head against the white pillar at the end of the porch railing. She was already posing for the cameras.

"We can do it right now." I held up my new notepad. She smiled her camera-shoot smile, a smile that barely rearranged her expression, except to make it wooden and artificial. Another of her careers was to be a world-famous model. That was in case the whole thing with the duke fell through. "I need a pencil." I ran to the office, snatched a pencil from the desk and ran back. I didn't want to lose this Ree-Jane opportunity. I sat in one of the rockers and rocked. "Okay. Let's see . . . what was your reaction when you heard about the events of that night?"

"What night?" She wasn't even looking at me; she was trying on different expressions for the cameras that would never come.

"The night of the shooting at Spirit Lake. When I—Emma Graham, I mean—was forced out on the lake in that rowboat?"

"Oh, that." She broke her pose long enough to twist a strand of hair. "That it never happened. At least not the way you said."

"Then tell the *Conservative* what you think *did* happen."

"I don't know. Maybe Ben Queen was there with his shotgun and you just happened along."

"'Happened along'? Why would I be out happening along the boat-house at midnight?"

"It wouldn't surprise me. You're really strange."

"Emma is."

"What?"

"You keep saying 'you.' I think it should be 'Emma' for the paper."

She shrugged in an exaggerated way, as if she wanted to shift the whole burden of being the fabulous Ree-Jane off her shoulders. I couldn't say I blamed her. I asked, "What do you think about Ben Queen?"

"He just got out of jail after eighteen years. He was in for murdering his wife, Rose."

I could tell she was relieved to deal with a fact, although I was asking for opinion. "Are you sure he did that?"

She gave me a blank stare. "He got convicted, didn't he?"

"Nobody in Cold Flat Junction believes he killed her. He loved her too much." It was truly a beautiful story, the one of Rose Devereau and Ben Queen.

She flapped her hand at me. "Do you believe everything you hear?"

Pretty much. It saves trying to figure things out. "His brother and sister-in-law said it was impossible."

"Well, they *would* say, wouldn't they?" One thing Ree-Jane had mastered was sneering. She sneered.

I didn't want her to get so agitated she'd stop, so I agreed that the Queens would defend Ben. "But if you don't believe my—Emma Graham's—version of what happened, then who do you think shot Fern Queen over by White's Bridge?"

"Why, he did, of course."

"His own daughter?"

Ree-Jane picked at a little loose nail polish. "It happens."

She made killing off your children sound like needing a manicure. Maybe for the Greeks it was. I knew something about them from having to listen to Will and Mill about that damned Do-X-machine in their production. But Ree-Jane?

"Why? Why would he kill his daughter, Fern?"

"Obviously, so she wouldn't tell where he was." Her tone was so self-satisfied.

"But nobody was looking for him before Fern was murdered."

Again, she flapped her hand dismissively. "You just want to argue."

Somebody better want to if they were talking to Ree-Jane.

6

It was too late to go to Cold Flat Junction and be back in time to serve dinner, so I decided to walk over to the Belle Ruin. There was a long, long driveway, gone weedy and rutted, that led to the remains of the hotel. Standing at the end of the drive was a broken statue of a loosely robed woman, arms missing, and with a weather-pocked face, tiny holes running down which reminded me of tears.

What was left of the hotel was its foundation, its skeleton and not really much of that. It was as if God had walked in with a gun and blown its brains out. It had burned almost to the ground in a "great conflagration," my mother called it. Miraculously, no one had died in the fire. Strangely, the huge ballroom had not been demolished, although most of its ceiling now was the sky. Practically all of the floor remained, and the walls on three sides, and even a few pieces of velvet-upholstered furniture that no one had since stolen.

Maybe you could see the leftover glamour in what remained of the ballroom. Here there had been dancing on a grand scale to a live dance band. The pine floor was still smooth and I could dance around on it, sweeping aside the massed dead leaves and twigs, and pretend I had a partner.

I think a little of that which was left got tugged away between times I was here, picked up and carried off by thieves, who were probably wind and weather, at least there seemed less of it each time. Another post from the porte cochere, another piece of intricately carved molding, as if what remained was giving in like a long, exhausted sigh.

My mother tells me there had once been half a dozen hotels in Spirit Lake; it had always been a summer resort for the wealthy. As the wealthy and I had never been on especially good terms, my imagination was let loose on the guests of the Belle Ruin—women walking about in waterfalls of diamonds and twirling silk parasols; men with money stuck to their fingertips, trailing hundred-dollar bills in their wake.

It has been named, Miss Llewelyn thought, after a town in France— Rouen. She believed the owner had been French. It was a name to deal with. Ree-Jane liked to work it into conversation to show off her French accent (the one she didn't have). "Oh? You've never heard of the Belle Rouen? The Belle Rouen has an interesting history . . ." As if she knew.

Except for the hunters, I must have been the only one to come here. It is strangely different from the rest of the woods around, but I could not say why. Once I had surprised a doe and her fawn across the clearing that were quietly drinking from that pool of water pictured on the postcard. They regarded me with shocked eyes and froze for a moment. I waved, which sent them flying deep into the trees. That made me sad, that they felt I was chasing them off. I don't know what I expected—that they'd wave back? For someone who spends a lot of time fooling around outdoors in empty places, you'd think I'd know more about wildlife.

I listened in the cold stillness and crossed my arms and rubbed them. But it was not a real, outside cold, a drop in temperature, a rise of wind, a gust of rain. It was inside cold, the kind I've heard a person feels when a ghost crosses a doorsill. If there were any ghosts around, my inside temperature would be the last thing I'd be worried about. Anyway, I don't believe in ghosts, and they wouldn't be interested in me if I did believe in them.

In addition to the diagram Miss Llewelyn had drawn, I had the postcards I had purchased. The museum had copied them from the originals to sell to visitors, as they had done with many of the old landmarks that were mostly now gone. This postcard showed the front of the hotel: its big circular drive with its wide, covered entry and its sweeping stairs. The Belle Ruin was three times the size of the Hotel Paradise.

Once in winter I was here. It was dusk, quickly getting dark beneath a full moon. I liked to imagine those Belle Ruin guests in their diamonds and silks and white winged collars, twirling on a floor of snow. I am good at hearing music in my mind, and so the orchestra played only my requests. I could step into the ballroom and dance myself, which I did, on the snowy floor (clumsy, with my boots on). I danced with one of the younger, handsomer guests and I could see along the edge of the floor all of the girls who had no partners regarding me sadly. At the rear of this little band of wallflowers stood Ree-Jane, looking furious. I nodded to her, graciously.

The music ended and I shuffled off through the snow.

In that winter was another time I had seen deer. This one had big antlers; he had been drinking from the pool of water formed by the end of a narrow stream. He was so peaceable, looking up and around and then dipping his head again. I stood in stiff stillness, wondering why hunters were so keen on killing deer. Were they jealous? Why were they so proud of their trophies? There was no competition in hunting. It was like a one-sided war, where the enemy had put down their guns and fled. Why shoot a fleeing soldier? I could see a hunter stepping up and shooting that deer as he drank from the pool. But what kind of contest was that? What kind of victory?

I remembered that winter silence. I was as still as the silence itself. I imagined myself dissolving, my body evaporating and me floating in the vapor.

I would like to see them again, the deer family.

I think I half expected to see the Girl step out of these woods, just as she had stepped out of the trees around the old Devereau house. I had seen her now five times: once boarding a train in Cold Flat Junction and then again at the railroad station; once on the streets of La Porte; once across Spirit Lake; and once near the Devereau place. There, she had been looking straight at me, I was certain.

I was sure she was Ben Queen's granddaughter, for she looked exactly like Rose Devereau Queen, exactly. He said she wasn't, but I supposed he was just trying to protect her because he suspected she was the one who'd shot Fern, her mother.

Or rather I should say I suspected it, and I'd been wrong, for the Girl hadn't shot her. That nobody else had seen the Girl except me I could tell worried Ben Queen in the short time he'd been with me. It had worried the Sheriff, too. It was even beginning to worry me. As I stood under a sweet-smelling pine, looking into the woods at the place where I'd spotted the deer, a new thought occurred to me: Was she following me?

I just said, didn't I, that I wasn't afraid of ghosts?

I think I lied. It wouldn't be the first time.

Ree-Jane had a small phonograph in a case with a handle that she refused to let me borrow. She said she'd rent it to me as long as it stayed in her room. I said that wasn't much of a rental plan, but then it wasn't much of a phonograph, either. That made her really mad, and she went off to tell her mother. It was hard for me to imagine "telling on" anybody, and I was twelve. But here was a next-to-seventeen-year-old doing it.

Naturally I did not tell her I wanted to take it to the Belle Ruin.

Then I remembered the Waitresses and dancing in their rooms to records like "Tales from the Vienna Woods" and "Moonglow." Why these wisps of songs clung to my mind like cobwebs, I don't know—or I do know: it was because the Waitresses knew I wasn't allowed to go to the dances and so they made one up and dressed me in the blue gown with the tulle skirt. I had only been five or six years old, but no wonder I remembered the Waitresses and "Moonglow."

Their phonograph still worked and much better than Ree-Jane's, even though hers was fairly new, and it was easier to carry. In the kitchen, I wiped it off with a damp rag and carried it through the hotel until I saw Ree-Jane on the porch, rocking and talking to herself. I made myself conspicuous, walking on by her, swinging the phonograph a little and whistling.

She skidded the chair to a halt. "Have you been in my *room*?"

As both the phonographs were the same size and had dark cases, naturally she took it for hers. I frowned, perplexed—or so it would appear—and said, "*Why* would I want to go in your room? Oh, you mean this?" I held it up. "This is mine, not yours."

Neither Ree-Jane nor her mother was a master of the quick retort. When stuck for one, both of them opened and closed their mouths several times, their lips bunched like fish lips. She could think of nothing insulting or biting to say. I excused myself and walked on down the porch steps.

Ree-Jane called after me: "If you think I'm giving back your rent money, you're crazy!"

As if I thought she ever would.

It was Will who'd discovered the midnight-blue tulle gown in one of the storage rooms. I was shocked to find it had been there all of these years and I not know it. I thought that if the Waitresses had left the dress behind, they might have left other things, too. That's how I found the phonograph and the records.

So I had brought the phonograph and "South American Way" and was doing my Carmen Miranda impersonation, at which I'd gotten very good. I could swing my hips and circle one hand around the other just like she did. Even Will and Mill were impressed. (I thought of taking a trip down Argentine way, as I'd had such a good time on my trip to Miami Beach.)

So I danced in what was left of the ballroom and all the while thinking of the Waitresses. Where had they gone? Why had they left in such a hurry they didn't take their phonograph and records and blue gown with them?

Wherever I turn, there's a mystery.

7

I was in the kitchen arranging salads. My mother told me to please remember the black olives should be sliced before adding them and for heaven's sake to remember not to put the Roquefort dressing on Miss Bertha's salad for she hated it. I thanked her for reminding me and scooped off the top layer of one salad and added a spoonful of Roquefort dressing. Then I put back the layer of lettuce, the pepper and onion rings, arranging them so that the dressing was invisible.

My mother called to Walter (as if he wasn't only a few feet away), "I need that turkey platter!"

Walter would sometimes be listening to us and wiping the same dish again and again. "Here it is," he said in his slow, solemn voice.

She took it and started arranging thin slices of ham, which she rolled around her special mango-pecan cream cheese. She was making canapés for the Baums, who'd all be drunk even before they got to their own cocktail party. There would also be little sausages for dipping in rum-and-orange sauce, Mrs. Davidow's favorite, which wasn't surprising.

As I was sprinkling the black olives over the salads, Mrs. Davidow's voice came wailing from the back office window across the yard to the side door of the kitchen, which was directly opposite the office. She needed Will to carry bags. My mother told me to find him, wherever he was. Didn't she know where he was? Where he always is, up in the Big Garage.

I didn't like going up to the Big Garage, for it meant hanging around by the closed door while Will and Mill acted mysterious. I don't think Will did this with everybody, but he certainly did with me. There was a door to the right of the huge garage doors, the ones cars drove through, but which are always closed since it wasn't used for cars anymore.

An inch was all Will would give me. Through the opening I saw only his eyes and darkness beyond. Everything stilled—piano playing, voices, singing, laughing. All were still. It was as if the whole world—rocks, trees, gravel—might come rolling in before he could stop it. They did this even though I was in their production and knew what was going on. Secretiveness was just second nature to them.

"What?"

"You're to come and bellhop."

He gave a giant sigh.

"It's just too bad to interrupt, but some of us have to *work* for a living." I pointed to my white apron.

Will opened the door a little wider, but not much, and came out. He shut the door tightly behind him. The piano playing and singing resumed. Mill was what you would call a prodigy. He was a genius when it came to anything musical; he could also play the guitar, the trombone and the flute, besides the piano. He had been coming here every summer I could remember.

As we walked Will said nothing. Probably his mind was back there in the Big Garage with their production of *Medea: The Musical*. I thought it was just crazy that they were writing songs for it. I said, "Don't you suppose if the Greeks had wanted it to be a musical, they'd have made it one?"

"They weren't very musical."

This was such a lie, I just stopped and stared at him. He didn't know any more about the Greeks than Walter did.

"It's true," he said. "They were great thinkers, you really couldn't beat them for their thinking, but deaf to music."

He sounded so self-satisfied I wanted to kick him. Will had an answer for everything. "You don't *know* that. I'm sure some of them were just as musically inclined as Mill."

He laughed abruptly. "Don't be ridiculous. No one is that musically inclined."

"Well, they had trumpets and things to play, didn't they? And pianos?" That didn't sound quite right.

"Pianos? *Pfff.*" This blubbery movement of his lips was meant to scoff at me. "Lyres, they played a lot of lyres, but that was pretty much it."

Oh, *honestly.* I set my hands on my hips and faced him. "Do you ever, *ever,* admit to being wrong about a thing?"

Will chewed his gum slowly, even thoughtfully. "Of course. When I'm wrong about a thing. I'm not wrong about the lyres." He wheeled around and headed for the back door of the east wing, so there was nothing for me to do but head on into the kitchen.

There was no one who could walk around with more starch in them than our head waitress, Vera. She was stiff right down to the roots of her hair, which she wore pulled up on both sides and rolled under. She always put on a black uniform with long sleeves and white cuffs, and over it a gauzy white apron, starched to stand up. The rest of us wore dusty blue or white uniforms. For a little while we had to wear caps the shape of tiaras. The caps had come about after Miss Bertha had found a hair in her eggs Benedict and thrown a fit.

No one knew whose hair it was and so we all were supposed to wear these caps that pushed our hair away from our faces. Vera had been wearing a cap all along to complete her head waitress image. Even so, I think the hair was Vera's because it was black and she was the only one with black hair. Although the hair might simply have been "dark" and that would take in my mother, too. But the idea of suggesting my mother had let a hair drop over the eggs Benedict would take a lot more courage than anyone had.

The caps came off after a week because everyone forgot them and it was a hard rule to enforce. I gave mine to Walter, who also had black hair, telling him it could have been his hair (which it obviously couldn't). I blamed things on Walter a lot, but so did my mother and Mrs. Davidow. Lola liked to yell at him for things like leaving a bag of groceries in the back of her station wagon. I never yelled at him; when I blamed him for something it was always with a quiet voice. I figured he needed somebody on his side.

We did not need a head waitress. There were only me and Anna Paugh for Vera to head up, plus whoever we got in on a temporary basis when there were a lot more dinner guests. Anna Paugh was small and without any of Vera's airs. The head waitress (we foot waitresses were informed) always decided on which of us served which guests, and this meant Vera got the best tips. When I complained, my mother said she deserves them, for look at how much trouble she takes doing table checking and seeing everything is perfect. I told my mother any fool could do the table checking; I did it myself when I went around with the butter patties. Fork on left, knife and spoons on right, water glass above knife. I could do it in my sleep. My mother then argued that Vera doesn't live in and doesn't get part of her pay in room and board. Meaning, I did.

I informed my mother that I was *supposed* to get room and board, or had she forgotten? "I'm even supposed to get the American plan, *unmodified.*"

My mother went back to whipping up meringue for her Angel Pie and I became so engrossed in the folding of the meringue into the lemon mixture I forgot all about tips. I was just glad I got room and board.

Vera might have been the perfect waitress to the guests, but she clearly wasn't to me. No, the perfect Waitresses had come and gone years ago. My mother could not remember their names. I don't think she liked them very much, probably because they were happy. There are a lot of people who aren't really into happiness and I fear my mother is one of them. Strangely, Lola Davidow wasn't. She seemed many times on the brink of happiness, but that could just have been "my old friend Jim Beam at the wheel." That's what she said, and laughed.

Once in a while I went with Mrs. Davidow to the florist we used, a big place with two greenhouses, and one sort of icy room that I liked to go into where flowers were kept. I liked the chilliness of it. One time I remember Mr. Ream, the florist, had shown Mrs. Davidow a huge vase of birds-of-paradise. "Too showy," she remarked.

Birds-of-paradise. That's what I think of when the Waitresses come to mind, as they often do. All three were pretty—at least, I think there were three. I had been only five when they'd fluttered in, and though I can't remember except in fits and starts, I imagine them lighting up the dining room. They couldn't always have been hurrying with trays back and forth, yet the rush and the hurry seemed to have been imprinted on my mind.

Vera said, haughtily, "They were flighty, those girls."

But that was the whole point! They fairly flew about, rushing in and out of one another's rooms. The one occasion that's clear in my mind is when they dressed me up for our Saturday-night dance that I of course was too little to go to. It was a deep blue gown with something silver, sequins perhaps, tossed like the Milky Way across the skirt. It was oceans too big for me, but I thought it was beautiful. They made up my face a little with a dusting of powdery rouge and pearl pink lipstick. Then they put a record on the phonograph and we danced, all of us, twirling from room to room.

"Too flighty." I can still here Vera saying this. "Too familiar," said my mother. "And much too colorful."

Yes, that was a good description of the Waitresses.

The rooms they occupied were the small ones over the laundry room, up a flight of back stairs. Once in a while I would go up there and walk around. They were empty except for a few old chairs and tables, dusty and unused. I think I was looking for some belongings they had left behind. But it was Will who'd found the blue evening gown which he'd intended to use in their production until I'd cleverly gotten it away from him. It's the people who place no value on a thing who always seem to find it.

Four new guests had come in, two couples who wanted to eat late, which irritated my mother, as they'd be running into the Baum dinner party. It was hard juggling two groups of people with two different menus. Also, it meant I'd be stuck with them, which irritated me. I scooped Roquefort dressing onto Mrs. Fulbright's salad and thought about the Belle Ruin. "Rouen": my mother also pronounced it correctly and without all the neck-stretching gurgles that Ree-Jane used. My mother did tell me about the rich, elaborate menus, the excellence of the crème brûlée, the Calvados gelée, the poached salmon in Chardonnay. I almost forgot about the Belle Ruin itself in listening to this list of dishes that went on, making me think my mother could taste the words. When I asked her about the kidnapped baby, she said, "What baby?"

I stood at the long white enamel counter where the dinners were placed ready to go into the dining room and asked, "How can you remember the crème brûlée and not about the baby?"

"'Crème,' not 'cream.'" She was arranging sprigs of mint around the most gorgeous mold of pineapple and lime mousse that I'd ever seen. Her eyes flickered up from the mold, and she looked off into some distance and added, "Oh, yes." *Oh, yes* was the sum and substance of it.

A voice came from the shadows. Walter's. I was amazed that Walter would be a source of information. "Ma told me. Somebody come in the middle of the night and stole these people's baby."

My mother looked up from her mint sprig arrangement and nodded and said, "That baby, yes."

How many babies were there?

She went back to the mint sprigs. "Yes, people said it was like the Lindbergh case."

Now she remembered. There were times I thought my mother didn't want to remember.

It was way past time for Aurora Paradise's predinner drink. With Lola Davidow going back and forth to the liquor supply in the back office, there wasn't an opportunity to sneak out any of the Wild Turkey or Jim Beam for Aurora.

Fortunately, there was a leftover mint julep in the icebox sitting right on top of the block of ice. Mrs. Davidow had made mint juleps for the Baum party. She was sitting at their table now, squeezed in between Mayor Sims's wife and Helen Baum. Everyone was so drunk they didn't know Mrs. Davidow hadn't been invited (including Mrs. Davidow), so Vera, her look scoured in disapproval, had done a makeshift setting for her.

They were all in there laughing uproariously as Vera came back to the kitchen. My mother's expression matched Vera's; she said there were only ten filets, and now Walter would have to dig another out of the deep freeze in the little kitchen. Why my mother was surprised that Mrs. Davidow had joined the party, I don't know. She was always including herself.

I removed the lone mint julep and grabbed up some mint sprigs while my mother was turned away to light up the broiler. I had already dropped a couple of maraschino cherries in the drink. I don't think that was good for the julep, but the touch of red was pretty. The julep had watered down some, but that didn't make any difference as it was sheer ice and fiery bourbon to begin with. With, of course, a minty syrup. I put the frosty glass on a small tray and passed through the dining room, just in time to witness Miss Bertha's forking up lettuce and a mouthful of Roquefort dressing. She couldn't exactly shoot up from her chair, bent as she was, but she certainly struggled out of it, yelling. I hurried on, feeling lucky to see my plan in action.

"Something wrong?" I called over my shoulder. "Be right there . . ." but my voice trailed away. Since I was carrying a tray, which was a passport to anywhere, no one demanded I stop. The Baum party merely laughed and hooted the louder, the loudest hooter being Lola Davidow, as if she'd just landed in this strange place and had never seen Miss Bertha before. My tray balanced on my upraised palm (for I was good at this), I sailed on.

"Cocktail hour starts at five and it's near seven!"

Pointing out my failure to attend to her every whim was the standard greeting from Aurora Paradise. I could not complain, however, since I was the only one to get into her room on the fourth floor, except for an occasional visit from Lola Davidow, bringing an extra bottle of gin. For some reason I thought it spoke well of Mrs. Davidow that Aurora allowed her to visit at all.

"What is it?" She frowned at the glass that was still adorned with a few ice shards. "It's not a Cold Comfort!"

That was her favorite drink. "It's a mint julep. Made my special way." Made Lola Davidow's special way, that is. And Lola wasn't about to work with the sweat of her brow for Aurora, living up here on the top floor of the Hotel Paradise, drinks served to her and meals sent up either on the dumbwaiter or delivered by me. I continued taking credit: "You have to pack the glass with ice first, then pour a jigger of good bourbon over and stir and stir. Then fresh mint that's been cut with sugar. The mint, of course, must be bruised." Where on earth had I picked up that tidbit? It sounded good, and Aurora was really paying attention, as if she meant to whip up a dozen of these for her next soiree. She liked to talk about soirees she'd held.

"Bruised?"

"That's when you mash the mint to release the flavor. Then you take an iced-tea spoon and stir and stir some more until ice forms *on the outside.*"

Her black-crocheted mittens (with the fingers cut off) grasped the glass. "Well, my Lord. Well, I must say you don't spare yourself."

I stared. She was actually giving me credit for something? "A good mint julep has to be tooth-rattling cold. I mean *cold* cold. That's what they drink in Kentucky at the horse races. At the derby," I added, worldlywise.

She sipped through her straw and her lips stayed bunched even after she stopped. She squeezed her eyes shut. "Um-*umm.*" She un-bunched her lips and smacked them. Then she started singing,

> *"Carry me back to old Ken-tuck-y,*
> *There's where the cotton and the corn and taters ga-roooooow."*

She was really belting it out, and even though she'd got the wrong state in the song, I would not correct her because the song gave me that feeling of something lost. And she meant to sing it right to the end.

> *"There's where I la-bored so hard for old massa*
> *Day after daaaaay in the fields of yel-low cooorrrn."*

At this point I was afraid if it went on any longer I'd start to cry. And I'd never even been to Kentucky.

"Yes, you surely do make a fine julep, I'll say that. Got another?"

I should have foreseen this development. "You just started that one. I told you it's hard work, making one of those." I had placed the small tray under my arm. As always, I had not been invited to sit. She was in the same rocking chair, one filched from the front porch and gotten up to the fourth floor God knows how. There was also an office chair, one on casters that she liked to zoom around in.

I said, "I have some questions for you."

She flapped her free hand at me. "Lord, you always got questions. You're the most curious person I ever did meet."

"Well," I said slyly, "you want your name in the paper, don't you? I'm interviewing people and of course those people are part of my story."

With the straw, she drew up some more of the drink. "You talkin' about that story you been writin' for the paper? Mr. Abner Gumbrel"— her tone changed—"used to be sweet on me."

Aurora was ninety-one. Mr. Gumbrel was probably in his sixties, not more than seventy, at least. "Mr. Gumbrel's too young for you." I tried to imagine a life where sixty would be considered "too young." I couldn't.

"Oh, don't be foolish. Even if he is a few years younger, you never heard of a beautiful older woman leading on a younger man?"

There was never any sense in contradicting her; she'd just keep on. "Maybe. But that's not the point. Do you remember the Bell Ruin?" I nodded my head in that direction. "On the other side of Spirit Lake?"

"Of course." She punched at the glass with her straw. "Burned down when I was in my twenties." Slyly, she glanced at me to see if I was taking that.

"You'd've been a lot older than your twenties."

"No, I wouldn't. I've reached the bottom." She made gurgling noises with her straw.

"I was told there was a baby kidnapped out of there one night twenty-some years ago."

She started humming and fooling with her glass, raising it and waving it back and forth. "A kidnapping? That's in-ter-est-ing." More humming.

I'd say it was blackmail, but, of course, blackmail works two ways. "Answer my questions and I might get you another drink. I'm sup-posed to be waiting tables, you know."

"Questions about what?" She stirred around the ice with her straw.

I switched my tray to under my other arm. I'd have liked to sit down, but I didn't want to disturb my line of talk. "It was the night of one of their balls. I thought you might have been there, dancing." I had to remind myself that Aurora even then would have been an old lady nearly seventy, which was hard to believe.

She started rocking the chair, humming some more.

By now I should be used to her lying, but as it was impossible to tell right off, I assumed she was telling the truth, at least as far as she knew it. Right now she was holding her cold glass up to the window and the dying sun, reminding me of the empty glass.

I wasn't going to give in without more information. "Walter says a baby disappeared. What about that?"

"That man?" Walter was always "that man" to Aurora, never Walter. I had forgotten that she also admitted Walter to the fourth floor at times when I couldn't take up her drink or her dinner. "He ain't old enough to recall that baby."

"Sure he is." This time mix-up bothered me. It seemed to shuttle back and forth with nothing to stop or correct it. Would I be saying, seventy years from now, *Oh, yes, the Hotel Paradise. I lived there; I was even a waitress there.* "Anyway, Walter says his mother told him."

"Well, she was right. Someone creeped up a ladder and took the poor thing out of her crib. Just like the Lindbergh baby."

"That's what my mother compared it to."

"Oh, your mother, that Jen Graham! What's she know about it?"

My mother wasn't Aurora's favorite person. My mother had married into the Hotel Paradise and into a long complicated list of relations that Maud had always said sounded like *Bleak House.* I would have to read that book some day and maybe learn a little about what was going on with the Paradise–Graham families.

She had set her glass down on the small table that held her playing cards and a couple of tricks, like the walnut shells and the pea. I had refused to play this game anymore, for she always cheated. Since I had to get back to the dining room anyway, I might as well get her another drink.

I picked up the glass. "It will take a little time." I wondered if Miss Bertha had settled down by now.

I managed to make an Appledew because it took only one kind of liquor—Dewar's scotch—which I was able to pour into the empty glass while Mrs. Davidow was out on the porch with the Baums, still there. There and just as loud. I took the glass to the kitchen and put in ice and apple juice.

My mother wanted to know if I'd stopped into the Orion to catch a movie. My mother could be sarcastic at times. Walter always appreciated these remarks and laughed as if he had water up his nose.

"As you *know,* I was with Aurora Paradise."

"All this time? And it's *Great-aunt* Aurora. I won't have you calling adults by their first names. It's ill bred."

I stood there with my face completely blank and let my mind go on. *LolaLolaLola. AuroraAurora,* and so forth. "I call Walter, Walter don't I?" This, I knew, was different.

"That's different." She turned to take a chicken breast from the roaster keeping it hot.

The difference was "breeding." Breeding was one of my mother's favorite topics. To hear her go on, you'd think the whole world was a kind of dog show. While she assembled the fried chicken, mashed potatoes and the greenest peas this side of the Emerald City, I put my hands on the counter opposite her and pulled myself upward, doing a little dance, and considered breeding. Walter was not well bred, according to my mother's standards.

"Is Ree-Jane?" I asked.

"Is she what? Don't call her that. She hates it."

"But it was her idea. Don't you remember this French comedienne she said she was naming herself after? *Rejane,* except I'm not pronouncing it right, which is the problem. I can't help it if I don't know French."

My mother slid me a dark glance.

I stopped supporting my weight on my hands and got a napkin and silverware for the tray. I always liked the way my mother would remove any edge of grease from a plate with the hem of her apron. Completely unsanitary, but artistic. Her plates of food looked sculpted.

"Take this dessert in to Miss Bertha, and then take Aurora's tray up."

It was Chocolate Feather Cake, one of my mother's signature desserts. I only wished I'd had a feather to bury in Miss Bertha's.

8

Aurora pulled the Appledew up through the straw until her cheeks collapsed and she looked like a death's head with her deep-set sunken eyes and parched skin. "Excellent!"

"I had to sneak it out of Mrs. Davidow's supply while she's with the Baums. The Baums had another dinner party."

"Helene Baum! Never could stand that woman. Gate crasher, social climber."

"There's no society to climb around here, is there?"

Aurora picked up the glass again. "Of course there is; there's always a ladder; there's a social ladder in hell."

The drink was half gone by now. I always wondered how a person as old as Aurora Paradise managed to stay put after a couple of these drinks. "Now you can answer my question."

"Hmm?" She drew in on the straw with such force her sunken cheeks nearly met behind her nose. "What question's that, miss?"

I sighed. She would pretend to forget; she would put all kinds of obstacles in my path just to get the better of me. "You know. About the kidnapped baby."

"What baby?"

"At the Belle Ruin."

She sniffed at her plate. "That chicken looks real good. I gave Jen Graham the recipe, even showed her just how to batter it and all."

That was such a lie. The only one who could show my mother anything about cooking was God. Aurora was just doing this to keep from talking about what I wanted to talk about. I was gritting my teeth so hard they'd soon be worn down to stubs.

"And Angel Pie. Um-*umm*!"

"So tell me about that night."

Her look was sly as her mittened fingers stirred the straw around in her drink. "Well . . ."

I knew where I'd made my mistake: instead of trying to remember what actually had happened, she could just as easily make things up. It would be hard. It would be hard for me to tell the difference, so I'd have to pay close attention, keeping in mind what Miss Llewelyn had told me.

She began: "It happened when one of those dances was going on; it was late at night—"

(True.)

"—real stormy, with sheets of rain and thunder and lightning—"

(Lie.)

"—and the mother and father left the baby girl—"

(True.)

"—she was crippled, you know—"

(Lie.)

"—with the nanny—"

(Half true.)

"—who was entertaining her boyfriend in the next room—"

(Lie.)

"—and never heard a thing."

(True.)

Aurora ignored her dinner now and set out her cards for solitaire and was slapping the jack of hearts down on the queen of diamonds just to get me off the kidnapped baby and on to her cheating. I really hated that cheating when she was the only one playing. It was one of her pointless things to do. But I didn't react. "Go on."

She sighed, being so put upon, and picked up a chicken wing. I never knew anyone to prefer chicken wings, as you had to fight for every last morsel. I figured she liked the challenge. "The police here thought it must be somebody outside the hotel because of the ladder."

(True. Nine of clubs on ten of spades.)

"Um." Her lips pursed. "But the nanny had been with them for years—"

(Lie! Lie! My mind went off like one of Greg's pinball machines yelling tilt! tilt!)

"Wait a minute. This baby was their first child! Why would they have had a nanny before her?" I watched the jack of diamonds being shifted over to the queen of clubs.

Aurora shrugged. "Well, maybe she wasn't really a nanny. Maybe it was one of the local girls just called in to babysit. Anyway, the person was so upset, the police even didn't think she had anything to do with it. Now, I remember!—"

Slap went the two of hearts on the three of diamonds.

"It was that Spiker girl!"

A local? I hoped this was the truth. "You mean one of the Spirit Lake Spikers?"

She nodded. "One of them."

"Which one?" This was exciting news, for the Spikers never left Spirit Lake, as far as I could see. Actually, no one left Spirit Lake. That was a chilling thought.

"Don't remember." She was riffling the pack of cards, looking for a new card to cheat with and forking up her mashed potatoes as she considered the cards.

I was frustrated. I switched the tray back and forth from under one arm to the other. "Well, what about ransom? There must've been a ransom demand."

"Not to my knowledge."

True, I'd say For if the whole thing had kept on, I didn't see how it could not have been in the newspapers. It was hard enough believing it was kept quiet anyway. I said so.

"Girl, you are such a naïve person. You never heard of hush money? You don't know there are crooked cops and that sheriff was as crooked as any of them? Why, money'll buy you anything."

"But what about the guests?"

"What about 'em? They didn't need to know."

"But there were all those people; they'd want to know why the police came."

"Police." She moved a ten of hearts from its row over to the jack of diamonds. "That sheriff, Carl Mooma, and his dep'ty was almost as bad. Couldn't light a fire in hell, those two."

"You mean Donny Mooma is some relation?"

"There's hundreds of them."

I dropped that subject and said, "Then you were there."

She nodded. "I was—I reckon I was in my thirties at the time."

I just looked at her. "It's only twenty-two or -three years ago." How could anyone past ninety still be lying about her age? "So what you're saying is really all hearsay." This was a word I'd lately grown familiar with.

"Hearsay!" said Aurora. "Miss Smartypants, you weren't there, were you?"

"But neither were you." I'd got it now: the way to get information out of her was to deny she'd done this or that.

She slapped down a card. "I most certainly was. I was right there when that flabby Mooma was putting questions to the staff—the bell-boys and so forth."

I frowned. What was she talking about? "You didn't work at the Belle Ruin, did you?"

"No, of *course* not. I put on a big apron over my gown and pretended I was one of the housekeepers." Her smile was wicked. "Got to get up pretty early in the mornin' to beat Aurora Paradise!" She pointed. "See that trunk?" She pointed to the big steamer trunk that she claimed had gone with her all around the world. It was covered with stickers that fascinated me. Now, instead of getting out of her chair—she was the laziest human I'd ever come across except for Ree-Jane—she jerked it around to the trunk. "The dress I wore to that dance is in here. You wait." She batted about through the clothes. The gowns were yellow watered silk; black satin that would have fit like a glove; pale blue velvet with a neckline strewn with pearls; and a dark blue chiffon that lifted like wings when she shoved it out of the way.

The trunk opened like the entrance to a little room. Drawers marched down both sides with necklaces spilling from one and long white gloves from another. I'd like nothing better than to go through the trunk's contents, holding dresses up to me and looking in the long, thin oval mirror back in a corner.

Aurora was holding up a dressy pink silk with a pleated skirt and silver embroidery decorating the top. "Here's what I wore."

"That's beautiful," I said, sincerely.

She held it up to her. "I still remember dancing all night"—here she reached out her arms and hummed—"with every man there. Oh! I was popular!" Humming, humming.

Probably, she was. From stories I heard, even from Ben Queen himself, who'd known her. Actually, I loved the idea of her putting on an apron so she could talk to the police. "So since you were there, what else did the police do?"

"Perhaps another drink would refresh my memory." She sat there looking prissy and pleased as punch.

I moved my tray from one arm to the other. "I can't get any more drinks because Mrs. Davidow's run out of everything."

She cocked her head and looked at me. We both knew just how likely that was. "Oh, do declare? Well, you need to keep a stash for emergencies, then."

"Me with a stash. That would really look good. Regina Jane Davidow says I'm on my way already to being an alcoholic, just making you these drinks." Aurora hated, loathed Ree-Jane, which was one of the things in her favor.

"That floozy? That dumb blonde don't know enough to come in out of the rain. I'll say this for you: anyone can put up with that simpering little tart must be made of strong stuff. Nerves of steel. Now"—she flicked her fingers off her thumb at me—"Angel Pie!"

I have to admit I was so surprised on getting a compliment out of Aurora Paradise I just stood there, mouth slightly open.

"Tell me what else the police did."

"Did about what?"

I gritted my teeth. "You know what!"

She squinted her eyes, looking for all the world as if she were trying to remember who I was and where she might have seen me before and forked up the Angel Pie, her favorite (and mine).

9

"What was Miss Bertha yelling about before?"

"Roquefort dressing." Another dark look slid my way and stayed. "The dressing wasn't on top of the salad, where she'd see it. It was in the middle, layered under the top, as if it were deliberately hidden."

I made up a puzzled frown for my face and slowly shook my head. "That's strange. I can't think how it could've happened, unless maybe Paul—" He was seven or eight, maybe nine. No one really knew, including his mother, our part-time dishwasher Will and Mill kept him up in the Big Garage, rehearsing.

"Paul hasn't been in here tonight."

"But Will and Mill came for dinner, didn't they?"

"No. Walter took them their dinners."

Room service? Since when? I remember once a guest had asked for a sandwich and coffee to be delivered to his room. Lola Davidow had said, "Not unless it grows legs and walks." (Lola considered the hotel her home.)

From the shadows, which Walter seemed to pack around with him, came the remark "That play they're doin' looks like it's good. June's up on the stage in a white bride's dress. With all the singin' and all, I bet it's good." He wiped the platter.

June! I squinched my eyes shut. If my mother heard that June

Sikes was in the production, there'd be an explosion that would send the chicken wings flying all over the kitchen. But she missed the name, thank heavens. Will clearly knew our mother would come to see this play. I guess he also knew that for her to yell and stomp out during the performance would have been a mark of poor breeding she could never have borne.

I was just glad we were off the Roquefort dressing subject. I stood and looked at the plates my mother was fixing and realized I was near starving. Since I never got white meat of chicken, I was having the meat loaf. Ree-Jane always got the chicken breast. I recall one dinner-time when at the family table (where Mrs. Davidow had her glass of Dewar's and that I had named Dew Drop Inn), Anna Paugh, our third waitress, had mistakenly set my chicken leg in front of Ree-Jane and given me her white meat. Then I had hurriedly taken a bite before Lola Davidow had banged her fist on the table and yelled at Anna Paugh that "Jane" was always to get white meat and to change the plates, even though my chicken was bitten into. Talk about breeding.

Anyway, I loved the meat loaf. As my mother was cutting off a thick piece, I took a teaspoon and made a well in my mashed potatoes, sort of like fishing through a cloud, and asked her to put some gravy in it. She would not do it unless asked, for she considered it common to eat mashed potatoes this way. But with a sigh for my commonness, she ladled the gravy into the well. I remember once a woman who'd worn a beautiful brownish-gold satin gown to one of our Saturday-night dances. That was the shimmery brown of the gravy.

The other plate was for Walter. He lumbered over when my mother told him to get his plate, a dishtowel tossed over his shoulder. I was a little surprised he wasn't told to take it off, but I guess my mother was too irritated with still dishing out dinners at this hour and didn't notice or didn't care.

There was something about the careless way he'd flung the dish-towel that suddenly made Walter, the closest thing the Hotel Paradise had to a slave, seem a free man, freer than me, certainly, free from all the petty little things that troubled me. Yet Walter was picked on and criticized every day, in such a way as to make clear it was done just for the sake of doing it. He must have turned all of the unpleasantness into something unharmful the way people long ago tried to turn metal into gold. They couldn't, but Walter could. I thought this was worth pondering further and would later.

I took my plate over to the round table where the help ate, which was just inside that side screen door (where business in the kitchen and in the back office was shouted across the backyard.) Out of that door I could see the evening star. Of course that wouldn't be its real name; that would be something scientific. I called it the evening star. On the few occasions I'd been in the kitchen really early, I'd looked out and seen it again, only now it was the morning star. I guess the two stars were different, but I loved to think of that star hanging around both in a soft dawn sky and in a black velvet one, day and night, shining. I would think of climbing a mountain by that star (Ree-Jane was going to be a famous mountain climber) or of being on a boat (Ree-Jane was getting married on the *Queen Mary*) on the choppy hard gray sea in wind and rain and steering home by the light of that star. It was a mystery to me how that star clung to the sky.

But I guess one unfailing star was worth its mystery. I could sit here and look and be glad I was just the help.

Walter came over and got his plate of chicken and potatoes and thanked "Miss Jen," as he always did. Ree-Jane called him a retard, and my mother told her never to use that word. Ree-Jane wasn't used to being told off. My mother said Walter was a little slow, and I said, well, he's come to the right place.

Then I remembered what Walter's mother had said about the baby at the Belle Ruin.

"The Baby at the Belle Rouen": it sounded like the title of something—a book or a song or a play. It sounded unreal, too perfect a phrase to mean anything true. I thought I'd slip around my real question by asking something not as pointed: "Did your mother ever work at the Belle Ruin?"

"That big hotel you was talkin' about? Sure did, lots a times. She washed dishes, too, just like me."

He acted almost proud that he was following family tradition here. "Then it wasn't a permanent job? I mean, like yours?"

"No. She'd go there when it was real crowded and they needed extra help." He chewed on his drumstick.

"You mean like holidays and so forth?"

He nodded. "That's right. And them dances. She was always called to work then."

My roundabout way paid off. "Oh, really? Then was she over there at the dance the night the baby was kidnapped?" I tried to be casual, pretending it was neither here nor there to me. Yet why was I pretending? Because I'd learned that it's much safer if you don't let on how you feel or what you really want to know.

"Uh-huh." Walter wiped his mouth with his paper napkin. "Sure was. Police asked her questions and all. She had it writ down somewheres in one of her diaries. Mom always kept account of things in her diaries. Must be a dozen of 'em."

My eyes widened as if dazzled. The very *idea* dazzled me. Something about this kidnapping not only recalled but *written down*. I couldn't eat; I stared at the air.

Walter asked, "What's wrong? You look like you seen a ghost."

Quickly, I closed my gaping mouth and staring eyes. "Oh, I was just thinking of something . . . ghostly." I looked at him, afraid to ask. So many things could have happened to a diary—fire, mice or simple carelessness.

"Well, you can read it if you want, whatever diary it was in."

A book. To think there was a written account to read of an event instead of having to depend on memory, which had to be pulled to the surface like Mary-Evelyn's poor body from Spirit Lake, or like the broken words of Ulub, telling me what he remembered.

I thought of Mary-Evelyn Devereau, who'd been drowned, and Rose, who'd been stabbed a dozen times, and her daughter Fern, who'd been shot, and of Ben Queen, who'd been eighteen years in prison. What I thought was how a book, something written down they could have read, might have saved them. *Rose, here is a book about children like Fern and what they could do to others and to themselves.* Or, *Mary-Evelyn, the Devereau sisters are dangerous. Get out! Run away!* Or, *Ben, do not leave Fern alone with her mother, not for a moment, not ever.*

Something noted down, something written—a message, a page, a book. Like the notebook Dr. McComb had written in based on the account Ulub had tried so hard to tell him of what had happened at the Devereau place. Neither of the Wood boys, Ulub or Ubub, could speak clear enough for anyone to understand them. Most of the time, a person had to fill in the words himself. Still, there was a written record of the Devereaus and Mary-Evelyn.

If all of this had happened to these people because there'd been nothing to tell them of the danger they were in, then why should I have it any easier? Why shouldn't I have to put bits and pieces together to form some kind of answer? Why shouldn't I have to squeeze my way in through doors? Why shouldn't I have to pay Rebecca Calhoun five dollars to get information about the Devereau sisters? Why shouldn't I have to be trapped in a leaky boat on Spirit Lake? Why shouldn't I have to *try*?

"I don't know if I should read your mom's personal diary, though."

"Oh, she'd not mind, her bein' dead and all."

"Well," I said, "did your mom ever talk about it later on? I mean years after it happened? It wouldn't be something she'd forget, that's for sure."

He held his drumstick up like a baton as he tried to remember. "Yeah, she did. Said it was one of them Spiker girls that did the babysittin' that night on account of their reg'lar girl—a nurse, I think—never come with them."

"Why not?" That was interesting in itself.

Walter shrugged. "She was sick or somethin'."

I watched Walter slowly eat his drumstick and thought about this. "Well, there was all them people at that dance. You can imagine."

No, I couldn't.

It was kind of convenient, wasn't it, that the baby nurse didn't happen to be there that night? Kind of convenient that the baby, on that one night, was left all alone?

Maybe I *could* imagine.

10

The next morning after my stack of corn cakes and eggs over easy, I told my mother I had to interview some people and could Walter serve lunch to Miss Bertha and Mrs. Fulbright?

They liked Walter for some reason. So did Aurora Paradise (and she didn't like anyone, except, possibly, me). They did not seem to mind that Walter was slow. I liked Walter, too, even though sometimes I could have kicked him. I think people liked him because he was so agreeable, and they could get him to do nearly anything.

My mother said yes. It was so nice being a reporter; it got me what I wanted; it opened doors. Whenever I got the chance, I mentioned this to Ree-Jane, making her stomp off.

When I called up Axel's Taxis, I told the dispatcher to be sure and have Axel himself pick me up, as I always did, and she said, "Abs-i-tively."

And as always happened, Delbert came. On the way into La Porte he made all kinds of jokes about me always "gallivantin'" around. I said that I sure never "gallivanted" with Axel, and why didn't Axel ever pick me up?

"Axel, he's just so busy. Usually, he takes the fares a ways out. Lake Noir, that kinda thing."

"Then why does your dispatcher tell me he'll pick me up all the time when I ask?"

"Prob'ly at that moment he don't have no fares, is why."

Delbert was trying to meet my eyes in the rearview mirror, craning his neck, stretching up, which he had to do because I'd slid down in my seat. I said, "If he takes the long-distance fares, then how come he didn't drive me to Hebrides that day?"

We were passing Arturo's Restaurant, where the neon sign that was half burned out wasn't flashing at all as it usually did, not even its ART EAT letters. I was afraid maybe something had happened to Arturo and I kept my eyes on the sign long past it.

Delbert asked, "So how come you don't want me to pick you up? Ain't my drivin' good enough?"

"It's okay. I just wondered why sometimes it's not Axel."

"Because if my drivin' don't suit you, well, I won't come."

Oh, how boring. "You weren't listening. I just said your driving's okay."

"Well," he said, in a grumpy way that sounded as if he meant not to speak to me again. But life was not that kind. "You takin' the train to Cold Flat Junction again?"

I gritted my teeth, for I hated anyone to know my business. I grunted, "Umph," which could have been yes or could have been anything else.

Delbert waited for a better answer, searching me out in the rearview mirror. "'Cause if you are, you could get the afternoon train, the one that stops in Spirit Lake." I didn't answer, and by this time we were on Second Street and nearly at the station.

11

Cold Flat Junction was about twelve miles from La Porte and kind of out in the middle of nowhere. That's a strange thing for a whole little town to be. The town itself should have been the "somewhere" that a house or a farm or a person could have been near. But "nowhere" really fit Cold Flat Junction. I always got the feeling it was just passing through the landscape, on its way to a better place.

As I always did, I stood on the Cold Flat Junction platform and looked across the tracks and off into the distance to that dark blue line of trees where the woods began. There were no houses over there, no businesses; they were all on this side. So the dusty land was completely empty until it reached that line of trees.

The Windy Run Diner was on Windy Run Road, called that because it acted as a tunnel for the wind train to scream through. I think the wind could get itself really worked up here because there wasn't anything to stop it.

I always stopped in the diner for information, although I never was direct about what I wanted to know. This is one thing about me: I try to get answers, but in a roundabout way. I don't know why I'm like this. Of course, I'd tell myself that being only twelve, people would hardly take me seriously, so I try to be vague about what I want to know.

The thing was, the customers in the Windy Run Diner were always so eager to talk to a stranger, or near stranger, anyone not from the Junction itself, that I'd gotten a lot of information from them in the half dozen times I'd been here. I'd gotten it under what is called false pretenses, which never bothered me, but it meant I had to make up the pretenses. Now that I was working for the paper, I wouldn't have to bother with pretense. Not only that, but I was famous, and people tend to overlook how much you lie when you're famous.

From the station I cut across acres of emptiness on a path worn down by other feet taking this shortcut, such as it was. I passed the Esso station and crossed Windy Run Road.

They were all in their usual diner places at the counter, and I found this restful, for it meant that the image I was carrying around in my head was exactly as it should be: Billy, Don Joe, the heavyset woman in the dark glasses and the others were sitting in the same places they always did.

"Would ya look what the cat dragged in!" called out Don Joe.

I didn't take it personally; I just smiled and sat on my usual stool where the counter curved and met the wall. From there I could see all of them without having to look sideways and around.

"I do declare," Evren said.

Louise Snell, the proprietor, said, "You've had quite a time of it, hon!" PROP. is what her badge said, and I wondered, since I'd never seen any other waitresses, why she had to wear an identity badge.

"Come on," said Billy, "tell us about you gettin' shot at! Why, when Don Joe here brought in the newspaper, we couldn't hardly talk about anything else for days."

More like years is what it'll come to in the end. "Well, it's all in the *Conservative*. There's not much else to tell." I said this modestly, not adding that that was my problem with part three of my story—there wasn't much else to tell.

Louise Snell was getting me a Coke without my even asking. I leaned over the counter to look at the pies in the glass case. I reminded myself that not much over an hour ago I'd eaten a stack of corn cakes with enough syrup on them to drown a cow. That done, I asked Louise Snell for a piece of coconut custard.

"Yeah, but we want to hear the story direct from the horse's mouth," said Billy, fingering a cigarette out of his shirt pocket and laughing a phlegmy laugh.

"You musta been scared shit—I mean, scared to death," said Don Joe. Those three—Billy, Don Joe and Evren—sat side by side down the counter.

I had a big bite of pie in my mouth that even my mother might like the recipe for and only nodded.

"You said in the paper if it wasn't for Ben Queen, you'd be good as dead."

Evren put in, "We always knowed Ben Queen was the kinda person to do that. Yessir, he ain't never killed nobody. He's the kind that keeps people from killing."

I said, "He saved my life, that's for sure." I forked up more pie.

Don Joe frowned. "Why in hell's that Sheriff in La Porte still lookin' for Ben, anyway? Now he knows it wasn't him killed Fern."

"Well, he doesn't exactly *know* it. I mean, I told him, but the Sheriff says there's a hearsay problem. It would be hearsay in court, that is."

They all looked at each other as if this was the strangest thing they'd ever heard.

"Hearsay?" said Billy. "The killer done confessed to you. That sounds pretty much like you heard it, don't it?"

"That's just it. That's hearsay. There wasn't anybody else to hear it, too. I'm a . . . minor." I certainly wasn't going to say I was twelve or just a kid or I wasn't sure anything I said was right.

Louise Snell hooted at that and lit herself a cigarette. "You nearly get yourself shot and that Sheriff DeGheyn says you might have got it wrong. Good Lord, I always thought Sam DeGheyn was the smartest cop around." She shook her head.

Of course, the Sheriff hadn't really said that, nothing about my age, but I let it stand. I even wondered if that might be the problem, but he didn't want to say so.

Billy blew a smoke ring and looked considering. "I thought you was from somewhere else, not a local."

The first time I'd come into the Windy Run Diner, that's what I told them, that the car had broken down and was getting fixed. The next two times, since I figured they were wondering why I was still around, I made up a story about being on vacation. I'd told them so many made-up stories, I hardly knew myself anymore. "Oh, you must've misunderstood. I meant I was somewhere else that day." If they believed that, they'd believe anything. "Shopping over in Hebrides." I rushed ahead to stomp out the "nonlocal" topic. "I've just come by today to talk to people and see if I can get any more information about Ben Queen. I mean, that's one thing. Nobody knows where he is."

Billy smoked and squinted at the chocolate cake high on a glass cake server. Don Joe and Evren, both wearing their tan-striped feed caps, pursed their lips. I think this was their thinking mode.

Louise Snell said, "I can't imagine where Ben's got to."

I asked, "Don't you think he's still around here someplace?" I certainly did. I think I might be the only person who had any idea at all.

They all looked at me. "Like where?"

Billy said, "I bet he's holed up over to Lou Landis's."

He'd said that before and been wrong. They were wrong this time, too. I was pretty sure. Ben Queen might still be at the old Devereau place, where he'd been the first time I'd seen him. My straw was making gurgling noises in my empty Coke glass, something I realized I was too old to do now, and I stopped.

Louise Snell stabbed out her cigarette. "Why would he stay with the police looking for him?"

I studied the crumbs of my coconut custard pie. I was thinking about the Girl, but not wanting to talk about her. It was as if I didn't want to share her with anyone. No, it was more as if I was afraid talking about her would make her disappear, like the rings that would form in lake water when I'd skip stones. But how would I find out who she was if I didn't ask about her? Maybe through my roundabout way.

I asked, "Did you know Fern Queen well?"

Billy nodded. "Sure did. Fern, she was peculiar." He made a circle around his temple with his finger.

"The poor girl was some retarded, that's what," said the woman in the thick glasses.

Just then Mervin came in with his bossy wife. They said hello to everyone and took their places in the middle one of the three booths lined up against the wall. She was on the side whose back was toward me, so I couldn't see her well. Mervin nodded to me and I returned the nod.

Billy was back on Fern. "Re-tarded a lot, that's what."

Mervin raised his voice to be heard. He had gotten to be a lot more mouthy since the first time I'd seen him in here. I wondered if I was having an effect. The customers at the counter seemed to think the booth people should keep to themselves. He said, "Who you talking about?"

His wife, who never contributed anything except to hit Mervin, gave his arm a little keep-quiet slap.

"No one in particular," said Billy, more to the cake stand than anyone.

I thought it was really spiteful to cut Mervin out. His wife was hard enough to bear without the rest of them being hard on him. "Fern Queen," I said to him, and it earned me a lot of sour looks. "I was just asking about her."

Mervin smiled. "Aren't you the one that got shot at and wrote that story for the paper? You're that famous girl."

Even his wife turned to look at the famous girl. But she didn't look especially impressed.

Mervin said, "You done good, girl. You really did!"

I thanked him. Really, he was the only one who wasn't trying to make a joke of what had happened.

Mervin went on: "Well, as far as concerns Fern Queen—"

Billy interrupted before Mervin could get it out. Twirling around on his stool, he said, "Now, Mervin, you never even knew Fern Queen. We're talkin' here about twenty years ago. Correct me if I'm wrong, but you ain't been in the Junction more'n sixteen or seventeen." Pleased with his point, Billy twirled back and drank his coffee.

"I was here when she come back from that trip. That wasn't twenty years ago. That was after her mother got killed."

"What trip was that?" asked Don Joe. Evren nodded as if he'd asked it, too.

"You must recall she was gone for months."

"He's right, Billy," said the woman with glasses.

"I guess I know that." Billy was irritated Mervin was claiming any part in the knowing-Fern Queen story.

"That's when I knew her." Mervin was not giving up.

Louise Snell had placed their "usual" on the table before them and walked back to stand in front of the pie case. Her walk was very soft because of the rubber soles on her shoes.

"What was she like?" I asked Mervin, trying to see into the booth around where Billy and the others blocked the view.

"Fern? Just a regular person, far as I could tell. Kinda jumpy . . . well, wait, let me just think on this a little." He thought.

Don Joe stepped into the thinking vacuum and said, "She did have a temper, Fern did. Fought with everyone, specially her mama."

"Rose," said Billy, as if he had some claim on her.

I recalled last time I'd been here when Rose's name came up, Billy got kind of misty eyed. But there was no surprise in that, for Rose Devereau Queen had been beautiful, "parade-stopping beautiful," is what Aurora Paradise had said.

Suddenly I asked, "Have you seen a girl around that looks like Rose Queen?"

This surprised all of them, me most of all, for I didn't want to talk about her.

"Like Rose?" said Billy. "Hell, no. Why you asking that?"

I shrugged and brushed it off. "Probably, I'm wrong. I just thought I saw someone like that."

"Can't imagine we'd not of noticed someone looked like Rose." He frowned and tapped ash off his cigarette with his little finger. "I'm sure I'd've noticed anyone looked like her. Why I remember—"

He, or his memory, stopped.

"Yeah, I guess we all remember Rose," said Don Joe.

Nobody spoke as we all joined in whatever Rose memory each of us had.

Rose Devereau Queen had been murdered here in Cold Flat Junction twenty years ago. She had been the youngest of the Devereau sisters, younger by a good fifteen years. She had run off with Ben Queen when she was twenty years old. Running was the only way to get away from the Devereaus. They were the sort of women who hated happiness because they had none and would have locked Rose in her room before they'd have seen her find any. Looking at their picture always put me in mind of dry leaves, dry petals, dry wind. Just looking at them made me thirsty, and if there was such a thing as the milk of human kindness, none of it ran in the veins of the three Devereau sisters.

There was another Devereau, though. Mary-Evelyn Devereau had drowned in Spirit Lake when she was only twelve. She had not drowned by accident, either, a fact I'd always known and got in deep trouble proving. For knowing what I knew, Mary-Evelyn's killer tried to kill me, too. Strangers to this area think it's pretty dull here and that nothing happens. They should stop awhile and look around.

Mary-Evelyn: there's always a scapegoat, Ben Queen had told me, always one the others have to go against and make miserable so as to unload their own misery. Mary-Evelyn had been one; Ben Queen was another. He got convicted of murdering his wife Rose when anyone with eyes in their head could see he hadn't done it. But maybe that's part of it, of scapegoating—that the people who make you out a scapegoat are blind. Ben Queen said that the actual goat was loaded down with all manner of things, pots and pans, tools. It was as if people were off-loading their anger and meanness onto this goat, which they then drove into the hills.

Rose Devereau got free of them; Mary-Evelyn didn't. In a way, maybe Rose didn't, either. Murder may dog some people's footsteps, waiting to happen—if not then, maybe now, or maybe later, but eventually, it's going to happen. It's like the Greeks, as I said before. It just seems with the Greeks, it's kill and be killed in revenge. Then another of them takes his revenge, then another takes *his* on the one who just did, and you can see it just goes on and on forever.

And into all this kill and be killed fray, in walks the Girl who looks like Rose Devereau that nobody but me appears to have seen. In she walks, and who is she?

"Thing is," said Billy, still pondering on this, "Rose and Ben, they only had Fern, and Fern never—"

In my mind I finished it for him: "Never had no kids" is what Jude Stemple over in Flyback Hollow had said.

"—she never had any kids," Billy said.

I had opened my mouth to ask what I'd thought of asking Jude Stemple, but Louise Snell asked it for me: "How do you know?"

Billy blinked.

Louise said, "That time Fern went away that Mervin's talking about. She was gone for months, wasn't she?" Louise Snell was refilling the coffee cups at the counter, and she picked up my empty Coke glass, too, for a refill.

The heavyset woman pushed her thick glasses up on her nose and nodded. "It's possible, it surely is."

Don Joe protested. "We'd of knowed, Louise. Queens would of knowed and that Sheba never could keep her jaws from clackin' over gossip."

Louise Snell said, "Not her own gossip; that'd be a secret she could of kept."

Billy blinked again, as if his eyes feared the light and looking as if he didn't understand her, but I did up to a point. Fern would have been one of those girls like June Sikes and Toya Tidewater, who just went with any man who came along and our mother said we were to have nothing to do with them. She would have done better to remind Will of this, seeing June was up in the Big Garage playing Medea.

Billy and Don Joe (and Evren, only because the others were doing it) stared at me. Billy said, "So what you're sayin' is this girl you saw is Fern Queen's daughter? And Ben Queen's granddaughter?" Billy shook his head, not in denial but in surprise. "How could that happen and we not know?"

Louise Snell said, "Because you never thought about it, Billy."

Billy cast his eyes down, tapping ash off his cigarette again, as if the only important thing here was that he'd never thought about it. "Well."

It was as if the Girl might be worn away by a constant rubbing of words. In a way, it scared me, as if I, being the one person who'd guessed who she was, was responsible for keeping her out of harm's way, even though I'd guessed wrong. That upset me. I frowned.

I was not about to tell them of the other times I'd seen her, for speculation then could wear on through the whole afternoon. In the few seconds of silence that ticked over, I got them onto another subject.

"Do you all know about that old hotel called the Belle Ruin?"

"Oh, goodness yes!" said Louise Snell, happily slapping her hand on the counter, as if the memory were so pleasant she just had to do something physical. "That big old place the other side of the highway from Spirit Lake. Burned down around that same time, didn't it?"

"Same time's what?"

"As when Rose was murdered."

"Not exactly," said Don Joe. "That old place burned down a few years before."

"Place was near all timber. Wiring probably all old and haywire," said Evren.

I didn't especially want to get into hotels with bad wiring.

"Does that hotel figure in your story now?" asked Billy.

"Yes." I told them, not knowing whether it would or wouldn't. I had the strangest feeling that I was running up my story in much the way my mother could run up a curtain, or Miss Flagler, who owned the gift shop in La Porte, ran up a dress. She was gifted; she could take a length of organdy or chiffon and fashion it into something as delicate as a cloud or a rainbow.

"Belle Ruin," said Louise Snell. "I know *belle* means beautiful, but why somebody'd call a hotel a beautiful ruin, I can't imagine."

I did not tell them that it wasn't "ruin," but "Rouen" and had just been mispronounced for so long by everybody (but Ree-Jane, according to her) it had come to be known as ruin. As for me, I liked it, the beautiful ruin, with its weeping statue, its tears of stone.

"Really rich people went there. They came in on the train. It was before there were so many cars, people used the trains." Louise Snell was looking dreamily beyond the short-curtained window above Mervin's booth. "There were these wonderful dances."

I sat with my elbows on the counter and my chin on my fists.

"I remember the train had a stop just for the hotel itself. It was that exclusive. There's not much there anymore, I guess. I was, what, in my twenties?"

"Oh, come on, Louise! You ain't but in your thirties now!"

I guessed that was supposed to be funny; I have never figured out why some people think joking about age is so funny. Twelve isn't funny, I can tell you that. But I wished Billy'd stop interrupting.

I hoped for a moment that Louise Snell was going to tell a story herself. I was always interested in anybody's past, not having much of a one of my own. But she didn't go on. She stopped and pried a cigarette out of her pack lying on the counter, and looking off as if she were seeing dancers through the rising smoke from Billy's and her cigarettes.

"Did you ever go to one of the balls?"

"I did, once." She looked off again, in a dreamy way. "I had a sea green gown and my boyfriend brought me a wrist corsage. Gardenias and sweet peas, that was it. Those dances were really something; they had a professional band in. It was crowded; you'd think everyone who lived within ten square miles must have been in attendance."

"Were there a lot of playboys?"

"*Playboys?*" Louise laughed. "Hon, only playboys I ever seen are Billy and Don Joe."

They thought this uproarious. I guess it was an amusing notion, but I was angry with myself for interrupting Louise Snell's story. I asked, "Were you there the night that baby got kidnapped?"

"No, ma'am, I wasn't. But then I only went to that one dance." She started wiping down the counter with an old cloth that made me think of Dwayne's oily rag. They seemed to go together, somehow. Maybe wiping away dreams, getting down to the dirt of living.

12

I should have been writing up my interviews with the Queens and the people in the Windy Run Diner. But this way, I was getting material not only for "The Spirit Lake Tragedy and Aftermath," but also for what I might call "The Stolen Baby." No (I told myself), wait: "The Stolen Baby: Another Lindbergh Case?" That would get readers who were used only to "La Porte High School Spring Prom Is Big Success" or "Covered-Dish Supper at Baptist Church Draws Many."

I decided I was on the right track.

Dr. McComb lived on the exact other side of town, not precisely in town but at the very end of Valley Road, where it broke off from Red Bird. He could almost have been living on both, which were fairly isolated. I knew I would need something to sustain me, so the next morning I did stop in at the Rainbow after all.

It was only eleven, but the coffee and early-lunch customers were lined up on their usual stools, including Ubub and Ulub, who, instead of being made fun of, were now accepted as the important figures they were; had it not been for the Wood boys, none of the Devereau mystery would have been solved. Had it not been for the Wood boys and *me*, that is.

As usual, Shirl was on her stool by the cash register, smoking and watching for some behavior she could complain about. It would be interesting to sit her down with Miss Bertha and take bets. Dodge Haines and Mayor Sims said hello and when was I going to interview *them*? I said I wasn't. Ubub and Ulub both said, "Nul-oh," which was their version of hello. Maud was making a shake, holding the aluminum cup fast to the mixer, for otherwise it would have vibrated so hard it could have walked out the door. She winked at me.

I sat down in one of the booths at the rear, thinking it was really nice to walk into a place and create a stir. The Sheriff always came in at eleven for his coffee, which was *not* the reason I did, but it would give me a chance to let him know I still was hardly speaking to him. I could not make that clear enough.

The booths were a beautiful dark wood, with backs so high you had to lean into the aisle to see people coming. I liked them because they provided privacy. So I didn't see the Sheriff until he was right there. It gave me a start, even though I was used to him being in here. He said hi as natural as could be and I said hi back. It was important that he know I was indifferent. He smiled in that way that illuminated everything within a country mile; I smiled my cheap version of a smile, a sort of rubber banding of the lips that lasted exactly one second. I just wished I had a book or the newspaper so I could begin reading and let him know I was ignoring him.

"When's the next installment, Emma?"

"Maybe next week." "The Spirit Lake Tragedy" was not getting printed up with any regularity, for I had missed last week. The second part had appeared in the *Conservative* a week ago. "But I don't know. I've got writer's block." Now, why was I giving him extra information? You'd think I was looking for sympathy, too, which I wasn't. I pressed my lips together.

He had taken off his sunglasses as he sat down and shoved one stem into his uniform shirt pocket. He gave me one of his blue, blue looks. "I expect that happens to all writers. Hemingway had it; so did Faulkner."

I would have to check this out with Dwayne. I was about to mention this—that Dwayne Hayden knew all about William Faulkner— just to let the Sheriff know I talked to Dwayne all the time, but then Maud came along with coffee for him and a Coke for me and a plate of doughnuts, including the new kind with the sprinkles.

"Emma's got writer's block. Thanks," he added as she set the cup down in front of him.

I said, "I didn't mean it was some *big thing*."

They nodded as if they were both reading my mind. Why did they often appear to be on the exact wavelength? Even bickering, they were. She was the one who bickered, but he was the one who caused it. I wondered if he knew about the "nobody-you-know" person she'd gone to the Silver Pear with.

"I was thinking maybe I could put in it about the Belle Ruin," I said. Had I been thinking that?

Maud's eyebrows inched up. "That old hotel? Or, at least, it used to be."

"Belle Rouen," said the Sheriff, to my surprise pronouncing it correctly, in the French way. He turned to look at Maud as he said this. There was a lapse of two seconds as he did this, looked at her, not having anything to do with a hotel. Then he said, "Burned down. Some said arson."

Maud went on being surprised, as if there was a whole world of discoveries yet to make. "Where was it?"

"The other side of Spirit Lake, across the highway," he said. "There's a big piece of woods out there hunters call a deer park. There are so many deer you'd have to be blind not to hit one."

"I hate hunting. So what was this hotel like?"

I answered that. "It was a big, big resort that had two golf courses and an enormous ballroom. The dance floor is still there. Its name was the Belle R-o-u-e-n. French. People call it Belle Ruin, though; I mean, anyone who's ever heard of it. Except for Ree-Jane Davidow. She tries to say 'Rouen,' but she can't."

"She can't even say 'Belle.'" Maud lit up a cigarette.

The Sheriff nodded at me this time. But the look didn't linger. He said, "Very thick with pine trees, the branches come down to the ground so that it's like looking at a place through a web or a lattice."

I was surprised. "You mean you've been there? You've seen it?"

He laughed. "Well, sure. I'm interested in around here."

Really, I was so surprised I forgot about the last doughnut, which is saying something. "Do you see deer?" I asked him.

"Yeah. If you sit and never mind them, then you see them."

He lit a cigarette as if he hadn't just told me something fantastic, at least to me. It was more to do with other things beyond the Belle Ruin and the stolen baby. But I wasn't sure what. Maybe I was wrong about me and the Sheriff not being on the same wavelength.

I must have looked at him for a long time because Maud asked, "What's wrong, Emma? Do you want some chili?"

Maud (like my mother) thought food did a lot more than just fill you up. I said, "No, thank you." Then I turned back to the Sheriff and asked, "Do you know about the baby that was kidnapped?"

The Sheriff said, "I heard about it, but there's not much in the files."

"Well, tell me the 'not much,'" said Maud. "When was this?"

I said, "It was just a couple of years before the Devereau case. There was this couple named Slade. Morris and Imogen Slade. They had a baby that wasn't much more than a few months old. On the night of one of the Belle Ruin's dances they got a local girl just to stay with the baby for a few hours in the hotel so they could go down to the dance. The babysitter was a Spiker girl."

"Is she still around?"

"I don't know," I said. "I don't know what Spiker it was, either. She'd probably be in her late thirties, maybe early forties now, wouldn't she? The parents would have gotten someone old enough to have good sense."

The Sheriff said, "Older than twelve, you mean. You're certainly up on this place. Where'd you get your information?"

"The historical society and Miss Llewelyn who runs it was one source." I liked "sources" instead of names. I wished I had one or two to protect. "This Spiker girl must have been eighteen or nineteen, at least. The baby was in its crib, and while this girl was out of the room, making a phone call down the hall, someone could have climbed a ladder, come through the window and stolen the baby."

"Lord's sakes," said Maud, more breathing it than saying it.

I continued. "Of course, the hotel owner called the police. They came and questioned people but didn't do much else. The sheriff found the ladder still under the window. There wasn't any ransom demand, at least no one around here heard of any. And listen to this: the Woodruffs must've paid off the sheriff to keep the whole thing quiet. He was a

Mooma, too." I looked at the Sheriff. "Of course, this is all *hearsay*. It's hearsay twice over because the person I heard it from heard it himself from somebody who'd been there. Both sources being very dependable, though." That was a laugh. I drank up my Coke. "Except they're hearsayists."

The Sheriff did not comment on the hearsay aspect of the story. He just said, "This ladder. I assume the police looked for prints?"

I sighed. "Well, of *course*. I was just getting to that." No. I wasn't. I'd never even thought of it. "I don't know what fingerprints turned up. There'd be hotel employees who handled it, I guess. Someone who washed windows and things like that. The kind of fingerprints you'd expect to find. There's a name for that kind—"

"Elimination prints," said the Sheriff. "My question is really why it was assumed it was someone on the outside. The ladder could have been put there just to make it look as if the kidnapping was done by a person on the outside."

"The police said that was a possibility, too."

Maud frowned. "I don't see what that solves; either way he could still have been a guest."

"You're right. It—"

"It would just put it in a different light, that's all."

She asked, "What did the case file say, anyway?"

"It's been some time since I read it. But I'm sure there's no more in it than the date and a brief statement about the alleged kidnapping. Probably, it was never followed up on. Where'd you hear this story, Emma?"

"From Walter and some from Aurora Paradise." Talk about elimination.

"Fellow who works in your mom's kitchen?"

"Yes. Why? I guess you think he's retarded, too? Well, he *isn't*." I wasn't defending Walter; I was defending myself for listening to Walter, in case anyone thought I was just as dumb as Walter.

"No, I don't think that. You're really tetchy today, aren't you?" the Sheriff said.

Today? Tetchy *today*? Hadn't he noticed I'd been tetchy ever since the hearsay business? Had it all gone to waste?

"So Walter's mother worked at the hotel?"

I nodded. "She was one of the dishwashers. Extra help. She came in whenever there was a dance or something."

The Sheriff was thinking.

"His mother's dead now," I added. I didn't say anything about the diaries. I wasn't sure why.

He said, "Walter lives alone, doesn't he?"

Even Maud gave the Sheriff a strange look at that.

"Yes," I said. "But so what?"

"So what is right," said Maud. "Are you going to make a case for all people who live alone, that they're subject to delusions?"

Maud lived alone.

"Of course not," the Sheriff said. "Both of you read so many things into what I say—"

"That's because you say so many readable things, right?"

She had turned to me. I was delighted at being lumped with Maud, if I had to be lumped at all.

The Sheriff by now looked sad. "No. I was only thinking Walter must be lonely."

"And that could be driving him crazy and making him imagine things."

"All I meant was what I said."

"Maud!" That was Shirl calling. She usually did sooner or later. I thought sometimes Shirl got desperate if Maud wasn't where she could see and hear her. Maud got up and walked off.

In all of this exchange, I guess I'd have to admit I'd started speaking to the Sheriff again, which was easier than not. "What I don't understand is why the police didn't do more and why this Woodruff father didn't want the papers reporting the details."

"Have you asked Abner Gumbrel?"

"Well, no. But of course I'm going to."

"Probably there might be a record somewhere, a story filed and then not printed, or something. It was Abner's father's, Asa's, paper, remember."

At this point, Miss Isabel Barnett had come back to sit in the booth she always favored, across the aisle from ours. The Sheriff smiled and nodded and looked as if he wished he had his visored cap on so he could tip it. I smiled, too; I really liked Miss Isabel Barnett, who was really sweet and treated me as if I had a brain in my head, which most adults didn't. It didn't bother me at all she was a kleptomaniac. For some reason, she was only interested in McCrory's Five-and-Dime and taking inexpensive items, like a lipstick, Pond's pressed powder, or Evening in Paris cologne. Or hair ribbon. Miss Isabel Barnett was the richest person in town, so it wasn't need that drove her to it.

"Something in her life that didn't work." That's what the Sheriff had said once. He had an agreement with Mr. Toomey, who managed the dime store, that Miss Barnett would give the Sheriff enough money to cover the things she'd taken, money which he would pass along to Mr. Toomey. It was punishment enough (he thought) that she had to face the Sheriff sometimes; to make her face a judge, or have these little thefts of hers publicized in the paper would be too much for Miss Isabel to bear. There was no gossip about her, either. I don't know how the Sheriff managed that, but he did. Even mad at him, I still say he should be mayor, at the very least. He should run the town. Maybe he should run the world.

Miss Isabel Barnett removed her small straw hat and gloves and took the menu from its aluminum holder behind the sugar jar.

He turned back to me. "Is the Belle Ruin something else you want to write about?"

I shrugged. "I'm just interested, is all. Can't I be plain curious?"

"Emma, you're not plain anything."

I pursed my lips. Was that a compliment? Of course I'd rather step in a cow patty than ask. "After all, wouldn't anyone be? It's about a stolen baby, even if it did happen a long time ago."

"Not because you think that it has something to do with the Devereaus and the Queens? Ben Queen, for instance?"

"No."

He shoved his cup aside and leaned over the table as if to tell me something in great confidence. "I'm still looking for him, Emma."

He meant Ben Queen. That was no confidence; I already knew that. "Well, stop acting like I know where he is. I don't." Not now, I didn't. Before, he was at the Devereau house. I doubt he would have kept staying there after the police were swarming all over the lake and woods the night I was *shot* at. The Sheriff and I were about to be back at the same point we were when I stopped speaking to him.

Then I thought of what Maud had said, that being right wasn't worth it, not to lose a friend over. "I haven't seen him since *he saved my life.*" I thought that deserved some emphasis, in case the Sheriff had forgotten it. "That's where he was. I don't know where he is now." That at least was true. "He could be a world away." That gave me a chill, saying that, for I didn't want Ben Queen to be a world away; I wanted him here, watching out for me.

The face of my father, barely remembered, flared up in my mind like a Fourth of July candle. I looked down at the table and my undrunk Coke.

The Sheriff said, "Emma, let me explain about hearsay evidence."

That *word*. My hands sprang to my ears almost of their own accord.

He clamped his hand on my wrist. "Get your hands down and listen!" It nearly came out as a hiss.

I uncovered my ears, embarrassed at being so babyish. "Well?" I said stiffly.

"Look: Even though Ben Queen got his prints on that shotgun he used to save your life—for which I'll feel eternally indebted to him— he still killed someone. And I've got to find him for that reason alone."

My jaw had dropped at "eternally indebted." For saving *me*? The Sheriff cared that much? I could hardly find words, my brain seemed turned to mush. I cleared my throat. "Do you think he killed Fern? I know he didn't."

"No. But the trouble is and was that the woman who shot at you was crazy. The woman was *insane*, Emma. She could have owned up to a hundred things she didn't actually do. I'm not saying that's the case, but do you understand it was possible?"

I guess I did. It made some kind of sense. "Well, but what about a deathbed confession?"

He shook his head. "What she told you wasn't that. She didn't plan on dying, that's for certain. She thought she'd won."

"Oh." Yes, that was true. "*Our Rose*," they called her. When the truth of it was that all of the Devereau sisters hated Rose because she'd

escaped from their shadowy life and that shadowy house. She'd escaped with Ben Queen. "Rose Queen," I said. "That's where all of these
murders really began. Ben didn't kill Rose; Fern did."

He looked away.

"Are you telling me you don't believe that?"

"I could. Or couldn't. This is where hearsay kicks in. No one was
there when Rose was murdered. No one bore witness to it, so anyone
who claimed to know could only believe it on the basis of things they
heard." He flattened his palm against air to keep me from speaking
while he finished his thought. "Personally, I'd say it makes a lot more
sense that Fern killed her mother, given Rose was talking Ben into
sending the child away. How old would Fern have been then? In her
teens? Fern was a handful; she was as bad as the Devereau sisters.
Some gene might have come down through her mother and blasted the
girl to kingdom come. It makes more sense than Ben Queen killing
Rose. From all I hear, he worshipped the ground she walked on. Fern
had motive; Ben didn't. But this still has to be looked into; I have to
find him. Ben's only making it harder on himself by hiding out."

"You can hardly blame him! He's a scapegoat; he's blamed for everything. The police are sure he killed Fern only because they think he
killed Rose."

"I'm police. And I'm not sure."

The Sheriff's smile was almost harder on me at that moment than
any anger.

"But what reason would he have for killing Fern?"

"Maybe because he knew she killed Rose. Because he'd gun down
anyone, including his daughter, for that. She'd been nothing but a sor-
row to both of them. That's what I thought until what happened to
you. That changed my mind."

"You mean you *did* believe me?"

"Of course. You just never let me finish my sentence. You never let
me explain."

"Oh." I tried looking everywhere but at him. I looked at Miss Isabel Barnett, who looked at us and smiled. I waved to her. "Well, all
right, then. I guess I can start talking to you again."

He adjusted his cap and put his black sunglasses back on. "Oh?
Did you stop?"

Then he left before I could say anything back. I pounded my fist on the table and Miss Isabel Barnett looked over at me.

"Hi, Miss Barnett. I'm sorry. Something just made me do that."

"Emma, you sound a little frustrated."

There are two reasons why I like her. One, she knows I'm Emma and not Ree-Jane. Two, because she gets to the point right away. This is unusual, I think. "Well, I am."

"I can certainly understand that."

"You can?"

She was eating a grilled-cheese sandwich and french fries. The french fry she dipped carefully into a little paper cup of ketchup.

"In this world? Of course, it's understandable. Hard to make it through a single day without your nerves getting in a mess." She ate her french fry.

How did she manage to make a french fry look elegant?

A woman with a baby had walked back to peer in the booths, probably looking for somebody. When she turned, we could see the baby. Its tiny forehead was lined with a frown.

"Now that is the most worried-looking baby I have ever seen." Miss Barnett looked over at me. "You see, even a baby can get frustrated."

I wondered how old Miss Barnett was. I bet she was older than she looked. Her fine skin, which looked almost as shimmery as my mother's pearl necklace, made her look younger. She would have been around when the Belle Ruin burned down and the other baby disappeared. A person like Miss Barnett would remember details, I thought. After all, she had to remember all that stuff she shoplifted from the five-and-dime in order to report to the Sheriff. ("*Tangee lipstick in coral; Evening in Paris perfume, one and a half ounces.*")

"You've lived here all your life, haven't you?"

"Indeed I have."

Another french fry was dipped and bitten. For some reason, I saw the ghost of Vera standing by the booth, pointing at the french fries, and saying, "*That is not good manners.*" And could my mother possibly whisper "*Breeding*" and look askance. No, I didn't think so. I wondered what was in Miss Barnett's life "that didn't work," as the Sheriff had said, that made her shoplift. "Do you miss being young?"

She looked slightly startled, but then withdrew that look, as if to express surprise at a question might embarrass the person who asked it. Now *there,* I thought, was *breeding.* I should tell my mother.

She reflected. "Often I do, yes. Although I wouldn't say when the hotel was there I was exactly young. When I could swim in Lake Noir without tiring, when I could go to dances, when I was pretty. Yes, that was nice; I miss that; that was fun." She sighed. "But then there are things that you have when you're old, like being able to spend money any way you want, to turn down invitations from people you don't like, and not to have to tell anyone where you're going."

Tell anyone where you're *going*? Why would you do that anyway? "You must have had a really strict childhood, Miss Barnett." She merely smiled, and I went on. "Do you remember the Belle Ruin? That big hotel that burned down? In the deer park near Spirit Lake?"

"Ah!" She crossed her hands on her chest. She was wearing a navy-blue polka-dot dress. "The Belle Rouen. I most certainly do remember. We would go there for dinner. The most beautiful dining room. Then there were the balls. The ballroom was huge. A twelve-piece dance band played for us. You could dance all night, or so it seemed." She laughed and picked up the last quarter of her grilled cheese. It was cold. She put it down.

"Do you remember on one of those dance nights the police came because a baby was kidnapped?"

"Yes, I remember the police coming, but I had no idea as to why they'd come. I recall I went to the ladies' room and had to walk across the lobby to get to it. The sheriff and his deputy were there, and I think a couple of state troopers. But I didn't know why: I thought perhaps an automobile accident. Then I learned about the baby."

"The parents' name was Slade. She'd been Imogen Woodruff."

"They weren't La Porte people, were they, the Woodruffs?" She thought this over, her long fingers on her forehead. "But the Slades were."

I didn't say anything about the Woodruffs' wanting the whole thing kept quiet. The more I thought about that, the more peculiar it seemed, wanting it hushed up.

"But after a few days, I don't remember hearing any more," she said, sounding troubled by this lack of news.

"They left town. There was never much publicity about it."

She frowned slightly. "Was the baby never found?"

"I don't think so. I heard they went back to New York."

She shook her head. "It was quite awful." Her french fries were gone, but I don't think that's what she looked sad about.

"That gorgeous ballroom. And the gowns! Well, we were all dressed to kill."

I hoped not.

"Such beautiful clothes, such beautiful people. I can't imagine where they've gone, those people, for some of them were surely from around here. One would almost think some places vanish and take the people with them."

I sat back with a thump and thought of the Hotel Paradise. Would it take me with it?

13

I don't know why I felt too tired to walk all the way to Dr. McComb's house, but I did. I rounded the corner and headed down the street to the taxi stand. I passed the stationery store, which was always so dark you couldn't see inside it unless you went in, and the jeweler's, and the Prime Cut, where one of the girls there was stuck doing Helene Baum's hair. I sympathized. But not enough just to walk on by. I stood right in front of the window until Helene looked toward it, then I quickly moved away. This would make her wonder what was going on. Had she seen me or hadn't she? Had she seen anybody? It was just something to do.

As I neared the next corner, I stopped cold. A block down there on Second Street, a cab was pulling up in front of the office and Axel himself got out and went in.

Here was my chance! I ran, bumping into the mayor's wife, a baby carriage and old Mr. Nasalrod. I crossed the street and kind of burst through the door of Axel's Taxis.

"Whoa!" said Delbert. "Where's the fire?"

"Where's Axel?" Breathing hard, I looked around the small room, hardly believing my eyes. The dispatcher said, "Why, honey, he had to take blood up to the hospital. You know, serum or whatever."

"But he just walked in! I saw him! And his taxi's out front!"

"Yes, he did, but he went out the back door so he could just walk up the back stairs of Frazee's store. That's where the blood is; I mean, Ben Frazee was keeping it in his icebox freezer."

"His cab's right out there." I pointed as I turned.

No, it wasn't. "It's gone!"

"Well, like I said, he was in an awful rush. Blood don't keep, as you know."

Delbert, toothpick rolling around his mouth, said, "Just be glad it ain't your blood is all." He laughed his wheezy laugh. That was his idea of funny.

"Now, Delbert he can take you wherever you want."

"Yeah, I will, only not to Hebrides like that one time. I got to be back this year." Laugh, laugh, he nearly died.

I was completely deflated, as tired as if someone had kicked me around the block. "Oh, all right. I need to go to Dr. McComb's house."

Delbert looked up at the ceiling as if a map of La Porte were drawn there. "Now, lemme see, don't he live near the country club?"

"Delbert, you drove me there awhile back. Don't you remember Valley Road? It's where Red Bird Road splits off."

"Ain't that what I said? Country club's just off Red Bird Road and Valley Road."

"Well, not exactly, Delbert," the dispatcher said. "The country club's on Country Club Road. That makes sense, don't it?"

"I said *off* Red Bird Road, didn't I? I didn't say *on* it. Any fool'd know if there's a road called Country Club Road, then the country club's goin' t' be on it."

I put my head in my hands. It was worse than the Windy Run Diner.

Delbert found Valley Road and complained all along it about the potholes and sand and gravel that the town ought to take care of. Probably the town didn't because so few people lived on it. Dr. McComb's house was the biggest; then there were the trailer home with the plastic flamingos and another small boxy house.

When he stopped to let me out, Delbert wanted to know how long I'd be and should he wait. For an extra charge, of course. I mentioned how he'd gone on and on about the extra charge for waiting the day when he waited for me at the library and I didn't want to hear about the extra charge again. "No, you don't have to wait."

Leaning across the seat he said, "Because if I did it'd be extra."

I knew if I so much as answered he'd go on and on like before, so I shut up.

The house sat back from the road in tall grass and dandelions, looking pleasantly unkempt. Dr. McComb lived here alone except for a female relative, who could have been his sister or maybe his cousin. The first time I'd been at the house, she'd come into the room where I was waiting and sat down and said nothing, not even hello or "Who are you?" It was kind of nerve-racking and I didn't want to run into her again. Instead of knocking, I went around the house to the back, where Dr. McComb would probably be anyway. Behind the house, there was even more overgrowth—shrubs and small trees and tall, tall grass. The grass usually hid him and his butterfly net. He was a kind of expert on butterflies. I had read his book, well, part of it, a little of it, in the library.

The grass was so tall and thick with wildflowers and brush, I had to look carefully to make him out. I saw the net jut up and swish around. Then I saw his milkweed hair. I called out to him, probably disturbing the butterfly, and he turned around.

"Who's there?" he called back.

"It's me, Emma."

He waved his net, meaning for me to go out where he was. I didn't much care for wading through the weeds, but he was stalking something and would not want to leave the spot. I shoved my way through the high grass, Queen Anne's lace, dandelions, black-eyed Susans and coneflowers and finally caught up to him.

"You made me lose that one. Painted lady, one of my favorites, not easy to come by." He sighed for extra measure.

"I'm sorry." Which I wasn't. Butterflies were pretty, but boring. I had put in enough of my time learning something about them and even catching one that looked like the white lace in his book to bring here as a way of getting him to talk about the Devereaus. He was nice, though. And made really good brownies.

He sighed again. "Well, I don't see it now." He looked at his big wristwatch, the size of a turnip, and said, "Brownies ought to be done. Want one?"

What a question.

The brownie aroma curled like smoke around everything in the kitchen. The kitchen was much smaller than the hotel's, so that scents were more concentrated. I sat myself down on one of the white wooden chairs at the kitchen table and stuck my chin in my hands, prepared to smell the rich, chocolatey scent of the baking brownies as long as I could. I think the sense of smell is really underrated; I think it can toss up old times, jog the memory just as well as sight and sound can. Perfume, for instance: Mrs. Fulbright's flowery scent, or the winier cologne of Lola Davidow. Scents of a certain soap, early-morning grass or the sea of mint in the field beside the hotel. All of these smells will come back to haunt me when I'm grown. A hundred different smells that will come at me in a hundred different ways, for I'll have forgotten the things and people that carried them. What I'll know is that something or someone did.

I do not of course mean to say I'd rather smell the brownies than eat them, and Dr. McComb was now sifting powdered sugar over the top of the pan, which he let cool a little before he cut up the brownies into twelve pieces. Then he pushed his spatula under one to lift it out onto one of the small blue willow plates. There were cups and saucers laid out, too, and he offered me coffee, which I accepted as he was the only person in the world who offered. I put a lot of milk in, of course, not wanting my brain to be "stultified," as Will had warned me it would be if I drank coffee. Dr. McComb had warmed up the milk, too, and that way my drink was hot.

He poured coffee and milk into my cup, coffee into his own and then sat down and took the second best brownie. He knew it would have been really impolite for him to take the first best, so he didn't. I was the guest and happy to take it. We had them ranked: the ones in the middle row were best, though neither one of us said so. We tried to be casual about this.

"Come to interview me again? That's a cracking good account you're writing."

"Thanks. No, I just want some information about something else." For a moment I concentrated on the soft sugary top of my brownie, then I asked him if he knew about the Belle Ruin and if he was doctor here then.

"That huge hotel about a mile from Spirit Lake? Of course, I've been there. Why, it was all the thing back then. Real fancy, real high society, if there's such a thing around here. But of course that place attracted people from the cities. At least one president stayed there. Several opera stars and musicians. That was a crackerjack place, let me tell you. You know it burned down; that was over twenty-some years ago. It was several years before that business about the Devereau sisters. Poor little Mary-Evelyn." He shook his head sadly. "Terrible, awful thing."

I couldn't linger now over its awfulness. "That's right. What I want to know is about the kidnapped baby." I must admit, my eye was on an inside brownie.

He rubbed the heel of his hand around on his forehead as if to give his brain a good stirring. "Oh, yes. That baby that went missing, poor little tyke."

"Wasn't it stolen? Kidnapped?"

Dr. McComb studied his brownie. "It was never known what happened for sure. The police came from La Porte and also a couple of state troopers. They called me. Why, I don't know. There was no body to examine. I reckon the sheriff was afraid the mother might pass out or something. Why are you on about this? Isn't there enough excitement in your life that now you've got to look for more?"

I didn't answer as I didn't think it was a real question. I just picked up another brownie.

He went on. "The parents were beside themselves. The police couldn't get anything out of the mother, poor girl. She had to be medicated. The father wasn't much better. It was really the grandfather, the daughter's father, who took charge. Name of Woodruff. Had tons of money, I know that."

He eyed the brownie pan, then unwedged one of the middle ones.

"I can't understand why there wasn't more in the papers."

"I don't know, except this Woodruff might have tossed some money the reporters' way to keep them quiet." He drank his coffee.

"But why would he want it kept quiet? I just can't figure out any of it. It's like the baby just"—I slid my hand through empty air—"vanished off the face of the earth." The thought of this gave me goose bumps and I rubbed up and down my arm. "And there wasn't any ransom asked for."

"Not that we ever heard about, no. Believe me, with that loudmouthed Mooma, we'd have heard. Not Donny, of course. There are so many Moomas around, hard to keep them straight."

"Was he related to Donny?"

"I think that was his uncle," Dr. McComb said. "He was worse than Donny when it came to keeping secrets."

"Then words must've gushed out of him like that broken sewer pipe on Alder Street," I said.

Dr. McComb gave a little laugh as he ran his eye over the brownies, so I quickly went for the one that looked the plumpest along the side. "I'm just glad we have our Sheriff," I said.

"Yep. Sam DeGheyn's the smartest man in these parts. He's the smartest man I know."

I drank my milky coffee. It always pleased me to hear the Sheriff complimented. "Weren't they suspicious of the babysitter?"

"Nah. I even talked to her."

My eyes widened. "You did?"

He nodded. "Gloria Spiker. She was around twenty, nineteen, maybe. She was scared witless. That's not hard to do with the Spikers."

"Does she still live around here?"

"Gloria? Let me put on my thinking cap about that."

Dr. McComb actually did cover his balding head with his hand. With the other hand he took another brownie. "I could be wrong, but I think those particular Spikers moved to Cold Flat Junction. Gloria'd be in her thirties or forties, I guess. She was a silly girl, so she probably won't be much help to you."

"But she was the one *with* the baby. She must know more than anyone else, more than even the mother or father. They weren't there when their baby was stolen."

"Um. Well, she sure didn't have much information to impart." He took a big bite of his brownie.

"Could she have had something to do with the kidnapping?" I was excited by this idea. "Maybe she was the one inside. It might have been an inside job. You know."

Dr. McComb frowned. "Gloria Spiker an accomplice? Don't make me laugh. Gloria would have a hard time finding her own shoes. Anyway, what's this inside job stuff?"

"Just that the ladder could have been put there to make it look like it was somebody outside the hotel who kidnapped the baby."

"What ladder?"

"There was a very tall ladder put against the side of the building that went up to their room. Where the baby was."

"I don't remember any ladder. That way it sounds like the Lindbergh kidnapping."

Everybody said that. It was peculiar.

"Do you think the kidnapper could have told the Woodruffs to get rid of the police and the reporters? Not to talk to them? You see that a lot in movies and mystery books. Usually, though, it's a warning made at the time of the kidnapping."

We sat in silence for a while, looking at the brownie pan. I didn't think I could eat another one, but there was one with a lot of powdered sugar on it that looked really good.

Dr. McComb said, "There might have been a ransom demand later."

His hand was kind of crabbing along toward the pan.

"Why, though?" My own hand shot out as if it had a life of its own and took up the one I'd been coveting. I said, "Oh, I'm sorry. Did you want this one?"

He waved it away. "No, no."

I was the guest, after all. "Why would they wait?"

He lifted a smaller brownie from the side of the pan. "Maybe because it was too hot for them to do it at the time. They might've panicked."

I wasn't satisfied with this answer, but I didn't say so.

He stirred some cream into his coffee and tapped the spoon against the saucer. "I haven't thought about this in years. You know, there should be some people here still who were at that dance, people around my age. Miss Flyte, I wouldn't be surprised if she was there. And Ben Queen."

My mouth agape again, I said, "What about him?"

"I was just thinking how Ben might know something because he delivered over there to the Belle Ruin. It was mostly vegetables. You know, he and his dad delivered to the Hotel Paradise, too. They went to nearly all the hotels. They raised the best vegetables around." He shook his head. "Too bad the police are still looking for him. After all this even."

I said nothing, being afraid my voice might give away my feelings if I mentioned Ben Queen. "I've got to be getting back to the hotel." The clock on the wall said 1:10. Lunch that day wasn't to be served until 2:00 as Miss Bertha and Mrs. Fulbright were being driven somewhere by a relation of Mrs. Fulbright's. "Thank you for the brownies and coffee."

"You're perfectly welcome. Come back and tell me what you find out."

"I will."

Delbert was still there waiting in the cab.

I could hardly believe it. "I told you not to wait." I climbed in; I'd have to get a cab anyway, as I'd never get back in time if I walked. I'd pretty much used up excuses for not being there to wait tables. Being famous could get you only so far. *"Fame and a dime'll buy you a cup of coffee,"* Will liked to say now. I get minilectures on the subject. "You shouldn't be thinking of fame; no, you should be trying to perfect your art."

"My art? What art? I'm only writing for the *Conservative.*" I was much more down to earth than Will, even if I didn't have his imagination.

So I told Delbert to drive me back to the hotel. "And don't try charging me for waiting time, either," I said as he turned the car at the dead end of a field of graze where some cows chewed dreamily. I closed my eyes and thought about being a cow. It wasn't all that bad an existence, until the end of it. I opened my eyes and stared at the back of Delbert's head and his jutting ears.

"Thing is—" he started.

I groaned.

"—thing is I kind of fell asleep there in the car, so I can't charge you waiting time for that, I guess." He sounded uncertain.

I leaned my chin on the seat back. "Delbert, awake or asleep, you still couldn't charge me extra time because I told you *not to wait!*" What could be clearer than that?

He was silent, which in Delbert's case didn't mean he was thinking, only that he was silent. Then he said, "Well, now, I don't know about that. See—"

I slapped my hands over my ears, but it did no good; I could still hear his whiny voice.

"—see, you're back in the cab now. And I'm drivin' you back to the Hotel Paradise, ain't I?"

I knew he was looking in the rearview mirror, waiting for me to say, but I didn't. So he just went on. "So it's like you had this cab all along. Yeah, I could've charged waiting time."

"I *told* you not to *wait*!" Why was I arguing?

"Yeah, I know. But you got back into the cab, see. But since I went to sleep, 'course I done it on your time, so I won't charge you—hey! What in the Sam Hill you doin'—hey! You close that door!"

He slammed on the brakes and butted the car up near the flowerbed of the house with the pink flamingos. He'd only been going like fifteen miles per hour. I closed the door and sat back. I'd only opened it an inch or two, anyway.

His face was perspiring all over. "Girl, are you crazy? Openin' a door in a moving vehicle."

He said "vehicle" just like Mr. Slaw did: "ve-*hick*-le."

"What in tarnation are you tryin' to do?"

"To make you stop talking."

He slapped the steering wheel. "Oh, now, *there's* a reason for you!"

"There sure is."

He started up the car again, pulled from the shoulder, back onto Red Bird Road. The lady who owned the flamingos had come out to watch. I guess she'd never seen a car before. I waved. She just stood and watched the car down the road.

Delbert went right back to talking. "What I think's that next time you'd best get Axel to drive if my driving ain't satisfactory to you. Axel don't talk much, neither, so you two would hit it off."

I yawned, letting the opportunity pass to find out more about Axel. The thing was, of course, Delbert wouldn't know what I was talking about if I said Axel was driving a mystery cab, that whenever I saw it and him in it, there was never a passenger.

Delbert was still talking when I finished my own thoughts. I was good at thinking of something else when people talked to me, not as good as Will, but then he was a master. Delbert was still going on about Axel's driving me to and from the hotel when we bumped up the gravel drive and under the porte cochere. I told him he could keep the change, the change amounting to twenty-five cents, which was more than anyone else would have paid him after having to listen to all that jawing he did.

It was 2:00 and I saw Miss Bertha walking in hunchback mode toward the dining room with Mrs. Fulbright. Miss Bertha was bent at the waist and in her steel gray dress, she looked and moved a lot like a turtle. I guess I should have felt sympathy for her, but as far as I could see, no one else did. Once when Mrs. Davidow was in the kitchen with her third martini of the evening, sitting on the big salad table with her legs crossed and swinging her foot, she had said someone really ought to feel sorry for Miss Bertha, and they all looked at me, even Walter. (Talk about your scapegoats!) As I was the one most in contact with Miss Bertha (someone had said), I should show her some compassion.

At the rate Miss Bertha was moving along now, I could get to the dining room long before they did. Mrs. Fulbright's walk was elegant and leisurely, her hand occasionally going to Miss Bertha's elbow in a kindly gesture of assistance and Miss Bertha slapping the hand away whenever it touched her.

"They've been friends since childhood," my mother had said. I had replied it was an insane miracle and then my mind swung to picturing Ree-Jane and me seventy years from now. Ree-Jane was the hunched-over one, and I was the elegant one.

I said, "Mrs. Fulbright must be having to pay penance for something she did to Miss Bertha. Maybe she drove her car into Miss Bertha and turned her into the Hunchback of Spirit Lake. So now to make up for it, she comes to our hotel every summer for all summer long with her victim."

My mother waved her cigarette around and told me to talk sense.

Why talk sense, considering the usual Hotel Paradise script? I went on to consider the punishment. Coming here every year, that was probably part of the penance. In my mind I heard Father Freeman, his head bowed, announcing the punishment. "Say ten Hail Marys and go to the Hotel Paradise every summer for the remainder of your life." I pictured Mrs. Fulbright, young and gay, dropping down like a leaf in a dead faint.

". . . Spanish omelets."

My mother was standing, hands on hips, behind the counter. "Where is your mind? Did you hear me?"

No, but I could figure it out. "We've got omelets for lunch." I was holding the red glass water pitcher that I didn't recall picking up. "Miss Bertha doesn't like the Spanish sauce. It's got peas in it." It could have a Spaniard in it for all I cared. I was just being argumentative. My mother already knew she hated peas.

"Then she can have a cheese omelet."

With my big tray holding the water pitcher, I shouldered my way through the swinging door and saw them just now taking their seats. Mrs. Fulbright said hello in her pleasant way; Miss Bertha grunted and moved everything on the table around, pushing the water glass away, the salt and the silverware. I poured water and listened to Miss Bertha *harrumph* as I told them the menu. "There are two kinds of omelets: Spanish"—Mrs. Fulbright brightened—"and cheese." When Miss Bertha looked relieved, I added, "Cheese and peas."

She flung herself backward so hard her hump nearly straightened out. "What do you mean peas? There's no such thing as peas in a cheese omelet."

I smiled in a kindly way. "Of course not. It's the cheese *sauce;* my mother, the cook, is trying out something new with the peas."

Miss Bertha sputtered and even spit a little. "Then you tell her to try leaving out the peas!"

"Now, Bertha," said Mrs. Fulbright, "I'm sure it will be delicious."

"Never heard of such a fool thing! Peas in cheese!"

I made my tone sorrowful. "Oh, but she can't leave out the peas. They're already in the sauce."

"Damndest fool thing! Jen Graham knows I hate peas."

I sighed. "You'd think she would. I'll see what I can do, Miss Bertha." I sailed away, back through the swing door and ordered one Spanish, one cheese omelet. With peas.

There wasn't much by way of entertainment at the Hotel Paradise.

14

I needed to catch the afternoon train to Cold Flat Junction and was saved from having to call Axel's for a cab (again), as Mrs. Davidow was going into La Porte and Alta Vista for "supplies." This usually meant a case of Jim Beam and Gordon's gin.

I prayed that Ree-Jane wouldn't want to go at the last minute, but my prayers as usual went unanswered. Ree-Jane came traipsing down the front porch steps just as her mother turned the key in the ignition. With one of her sneering smiles she opened the passenger door and told me to get in the back.

With a withering look at her, I climbed into the backseat. Even Mrs. Davidow shook her head at this and mumbled something I couldn't make out. But she didn't order Ree-Jane to get in the back herself.

Naturally, Ree-Jane had to know where I was going, so I made up an appointment with Mr. Gumbrel. "At the *Conservative* offices." Then I went on to rub it in. "To go over the piece I'm writing." She had been looking back over her shoulder, but now she turned away. She couldn't think up a retort, and it drove her crazy that *I* had pulled out the biggest plum of a reporting job, when *she* was the one Fate had earmarked for journalism fame.

When Mrs. Davidow dropped me off at the *Conservative,* I thanked her and ran upstairs, or halfway up, and then came down again. I had but a few minutes to run down the street and around the corner to the station to make the train. I flew.

When I stepped off the train onto the platform of the Cold Flat Junction station, I looked up and down it as I always did, hoping to see the Girl. I had seen her there twice before. The first time was around three weeks ago, when she had been sitting on one of the wooden benches against the brick wall of the station, facing toward the empty field beyond the track. I wondered if she saw the same thing I saw, and if she felt a pull to cross the tracks and walk over the field to that dark line of trees and vanish.

This made me shiver. I had never thought about vanishing before. Why would we, she and I, think about disappearing into the woods out there?

I had never thought about "we" before, either.

The Cold Flat Junction station was what I believe would be described as Victorian. It was intricately designed, no detail escaping the overall pattern. A filigreelike molding edged the roof that I'd seen on cottages in Spirit Lake that my mother called gingerbread style and was delicate and kind of pretty. La Porte's station is in the same style and has gone unappreciated, at least by me. But that train station is busy with passengers, suitcases at their feet, or walking up and down, searching through the engine steam for a passenger alighting or departing, looking for someone to say hello or good-bye to. The ticket window is almost always up to serve you, people greeting one another, throwing out names like hugs; or ladies stepping down from the train onto the little stool the conductor provides, meeting and hurrying, collecting bags and belongings—it almost leaves me breathless. I did not even know why I was thinking about it, why this scene sprang to mind—oh, but yes I did: it was because no one does those things here in the Cold Flat Junction station. There is no one to do them. Excepting me and the Girl, the only ones who are ever here. But that of course is nonsense; there must be other people who get on and off the train here; otherwise, why would it stop at all?

The beige blind over the ticket window was always down, at least when I'd been here. Dark wood benches in the waiting room positioned back to back ran the length of the room. Posters hung around the walls advertising all of the dangerous, exciting, storybook places you could go. Trains were pictured steaming into Florida somewhere or snaking along the cliff coast of Maine as if one wrong move would send the whole train into the sea. All of the bright holidays took just boarding the train and off you went. Except nobody seemed to go there anymore, at least not from the Cold Flat Junction station.

I don't know why I stood wasting my time studying the posters. It was not some overall longing to see these places that were advertised. Maybe I agreed with Father Freeman, who had said it was better to go to such places in mind rather than in body. I had gone that way to Miami Beach after all and found it better than the trip the others had described.

Perhaps it was the pictures of happy people going to happy places; perhaps it was the waiting room itself, as empty as the field across the track. I liked the emptiness, for life is so cluttered. I guess I am crazy. It just seemed a place to stop and look around and for no reason but to do it. I had thought this before I looked at that parched land. I left the waiting room and went to sit down on one of the benches just as the Girl had done. I wondered what she made of it. What she made of any of it. What *we* made of it.

I walked into the Windy Run Diner and took my usual stool at the counter and said hello, hello to all of them. Even Mervin's wife smiled and returned the greeting.

Billy pretended amazement at seeing me back here again. "Godamighty, girl, you been in here enough times you ought to move here." He thought that was very funny and laughed and nudged Don Joe beside him to do the same.

I'd like to say I thought over my reply, but I didn't. I just said it. "Yes, that's what we aim to do. My family, I mean. We're wondering if there're any houses around for sale."

You can imagine what kind of storm that would stir up! Here was a subject they could all get in on; it could involve not only houses for sale right now, but also people who were thinking of selling, or others who might sell if offered enough money or houses sold in the past. They could toss all of this around forever and a day. But I wasn't going to let them.

"Jim and Jolene Spiers," said Don Joe. "They're sellin' up, last I heard."

The heavyset woman wearing glasses (whose name I still didn't know) said, "Since when, Don Joe? Jim's not doin' any such a thing. I saw him not fifteen minutes ago walking up to Flyback Holler without a care in the world."

"Well, what in tarnation's that got to do with it, anyway?" said Don Joe. "He could be selling his house and walking to Flyback Holler without a care, for heaven's sake."

"A course he could," said Billy. "And I ain't never heard him say a word about sellin' his place."

Louise Snell was in her usual stance by the pie and cake shelves. "Mami Oster's going to live with her daughter out in Arizona is what I heard, so she'll be selling. That's a cute house. Mami's kept it up real nice. Four bedrooms and a separate dining room. With old Sam dead and the kids gone off, she sure doesn't need all that room and aggravation of keeping up such a big place. How many bedrooms do your folks need, honey?"

I was nodding off with my chin in my hands. "Bedrooms? Oh, I guess three or four. Or five."

Louise Snell asked, "Do you have any brothers or sisters?"

"Siblings," Mervin's wife said. She seemed to be really interested in my moving to Cold Flat Junction.

I thought for a second. "Just one, a brother. He's kind of deformed but he scoots around okay in his electric wheelchair."

Their condolences (and embarrassment at now knowing this family curse) were softly given: "Too bad," "What a shame," "Real sorry," "That's rough, ain't it?" I had put him in the wheelchair with his deformity so they wouldn't want to talk the subject to death. I changed the subject to what I really wanted to know. "Now, somebody told Ma (who would, if she ever heard me call her that, offer me a long lecture on breeding) that there's a woman named Gloria. . . . What's her name, now . . . oh, it used to be Spiker. Maybe she's gotten married since. Anyway, Ma heard this Gloria Spiker was selling her house."

"Gloria Spiker . . . yeah," said Don Joe. "Didn't she marry that Baker fellow?"

"Nah, you're thinkin' of Charlene Budd. She married Fred Baker. Far as I know." Billy batted the ash from his cigarette onto his empty pie plate. He would definitely be included in the good breeding lecture. "Now, Gloria, she married Cary Grant Calhoun. Had four or five kids. Cussed ones, too."

Surprised, I said, "Cary *Grant* Calhoun? Cary Grant's a movie star."

"Well, don't his ma know it?" said Billy. They laughed, giving one another nudges with their elbows. "His ma always claimed he looked just like Cary Grant, even when the child was just born. And that's who she named him after. Used to describe him as the handsomest man in Cold Flat Junction."

Louise Snell said, "That wouldn't be much accomplished, would it?"

I asked, "*Is* he handsome?" I already had my quota of handsome men: the Sheriff, Dwayne and Ben Queen. I could hardly believe there was another in the whole state, much less in Cold Flat Junction. "Does he look like Cary Grant?"

"No," said Mervin. "He looks like a Calhoun."

Evren put in his two cents. "He ain't handsome, for sure. Cary Grant Calhoun was ugly from a baby. 'Course, you couldn't ever get his mama to see it. Love is blind." He gave a snorty kind of giggle. "His ma claimed he was the handsomest baby in the forty-eight."

Don Joe held up his hands, palms out. "Evren, if you mean the forty-eight *states,* you'd best wake up. There's fifty of the damned things, as I got told a few days ago. Got told off for my dumbness." He looked at me.

The teller-offer, me. "That was about Alaska because you said if you was—were—Ben Queen you'd hightail it out of the country and go to Alaska."

"You'd be good as a *po*-lice witness," said Mervin, chuckling, "with your memory and all. They like people that remembers details."

Mervin got a slap on the arm from his wife for that. She never liked him speaking up for some reason.

Billy said, looking at me, "You were looking for Rebecca Calhoun that married Bewly Spiker, remember? Last time you was here?"

It was as if my diner friends were actually telling me what my life was all about and I was just going by what they said. "Then is this Gloria Spiker related to Bewly?"

"Hell, gal, all them Spikers is related—brothers sisters aunts cousins. Now Bewley he'd be Gloria's, what?, uncle?"

"Cary Grant Calhoun'd be Imogene's cousin," said Evren.

This got Evren a tired look from Billy, as if Evren were wearing him out. "Evren, you don't know that anymore'n you know how many kernels is on a cob."

"Yes, I do. I asked her if she was related to Cary Grant Calhoun and she *said* they was cousins." His head bobbed down on "said."

Louise Snell said, "It's just like the Spikers, Billy. There are so many Calhouns they'd stretch from here to Hebrides if you stood them end to end."

"And come back with a case of gin each," Don Joe just slapped the counter until his coffee sloshed over and Louise Snell sponged it off.

Well, I just got this sense of its being impossible to figure out who anyone really was. I asked, "Where does Gloria Spiker live? I mean, I'd like to just go see her house to tell Ma all about it." (I liked saying "Ma"; I sure never got to say it at home.)

"Over there in Red Coon Rock like you went to before," said Billy.

Mervin piped up, "It's the blue house, first you come to."

Billy swung around on his stool. "Mervin, you keep tryin' to sell that blue house as belonging to someone it don't. I told you before, that house is Wanda *Leroy's.*"

"It ain't any such a thing. You are mistaken here, Billy."

Mervin's wife hissed something at him.

Billy just rolled his eyes and turned to me. "Gloria Spiker's only two houses down from Imogene. It's kinda greeny-gray and there ain't no porch."

I intended to get out before Mervin started up about the blue house again. "Well, thank you all very much," I said, getting off my stool. "I'll just be going along there, then."

As I passed Mervin's booth, he leaned out a little and whispered, "Blue house." When I got to the door, Don Joe called to me to "let me know how much Gloria wanted for that old falling-down place" as he might just up and buy it himself.

I said I would, which I wouldn't.

15

Red Coon Rock was just past Flyback Hollow, where Jude Stemple and Louise Landis both lived. Jude Stemple didn't look like he'd have gone dancing at the Belle Ruin, but Louise Landis might have. Miss Landis had been Ben Queen's girlfriend before Rose Devereau came along. Still, she had remained his friend, which said a lot about her as I'm sure it had long been a case of unrequited love.

I walked along Dubois Road, past the Queen house—Ben's brother George and sister-in-law's place—and wondered if George and Sheba had ever themselves gone to the Belle Ruin. It seemed more likely they'd have worked there than danced there, given how fine a hotel it was, with the rich and socially prominent as its guests, ones who had come from other places expressly to stay "the season" at the Belle Ruin. There was a third class of people who might have pulled up under the Belle Ruin's handsome porte cochere: the extremely well bred. Bred to the bone, like my mother and anyone my mother set her seal of approval on, Louise Landis being one of them.

I got to the end of Dubois Road where the Kool-Aid stand—a folding table and chair—was still set up and the hand-lettered sign still read LEMONADE. The girl, younger than me, was not there and neither was the pitcher of Kool-Aid, so I figured she'd gone for more. She insisted that it was a lemonade *stand,* even if she was selling Kool-Aid. I had to agree that I had never seen a Kool-Aid stand as such. I could have argued it, but it wasn't like she had customers lined up and down Dubois Road. I figured business was bad enough without making her feel even worse. If the pitcher had been there, I'd have taken one of the little plastic cups and left her the five cents.

Just looking at the empty table made me sad. It was hard work sitting out here alone, hoping you'd sell enough Kool-Aid to buy yourself some small thing. It would have been harder still on such a day, looking as if it could rain at any moment, the sky the color of lead and just as heavy looking.

I looked all around, not for the girl, but at the land and the houses beyond Dubois Road where the white-painted grade school sat. I remembered the first time I'd come here, passing the school and the single boy standing on its playground with a basketball or volleyball. I recalled a woman in a dark dress coming out of the back door of the school, shading her eyes with her hand and staring off into the distance. Then there was the girl in the schoolyard on my second visit I played a game of pickup stix with. She said nothing all the while we played.

It was the utter stillness I thought about. Even in the Windy Run Diner, it seemed to underlie all of the talk; it had to do with all of them keeping to their same seats while the old world went on turning without them. They had stopped going along with it; when I was here, I stopped too, even though I was acting busy—looking up people, making up stories, hell-bent (as the Sheriff had called me) on finding things out. It reminded me of that game kids play, Statues, where the players have to freeze before the moment of discovery.

This all sounds unhappy, but it is not, not when stopping is really the only thing to do. I stayed there another moment and then walked on past the stone with RED COON ROCK in whitewashed letters, like a road sign.

There were a lot of trees here, oak and maple, all clustered around the few houses on this road. It was as if all the trees that had ever grown in Cold Flat Junction had gathered here, for all of it was treeless except for Red Coon Rock and Flyback Hollow. There were the woods way off across the empty field, but I didn't know if that was even part of Cold Flat Junction, it looked so far away. It was the lack of trees and the dust that made it look scalped, shorn of any shade. You had to be really vigilant (like the Queens) if you didn't want your lettuces and roses burning up.

But along here was lots of shade; it was cool and relaxing. I kicked little stones from the road and watched the dry beige earth dust my shoe and leg.

I passed the house where Imogene Calhoun lived and who'd told me about her sister Rebecca babysitting Mary-Evelyn Devereau. I wonder if finding out what really happened to Mary-Evelyn made thinking about it worse or better. For it was horrible; but then I had always suspected it had been. Still, I think not knowing would have been worse. No, I'm glad I found out, for it had led at least to some kind of justice—if that's not too heavy a word—and as far as most people were concerned, it showed Ben Queen was innocent.

There was always the Sheriff, though, who didn't think it was proved. Even just thinking of that made me kick harder, kick a stone to kingdom come. For as far as I'm concerned, anybody who shoots someone who's trying to shoot *me,* well, that person has innocence written all over him. While I stood, reminding myself that what the Sheriff had said did make sense, I saw the blue house. I saw it first through pine trees, and so its color was muted by dark green. But as I drew closer and set my feet on the narrow path to its door, I could see it plain. It was blue, all right. I don't have anything in my head to compare it with. Not the sky, certainly; not even the Sheriff's eyes. This house was a crazy bright and blinding blue, a blue that could really hurt your eyes if you looked at it too long.

I walked up the path to the porch with its white railing, and I could rest my eyes for a moment from all that blue. The house was very well kept. Potted pink geraniums in earthenware pots marched up the porch steps and there were hanging baskets of some purple flower I didn't know the name of. I knocked on the door.

When the woman opened it, I said, "Excuse me, ma'am"—"ma'am" being a form of address my mother told me was ill bred—"but are you Mrs. Gloria Calhoun?"

She held the door wider. "Well, yes, I am."

There's so little to do in Cold Flat Junction that even I counted as a source of entertainment.

"What can I do for you, miss—?"

"Emma. Emma Graham. The reason I'm here is because my mother, who's laid up with a cold, told me to accompany my aunt Aurora to Cold Flat Junction to see what houses might be available for sale. Aunt Aurora got a fierce headache and she stayed in the car and told me just to come see." I drew breath. "So one of the people in the Windy Row Diner told me you were thinking of selling your house. 'The big blue house in Red Coon Rock,' they said. Well, this certainly is blue! It's really pretty."

It was, too. She'd invited me in by now, and I was in the front room, and it seemed so fresh, as if all of the slipcovers and pillows and curtains had just been laundered. One of the curtains was blown inward by a small breeze. Even the air smelled washed. Yes, I would really like living here.

As she kind of smoothed her short oat-colored hair, Gloria Spiker Calhoun said, "Well, now, I can't imagine why they said that—oh, please sit down." She pointed to a bright-flowered chair. "Who was it told you that?"

She did not seem at all suspicious or even much bothered by this intrusion. She was quite pleasant, heavyset and smooth faced, and very clean and plain—just the sort of person, I decided, who would live in a house such as this.

I thanked her and as I sank into the armchair she'd indicated I realized I was tired. "I can't remember exactly which person at the diner told me you were selling your house, but I do recall someone named Mervin was the only one who knew where you lived. The others claimed somebody else lived in the blue house. So, you see, it could be the house for sale is this other person's."

She sighed and sat down in a dark green rocking chair that looked like it might have come from our hotel. "Mervin's the only one with the sense he was born with. You'd think they'd all know who lived in this house, as long as I've lived here. Would you like some milk?"

Milk? I frowned and then quickly wiped that from my face. "No, thank you. Then I guess I can tell my mother and aunt you don't want to sell. I don't blame you. It's so nice around here. My grandfather talked about it all the time. Before he passed." I'd picked up a few things here and there from the gospel meeting camp. "He used always to talk about the hotels around Spirit Lake. I guess it used to be a big summer resort."

"That's right. Big splashy place called the Belle Ruin was the best. A kind of French-y name because the owner I think was from a place in France with a name like that."

"I saw pictures of it in the historical society in La Porte. It was beautiful. Did you used to go there?"

She looked away and picked up an embroidery hoop with a needle stuck in the material. It was threaded with a silky green thread. The pattern looked like leaves. "Not really."

That made me shut my mouth, which had been open to step on the heels of a different reply, like "Oh, yes, I did some babysitting there." Still, her answer wasn't no, but not really. When she started on the embroidery I decided she was just too embarrassed to talk about it. The baby had been taken when she was supposed to be watching it. I chewed at my lower lip, thinking. "I read there was something really awful that happened there. Somebody was kidnapped? There was this huge ransom demand. I read it in the paper." That was stupid. The ransom demand couldn't have been reported in the paper because it never happened.

But Gloria said anyway, "That's wrong. There was never any ransom demand, at least as far as any of us heard." She started rocking briskly.

I waited for her to say something else, but she didn't. "I guess I must've read it wrong."

There was a long high note from somewhere and she said, "That'll be the kettle." She rose and dropped the embroidery back on the chair.

I sat there thinking, holding my fingers up to the light coming in through the window to see my fingernails go transparent and wondered what it would be like to be kidnapped. If you were a baby, you probably couldn't tell the difference, so it shouldn't be too bad if they gave you back after a while. All I mean is a baby wouldn't know it was being kidnapped as long as they gave it food and blankets and, I guess, changed its diaper. Would a kidnapper change a diaper? I couldn't picture that. Now, at my age, if a person was kidnapped it might even be kind of exciting, kind of like camping out. Kind of like getting away from Ree-Jane. Then I pictured Ree-Jane being kidnapped, and that was pleasant. No one would pay a ransom; we'd all just shrug our shoulders and say, "That's life."

I looked around the room for a photo of Cary Grant Calhoun, but didn't see one. Or at least not of anyone who looked like Cary Grant. There was a cluster of little framed pictures on a table across the room, and I got up to inspect them. They were mostly those gawky snapshots you take of people looking like anyone except themselves, stiff on porches and wearing snapshot smiles.

I went back to my chair. I reached up to the metal pull of the lamp by my chair and yanked it on and off several times. I could hear Gloria Calhoun fussing about in the kitchen.

If I were kidnapped would I be scared? Maybe, right at the beginning when they were pulling me out the window. I hoped they would not put me in the trunk of a car in case I had claustrophobia. The kidnappers would probably take me to a log cabin somewhere in the woods. I thought of Brokedown House. That would be excellent for a kidnapping, out near Lake Noir, with the only other house nearby being Mr. Butternut's. He would never go snooping around Brokedown House; he was too afraid of the place. Dwayne hunted rabbits around there, so he would probably come along and save me.

I jumped in my chair when Gloria came back with a tea tray. I told her it looked very nice, including the cookies. That was a lie because my mother makes the only good cookies around. Still, they looked better than Sheba Queen's cookies, but that wasn't much of a compliment.

In her big white apron, Gloria looked pretty calmed down, so I started in again as I put four sugar cubes in my cup. "This person that got kidnapped—"

"Wasn't a grown-up; it was a baby." She handed me my tea and re-sat herself.

"Oh, my *goodness*!" I said it as if I was shocked beyond measure, my hand dropping my spoon and flying up to my cheek. "That poor baby must have been scared to death!" But it wouldn't have been; I'd already worked that out.

Gloria sipped her tea and rocked in the agitated way of one who was keeping something back, but she let the embroidery lie in her lap.

"Now, I don't want you gossiping about this, about what I'm going to tell you." She gave me a sharp look.

"*Me?* I *never* gossip." I always gossiped.

She leaned forward as if she wanted to cut down on the space her words had to travel through, as if the very air might whisper them about. And that made me think of that Ink Spots' song called "Whispering Grass," where the grass was warned not to tell the trees. Because the grass had told the trees once before: *"Because you told the blabbering trees,"* which was my favorite line. I had no trouble believing all these things could talk—grass, trees, birds—because, frankly, I pretty much believed they did anyway. No, what bothered me was that the song never told me what they were whispering *about* and that was really annoying. What were the secrets that "the blabbering trees" had told "once before"? I had always thought this song to be very mysterious.

All of this went through my head as Gloria Calhoun smoothed her apron and folded her hands across her knees. She nodded. "It was Mr. and Mrs. Slade who were the parents. The baby, little Fay, was in the room that connected and Mrs. Slade said she was sleeping sound and not to disturb her as she'd had a fever. If anything happened to come get them as they'd be just downstairs in the ballroom." She picked up the teapot and poured us some more.

I added my four sugar cubes and said no thanks to the cookies. "Then what happened?"

"I'd brought a copy of *Photoplay* along and I sat and read it. It's funny, the things you remember around something important, isn't it? There was an article about Veronica—"

I cut her off, for I could see we might end up in Veronica Lakeland. I said, "So nothing happened for a while?"

"Nothing. Then about an hour and a half later, around ten P.M. it was, I needed to make a phone call to my best friend, Prunella Rice. We was to go to a show the next night at the old Limerick movie house that used to be in Hebrides and that's been closed for years. Well, the hotel didn't have phones in the rooms, not the way hotels have now—"

It was clear she'd never stayed at the Hotel Paradise.

"—they had them in the hall, two or three on each floor, and the one for this room was down the hall. So I left the door open in case the baby waked up and I went down and called Prunella." She put a little more milk in her tea and stirred slowly and bit her lip. "I was on the phone longer than I thought. Prunella was always such a chatterbox—"

(Uh-huh.)

"—I couldn't hang up on her. Well, I was gone for twenty minutes, I guess, and when I went back, Mr. Slade was there and the baby was gone."

"Mr. Slade? He was there?" First I'd heard about that.

"He'd come back to the room to get Mrs. Slade a shawl or some kind of wrap. Well, you can imagine!"

For once, I couldn't. "Was he furious, or what?"

"He was so mad he just turned ice cold. He got the manager or the owner to call the police."

Poor Gloria Calhoun. Even now more than twenty years later, she looked crushed, and I thought she'd start crying, but she didn't.

"Worst thing that ever happened to me."

Worst thing that ever happened to the baby, too, but I didn't say it. "That's terrible." I let a few ticks of the clock go by for sympathy, then said, "Well, how'd the kidnapper get in?"

"Through the window. There was a ladder leaning right up against their window. He came and went that way. Or they did."

"More than one? That would be kind of hard, the ladder and all."

"There were footprints on the ground around the ladder."

But anybody could make footprints.

I said, "There wasn't much in the papers after the first time it was reported. There wasn't anything about the ransom—" I just remembered I wasn't supposed to know anything about this kidnapping, but Gloria had forgotten that.

"That's because Mr. Woodruff—the old man, the one with all the money—didn't want it in the papers or the police doing anything because he thought they'd have a better chance of getting her back."

That's what kidnappers always put in ransom notes: *Do not tell the police if you want to see your daughter alive again.* Or wife or son. But here there was no ransom note. Maybe Mr. Woodruff thought that's what it would say.

"I just know they blamed me." Her head was lowered over her embroidery hoop but her hands didn't move.

"Didn't they have a baby nurse?"

Gloria shrugged. "Well, see, she was sick or something. She didn't come with them."

I thought that was quite a coincidence, the baby being sick and the nurse being sick on the very night the baby was kidnapped.

"What did you think happened?"

She looked at me as if surprised anyone would ask her opinion. "Well . . . that somebody just crawled up that ladder and"—she held her arms wide—"took the poor thing."

16

Late that afternoon, after I got back to Spirit Lake, I was at Slaw's Garage. Mr. Slaw was gone for the day, so nobody yelled. Besides Dwayne there was just You-Boy, who was dawdling over Ree-Jane's white convertible that I knew she had brought in just so she could see Dwayne. She made up stuff about funny noises coming from underneath the hood and so forth. Dwayne knew it; he didn't say so, but I knew he knew it. He just handed the car over to You-Boy, who liked it because it was a white Chrysler convertible.

When I came into the garage, You-Boy was sitting in the driver's seat, calling out to Dwayne that he was taking the car out for a little spin to see what was wrong with it. Dwayne called back for You-Boy to take his time. Which You-Boy certainly would.

I was sitting on the stacked-up tires and talking to Dwayne, who was on his wooden pallet underneath a Ford station wagon, clanging and banging away. I was telling him all about my visit to Gloria Spiker and all about the Belle Ruin.

"You sure you're saying that right?"

I gave a sigh huge enough for him to hear even under the car. "All I've told you and all you care about is how it's pronounced! You're as bad as Ree-Jane."

"Nobody's as bad as her, not even me."

I loved it when he said things about Ree-Jane.

"Not even you," he added.

I could've done without that.

"It's 'Rou-*en*,' right?"

I was surprised he seemed to know French pronunciation. But Dwayne was full of surprises. "Were you here back then?"

"No."

I'd just asked it to make him think I thought he looked old and haggard. Which made me laugh. It was really annoying that I couldn't get under Dwayne's skin. What I said rolled right off him like rain off a roof. I couldn't even pock the surface.

But he could always get a rise out of me. I liked to put this down to the difference between twelve and thirty-plus. But what it was, I guess, was that he was on to me. Still, he never *humored* me because I'm only twelve. "Well, don't you think it's important? It's what happened there. Don't you think Gloria Spiker's story is strange?"

"I think it's really sad, is what I think." *Clang clang.*

If Dwayne was going to go all soft on me I didn't know what I'd do. "Well, yes, it's *sad.*" I thought about the police, that old sheriff, another Mooma. "And what about the FBI?" I had just learned from Mrs. Davidow (of all people to know something useful) that the FBI got in on a kidnapping because it was a federal offense "If the kidnapper crossed state lines," she had said.

Dwayne said, "FBI don't put their pictures in the paper." *Clang.*

"Well, but I still think it's strange—the police and FBI are supposed to help. They help by telling the mom and dad—in movies, at least—that a family's chances of getting the kidnapped person back are zero, *zero,* if the family tries to do it without the police. They always make that point. So I don't see how this Woodruff and Slade family thought they'd succeed, if that's the reason they didn't want the police."

The tapping and clanging went on for a few seconds and then Dwayne rolled out. He got off the wooden pallet and stood wiping his hands on an oily rag. I have said before that all mechanics have an oily rag in the back pocket of their pants, learned, I guess, in mechanics school: *after every job you will wipe your hands on an oily rag. Let me demonstrate—*

Dwayne was wiping and frowning. He said, "Not if it was a family member."

I frowned. "You mean kidnapped?"

He shook his head. "I mean who did it. Old man Woodruff wouldn't want police investigating if it was a Slade, for instance, who did it."

Shocked, I slid off the tires. "One of *them*—?"

"If this Mr. Woodruff thought the kidnapper was his son-in-law he probably would want to keep it quiet."

"The nurse! She wasn't there because she told them she was sick. But maybe all the time she was in on it!"

Dwayne had raised the hood of the station wagon and positioned one of those caged lights under it. "Wasn't that Lindbergh nurse accused of doing that?"

"Everybody brings up that case."

"They do? That's only because he was a hero. Lindbergh was a hero, at least when that happened." He took out spark plugs and set each above the grille. He looked very serious about either the Lindberg case or the spark plugs. Probably the spark plugs, as Dwayne, it was said, didn't "fix" cars. He breathed new life into them. He was a *master* master mechanic.

In his other back pocket was stuffed one of his William Faulkner— "Billy" to him—books. He loved Faulkner. I had recently read part of *Light in August*—well, I read ten pages of it, looking for quotes to impress him. Actually the quotes impressed *me*. William Faulkner made up wonderful words, like "bugstumped." I could see the title of the book in Dwayne's pocket: *Sanctuary.* My mind seemed to fly, to race ahead of me, as if it was going on without me, not waiting for me to catch up. Did the baby's mother need "sanctuary"? Did the Girl? Or did I?

From under the hood, Dwayne's voice kind of ricocheted. "It's kind of superficial, ain't it?"

Dwayne said words like "ain't" just for effect.

"It's the ladder, the sleeping baby, the nurse." He stood up, looked at the row of spark plugs as if they, too, were tiny babies and he had to care for them. "You could find kidnappings like that all over. Just no hero or wealth to make them stand out. They aren't really alike." He'd turned to look at me.

He was over six feet, the same height as the Sheriff. If I had to, I wouldn't know how to choose between them. (Not that I cared about boys at all.) Dwayne was dark and he had really long eyelashes, long enough to web the skin beneath his eyes when the light hit his face at a certain slant, as the caged light was doing now. Why did he have those long eyelashes and me just these stubby little ones? It was infuriating. Dwayne was handsome enough without them. Me, I needed all the help I could get. I'd lost the train of thought by now. "What are you saying?"

He shrugged. "Just that kind of comparison can confuse the issue. It makes it easier to think about. People like that."

"Dwayne, what are you talking about? I wish you'd stop."

"Don't you just like to hear yourself talk sometimes?"

"No." I did, but I wasn't going to admit it.

I slid down from the tires. It was five-thirty and I had to be in the kitchen by six o'clock at the very latest. I should really have been there by now.

Dwayne held a spark plug at arm's length and up to the light, as if God might want a look and Dwayne was waiting for His opinion.

I've seen Mrs. Davidow do the same thing with a martini. She probably had better luck than Dwayne that way.

17

As I walked along the boardwalk between the Hotel Paradise and Slaw's Garage, I wasn't thinking of what things have in common, but of parts of things, bits of something I could not put together. These bits were circling around in my mind, but this state didn't last long. In the time it took me to walk from the gravel drive to the porch, my mind was once again flat as a pancake. There wasn't much around to fill it, either, as Ree-Jane was sitting on the porch, smoking a cigarette.

I was surprised to see her with a cigarette, but I didn't show it, since that's what she wanted. *Bowled over* was what she wanted. She was smoking in the same amateurish way that a few boys from school did, taking in a huge drag and letting some of the smoke out through their noses. It looked stupid, but I said nothing. Her mother was clearly not around.

"Been to Slaw's Garage again? Dwayne knows you have a crush on him."

Then she started this silent laugh of hers that shakes her body. It was fake and peculiar, but then everything about Ree-Jane is fake and peculiar. That she'd actually think I'd believe Dwayne said that showed me how little she knew about people. "I don't know if You-Boy's finished fixing your car yet. He took it out for a ride and never came back."

"You-Boy? He's not supposed to work on my car. *Dwayne* is!"

I smiled. "Well, you better say something to Abel Slaw, then. You-Boy's the one that works on it."

"You're just a no-good *liar*!"

I was opening the screen door when she got off this last comment.

Now, I never swear anywhere within hearing distance of my mother, for I can imagine the consequences. (Neither, surprisingly, does Will. He swears all over the Big Garage and once said "fucking" a short distance from the kitchen, but that's all I know of.)

So I did not take the word lightly when I said to Ree-Jane. "You're so full of shit." I then went into the cool darkness of the lobby.

She sprang to her feet and yelled, "You just wait until I tell Miss Jen!"

I nearly skipped my way to the kitchen, happy I had once again got the best of Ree-Jane. I even looked forward to her telling on me. Hadn't she learned anything in the years she'd lived here? Didn't she know yet my mother was always too busy to be bothered by what she herself hadn't witnessed? It was kind of like hearsay evidence, wasn't it?

Vera gave me a cutting glance for being late. It had meant she had had to do part of the predinner chores—taking in the butter patties and putting them on the butter plates, which she considered beneath her.

"I'm not getting paid to do these menial tasks," she said with a sniff.

"I'm not getting paid at all," I answered.

She fumed around the kitchen at that and I started on the salads. Back in his dishwater shadows, Walter tittered. He loved it when someone talked back smart to Vera, for she was awful to him when she wasn't treating him as if he were invisible.

There were six new guests, two staying in the hotel, four coming just for dinner. Vera would wait on the four; I'd take the two. Vera would have checked them out before she'd decided, so it wasn't hard to figure which table would leave the bigger tip.

As I arranged the crisp lettuce in the salad bowls, I thought about the Slades and Woodruff and what Dwayne had said. Could one of them have really been responsible? Why had Morris Slade come back to the room right then? All I knew about him was that he was a playboy. I asked my mother if she knew any Slades as I put the pepper rings on the lettuce. She was standing over a cast-iron pan that sizzled and spat around her deep-fried chicken.

"There are a lot of Slades, mostly in Hebrides. Why?"

"Well, do you recall that Woodruff family? The ones whose baby was kidnapped from the Belle Ruin?"

"'Rou-*en*,' not 'ruin.'"

"The baby's mother was married to Morris Slade, I was told."

My mother stopped shaking the pan and turned to look at me across the half mile (it seemed) of white porcelain that was her long counter and my big square salad table. "She was? Yes, I remember a wedding breakfast we did for a Woodruff girl, but I can't remember her name."

"It was Imogen Woodruff." Walter's voice came in its slumbery way. "Least, that's what Ma told me."

"Yes, I remember her. The wedding party was mostly, you know, fairly common. Well, they were Slades, weren't they?"

Not well bred, I added for her. "Then I wonder how he came to marry into this rich, *uncommon* New York family."

Back to shaking the pan, she said, "Oh, it happens. But if the Woodruffs were New Yorkers, New York *society*, the family probably just ignored the Slade relations. Which I do myself."

I shook my head and went back to the salads. If my mother measured ingredients for her food the way she does for people, there's no telling what we'd wind up with.

The Pink Elephant is a little room directly beneath the dining room. I can hear Miss Bertha's cane pounding around up there if I'm down here. I guess you could call it a basement room, though there wasn't any other basement. The Pink Elephant was called that because it was once where a few people would gather for cocktails (and why they needed one more place, I couldn't imagine) and probably get so drunk they'd see pink elephants. Somebody had a real sense of humor. Ha ha.

It was where I did my serious thinking. It was also where I had taken my trip to Miami Beach; the cardboard palm tree with its crepe paper fronds still stood near the picnic table, which was the only furniture in the room besides my collapsible beach chair. The walls were stone and painted pink; the floor was very hard packed earth. It was chilly and damp, which kept other people away, and that was fine with me. There was no electricity, so my light was a combination of a fat candle and a battery-powered lamp. (The candle was mostly for effect.)

I had a Whitman's Sampler box in which I placed anything that I thought especially valuable: a photo of Mary-Evelyn Devereau standing with her three aunts. They were all dead now, as far as I knew, and so was Mary-Evelyn. But that didn't mean they were no longer what people call a force to be reckoned with. Sometimes I think the force is stronger in the dead than in the living.

I sat for a pleasant minute imagining Miss Bertha in her coffin. Would her force be greater when she was dead? No. Miss Bertha didn't really have a force; she only had a bad temper.

Anyway.

In the box there was also Ben Queen's handkerchief that he had given me down by Crystal Spring when I'd started bawling. The handkerchief was, most of all, proof that he'd been there and that we'd talked about Mary-Evelyn. The second time I'd seen him, well, that needed no proof; that was something even I, with my wild imagination, could never have concocted.

I thought about him, Ben Queen, once married to beautiful Rose Devereau; Ben Queen, in prison for eighteen years for her murder, which I knew he did not commit; Ben Queen, who saved my life. And now the police were looking for him again for the murder of Fern.

Why was it the wrong people wound up with fate flying in their faces? Why didn't it happen instead to the Davidows? Or was that, I mean that it happened to you, what made you the right people?

18

The next morning, right after breakfast, with Miss Bertha demanding a jelly omelet that wasn't on the menu, I left for Mrs. Louderback's house, allowing myself time to stop by Britten's store to get a pack of Sno Balls. I would save them for later, as I had just had breakfast, which was Palm Beach pancakes. My mother made that name up, which she loves to do. The pancakes had bits of pineapple and mango in them and the syrup had pineapple and coconut. I ate all of this in a kind of dream, as I ate much of my mother's cooking. I had two helpings of the Palm Beach pancakes, all the while reminiscing about Miami Beach, as if I had ever been there.

I also wanted to see the Wood boys and Mr. Root to find out if they remembered the Belle Ruin. Mr. Root would have been in his middle years, I guessed. I had been very surprised to discover that once Mr. Root had been the boyfriend of Sheba Queen before George Queen came along.

As I rounded the corner of Britten's store, I saw the green bench and Mr. Root occupying it, as he did most days. It looks out over the highway and you can watch the traffic pass, what there was of it. When he saw me, he smiled, giving me a view of a few missing teeth. I called to him that I'd be out in a second and went into the store.

Mr. Britten, who did not break out a smile, was moving around with a clipboard, counting his stock, his cans and jars and bottles and boxes. Even my own job waiting tables was more interesting than Mr. Britten's, though he owned the place and that must have made up for a lot of boredom. He looked what you'd call in deadly earnest, as if he were counting bodies on a beach instead of cans of Spam and jars of jelly. Mr. Britten always wore a big wraparound apron like my mother's that could protect her clothes from anything, including a pie-throwing contest. Over the apron Mr. Britten always wore a dark brown cardigan. I don't think he liked me much. He liked Walter, who reported on Mr. Britten's joking manner: "Me and him, we're just a couple of cutups." Try as I might, I could not picture Walter and Mr. Britten cutting up.

I looked at the candy and "confections" shelves for the Sno Balls. There were two kinds, pink and white. I couldn't imagine getting anything but white, for why would anybody want a pink snowball? I asked Mr. Britten to get me out a packet, which he did, but really grudgingly, as if I were a thorn in his side instead of a customer. He really ought to watch it. After all, the Hotel Paradise was his biggest customer, even though he did have to wait awhile to get paid.

I let the screen door of Britten's slap shut behind me and walked down the steps and up to the green bench, where Mr. Root told me to set a spell and kind of swept his hand over the place beside him, dusting it off.

"Listen, Mr. Root, do you remember that big hotel near here called the Belle Ruin?"

"Sure, I do."

"But did you go there, to the Belle Ruin? Maybe to a dance?" I brightened. "Maybe you took Sheba Queen?" I could not really imagine Mr. Root or Sheba Queen in that circle of society that danced at the Belle Ruin. I just wanted to find out if he knew anything at all.

"Nah, we never went to no dances. She don't know how to dance, Sheba don't. Leastwise not back then. Anyway, we'd never get into that hotel; it was only for the swells."

"What about that baby being kidnapped there? Do you remember that happening?"

Mr. Root's eyes narrowed as he looked out over the highway. People called it the highway, and once it had been a highway, a major road, but then a new four-lane road had been built that didn't come any-where near Spirit Lake. I watched as a flatbed truck rumbled by, then a couple of cars. And *then,* Axel's taxicab! Axel in the driver's seat and nobody in the back. He would be on his way to some mystery destination to pick up a mystery fare.

"Yeah, I sure do remember that kidnapping," said Mr. Root. "Now that there was a tur'ble thing to have happen. They never caught the fellow that done it, neither."

I inched closer. "Here's the thing: it was hushed up; at least that's my understanding."

He turned. "How in hell—'scuse my French—does a person hush up a *kidnapping*? That don't sound right. Kidnappin', that's one of your *federal* offenses."

"This Mr. Woodruff—the baby's grandfather—what some think is he paid off reporters and I guess the publisher. And there was talk he maybe even bribed the police to be quiet."

"Publisher? That wouldn't have been Gumbrel, would it?"

"Not the present Mr. Gumbrel. His dad would've been publisher back then probably."

"Well, the one there now would know, wouldn't he?"

Of course. "I can't just walk into the *Conservative* office and ask, 'Hey, Mr. Gumbrel, was your father taking bribes?'"

Mr. Root chewed his tobacco in silence. "Still and all, you could ask him about the baby, see if he knows about that. Gumbrel's about the same age as me. He'd surely remember something. You asked the Wood boys? It was them knew about how Mary-Evelyn Devereau was treated. You know, it wouldn't surprise me if Ulub didn't have second sight."

"Second sight? You mean like someone who can see the future? Like Mrs. Louderback?" Which reminded me to check the time.

"That ain't second sight. Second sight's like being able to see things ordinary people can't." He smiled.

I could tell he was so pleased with himself knowing more than I did.

He went on, "Like knowing how they was treatin' poor Mary-Evelyn."

"But, Mr. Root, that was *first* sight. Ulub had actually seen some of it. Like them making Mary-Evelyn play the piano while they ate dinner. Ulub saw that through the window."

"Says he saw it."

"You don't believe him?"

"Now, sure I *believe* him, it's just a matter of first or second sight is all."

There came a shout from behind us, from the walk that led back to the Hotel Paradise, which I often took.

"Damn! Here they come now. Don't you say nothin' about this second sight stuff, hear?"

It was so ridiculous, it didn't even bear answering. Ulub Wood with second sight. Even if he did, how would he communicate it? It was hard enough understanding what he saw with his first sight.

The two brothers came walking toward us. One was tall with a thin face that looked like it had been hacked from whatever substance it came from. The other one, Ulub, was shorter and kind of square, neither fat nor thin, just solid and squarish. They both made greeting sounds—*Nuh-oh, Un-o*—accompanied by big smiles. I guess it was a cleft palate that made Ubub hard to understand. He could talk a little better, though, than Ulub, whose speech problems went way beyond cleft palates and stuttering. I had learned to make out words that a person often repeats—like "I," "me," "you," "and"—easy words. But Mr. Root could understand every word that Ulub spoke and repeat it to me, like a translator.

"'Lo, boys," he said. "Emma here needs t' ask you some things." He turned to me. "You know. About the hotel."

As if I might not remember what I'd said ten seconds ago. "Yes. The Belle Ruin."

Ulub kind of rolled his eyes and said, *"Beh-ooh-en. Beh u-en."*

Oh, I thought, if only a person could take a picture of a sound! I could not believe it, but Ulub sounded as if he were trying to give us the *French* pronunciation. It was the way he kept saying it. Wanting to let him know I understood, I said, "You're right, Ulub. Practically everybody says it wrong, they say 'Ruin.'" When Ulub said it, he sounded exactly like Ree-Jane and I could hardly wait to tell her.

Mr. Root, also wanting to give Ulub a pat on the back, said, "Emma's right. I can't never say a thing but 'Ruin.'"

Had God all along meant for Ulub to speak French? Stranger things had happened (like Aurora Paradise turning down a drink). Then I began to wonder: where had Ulub ever got hold of this French pronunciation? For as we said, only a handful of people seemed to know how to say it. Where had he heard "Rouen" to such an extent he made a point of it?

Around the Belle Rouen itself.

I began to tingle with excitement. "Ulub, did you ever work there?"

Ulub nodded. "Un a gowns."

Gowns? I looked at Mr. Root.

"Say again, Ulub."

Ulub's face contorted as if that might make it clearer. "Un a gu-*owns*."

"Well, shucks," said Mr. Root, flapping his hands at the ease of it all. "In the *grounds,* right? You worked around the hotel grounds."

Ulub nodded, and so did Ubub, who said, "Ee bof id."

"Both you fellas worked there?"

Ubub nodded as enthusiastically as his brother had.

I said, "What did the hotel people have you doing? Clearing out dead branches and stuff? Taking care of flower beds?"

Ulub nodded and said, "Een-eenin."

"Weeding," said Mr. Root. "They weeded the flower beds."

Ubub added. "Ut-now saw-icks."

This even stumped Mr. Root: "Fellas, could you say that onc't again?" He had a listening expression like he was listening for a winning number.

Ubub said, "Saw-icks, saw-*icks.*"

Mr. Root came up with it. "Salt licks! You boys put out salt licks for the deer."

They both nodded so hard I feared their heads would drop off. "Es, es. Eer ane," said Ulub.

Even I could work that out. "Deer came."

"Ay nint geh ot." Ulub looked sad.

Mr. Root translated. "They didn't get shot, right, Ulub? Not like they do now. I guess they had the deer park posted."

Ubub nodded. They were still standing by the bench and I moved over. So did Mr. Root. Four could squeeze onto the bench. Our moving was an invitation.

"Have a seat, come on, set," said Mr. Root. They did.

"What else did you do?" I asked.

Ulub looked up at the massed clouds as if watching for rain. He said, "Ee ouvn ins."

"Moved things," said Mr. Root. "Like furniture, that kind of stuff?"

"Nails n airs."

Tables and chairs? I wondered.

"Were you at the Belle Ruin—"

Ulub frowned at me.

"—I *mean* Rou-*en* when the hotel had its balls?"

Both of them were nodding before it was out of my mouth. I don't know why I didn't just ask about the kidnapping the moment they said they worked at the Belle Ruin. Maybe I thought a sudden pouncing would scare the truth away. Was that the reason for my roundabout questioning? I didn't know. Maybe it was because I didn't want the story to end, at least not soon. Well, one thing was sure: my story was a long time in the telling.

"At nine," said Ubub.

At nine?

"That night!" said Mr. Root.

Ulub said, "Es, es!"

"You talking 'bout that night the baby got took?"

Mr. Root was almost as excited as I was.

"Ee uz nare," said Ulub.

"You was there? Where? You was where?"

Both of the Woods seemed beside themselves in their eagerness that we understand them. "Ary ood."

Mr. Root frowned. Then his face cleared. "Carrying wood?"

Ulub nodded. "Er ire ace."

"For the fireplaces inside?"

They nodded, and then Ubub said, "Atter, atter." And both of them raised their arms in the air and made fists, which they raised one over one, as if they were climbing.

Ladder! I was nearly bug-eyed with excitement. "The ladder! You saw the ladder that went to the baby's window."

They nodded happily as if they'd waited a long time to tell this to somebody.

"Did you see who put it there?"

They shook their heads.

"Well, did you see someone *on* it?"

Again, they shook their heads.

I felt deflated. They didn't seem to know any more than what was in the police report. Now they waited upon me or Mr. Root to say something.

"E uz nare!"

"I know, that's what you said before. You were there."

They both shook their heads in what seemed to be frustration. I felt bad, for frustration was what they had to deal with every day of their lives.

Ulub made his hands into fists again and raised them as if rung by rung. "O un. O un," he said.

Even Mr. Root looked baffled. "You didn't see anybody climb that ladder. We know that."

Ulub clamped his hands over his ears. That meant he was really annoyed with us for not understanding. "E uz *nare*. E *saw* ut!"

Suddenly, I got it. "No one—it's not that you didn't *see* anyone climb the ladder, but that you saw that *no one* climbed it!"

"Es! Es!"

Mr. Root grumbled. "Well, I don't see what in the Sam Hill—"

I said to him, "Look, they were there when someone was supposed to have climbed the ladder, but no one did."

Mr. Root was a little put out that he hadn't understood the best part of the whole story and asked in a whiny voice, "Well, why didn't you fellas explain this to the *po*-lice?"

The three of us looked at him.

Was he kidding?

19

Imagine Ulub or Ubub trying to tell the police what they knew. If it had been the Sheriff, that would have been a different story. The Sheriff would trouble himself to listen to make sure he got it right.

As I made for Mrs. Louderback's, I thought about that old file that was sitting with all of the other forgotten cases in the Sheriff's files. In his office. Maybe he had said all that was in it, but maybe not.

I passed by big white Victorian houses with green shutters. White-house-green-shutters was a sort of rule in Spirit Lake. The houses looked nice and big and airy, but the sameness of them got a little tedious. Mrs. Louderback's was on the corner, a house not nearly as big, but still white and green shuttered.

As I knocked on the door I hoped the strange woman who answered it the other times I'd come wouldn't be here today. Does every old person who lives alone (like Dr. McComb) have a strange woman living with him or her? That wasn't much of an advertisement for old age.

Mrs. Louderback's strange woman did open the door. I said I was Emma Graham and had an appointment. She didn't look happy at seeing me again, but she did step back so that I could enter. Then she whisked away, silently, as if on a broom.

The waiting room, which was a parlor off the living room, had two other people sitting in it and I wondered if I was so late my appointment was handed off to these women. I really should have a wristwatch, and then wondered why. According to Dr. McComb, monarch butterflies had no trouble in finding Mexico in the winter or Canada in the summer. I should be able to find the Hotel Paradise kitchen at five-thirty then.

I sat down in a wooden chair, the rounded kind with arms. It was burnished, the wood, warm looking and I settled into it quite comfortably. I wondered if the two women across from me who looked as if they'd never spent a comfortable hour in their lives were related. I had never seen them before. In a place like Spirit Lake you'd think everybody would look familiar. They stared at me in the way people do if they've looked at everything else and now only wanted to set their looks on something new, no matter how unexciting.

This was quite rude of them, and I stared back, hard. Their look never wavered. They could both be blind and maybe had come to find out from Mrs. Louderback when they could see again. I picked up a copy of *Life* magazine and held it right out in front of my face. After a few minutes, I lowered it. They were still staring.

Thank heavens the door opened then and a tiny pale woman who reminded me of a teardrop came out. The two women rose together and both went in to Mrs. Louderback, who gave her readings in her kitchen, which I thought very cozy. The women were apparently hearing their fortune told together. How could Mrs. Louderback do that?

I was just as glad not to have to wait through two fortune-tellings. Each one took about a half hour. Maybe one of the women was there for moral support. I wondered if they had to pay four dollars instead of two. Anyway, there was no charge, really. We were supposed just to contribute whatever we felt like. I guess everyone felt like two dollars because that was what everyone contributed.

Mrs. Louderback used Tarot cards, which were very mysterious, especially the Hanged Man. My own card was the Orphans in a Storm (though that was not the card's exact name), at least I assumed it must be my card for it came up every time. None of the faces on the cards looked very happy, and I pointed this out. Mrs. Louderback said, "Happiness may not be the point." As I sat waiting and making spitballs from a page of *Life,* I thought happiness might not be her point but it was mine. I aimed another spitball just right so that it hit the chair opposite where one of the women had been sitting.

I was still wondering, why did they go in together? Maybe one of them, the one who wanted her fortune told, was deaf and dumb. I frowned. If she was deaf and dumb, what good did the future hold out for her anyway? Why waste her two dollars just to hear bad luck had come and bad luck was staying? Maybe Mrs. Louderback would tell her deafness and dumbness wasn't the point. I didn't much believe that handicapped people could lead "normal lives." What was normal about driving a car if you had no legs (although I would be the first to say that's pretty much how Mrs. Davidow drove anyway)? Or playing baseball from a wheelchair? Playing the piano with one hand? You were just getting the handicapped's hopes up by claiming all of this was normal.

I wish people would just tell the truth.

Ha. I should talk.

I spat another tiny wad of paper just as the door opened and the two women came out with exactly the same expression they'd worn going in.

Well, I could have told them. Then I remembered I had made up the deaf- and dumbness and they were actually normal. No, they weren't.

"Emma," said Mrs. Louderback, holding the door.

As the two passed me, there was that voodoo look again. I hadn't yet considered that. A curse. Maybe it took two of them to work a curse. Maybe I wouldn't be leading a normal life anymore.

"Emma." Mrs. Louderback repeated it. She's really a very nice and patient person. As I walked into the kitchen with her I asked, "Did you ever consider working with the handicapped? I think you'd really be good at it." But then I thought, she didn't seem to have done them much good.

I took my same seat in the kitchen, a white-painted chair on the other side of the kitchen table, which felt slightly warm as if the wood had been rubbed and buffed a million times. I wondered if Mrs. Louderback had anything in the oven. I didn't smell anything, but still there could have been something there cooling off like meringues. I loved meringues with a scoop of ice cream and some strawberry sauce.

"Is your mother well?" she asked, turning the deck of cards this way and that.

"Why? Isn't she?" I was a little alarmed.

Mrs. Louderback only laughed. "No, I don't see anything about Jen Graham in the cards. That's very funny, Emma."

Although my question had been sincere, I took credit for the funniness and just smiled.

She started laying out the cards, three facedown before me. One thing I liked about Mrs. Louderback was that she didn't ask a million questions. But then maybe she didn't have to. I looked down at the cards, and then I turned them over one by one. The Nine of Cups and, yep!—Orphans in a Storm. I was beginning to like the orphans, for I thought their view of life was more realistic than some of the others (like the woman with all those wands). "It's here again." I tapped the orphan card.

"My, that card does certainly follow you around, doesn't it?"

Like bad news, I didn't say. "Why? Why does it follow me around?"

She frowned. "It isn't really bad, you know."

The orphans probably wouldn't agree. They looked pretty cold and homeless.

She went on: "Well, for one thing, it means quest. A quest for something. And doesn't that apply to you real strongly?"

I didn't think I was questing. But maybe I was. I was looking for answers, for sure. This was a perfect opportunity to ask questions. "I guess so. See, I'm still writing up this story for the *Conservative*. Do you remember that hotel that burned down called the Belle Ruin?"

She had been slapping down rows of cards and stopped. "My goodness, yes. It was fortunate nobody was killed in that fire."

I ignored the Hanged Man, looking right at me in his upside-down way, and asked, "Then do you remember that baby being kidnapped?" I thought Mrs. Louderback might remember more than anyone because she probably had that second sight Mr. Root was so big on.

"I certainly do. It was tragic. We never heard how that came out. Whether the baby was found or not."

Mrs. Louderback concentrated on the backs of the cards she'd laid out. Maybe she could see straight through them.

"The thing is, there was hardly anything ever reported. I mean, what I heard was it was hushed up by the grandfather. His name was Woodruff."

"Oh, that old fool."

My ears seemed to have grown ears with that remark. I was astonished. "You knew him?"

"Lucien Woodruff? Of course. They'd come to Spirit Lake in the summers. They had a cottage across the highway. What street were they on? Let me think."

I didn't need her to think about the street name. I was flabbergasted the Woodruffs had lived here in Spirit Lake. Had my mother's head been so alight with recipes she couldn't recall this?

"Yes, there was him and that silly wife of his and sillier daughter. I was older than she was, but I probably didn't have a lot of good sense myself."

I couldn't imagine Mrs. Louderback without good sense.

"Still, I could tell a spoiled, silly girl when I met one."

"Tell me about her. Forget about the cards."

"Your character's more important than a lot of old gossip, Emma."

Oh, no, it wasn't. "We can do my future next time. It'll still be the same."

Mrs. Louderback couldn't help but laugh. "All right. Let's see. The family lived winters in New York City. They'd been coming to Spirit Lake summers and I think they even had a cottage on Lake Noir. Now that girl Imogen just made a fool of herself over every boy around."

"Did the boys like her?"

"Of course. She was pretty and had her own car and a lot of money."

Why hadn't somebody told me this? The people who'd been around back then, like Dr. McComb? And Aurora Paradise, for heaven's sake! She had to have had something to do with the Woodruffs because Aurora had something to do with everybody.

"You see, they had a lot of money. Lucien Woodruff was in railroads, the B&O and others. He was very rich. And when you're real rich, well, a girl's going to have fortune hunters around." She nodded with a kind of satisfaction. "The boy she finally married was Morris Slade. Morris Slade, now there was a devil-may-care fellow who knew a good thing when he saw it. There are still a few Slades around, mostly getting up to no good." She slapped a card down on the table.

She must have had personal experience with a Slade or two, but I didn't want to get sidetracked on that.

"And Morris was no different from the rest of them. Worse, if you must know."

"Then you knew him?"

"Not very well. I just knew of him mostly. He was a ladies' man, from what I heard. Real handsome. Morris and her, the Woodruff girl, two frivolous people, those two. I think her father probably had Morris working for him in New York City, but I doubt Morris did much work. There's people in this world think they can make it all on looks alone."

I wasn't one of them.

Mrs. Louderback looked at the big kitchen clock. "We've got a few minutes; let's see what's in your cards. Now, there's the Nine of Cups and that means Happiness." She smiled.

But I knew what the happiness card would come to . . . yes, here it was. The Three of Swords, the swords run through a big heart. "It doesn't look happy to me."

Mrs. Louderback frowned and tapped the card. "You may be getting unsettling news."

That's all the news I ever got, mostly from Ree-Jane. "But is that all about the Woodruffs? Didn't you ever wonder what happened to the baby? Her name was Fay."

"Yes, of course I wondered."

"Well, but you have these cards to tell you things."

She smiled "Not about someone who isn't here. I mean right here, in person. See, I'm not a medium. That's all I can tell you, really, about those people. Is it important?"

"I think so. It's all going to be part of my story."

But the thing about stories is, when you think you've wound things up (as I certainly thought that night at the lake) things just start unwinding again until you think you'll never be done.

I sighed. "Doesn't anything ever *end*?"

She laughed. "Maybe you don't want it to, ever think of that?"

I frowned at that, and thanked Mrs. Louderback and got up.

"Well, we didn't get to talk much about your cards."

I didn't want to come out and say talk wouldn't have done much good because they're always the same cards. Orphans. Hanged Man. Swords. Maybe they were trying to tell me something, but I don't really believe in cards. If I did, I'd have to believe the things Aurora Paradise tells me. That would be just about as dependable.

20

I did not have to serve lunch that day since Anna Paugh had come over to help my mother with some cakes and she told me she'd be glad to wait on Miss Bertha and Mrs. Fulbright. They were the only guests who'd be having lunch.

Carrying a Heather Gay Struther shopping bag, in case I could use it, I decided to walk to La Porte as I thought I could not stand another ride with Delbert. My purpose was to get hold of that old file about the kidnapping of the baby, and I had to get it from the Sheriff's office. I had been in one of the file drawers before, looking for what they had on the Devereau case—the drowning of Mary-Evelyn Devereau. There were cases stretching back decades. Not all of them, of course, but the more serious ones like murder or kidnapping.

La Porte is roughly two miles from Spirit Lake and the way is marked by empty land on one side of the highway and a few businesses on the other—Winnie Winkle Wash, Hi-Lo Market and Burt's Electrical Service. After these came heavily treed land on both sides until you got to Arturo's Restaurant with its flashing neon sign. The sign was back to flashing ART EAT (BLINK) ART EAT. This was my favorite sign, except for the Silver Pear out near Lake Noir. That sign was a big pear that cast its glittery light through the pines and turned them silver in the misty night.

By the time I got to the courthouse, it would be about time for

Donny Mooma's doughnut break. He wasn't supposed to leave the office unmanned. The Sheriff really gave Donny a dressing-down for leaving me alone there. Donny didn't like me at all and would never do me any favor, but then I wasn't asking for favors. All I wanted was for him to either collapse with a brain hemorrhage or leave. Since it was Maureen Kneff's day off—she was the secretary—that would leave only Donny to get rid of. Donny was ornery stubborn, but I was stubborn with a purpose; I could stick to it like glue.

Except for him, the office was empty. He was sitting at the Sheriff's desk in case some stranger should be passing and think he was the Sheriff.

"Sam ain't here," he said before I'd barely set foot inside.

"Okay, I'll wait."

"He don't like you in here after you abused police property."

I said nothing.

"You best be careful anymore." Donny squeaked back in the swivel chair and rocked a minute, probably trying to think up other things the Sheriff might've said.

I said, "Well, it's too bad you won that contest, then, if you can't leave the office."

He stopped rocking. "What contest?"

I shrugged and looked away. "Nothing."

He got up and came around to the other side of the desk, hitched a leg up on it and stared. "It must be somethin' or you wouldn't've said that about a contest."

I steepled my fingers and remained silent.

"Well?"

Sliding down in my chair, I stared up at the ceiling, raising my fingers as if I were looking through their latticework. "A box of doughnuts is what you won. Over at the Rainbow."

He flapped his hand at me and moved back to the chair. "You always been a bit barmy, you know that?"

And you and Ree-Jane should get together, I didn't say.

"Well, how'd I win the box?" He sounded uncertain.

"Because you bought the three thousandth doughnut. Ulub was runner-up. Anyway, it's not important; if you don't get there by three

P.M., runner-up gets the box." I sat up, saying brightly, "You want, I could get the box for you."

He looked at me with eyes narrow as slits. He was figuring I wouldn't do him a favor even if the heavens poured down angels for it. He figured something was wrong. He just didn't figure the right thing was wrong. He got up again. "Oh, no you ain't. How many's in it?"

"Twenty-four. Two dozen."

"Well, I know you, you'll just help yourself to whatever and give others away to your buddies. That's the only reason you'd go get that box." He looked at his watch. "I'll get 'em myself. You can't sit here in the office, though."

I made a face. "You want me going along with you, then?"

"No, I do not want you with me. You think I want you trailin' around after me actin' like you're in charge?"

"I want to see the Sheriff." I whined this out.

"Then you can just go sit on one of them benches in the corridor."

"Okay." I got up. We both trailed out. He closed the door and didn't lock it. They never did during the day. Couldn't Donny see the stupidity of this? I went over to a bench.

"It won't take me five minutes."

At least fifteen. When he disappeared down the stairs I went back into the office.

I crossed the room to the gray metal cabinets that lined one wall. I knew which drawer the old case files were in from having done this before: abusing police property. Inside of five minutes I found the Woodruff file and pulled it out. I would not attempt to read it while sitting on the floor (although I was tempted). I put it in the Heather Gay Struther shopping bag. I carefully closed the file drawer and also carefully closed the office door.

I decided not to wait for Donny.

I went to the Abigail Butte County Library, the safest place to read something you don't want other people to see. No one paid any attention to what you were reading in the library because everybody was reading, if only a newspaper. I took a chair at one of the deserted tables in the back and pulled the folder from the shopping bag.

There weren't many pages, just three, and the writing on the top page—couldn't they afford a typewriter back then?—was extremely hard to read because it was so small. It looked as if tiny fingers had written it. I could make out a few words—Woodruff, Belle Rouen, ballroom—but only because I had some knowledge of the case. I squinted hard. Then I walked up to the desk and the librarian, or rather, one of them for I didn't recognize this one. I was used to dealing with Miss Ruth Babbit, who was nice as pie. I asked this librarian for a magnifying glass.

"That's an unusual request," she said. "What's it for? I could try reading this thing for you." She adjusted her glasses as if they were magic glasses.

How nebby. Miss Ruth Babbit would *never* have suggested that; she would simply have handed over whatever she could find to help. "Oh, no, that's all right. I mean, just the magnifying glass will do. Miss Babbit has one. I've seen her use it."

But this lady seemed to have doubts, the way she pursed her lips, considering. "What is it that you're trying to read?"

I could hardly believe she'd be so nosy as to ask that again. I thought for a moment. "It's an account of my great-grandfather's expedition to Egypt. He died a long time ago there. That was after he helped exculpate a tomb."

Her smile was prissy. "You mean 'excavate.'"

Imagine. Here was an expedition to Egypt and all she could hit on was a word misused. "That's right, that's what I said."

"No. No, you said 'exculpate.'"

Now I put on a prissy smile. "I don't see how I could have because that's the wrong word, isn't it? You just misunderstood. Now, can I have the magnifying glass? Please?" She was really put out by this, I could tell, that I wouldn't admit my mistake. But she could hardly go on and on about it as if she were the language police. There were other people by now gathered in a line behind me. So she reached under to a shelf and brought out the big magnifying glass and put it on the counter.

"You're holding up the line," she said, accusingly.

I took the magnifying glass, said thank you and didn't mean it and walked back to my table. I was surprised she hadn't insisted on seeing what I was reading. I don't mind people being curious, as I was myself, but I hated nosiness.

Now, glass in hand, I could just make out the writing: Incident Report:

> Call come in from Belle Rouen Hotel at 10:03 p.m. Reporting abduction from room of Slade/Woodruff child/grandchild, four-month-old Fay Slade.

Why did the report insist on putting in old Mr. Woodruff's name as if he had as much right to the baby as his daughter? I guess he was that important.

> The parents, Morris and Imogen Slade, were in ballroom where ball was in progress. Baby Fay sleeping in crib when Gloria Spiker (babysitter) went down hall to make telephone call. Gone for around 20 minutes. Assumed abductor entered by means of a ladder shoved up to window. Room was on third floor. Nothing burgled nor broken insofar as could be determined. All help was interviewed, including kitchen help that was still there because of food being served.

Baby Fay. I sat, chin in hands and gazed off across the reading room, seeing the empty ballroom of the Belle Rouen and me in my deep blue gown and the Waitresses. We were twirling around like tiny figures atop a music box. I didn't know why I pictured this as it had nothing to do with Baby Fay or my mystery. But then it was my mind thought of it, wasn't it? So maybe it was connected to the story.

The Belle Rouen: I saw in my mind's eye its endless, empty corridors, high-ceilinged rooms without a breath of laughter to disturb them. It was empty; it was lonely; it was winter. I saw the two deer in the cold moonlight on a crust of snow, one drinking from the pond that hadn't yet frozen over, the other keeping watch. The deer park, the woods around, the empty hotel. The silence. I know many people think silence is lonely, but I don't. There are times I hunger for it.

There's the story I tell. There's the backstory that connects it to the

past. But then there's also the understory, the one I should pay more attention to, the one that comes to mind only in hints and brief flashes
of light that show whatever lies beneath the surface, like pebbles and
dark fronds I can see only when light strikes water in a certain way and
brings up images: the baby, the Waitresses, the Girl. These were connected in my mind for some reason.

It was the understory I wanted, wasn't it?

Or should I just let the pebbles and grasses lie there at the bottom,
undisturbed?

21

"Imogen Woodruff Slade," said Mr. Gumbrel. "Morris Slade. Humph! Been a long time since I thought of all that. Of course, I remember them and old man Woodruff. He'd be hard to forget. Real tyrant, he was."

I had come here from the library.

Mr. Gumbrel sat back in his desk chair and I could tell he was watching a scene in his mind and getting caught up in his story. I hoped it might be the understory, but I guess that's a story you have to dig out by yourself. You couldn't just be told it.

"Yes, I recall he threw a fit over Imogen marrying Morris Slade. Every girl in town was after that boy. Imogen just couldn't believe her good fortune, that out of all the girls, Morris chose her. Ha! And that's just what it was, wasn't it: 'good fortune.' That's what she had and Daddy knew it. So should she have. But she didn't. Oh, Imogen was a nice girl, all right, but niceness wasn't going to capture that lad! She was never lively enough for Morris, no, not by a long chalk."

Mr. Gumbrel looked lost in thinking about it. I said, "They were from New York, weren't they?"

He nodded. "Yes, indeedy. New York City."

The way he said it, it could have been a planet away.

"Used to come here a lot like plenty of other people. Lived in Spirit Lake awhile, then got themselves a big place out on Lake Noir."

He, like most people, pronounced it "Nor." Ree-Jane loved to correct people when they did this, saying, "Nu-woh, Nu-woh." The French language didn't have much chance around here except for Ree-Jane. But what I liked about the name was what it meant: Black Lake.

"Lake people," I said.

He nodded. "More of them back then than now. Richer, too. And they weren't so spoiled and tetchy as now." He ran a hand over a head from which the hair seemed to be evaporating rather than just falling out. Most of his head was bald. With a deep frown, he folded his arms across his chest.

The lake people were a special group who didn't mingle much with La Porte people; they came into town occasionally in a state of wide-eyed surprise that here we were, living so close to them. They had these glamorous houses of glass, studded around the shore, their lights winking like diamonds. Most of them lived on the far side of the lake. On the near side were much more modest cabins, one of them Maud Chadwick's, a little cottage with a long pier behind it where she liked to sit and smoke a cigarette and drink cocktails and read poetry. She was really big on poetry.

The lakers all flocked to the Silver Pear for dinner. Not many of us did, for it was too expensive. I had been there once with Mrs. Davidow for lunch. But it was really her past she wanted to have lunch with, not me. Over a few martinis she told me all about her fall from riches. I couldn't help but feel sorry for her at the Silver Pear because all she had to show from that happy time was Ree-Jane.

I said to Mr. Gumbrel, "What's strange is no one ever heard how it all turned out with the baby. Her name was Fay. Was she found? Was she dead? What happened?"

Mr. Gumbrel sat forward, arms still folded and looked at me like a fellow reporter, one he could confide in. For a minute I thought he was going to say whatever he told me was off the record. "Now, I'll tell you what I think, Emma. Why it was all swept under the rug and we never heard more. I think that one of them, or both of them, did it. Morris Slade and even Imogen herself."

My mouth dropped open; my eyes got big as saucers. That was what Dwayne had suggested. Here was Mr. Gumbrel saying it, too. "You mean Morris and Imogen stole their own *baby*?"

"I mean exactly that!"

"But . . . why?"

He shrugged. "Don't know."

"Well, I don't see how it could've been for the money. There was never any ransom note."

He shrugged again. "Far as we know there wasn't. They left; they fled the scene right after. Maybe one came when they got back to New York."

Well, that didn't make any sense at all. "Maybe there was a ransom note or a telephone call telling them not to talk to police or anyone and directing them to take a suitcase full of money to a certain spot." That's how it always was in movies. "After all, it was the hotel management that called the police."

"Could be." He said, "You know what? Maybe we should get Sam DeGheyn on this. He's the smartest policeman I know."

"It's too old a case. He's too busy looking for Ben Queen." I said this a little sarcastically, pointing out we knew that was a waste of time.

But Mr. Gumbrel was thinking his own thoughts and rubbing his jaw. I heard his day-old beard rasp. "But after the police were notified— like it or not—what was old man Woodruff's motive in keeping it quiet? Damn! I wish I'd found out more back when it happened."

"Did Mr. Woodruff pay the papers off to keep it quiet?" Hastily, I added, "Not the *Conservative*, of course."

"I'd think not. My daddy would have never taken a bribe, no ma'am. But I can't answer for anybody else. If the Woodruffs left for New York right away, and we heard nothing else much as to what happened Yes, they fled the scene. And that's mighty peculiar. To leave the place where it happened, where anybody in his right mind would stay." He shook his head.

They fled the scene.

There was something in that statement that really scared me, for then what happens next? I thought of Brokedown House, its paint-stuck windows, its banging screen doors, and I thought of the Belle

Ruin with its empty ballroom, its dead leaves drifting and what had been those echoing corridors.

They fled the scene.

They vanished.

My heart went cold at the thought of the places I had left and the ones I had yet to leave.

22

Lola Davidow was in the kitchen drinking a martini and tapping ash from her cigarette onto the floor. She was engaged in conversation with my mother. She was in laugh mode. Since I knew she'd be in the kitchen for a time, it was a perfect opportunity to raid the back office for whiskey, which I did. I filled a glass with ice and orange and pineapple juice, supposedly to drink myself, and went off through the dining room, made my stop at the back office and then climbed to the fourth floor.

"You took your time! I'm parched!" But it was, as always, worth it. Aurora smacked her lips. "That's a good Cold Comfort, but it needs a little more Southern Comfort." She smacked her lips again and said this thoughtfully, like my mother tasting the whiskey sauce for her bread pudding.

"Now tell me about the Belle Ruin."

"Everybody who was anybody around here went there for dinner. First-class restaurant they had there. I can still recall their veal medallions in brandy sauce."

I bet she could. But in my newfound concern for animals, I didn't want to discuss meats.

"What's for dinner, miss?"

"Fried chicken. Do you remember there was a baby kidnapped one night during a ball?"

"I surely remember those Belle Rouen balls! I danced all night—" Here she weaved right and left in her chair, arms out, one hand clamped around her drink that was fast disappearing. Only one drink and she was already dancing. "Oh, but I was popular back then! I was sought after!"

"What about the baby? It sounded pretty sought after, too."

She was already drawing the last of the drink through her straw. It was a record even for her.

"The one that was kidnapped," I reminded her.

Air was being noisily sucked up and I knew what she'd say. "How about another?" She smiled in a way she probably thought was winning.

It wasn't winning me. I moved my tray to under my other arm. "Not until you answer me about the baby." She saw I was standing firm on this and wasn't about to get the drink. "I know you remember. It was the Woodruff family."

"Oh, that Lucien Woodruff." Her hand waved him away. "Wanted to marry me—"

Who didn't, except maybe Will, Mill and Walter?

"—but he wasn't good enough. He was rich enough, yes, but there's more to life than money."

Tell me one thing.

"Yes, I met Lucien Woodruff, oh, forty years ago, it must be, when I was hardly into my twenties."

She went on as I shifted from one foot to the other, but I would have to let her impress me awhile, so I didn't interrupt as she told me again about all of her beaux. I looked around her room at the steamer trunk draped in gowns and the posters of the French Riviera and the Hôtel-de-Something and various cafés in Montmartre and on the Left Bank. I guess she had really been to Paris. I waited for the next noisy slurp and said, "Then you must've known Imogen and Morris Slade?"

She hooted at the ceiling as if I'd just brought off a magic trick. "Morris Slade! Why I haven't thought about Morris in years. There was a handsome boy. Younger than me by a good ten years—"

Forty, more like.

"—Morris was a real ladies' man. Imogen was just a colorless girl with a fortune. Lucien was dead set against that union! Well, Morris wasn't their social equal, was he? The Woodruffs were New York City so-ci-ety."

She was rolling her chair—this one had casters on it and she loved spinning about the room, often with a push from me. Oh, I could push, all right. The steamer trunk had drawers down each side and was lined inside with a faded flowery material. She rooted around and swore under her breath, or maybe she was just talking to herself, who knew?

Now she started pulling things out of the steamer trunk drawers—chiffon scarves, jewelry and small satin purses, the sort you'd carry if you were all dressed up in an evening gown. Gold, pink, black. The gowns were satin, silk and chiffon. Old-fashioned, maybe, but they were expensive and beautiful. Seeing all of this made me wonder how much of Aurora's tales about her colorful past were actually true. I put the tray down and went over and had her hand the things to me so they wouldn't be all over the floor.

She found what she wanted, a blue satin box with a blue tab on the top for opening it. It was filled with photos and snapshots she hadn't yet fixed in her album. "Here." She took a handful from the satin box, bunched them together and tapped the ends, shuffling them like a deck of cards. Then she went through these, one by one, the top one going on the bottom. I'd like to have seen them but I didn't want to say anything in case she might go back to her sly self and demand a drink first. She rolled back to her side table and started slapping down the snapshots, still like cards, like the blackjack dealer she claimed once to have been.

Tapping one of the snapshots with a bony finger, she said, "Here's Lucien Woodruff, if you're interested. This one's his poor daughter, Imogen. And the next is that up-to-no-good Morris Slade."

I took a step toward the table, completely thrilled. I had never expected pictures! But she held her arm straight out, palm flat in a STOP gesture. "Just a minute, miss! You can see 'em after I get my Cold Comfort." Then she folded her hands in her lap, looking smug enough to slap senseless.

"How can I be sure it's really the Woodruffs? They could as easily be a family of monkeys."

She smacked her lips as if the drink were already before her and said, "Well, I guess you have to take my word for it!"

Was she kidding? For every little thing I wanted in life it seemed I had to bargain or beg. I had to calculate and wheedle and pretend. Mostly it was bargaining, though, this for that, tit for tat. "Oh, hell!" I stomped my foot.

"Now, don't you use foul language around me, young lady!"

Foul language. She should talk. I turned with my tray and left the room. I stuck out my tongue at nothing but the blank wall and dark stairwell. This was, I know, really babyish; it's why I'd stopped doing it.

But why did everything have to be a card game, a gamble, a double or nothing or double down? It wasn't who was the sweetest, the nicest, the lovingest who won; it was the cleverest, the slyest, the trickiest.

So why was I complaining?

I had started training Walter how to make Cold Comforts, for I hated having to leave in the middle of Aurora's stories. The trouble with leaving in the middle was that when I went back she'd have forgotten, and I wouldn't hear the rest without propping her up again (so to speak) to tell it. It was very tiring.

"Now," I said to Walter, "the secret of a Cold Comfort is in the proportion of the whiskey to the fruit juice." We were in the back office, the tall glass refilled with orange and pineapple juice. Walter had checked to see where Mrs. Davidow was, and she was in the dining room eating her lobster and steak. "I use Jim Beam or Jack Daniel's, some brandy and Southern Comfort." Actually, I used anything around, but that didn't sound like a bartender.

Walter let out his sneezy laugh. "That's good."

"What?"

"That name you give it: Cold Comfort."

I was glad someone appreciated my cleverness. "Aurora likes it, too."

"She ought."

Usually, Walter had next to nothing to say, which was swell and I hoped these lessons weren't going to turn into an opportunity for conversation. I told myself I should be complimented that Walter was talkative around me. But what I wanted was the compliment without the talk, especially with those snapshots lined up on Aurora's table. Teaching Walter would take up precious time, but I wanted a stand-in for the times I couldn't take the drink up myself. There was a dumbwaiter in the office that went all the way up to her room. Sometimes that's the way her dinners would be sent to her. Naturally, it wasn't all this easy, for Mrs. Davidow could finish her dinner during all of this back-and-forthing.

I was making the Cold Comfort as I was describing it for Walter's sake. "The juice can be nearly any kind, but I generally use orange and pineapple."

"How about tomato?"

"Walter, that's just dumb."

He shrugged. "Well, you said any kind."

"It's any sweet kind."

"I've seen Mrs. Davidow put tomato juice in her drinks."

"That's those bloody Marys she likes at lunchtime." And sometimes breakfast.

"Well, but—"

I placed my hands on my hips and looked at him full face. "Walter, could we just concentrate here? Could we just focus? Now: I've already got the juice and ice in the glass. So you can pour the whiskey in. Usually I put the whiskey in first, then the ice and then the juice." I added some Jim Beam and Southern Comfort and then a little brandy. "Like I said, it can be just about any sweet juice; it's hardly ever the same drink twice. Just be sure you get the whiskey up to the halfway mark on the glass."

"That's lotsa whiskey, ain't it?"

"I agree. But that's what you do. You can't go wrong on the whiskey, I can tell you that. You can't really put in too much of this stuff." I tapped each bottle in turn. "Use any juice around, like apple or maybe cranberry, except you don't want it looking too dark, then"—I pierced a maraschino cherry with a toothpick—"you put this in and add one of these stirrers." I picked up one of the plastic stirrers with a hula girl on top. She was wearing a grass skirt and I thought she was cute.

"That toothpick done sunk."

I glared at him. He didn't have any bartending experience at all, yet here he was criticizing the way I did things. "I know, but it doesn't make any difference. I don't care if you use a toothpick or not."

"Pineapple cubes'd be nice, too."

"Walter—"

"And maybe a orange or lemon slice. Mrs. Davidow likes to put mint in hers."

I glowered. "In mint *juleps*. If you want to stick in a sprig of mint, that's fine with me. As long as you don't spend hours doing it and have Mrs. Davidow find you out." Honestly. I set the glass on the tray and huffed out, calling back, "Just make sure you put those bottles back where they were. Maybe what you should do is go back to the kitchen for a while, too."

"Yes, ma'am."

I stomped up to the second floor, recalled the pictures and went much more hurriedly to the third and fourth. The fourth floor, unlike the others, was not a long corridor running the length of the hotel. It was stunted, like rooms at the top of a tower: four rooms positioned around the stairwell. Aurora called these rooms her suite and she used them all, too—one was her bedroom, one her storeroom, one the sitting room where I served her drinks and meals. The fourth was her guest room, which didn't get an awful lot of business.

As I walked up the final flight of stairs, I heard Aurora singing to herself as she sometimes did. "Alice Blue Gown" was one of her favorites, but tonight it was the one about the swallows.

> "*. . . that's the day you promised to come back to me.*"

I stopped on the top step, feeling weighted down. I did not like songs about leave-taking.

> "*When you whispered, 'Farewell,' in Capistrano*
> '*Twas the day the swallows flew out to the sea.*"

I felt rooted on the landing, overcome with an inexpressible sadness. I could see them, the swallows, a cloud of them rising, their wings stretched and winking in the sunlight.

Where were they going? It was the swiftness of their rise into the air that was so hard to watch. No warning. Just good-bye.

I straightened myself out and with my tray steady, walked into her room.

Very few people were admitted to the fourth floor—only me and Walter and on rare occasions Mrs. Davidow. Another person who could come up here was Anna Paugh. But never Vera ("that chicken-necked sourpuss") or Ree-Jane ("bottle-blond spoiled brat"). Actually, Ree-Jane's hair was natural blond, but I didn't bother telling this to Aurora.

She snatched her drink from the tray, took a sip and pronounced it good, then handed me the three snapshots she'd lined up.

Lucien Woodruff (I decided) did not look what his age must have been, for he was a straight-standing man with a square head and neat mustache and bright-looking eyes under eyebrows that ran straight instead of curving.

"Fine specimen of a man, wasn't he?"

I nodded and went on to Imogen, who looked like him, I mean, as much as a woman can resemble a man. The square jaw and straight-across eyebrows didn't look all that good on her, and she didn't have his haughty posture. She was holding a baby wrapped up like an ear of corn in her tiny peaked cap with a glossy tassle.

"How old was the baby here?"

"Oh, a few weeks, I guess. They were at the Belle Rouen, right before they went back to New York City."

"Was the baby cute?"

She frowned, as if I were taxing her mind too much. "No. All babies look alike, don't they? Kind of unformed faces like a plate of mashed potatoes."

So this was Morris Slade. There was no doubt he was handsome, a catch-your-breath handsome, with fair hair and light eyes and a lit-up smile. "He's sure good-looking," I said. The longer I looked at the picture, the more he reminded me of someone. I squinted. "He looks like someone I've seen before."

"There's Slades all over. You've seen Slades. Most of 'em now live over in Bitterroot, but there's always been Slades around this neck of the woods. Now, Morris got those looks from his mama; his dad was a drunk and a womanizer. Funny about looks, the way they skip around.

My own mother was plain as a biscuit, but my grandmamma was a beauty. So you can see that the good looks danced right by my mama and came to me."

Uh-huh.

"Augusta"—this was her sister—"she looked like our daddy. Didn't get a speck of Grandma's looks; well, there wasn't enough to go around."

When she looked off toward the window, holding hard to her Cold Comfort, I shoved the picture of Morris Slade into a pocket of my jeans. I laid the others facedown in the blue satin box. "Can I see some more snapshots tomorrow?"

"Depends," she said without turning her face from the window.

It was just something to say, something a little cantankerous, something to keep me in suspense. To her, it was all a shell game.

23

After breakfast, my stomach resisting that sixth half of apricot-stuffed French toast, powder sugared and maple syruped, I decided to walk into La Porte instead of taking a cab. I could work off the French toast and also not have to put up with Delbert's blabbing about all the trouble I put him to. Like making him drive a cab.

I scuffed along the side of the highway that never did seem to have much traffic, thinking again of Morris Slade. One thing was certain: Miss Flyte and Miss Flagler would have known him, and known the Woodruffs and the Belle Ruin into the bargain.

The Oak Tree Gift Shoppe (Miss Flagler's business) and the Candlewick (Miss Flyte's shop) were on the same side of the street across from and down some from the courthouse. The Rainbow Café was directly across from the courthouse, which made it easy for Donny Mooma, as he had to cross only one street and hold up traffic in his emergency trips for Shirl's doughnuts.

The gift shop and candle shop were separated by a narrow alley and the side doors of each shop opened onto it. They were directly across from each other so that Miss Flyte and Miss Flagler could just "slip across" (they said) to visit without having to go out of their front doors. I wondered why the side doors struck them as an advantage.

Miss Flagler's shop didn't seem to do much business. I believe that there was "money somewhere" (according to Mrs. Davidow, who could always find the "somewhere" of money) said that Miss Flagler was very "genteel." For my mother, this was another stand-in for "well bred." This hinted at family money, although one could of course be poor and well bred. There was plenty of proof of this. There were some very wealthy people in La Porte, such as Miss Isabel Barnett and Miss Ruth Porte, whose great-granddad settled the town. I do not know what "settling" entailed and don't really care. I have never had a liking for history and hate when I have history class in school.

Anyway, I often join Miss Flyte and Miss Flagler when they have their morning coffee or afternoon tea. As it was getting on for ten A.M., they would probably be having morning coffee soon. Sometimes Miss Flagler went to Miss Flyte's and other times it was the other way around. They took turns.

The GONE FOR FIFTEEN MINUTES cardboard clock was stuck in the corner of the Oak Tree's little window, but the door was never locked and I just went in. I loved this shop. If I felt crazy or harried, just stepping into it would calm me down. Perhaps this was because the shop itself was small and sold small items. There were pearl earrings, tiny silver crosses on silver chains, silver baby rattles and teething rings, little enameled boxes. The shop was so tiny that more than one or two customers at a time would crowd it. I rarely saw a customer in it and so I was left alone to look at porcelain-handled letter openers and linen handkerchiefs. When I needed a gift, I always came here.

I lifted the small brass bell and shook it a little. In a minute Miss Flagler came to the beaded curtain that separates the shop from her personal rooms and invited me back.

"Miss Flyte's here," she added, as if that was news.

Miss Flyte said hello and smiled as if delighted to see me. For some reason we three got along really well. We all exchanged information that was mutually helpful. Miss Flagler offered me cocoa, as usual.

I love cocoa with marshmallows and after checking in on the French toast fullness of my stomach, I accepted. I sat in my usual chair at the kitchen table, its position below a low shelf where Miss Flagler's cat, Albertine, liked to relax. Albertine liked me sitting there, for she could reach her head down a little and chew my hair. It was a surprisingly comforting feeling. But, of course, Miss Flagler always told her to stop, which Albertine did for a minute and then started chewing again.

My cocoa was set before me and I stirred it to keep a skin from forming. Miss Flagler put down a little dish of marshmallows for me, which I thought was extra nice, and I deposited three into the cup. I tapped the spoon and put it in the saucer. "I'm writing this story for the paper—"

"Oh, my goodness, yes," said Miss Flagler. "We've been following it. It's very suspenseful, Emma. You're an excellent writer."

"Thank you. Now, I need some information that you might be able to help me with." I did not bother using the "interview" excuse, for the two of them had never needed a reason before they started talking. They weren't suspicious, which was, in my experience, unusual in adults, most of them looking at kids as if they all had knives behind their backs.

"We'd be glad to help. What did you want to know?" Miss Flyte was spooning sugar into her coffee. She added thick cream.

I loved this kitchen even more than Dr. McComb's or Mrs. Louderback's. It was very clean and bright and smelled like baking bread. Miss Flagler's homemade walnut cookies were the only cookies I liked to eat besides my mother's. The wooden kitchen chairs were painted different colors—buttercup yellow, sky blue and aqua—which I thought showed Miss Flagler's youthful side. And the kitchen was restful. I imagined the clock on the wall ticking more slowly and the pages of the calendar above the table turning more reluctantly. There is a lot that's attractive about Miss Flagler's life, spent among silver and lavender. It's peaceful. I think it's the kind of quietness you hear when the moon at night is pulling against the sea.

"It's about the Woodruffs. If you remember them."

"Oh, my, yes. They would come in the summertime. They had a house out at Lake Noir and I think another big Victorian in Spirit Lake."

"They were rich, weren't they?"

"Very. The girl, the daughter, went to a fancy school in New York. I never cared for her much. She seemed sulky and spoiled. She and her mother—a little, faded woman—used to come into the shop. The girl would insist on being bought this and that. And she was nearly twenty! She acted more like six."

"Didn't she have money of her own?"

"I'm sure she did. But you know how selfish people always want to use other people's money."

Oh, I certainly did. Just look at Ree-Jane and the way she tricked me into paying for taxis and sodas.

Miss Flyte said, "She came into a large amount of money, a fortune, when she was twenty-one. And got married right after. Married a boy named Morris Slade. Had a reputation, that one." Yet she smiled, as if she kind of liked the reputation.

"When the baby was three or four months old, it was kidnapped," said Miss Flagler. "Right out from under them in their room at the Belle Rouen Hotel."

Her accent was halfway to French. "That's what I was wondering about." I hitched my chair a little closer to the table. "Were you there that night?"

"No." Miss Flagler looked a bit mournful, either for the kidnapped baby or for missing out on the excitement.

"No, we weren't." Miss Flyte sighed. "Well, it was the most *dreadful* shock! But nothing ever came of it. I mean, the kidnapper was never apprehended nor the baby, as far as I know, ever brought back."

Miss Flagler put in, "They went home to New York and never came back to La Porte. Some people from out of town bought their house."

"But Morris, he came back. Remember?"

Miss Flagler nodded. "Oh, yes. Morris and the Woodruff girl—what was her name? Imogen? Yes, Imogen—separated and I expect divorced. The fate of that poor baby was just such a strain, I imagine, that their marriage couldn't survive it."

"Don't be so romantic, Serena. Those two would never have lasted as a couple. They were always bickering and fighting. Famous for it, they were. It was probably just as well they had a full-time nurse to take care of the baby. I wonder if Imogen Woodruff ever changed a diaper."

"Morris Slade," said Miss Flagler, "was no better than she was in that way. Everyone reckoned he married her for her money. Well, it was obvious to everyone but her. The father certainly knew it. There must've been one of those prewhat'd'you call them? Premarriage agreements?"

"Prenuptial," said Miss Flyte. "So that he couldn't get his hands on her money if they divorced."

Miss Flagler poured more coffee into both cups, then rose to get the cocoa pan to pour me some more. "All I know is, when Morris returned he was throwing money around all over the place. Going with two girls at once. He was definitely one for the ladies. It wouldn't surprise me if Woodruff just paid him to leave."

"But if there was this prenuptial agreement, Morris Slade wouldn't have inherited anything anyway. So I'd think he'd have been running as soon as that poor baby went missing. He did have a kind of love for her, no matter what else bad we say." Miss Flyte took another cookie and broke it in two. It snapped in the stillness.

I could not get over the fact that nothing else was heard about the baby. "How could the police just stop looking?"

"Oh, that old Carl Mooma, he was as corrupt as a public servant can be."

I frowned. How many chances did you get at corruption in La Porte? "There's nothing around here to corrupt a person."

They both tittered, thinking I was joking, when actually I was serious. "What I heard was Mr. Woodruff paid the police off, but I don't know what for exactly."

"Not to ask questions, probably. Just to keep the pot simmering but not let it overflow."

"I heard that it was to keep the Federal Bureau of Investigation out of it," said Miss Flagler. "Kidnapping's a federal offense."

I said, "So that sheriff didn't do anything?"

Miss Flagler shook her head. "He went around saying it was out of his jurisdiction. 'That case is out of my jurisdiction.' He kept saying it as if he'd learned a new word."

"Then whose jurisdiction was it?"

"It was his, of course; that hotel isn't more than four miles from here."

Again, we sat in silence for a few moments, considering.

Then I said, "Everyone I've talked to says it was like the Lindbergh case."

"That's exactly right," said Miss Flagler.

"Yes."

I thought of Dwayne. *"Sounds staged to me."* I said that. "To make it look like a stranger did it, when it was really somebody inside—on the inside."

"That's certainly possible, isn't it, Serena?" said Miss Flyte.

Miss Flagler's forehead wrinkled in thought. Old skin to me looks like it's been washed so much it looks transparent.

"What if *he* did it? Morris Slade?" I said.

"Shocking notion, Emma." Miss Flagler gasped.

Miss Flyte looked thoughtful. "There wasn't any ransom demand, though, and money's surely behind a kidnapping."

"*We* never heard of one, but how do we know? That could have been part of keeping the whole thing quiet. I mean, that the baby's own father kidnapped her for ransom."

There was a silence. Then Miss Flyte said, with a pained look, "But the baby?"

"Yes, what happened to that baby?" asked Miss Flagler. "Do you suppose that's why they left so suddenly?"

"And took the baby back to New York?"

Again, we stopped talking, as if honoring some memory.

Miss Flyte said, "If that's so, really, it's the most wicked thing . . ." She sighed. "Well, the Slades were never the best family in La Porte, for sure. I guess not even a Souder can get free of the Slade genes."

What was she talking about? "Do you mean the drugstore Souders? The Souder's Pharmacy ones?"

Miss Flyte nodded and took a tiny bite out of her cookie. "The Souders were a fine family. Not many of them left. They were well-bred, well-spoken people. Very intelligent. Well, you can tell from the Devereau women, even if most of them were murderers. They were well bred; no one'd deny that."

I'm sure my mother would appreciate that distinction. But I couldn't understand what Miss Flyte had said. "How do the Devereaus come into it? What did they have to do with the Slades?"

"How? Well, it was their mother, wasn't it? Alice Souder?"

It hit me. I got up so quickly I scared Albertine down from her shelf. "Are you saying—?" I could scarcely breathe.

They looked alarmed.

"Are you saying Morris Slade was related to the Devereau sisters?"

They looked at each other and then back at me. "Why, yes, he'd have been a half-brother, wouldn't he? It's always so difficult keeping that step-relation and half-relation straight. They had the same mother: Alice Souder. When Mr. Devereau died—the Devereau sisters were his and Alice's—but when he died Alice married William Slade. A step down in the world, you ask me."

I just stood there, my mind swimming with the Slades, the Souders, the Devereaus, swimming with the very *idea*. "Thank you. Thank you very much, Miss Flagler, but I've got to run."

Which I did, literally, them calling after me, "Emma, Emma!" My own name sounded strange in my ears, as if I'd suddenly fallen into a place where there were no Emmas.

I shot up the street, once or twice bumping into people who were all going in slow motion, it seemed to me, and entered the Rainbow Café.

"Slow down!" called Shirl, from her cash-register stool. To the several regulars at the counter who spoke to me I mumbled several hellos, moving toward the back.

Until Maud grabbed my arm. "Whoa!"

It was eleven A.M.; the Sheriff should be here. "Is he here?"

"You mean Sam? No, he's over at the court—"

The courthouse. I wheeled and ran out of the Rainbow.

I seemed to take the high, wide steps two or even three at a time. Any faster I'd be flying like the starlings wheeling across the sky or the swallows suddenly flying out to sea. I raced down the marble corridor to the Sheriff's office and found him standing behind his desk, reading some file.

When I walked in the door, Donny turned on me. "That was a pack of lies about that contest! There wasn't no contest. You better watch it, or I'll run you in!"

I tried to look both puzzled and sorry. "There wasn't? I guess I just misunderstood."

I must have looked pretty desperate. "What's wrong, Emma?"

"I found out—" I stopped. Why did I stop?

The Sheriff came around his desk. "Found out what?"

"I wanted to tell you—" Exactly what? This was nothing he'd really care about; why should he? It wasn't a police matter; no crime had been committed. "The stolen baby—"

Donny guffawed and felt a razor look slide his way.

The Sheriff turned back to me. "You've lost me, Emma. You talking about the Slades?"

Maybe it was because of sneering Donny reminding me of Mrs. Davidow and Ree-Jane, even of my brother, that had me blushing so ashamedly I couldn't go on. But what had I to be ashamed of? Rushed in here as if I had a ten-car accident to report? No. It was because I had something to tell that made an enormous difference to me. I felt it shouldn't have. I felt nothing should make an enormous difference to me. That was part of it.

The rest was, well, I honestly wasn't sure I wanted anyone else to know.

24

I went again to the *Conservative* offices on Second Street and found Mr. Gumbrel at his desk. He actually brightened when he saw me; I wasn't used to brightening people and it made me feel better.

"You finished next week's episode, Emma?"

"I've just got to go over it again," I said. I hadn't written a word since I'd last seen him. "I need to check on a few things for the back-story." How I loved that word! "Like Rose Queen's murder and so forth." How could there be anything as lame as a "so forth" after Rose had been stabbed five or six times and blood everywhere?

"Sure. You still trying to help Ben Queen?"

I nodded. That wasn't the reason for the visit, though.

Mr. Gumbrel shook his head. "I don't see why Sam DeGheyn is being so stubborn on that point, not after Ben's saving your life."

"Well, I guess he can't let his feelings interfere with his job," I said, being really big about it.

But Mr. Gumbrel still *humphed* around about it as we left his office and he led me back to a musty room that I was by now familiar with. I liked the smell of old ink and old paper. The age of it was comforting, as if these newspapers would continue on as long as I needed them.

He said, "You're about the only one who comes back here any-more. I guess we don't write much that requires research now." He looked off across stacks of papers and metal shelves and sighed.

I guess he was thinking of a better, research-filled time than now. He stood with his hands in his pockets and I felt kind of sad for him because I liked him. If for no other reason than because he had told Ree-Jane, no, she couldn't write a column for the paper, that she'd had no experience beyond the paragraph she'd done about the tennis tournament. That wouldn't have gotten in either except Lola Davidow had worn him down over drinks and gotten him to promise he would publish a small piece on the annual tennis tournament that was held in Spirit Lake every summer. He'd told Ree-Jane she didn't know enough about tennis, or anything else, come to think of it, to write for the *Conservative*.

This honesty was one thing I liked about Mr. Gumbrel and would, of course, have liked it about anyone else who said similar things about Ree-Jane. It's maybe the main thing Aurora Paradise had going for her; throwing that chicken wing at Ree-Jane had upped her popularity with me considerably.

We were standing by a table stacked with magazines; it looked like *Life* mostly. The top one had the most beautiful cover, a Christmas issue with snow falling against a red background. A woman dressed in red was putting cards into a mailbox. The thing was that her red outfit blended into the red background so that you couldn't tell where one began and the other ended. "I really like that," I said.

Mr. Gumbrel looked. "Oh, yes, that's one of Coles Phillips's Fadeaway Girls. He was famous for that technique. Probably more of them in those stacks." He nodded at the other magazines. Then he steered me toward the shelves at the rear of the room and I told him I knew where these issues were as I'd looked through them before.

"I'll leave you to it, then." He walked off.

I knelt down in front of one of the bottom shelves and dragged out several copies of the old paper. I didn't have to read through a lot because the Ben Queen story headlined at least three of the issues. What I wanted was not words but pictures. I wanted to look at the picture of Rose Queen that had been run; it was a formal photograph of Rose a few years before she was murdered that had been taken by a local photographer. The only other pictures I had seen of her was a snapshot Aurora had and a photograph of all the Devereau sisters much younger, hanging on the wall in their old house, now vacant.

I found the twenty-year-old issue of the paper. The paper's name was different—*The Conservative Arm*—and printed in much fancier type, the two capitals, the "C" and the "A," looking as if tiny leaves were growing out of them. The awful headline glared up at me:

COLD FLAT JUNCTION WOMAN
BRUTALLY MURDERED

and there was Rose's picture just beneath the banner and beside the column that gave the account of the murder. Below hers were smaller photos of Ben Queen and their daughter, Fern. I rested my eyes on Rose's picture. She wore a dress with a sweetheart neckline and a small cross on a delicate chain that looked as if it had come from the Oak Tree Gift Shoppe. Her hair was to her shoulders; it was very light and shiny, almost transparent, almost as if you could see through it. I took the snapshot from my back pocket and laid it right beside Rose's picture. They looked so much alike they could have been twins. Rose Devereau Queen and Morris Slade.

That's who he had reminded me of, but it hadn't come to me of course because I was assuming he reminded me of another man. "As much as a woman can resemble a man." That's what I said when I was looking at Aurora's snapshots of old Mr. Woodruff and his daughter, Imogen.

Rose would have been older than Morris, fifteen years or so. I wondered what Mr. Devereau had looked like. I had never seen a picture of him. The three Devereau daughters must have looked like him, for they certainly did not appear to have taken after their mother, Alice Souder. Looks can skip around as Aurora had said. (My brother looks like our father, but I don't look like either of my parents. Maybe I look like some aunt somewhere.)

But Morris Slade? He was the spitting image of Rose and Alice Souder, mother of both of them.

The most vicious slaying these parts have ever seen—

the report went on. That didn't strike me as the most objective reporting. It wasn't even good writing. If it hadn't been twenty-two years ago,

I'd think Ree-Jane was working for the paper. That was her kind of language.

———

—occurred yesterday afternoon on the property of Mr. and Mrs. George Queen when their sister-in-law, Rose Devereau Queen, was found brutally stabbed to death in the barn behind the house.

———

The account went on to describe the attack and ended with the dark note that the victim's husband, Ben Queen, could not be found.

That was such a lie. I'd found out myself that Ben Queen was in Hebrides at the feed store where he went every week for supplies. If I could find it out, the police surely could have, if they hadn't been so dead set on arresting Ben Queen. The police *should* have found out.

But Ben Queen never defended himself; he never offered an alibi; he never spoke at his trial.

This always made me want to cry, his silence, because I knew what that kind of silence paid for.

In charge of the investigation (such as it was) was State Trooper Willard Plum and Sheriff Mooma, who said, "We won't rest until this brutal killer is brought to justice." All Sheriff Mooma did was rest. He was sheriff after that for nearly ten years and "bone lazy" according to Aurora Paradise.

Finally, I put up the paper and shoved the stack I'd taken it from back on the shelf. I sat looking at nothing except the gray cinder-block wall. I reached out and put my hand on it; I don't know why. It was cold and hard. Maybe I'd been afraid my hand would go through it. Maybe I felt I'd been dealing with ghosts too long.

I sat there wondering. Of all the crazy things to think of just then, I thought of the Big Garage and *Medea*. But that was because this whole Devereau–Queen–Slade case was all so Greek! Revenge after revenge after revenge. Mary-Evelyn Devereau is murdered, and after that, almost as if it were a punishment for her letting it happen, Rose is murdered by her daughter, Fern; then after *that*, Fern is murdered—and I had been so sure she was murdered by the Girl who I thought to be Fern's daughter.

What had Been Queen to do with her, then? She wasn't the grand-daughter he wanted to take the blame for—

Or had he made the same mistake as me?

With a jerk, I looked up. My head had grown so heavy with trying to concentrate I had nearly dozed off.

What if he had seen her? What if he had assumed she was Fern's child because of the way she looked? He knew Fern had gone away from Cold Flat Junction several years after the murder of Rose. The Queens would have told him—Sheba would, even if George wouldn't, want Ben to know because he would have thought to spare him more pain. But Sheba, she wasn't interested in sparing pain; she loved gossip and secrets more than either her husband or brother-in-law. She wouldn't have kept quiet about Fern's "condition."

Then what had happened to Fern's baby? Maybe it was what they called stillborn (whatever that meant it didn't sound good) or maybe somebody'd adopted it or she'd sent it to an orphanage.

It wasn't easy being a baby, no, it wasn't. And it was even harder, I bet, being a stolen baby.

I sighed and rose and walked to the door, stopping to look again at the *Life* magazine and the wonderful illustration, red fading into red.

A stolen baby. A Fadeaway girl.

25

I didn't mind, as much as I thought I would, being wrong about the Girl. That was because I now had solved the mystery twice and I had not been wrong about her being connected to Rose Devereau when she was Rose Souder. This second solution was even more thrilling, for it is not every day you come up with an answer to a crime that no one else has solved, including police and maybe even New York City police. No, it wasn't every day you did that.

Of course, to be fair, the police hadn't seen the Girl and I had. And I guess you had to see her to get yourself thinking. Other people must have seen her—on the train, in La Porte—but she hadn't registered. *Who is that girl? Haven't I seen her somewhere before? Doesn't she remind me of someone? A face in a picture?*

And then I had seen her several times. And you had to be as interested as I was in lost people, people who vanished almost before your eyes, people who seemed alone and without help, people who got robbed of everything, even their names.

Not only people, either, but animals and landscapes, like that far field across from the Cold Flat Junction railroad station, that line of navy-blue trees, a landscape of forgetting is how it looks to me. The hotel cat, who can lose himself in morning fog, or the deer in winter, drinking from the stream's end, and even the river itself.

Suddenly, without warning, I knew that something had gone, that it wasn't me just imagining something had vanished before my eyes. No, something really had. I got scared and got up all of a sudden. It was too much to take in: the Girl, the stolen baby, vanished people, the deer, the old hotel. I stopped looking at newspapers and left the office.

I had stopped myself telling the Sheriff about what I'd discovered about the Girl. Would he care anymore about something that had happened when he wasn't even the sheriff? Well, he cared about Ben Queen, didn't he? Or at least about finding him. Which wasn't the same thing. But I don't think he cared so much about the truth of the whole thing. If he did, he would've gone over to Hebrides and talked to Smitty at Smith's Feed and Garden Supply and found that Ben Queen had an alibi even if he didn't use it. Well, it was clear why he hadn't used it—because of Fern.

I was getting testier and testier, walking along, kicking at a pebble on the sidewalk, headed for the Rainbow Café. I was hungry from all of this thinking. Or maybe from all this feeling. Because back there with the newspapers, when I felt something had gone out of my life, my mind (or maybe my heart) flew to thoughts of my mother's ham pinwheels and Angel Pie. It seems a funny thing to think of food, but I was hungry without being hungry. I was starved or I was thirsty or I was hollow. I didn't know what I was.

As I passed Souder's Pharmacy, I lingered in front of the window. The display was always the same: Vitalis hair tonic, Evening in Paris cologne, a little silver compact opened and a tiny trail of pale powder beside a pair of long blue satin evening gloves. They went with the cologne and powder. They would have been popular with the women who danced at the Belle Ruin.

You could barely see into the pharmacy, it was so dark inside; it was made dark by all the dark wood and the lack of overhead lights and shadows cast by the ceiling fan. Old Mr. Souder, who did up the prescriptions still, even though his hands shook, hardly ever came out from the back, and it was left to Mrs. Souder to take care of the soda fountain and sell the Vitalis and the cologne. I thought of stopping off for a chocolate soda; that way I could ask Mrs. Souder about Morris Slade, for he would have been some relation to her. But I knew perfectly well Mrs. Souder would no more talk to me, twelve years old, than to a doorknob. Asking her questions was just my excuse for getting a soda. I slumped along, thinking how pathetic it was a chocolate soda was all it took to lift me out of the doldrums. I wondered what a doldrum actually was, and sighed, and walked on up the street to the Rainbow Café.

26

I said hello to Shirl, who was bringing down two fingers on the keys of the cash register; the drawer sprang forward, as if it too wanted to get a punch in. She didn't hello back.

Wanda must have been on her three-minute break, for she was standing behind the soda fountain eating a rainbow-sprinkled doughnut and with a cup of coffee in her other hand.

"Hi, Wanda," I said as I crawled up on one of the imitation leather stools beside Dodge Haines, who started chortling and nudging me in the ribs as if we were best buddies. Maybe that's why I liked the Windy Run Diner customers. At least they didn't get physical with a person.

"Hi, hon." She put down her coffee cup and put her doughnut on a napkin. "What can I get for you?"

"No, Wanda. Looks like you're on your break. You shouldn't be waiting on anyone."

She flapped her hand. "Oh, it's all up 'cept for half a minute. That's okay."

But in half a minute a person could do a lot. I said this. "You could dive into Lake Noir, say 'I do,' shoot Shirl—"

Wanda just thought that was the funniest. She doubled over laughing. For some reason, being around a person like Wanda made me feel good. Maybe it was because she found me worth waiting on, even during her three-minute break. I don't know.

I leaned back as far as I could, looking down the aisle between the booths, but I couldn't see who was in the last one, the one reserved for the help. "The Sheriff here, Wanda?"

I slipped off the stool and said hello in passing to Mayor Sims and Buddy Dubois who were the only others at the counter in this off-hour and walked back to the booths.

I couldn't believe it. I stopped cold.

The Sheriff was there all right, in the back booth. He was sitting across from Ree-Jane, who looked like the cat who'd swallowed the canary when she saw me. *Ree-Jane!* This wasn't the porch or the dining room or her room filled with Heather Gay Struther clothes, or even Slaw's Garage. This was *the back booth of Shirl's.*

I let on nothing. I was the Star of feeling-hiding. If they gave out Academy Awards for disguising feelings I would have a row of them on my dresser. I was the one. I was the It girl.

So I put on a smile. "Hello," to the Sheriff; to Ree-Jane, "What are you doing here?" But bored, as if I couldn't care less whether she was or wasn't here.

Now, Perry Mason has taught me one thing. Don't ask questions you don't know how somebody will answer.

"I made a discovery I thought Sam should know about."

Sam. Her smug smile.

The Sheriff reached toward an object on the table and so did Ree-Jane, her hand actually on top of his.

Something was crazy.

The Sheriff pulled back his hand and with it whatever was wrapped in the napkin.

She said, "Do you think it's a good idea telling, you know—?"

She tilted her head toward me—"you know"—as if I was simple and couldn't understand what she meant as long as she didn't name me. I gritted my teeth hard, but I still managed to keep my face bland.

The Sheriff said, "A better idea I can't imagine. It's Emma here who's been writing the whole account up; she's the first person who should see this." He folded back the napkin.

I could hardly believe my eyes. Inside it was a gun and the Artist George tube that I had returned to the little alcove in the spring near the Devereau house. My mouth dropped open. I made little noises that

I meant to be words but couldn't shape them. I knew then how Ubub must feel. I stared at her and her simpering smile.

"Regina Jane, here—" began the Sheriff.

She leaned toward him. "R.J., Sam. These days I'm called R.J."

Was the Rainbow Café today to be nothing but surprises? *R.J.?*

The Sheriff went on, basically ignoring her. "I was saying, Regina Jane here brought these two items to me. Says she found them at Crystal Spring, over there by Spirit Lake. Says there's a hollowed-out place in the rocks around the spring where a cup is kept for people to drink from. This little tube thing was behind it. And behind *it* was this pistol."

In the palm of his hand, the gun looked like a toy, just like it had in Ben Queen's hand the time I'd first seen him. I stared at them, my eyes going back and forth from gun to Artist George, one of the characters from the Mr. Ree game. I was sure it was the Girl who'd left it in that hollowed-out place in the stone. Though there had been no actual message rolled up in the tube, the tube itself was a message of some sort. I just hadn't unriddled it yet. But the first and last time I'd seen the gun was when Ben Queen had picked it up from the chair in the Devereau house and stuck it in his pocket. I looked up. What was Ree-Jane doing at Spirit Lake? I mean, she never goes there; she's too lazy to walk three quarters of a mile.

Then I remembered that feeling someone was following me. *She was!* I was so furious I could feel my face go blotchy red. I never blushed prettily.

"What's the matter?" she asked with that sneer disguised as a smile. "I was investigating." She held up a brown leather notebook. "Taking notes. I just *know* there're things missing from your report. See"—here she held up the hollow tube with Artist George's head stuck on top of it. She pulled out the head—"this is what I bet Ben Queen is using to communicate with somebody."

It was clear who she thought the "somebody" was.

She went on. "And the gun's his, too, I bet. I bet it's the one that killed that poor Fern Queen." She lay her hand on her forehead and closed her eyes as if she really gave a damn. "Imagine, a parent killing his own *daughter*!"

I knew at least one mother who'd probably do that one of these days. I was afraid to lift my head and look at the Sheriff. Ree-Jane had invaded me, taken my private place and I was so furious I thought I'd explode into bits and pieces that would career around the Rainbow. The heat and redness had drained from my face and now it was pale to white. Without even thinking, I inched closer to the Sheriff. I needed somebody human (as opposed to Ree-Jane) to lean against. Tears and sobs were building up in me like lava from that volcano somewhere in Italy that erupted and covered a whole town and turned the people into statues. I comforted myself with the thought of Ree-Jane turned to black stone with that silly smile on her face. I had gone cold in order to freeze the tears before they got to my eyes, so now I could feel them as tiny icicles in my throat.

The Sheriff felt warm where my shoulder touched his arm. I chanced a look at him; he was looking at Ree-Jane and he did not look pleased. His face had that granite look of statues, and I was afraid maybe I'd done it—erupted and overflowed down the awful mountain and turned him into stone. He looked like he was trying to control himself, which meant he was mad at her, too. Then he relaxed a little and put his arm around my shoulders. His arm. My shoulders. It almost made up for being born. I sat up so spanking straight and twangy you could have shot an arrow with me. He patted my shoulder, removed his arm (but not its ghost), leaned toward her across the table and said in a deadly soft voice, "Thing is, Regina Jane, neither one of these—the tube, the gun—is significant as evidence—"

Oh, *joy!* Now it was Ree-Jane's turn to go blotchy!

"—because this"—he held up the hollow tube—"is a kid's way of sending messages."

(I wasn't sure I liked that much.)

"Not a man like Ben Queen. *This*"—he held up the gun—"isn't the murder weapon."

Her mouth fell open. (Actually, mine would have, too, except I quickly paralyzed my jaw. But it might have been like looking in a mirror, except I'm prettier, if I do say it myself.) "What do you *mean*? It's his gun! I know it is!" Her cranky voice made itself heard.

"Then you don't know squat about guns." He pushed the gun down in his belt, much like Ben Queen had done. "I'm taking it anyway. A kid shouldn't be walking around with a gun."

A *kid, a kid!* Even though I was sitting in a booth, I could hardly keep from jumping up and down.

Ree-Jane was livid. She was turning, right before my eyes, into a witch melting. Her mouth drooped, rid at last of the smile.

And it seemed the Sheriff was not yet done!

"You ought to watch yourself, Regina Jane. If you continue to mess around like this, I might have to cite you for obstructing a police investigation. We can't have people going off on their own tangents, certainly not kids."

He said it again!

"Unless it's Emma, here, but all this was thrust upon her and I must say her own actions were nothing short of heroic."

I think right then I knew what "swoon" meant. I fell against the high back of the booth, but I couldn't swoon because I didn't want to miss one lick of what the Sheriff was saying.

"Imagine, Regina Jane, just imagine walking through that dark wood with a crazy person behind you and you—"

"With a gun," I reminded him. "A crazy person with a gun." You wouldn't think he'd forget that detail.

He nodded and seemed to be biting his lip. "With a gun, right."

Melt, melt. Ree-Jane was slipping slowly down in the booth, looking more and more liquid.

"Do you think you could have done that? I sincerely doubt it."

Right now I had my two fists up to my mouth, I guess to hold something in—whoops of laughter or screams of triumph. Ree-Jane was completely flummoxed by where she'd gone wrong. It was really bad on her.

The Sheriff said he had to leave and I got up from the booth to let him out.

I'll say this for Ree-Jane: she at least had the sauce to give him a disbelieving look and even call back a little of the sneer. "How do you know that's not the gun?"

Yes, I'll give her credit for wheeling out another stupid question. You'd think she'd have learned and been silenced. Not her.

The Sheriff stood there, adjusting his black sunglasses. "Because I'm the Sheriff."

I have *never* heard the Sheriff say anything even remotely conceited. But now he pulled up his holster belt and folded a stick of old
Teaberry gum into his mouth (I know it was old because I gave it to
him a week ago and he only chews gum when I give it to him, for some
reason). With his thumbs tucked into his belt like Donny Mooma, he
added, "That's how." He swaggered out.

A new song was playing on the jukebox, Patsy Cline wailing

> "PARDON ME IF I'M SENTIMENTAL
>
> WHEN WE SAY GOOD-BYE"

and I thought it a nice touch for the Sheriff's exit.

I was left over, so she glared at me with her mouth working and
trying to frame a huge putdown. "You think you're so smart!"

I winced at the childish insult and almost felt sorry for her. Then
she flounced out of the booth in her new, blue Heather Gay Struther
dress and walked out and didn't answer Buddy Dubois or Dodge
Haines, who greeted her. "Hey, Ree-Jane!"

Patsy went wailing on:

> ". . . NOW AND THEN, THERE'S A FOOL SUCH AS I."

And that was a nice touch for Ree-Jane's exit. Only the song was
much too pretty.

There wasn't much glee in my life, but that half hour in the Rainbow contained enough to last me the rest of it.

I waved good-bye to Wanda, and she waved back, both of us
wreathed in smiles.

Our funky old lives were on their three-minute breaks.

27

I really wanted to talk to the Sheriff now, for if he didn't think this gun shot Fern, maybe he'd changed his mind about Ben Queen. It certainly sounded as if he was defending him a little bit ago. So I went back into the Rainbow and had Wanda bag a half dozen doughnuts for me. I took my bag of doughnuts and went across the street to the courthouse, hoping the Sheriff was there now and that Donny wasn't.

That was hope wasted.

Donny was tilted back in the Sheriff's chair with his big booted feet up on the Sheriff's desk. He always made sure his holster was in plain view, even sitting down. Dwayne called him a cowboy, for some reason. I said Donny couldn't even cowboy a horse. He was short and stick thin and I supposed all of his blustering about and using his authority every chance he got (like once drawing his gun on an old dog and ordering people on the sidewalk, *Stay back, stay back, we got us a rabid animal here!* and then Mayor Sims's wife, whose dog it was—everybody knew Timmy—came out of the gift shop and told Donny not to be foolish, Timmy'd just got hold of a bar of Miss Flagler's lavender soap, and Donny had slunk away). It was probably because standing next to the Sheriff gave him such a total complex he just went to the other extreme and blustered and swaggered and stopped cars when he wanted to cross the street just to show off he could.

When I walked in the door, he said, "Ain't seen you for at *least* a day." He flapped his hand at me. "Sam ain't here."

"He was just in the Rainbow. Where is he?"

"I ain't at liberty to say. Whatcha got there?" He nodded at the white bag that he perfectly well knew was from the Rainbow. I held up the bag. "I got some for you and the Sheriff and me. There's half a dozen and you can have them all, since you didn't win any."

He stuck his neck out like a turtle. "Got any of the new kind, the ones with them little crinkles on 'em?"

"Yes. There's a couple with all different colors and a couple chocolate-sprinkled—crinkled—ones."

He dropped his feet from the desk again and motioned me over with a broad wave of his arm. "Well, bring 'em here, girl. I ain't got all day. Sam's over to Hebrides and I'm here by myself with a mountain of work." He peered into the bag, stuck his hand in and pulled out one with colored sprinkles *and* with chocolate sprinkles.

I didn't care. For the information the Sheriff had gone to Hebrides, Donny could have the whole sack. If the Sheriff had gone there, it might have been to interview Smitty, the old man who owned Smith's Feed and Garden Supply and who could be an alibi for Ben Queen for the time Rose Queen was murdered. I was bursting to know. But Donny'd never tell me, just because he knew I wanted to know. I set the bag on the desk. "Oh, well, he must've gone to talk to Miss Stump."

Chomping away, Donny said, mouth full, "Who the Sam Hill's *that*?"

"Miss Jean W. Stump? She owns the little dressmaking goods store. It just occurred to me that's who he went to see because I saw him write down her initials in his notebook: *J.W.S.*"

"Ha ha *ha*!" He said, singsonglike, as he ate the rest of his chocolate-sprinkled doughnut. "Shows how much you know." Cross-eyed, he tried to see the sprinkles across the doughnut's surface. "Them initials stand for J. W. *Smith*. He owns the feed store." He chomped away for a while, then said, "You think you're so smart, don't you?"

Uh-huh.

I felt like marching right back to the Rainbow and buying Wanda a dozen doughnuts for introducing me to the crinkled ones. I honestly believed they hypnotized people into giving you what you wanted. Maybe I could catch her on her three-minute break again one day.

28

The day had been so thrilling I was even able to put up with Delbert in the taxi back to the hotel. By "put up with" I don't mean converse with (what day could ever be that thrilling?), but just that I didn't pull back my mouth with my fingers and stick out my tongue at his back. No, I rode quietly and, for me, in a dignified manner, sitting upright instead of sliding down in the backseat so he couldn't see me in his rearview mirror. I even answered some of his dumb questions with an *uh-huh* or *nu-huh* or with actual words. But mostly I just remembered Ree-Jane's horrible humiliation, smiling so broadly Delbert asked me why I was so happy (one of the questions I answered with words).

"I'm not," I said, which was really stupid, because of course he asked why I was smiling if I wasn't. "I'm doing a few face exercises is all."

"Well, you sure do look awful happy."

At this point I nearly dropped to the floor of the cab in an exaggerated version of even my moves. Why hadn't I simply told him I'd found a twenty-dollar bill on the sidewalk, which would have satisfied him as a reason for happiness and also allowed him to go on talking to himself without bothering me?

"I found twenty dollars on the sidewalk."

"Well, that's good luck, but maybe you should've turned it in."

"Delbert, that is the dumbest thing I ever heard! Turn it in to who?"

He shrugged. "Police maybe. You got to be honest in this life is what I think. It's the only thing that gets you through."

I could just hear him smacking his mental lips over all this wisdom. "No, it isn't. Making things up is what gets you through."

"Telling lies? That ain't no way to live your life."

"Did I say lies?" Though I had to admit it wasn't a bad idea. Look at Aurora Paradise: happy as a clam lying about the present, the past and which walnut shell the dried pea was under. "What I mean is *making up* things. That's what my brother does. He and his friend spend nearly their entire lives in the Big Garage making up plays. He's happy." I don't know if he was happy, but he was certainly crazy.

"Well, but you can't live in some never-never land. You got to face reality."

"Reality? Who even knows what that is? Nobody does." That was clever of me and I smacked my mental lips.

Delbert hit the steering wheel. "Right here! This here's reality! Ain't nothin' realer than drivin' this old cab."

I smiled my sneaky smile. "Oh, is that so? Let's just ask Axel about that."

We were tire crunching up the hotel driveway. "Axel? Well, it's his cab company. I guess he knows it's real. So go on, ask him." Delbert halted the cab under the porte cochere. I leaned forward with the fare and his small tip and rested my chin on top of the seat. "I would, only I can never find him."

I hopped out of the cab and went up the porch steps, thinking that I'd just had a conversation with Delbert. I stood gazing through the screen door at shadowy outlines of front desk and carpet and flowered, chintz-covered chairs. Did this mean I was getting more patient? More grown up? Older? My birthday would be here soon. Did that mean things like conversing with Delbert would now be a way of life?

Oh, please, please, please, let my birthday go by with no one knowing, especially me. I prayed to whatever deus ex machina was swaying up there way over my head. If growing up means talking to

Delbert and being patient with Miss Bertha for the rest of my life, do not let me turn thirteen.

I went into the pleasantly cool lobby, where I wouldn't at all have minded spending the rest of my life. And this was about as far from reality as a person could get.

29

The salads would have to wait. It was time for Aurora's cocktail and I wanted to make it good and strong to get her talking. What I really needed was one of those machines the police use for separating truth from lies. It would be about four to one in favor of lies in Aurora's case, which was the same parts of rum and juice I was using for this drink.

Mrs. Davidow's office supply was way down on Southern Comfort and Jim Beam and out of Gordon's gin, so I would have had to empty bottles if I used them. Lola Davidow would know someone had been raiding her liquor and she would start locking it up. There was a rum named Montecristo, and it looked strong enough to flatten an army. It was dark as molasses and nearly full because Mrs. Davidow didn't care much for rum. The only rum she liked was in my mother's rum buns and the rum-and-orange sauce for little sausages, and who could argue with that? Making this drink brought the level down, but the bottle had been stuck back on the shelf behind all the others, so she probably wouldn't notice.

She was gone from the hotel right now, and I figured, given the lack of gin, she'd have gone to Alta Vista, even though she'd just recently gone there. They must have been out of Gordon's. Alta Vista was a little town just over the state line where there was a state liquor store. I'd gone with her a few times, which had been really pleasant for her frame of mind was always excellent headed for Alta Vista. Well, it's no worse than me heading for the kitchen for ham pinwheels or buckwheat cakes.

The drink was actually quite pretty. It had a bronze look, a pink cast from a few strawberries I'd mashed around, and with the maraschino cherry floating atop it, it made me think of the sun going down over Miami Beach. I stood holding the little tray with the drink on it and thought about my trip there. Watching Ree-Jane in an old brown dress, dancing with a squat little partner, and me with the handsome heir to the Rony Plaza, I tried to decide which, that night or this glee-filled day today, which was the best of the two. Of course, my Miami Beach trip had been all in my mind. But I had been really happy down in the Pink Elephant with my cutout palm tree and the record player playing "Tangerine" and other songs the heir to the Rony Plaza and I danced to . . . well, it was a hard decision.

As I stood with the small tray in my hands, I gazed up at the heir, who said my name: *"Emma!"* I smiled before I realized, no, it wasn't him, it was someone in the room. It was Vera.

"What are you doing standing there with that tray? What's that drink? Who's it for? Why aren't you making the *salads*? Don't you know it's *nearly six*?"

I waited to see if the run of questions was over, and deciding it was (although her mouth was still working out something), I said, "I'm taking this up to Aunt Aurora. You know how she gets." Vera certainly did; Aurora Paradise threw a dish of rhubarb at her once. The memory made me smile almost as much as when she threw a chicken wing at Ree-Jane.

Vera pursed her mouth, bright with lipstick, so it looked a little like the cherry in the glass, and said, "Hurry up, then. I can't be expected to do the salads along with everything else."

I had no idea what "everything else" was, since Vera didn't set the tables (except when there was a dinner party), didn't take the butter patties around and didn't fill the ice-water pitchers. "Well, then, I'd better take this up to her before she comes down and gets it herself."

Vera actually took a step back. Until that moment I hadn't realized what a threat I'd been passing up. Aurora's suddenly appearing downstairs could scare the pants off anybody except: a person with nerves of steel (my mother); a person with gumption (me); a person who didn't live in this world (Will); a person who didn't know what he should be afraid of anyway (Walter); a person who'd just finished five martinis (Mrs. Davidow). I could go on with the list, but I sailed out of the kitchen holding the tray up on the flat of my hand, just to annoy Vera, who thought she was Queen of the Trays. I smiled. It sounded like one of the Tarot cards.

"What's this?" Aurora held the drink up to the light and shook it a little.

"It's new. It's *really* popular in Miami Beach."

"How would you know what they drink in Miami Beach? You never been there."

"Yes, I have, too." In a manner of speaking. Or being.

She sipped it and her face glowed. "Well! Now *that's* a drink! Got a little rum in it."

"You could say that."

"What's it called?"

I had forgotten to give it a name. I chewed my lip. "The Count of Monte Cristo. In Miami Beach," I added.

"The Count of Monte Cristo in Miami Beach? Now, there's a peculiar name."

"It is, isn't it? But you know how Miami Beachers are. See, it's made from Montecristo rum. And it was invented there. They call it The Count for short and it's so strong it'll blow your iron mask off." I puffed up my cheeks and went, "*Pffffff.*"

Aurora had really reduced the contents of the glass. "That ain't the Count of Monte Cristo, girl; that's the Man in the Iron Mask."

I put on a pained look, pained by her ignorance. "There's more than one mask to go around. The count of Monte Cristo wore one, too. It was black." I was beginning to understand Will; a person could spend all day and all night doing this.

"I have a couple of questions," I said.

She smacked the glass down and folded her arms across her chest. "Depends. Don't expect me to betray any confidences."

Who would ever confide in Aurora? "This isn't a confidence."

"What ain't?"

"It's about the Belle Ruin Hotel. Do you remember the outside was being painted that summer the Slade baby disappeared?"

Astounded, she looked at me, stretching her neck as if to bring her eyes closer. "Why in God's name would I remember a fool thing like that? You're addled. You been doin' tables too long side by side with that headwaitress. She's like a case of whiplash. You have my sympathy, miss." Aurora picked up her glass again and set about rocking primly.

"Thank you. But do you remember about the painting?"

"Girl, did I spend my flaming youth keeping track of when people painted their houses and hotels?" Here she shot her long skinny arms into the air and gazed at the ceiling. "I was too busy *living*!" Then her whole upper body squirmed and turned as if she were doing some exotic dance like a tango.

I hoped that wasn't what living was. "What I want to know is who did the painting?"

"Oh, that." She rattled the last bit of her drink up the straw. "Now, that would've been Ruby Stuck. Best house painter in the business."

"Ruby? It was a woman?" That surprised me.

Aurora frowned and shook her head as if trying to free it from the sight of me. "No, no, don't be simple. *Reuben's* his name. Right strappin' man, set his sights on me." She fiddled with the cuffs of her gray silk dress.

"I'm sure. Was he your age then?" She'd lie about her own age, but probably not his.

"Just about. He'd've been in his early forties, I guess. I, of course, was younger."

Had Aurora ever learned to add? No, and she thought no one else had, either. So if Reuben Stuck was in his early forties back then, he'd be sixty-something now.

"I guess he wanted to marry you, too."

"Naturally."

There was nothing much to shake, but she shook what she had. I had to admit, though I didn't want to, I couldn't help but admire Aurora. Imagine having this much energy at age ninety-one. "Did he live around here?"

"No, that family's Cold Flat Junction people. For all I know, Ruby still lives there."

I felt like shooting *my* arms in the air! But I maintained my serious and unruffled stance. Cold Flat Junction was even better than if he lived in Spirit Lake because it was smaller and because there I had my own little other life with my band of informants.

I put out my hand. "I'll get you another drink. Just remember, they're pretty strong."

"Oh, I hope so, I hope so." She went back to fiddling with her cuff.

I got Walter to deliver the second drink to Aurora and sat in the kitchen when I'd finished with Miss Bertha. She'd raised an awful ruckus because her salad was "on fire." I had found a little jar of serrano peppers. She'd shot out of her chair so fast she all but straightened her hump. Looking at the red pepper you couldn't tell the difference between it and a slice of pimento. When her mouth splattered down on it and she shot up from the table, I was quickly at her side saying, "Oh, Miss Bertha, what is it?" in my most sympathetic voice (which isn't very), and removed the salad from the table. This I marched right into the kitchen to where Walter was polishing one of his big platters around and around, hypnotized by it. I told him, Quick! Get rid of the evidence.

My mother had gone into the dining room to "minister" to— meaning shut up—Miss Bertha and inspect whatever it was she had eaten. The only salad she had to look at was Mrs. Fulbright's, which, of course, was salad as usual.

It was really quite a bit of fun and a nice way to cap off my day. Or almost.

When I went up to my room, there was a note on my bed telling me to come to the Big Garage. It was after eight-thirty and all I wanted to do was listen to my records.

Mill was teaching June a new song and I wondered what else had been added to the script. June had a terrible voice.

Will had a ladder up at the end of the stage and he was standing on one of the top rungs and hanging the last of the curtain hooks. He'd coated the rope with some kind of wax and something hardened to keep the coating on. That way the hooks would slide along.

What I could never understand about my brother was, he would pay attention to tiny details like this but didn't seem to care what sex Medea's children were. I had told him that they should be two boys, not a boy and a girl. Did that bother him? No.

"It doesn't make any difference, does it? As long as she kills both of them. Tries to, I mean."

"That's like saying it doesn't make any difference if Hamlet is a woman!"

Scraping around in the wax container, he stopped and seemed to be thinking. "Interesting idea."

Right now I was holding the rolled-up script to his face. "Betsy! Whoever heard of Greek kids named 'Betsy' and 'Jason Junior'? In the real play, they don't even have names. They're just referred to as the 'boys.'"

"All you do is criticize, you know that?" He set down the jar. "Look, they've got to have names—"

"The playwright what's-his-name didn't think so. But of course he was only a *Greek,* and it's only a *Greek* play, so how would he know! You know what I wonder? I wonder if you ever even read this play."

Big sigh. "Of course we did. The highlights, anyway."

My mouth was agape. "The *highlights*? You two are putting on a play you haven't even *read*?"

Will let loose another sigh that could have taken on half the sorrows of the whole wide world. "You just don't get it, do you? This is *Art* with a capital *A* we've got here. This is an interpretation. Every creative person would do it differently. The audience is here and now. It's not back then and there. That was Greek society. You've got to move with the times. If Euripedes was alive today, he'd be *us.*" He waved his arm to take in Mill, June and maybe even Paul.

I had never in my life heard anything more outrageous.

June was singing what sounded more like dying:

"*In some se-cluuu-ded arboretum,*"

Behind her were three kids, two of June's little sisters, Twinkie and Annie, and another child I didn't know. I'd never seen her before.

"Why are they here?"

"They're the Hummers."

"Who?"

"The Hummers. We needed a Greek chorus but we didn't have enough people, so we decided on Hummers. They stand behind actors and hum during songs. Mill thought of it."

I tried leaning into his face. "This play's on day after tomorrow, remember? You can't just keep on making changes!"

"Art evolves."

I wanted to tear out my hair. Noticing the third girl, I asked again, "Who's that other girl?"

"Her? She's a guest. She came in this morning."

"One of ours?"

That was obvious, so he didn't answer.

"Well, but do her parents know?"

He looked at me and shook his head. "If everyone worried about every little thing the way you do, people would never get anything done."

"Every little *thing*? You *kidnap* one of the guests' children and that's a 'little thing'? It's nearly nine o'clock and she didn't have any dinner. I sure didn't see her in the dining room!"

"Oh, for fuck's sake! Yes, she did. Walter brought hers when he brought all of ours. And we didn't kidnap her. She was just wandering around the croquet court like a little drunk and we asked her if she wanted to be in a play. I don't think she's got all her marbles."

"*Now* she hasn't, not after you've been at her. She doesn't look any more than five or six. How long has she been in the garage?"

"Awhile." He cocked his ear toward the stage. "That's the duet. Gotta go!"

"What—" He didn't answer but then what difference did it make?

He ran up the steps to the stage.

Mill shut June up while he made adjustments to his various instruments: these were the piano, the clarinet, a tin drum, a cowbell, an old washboard from our laundry room and a couple of things that clattered like those noisemakers you see at parties. All of these Mill would play himself with a little bit of help from Chuck, who was also working the colored lights. Right now he trilled on the clarinet and rippled the piano keys by way of introduction. Will, who had a fairly booming voice, and June, who had a thin one, sang:

"In some se-cluuu-ded arboretum,
  That overlooks the Colosseum—"

Arboretum? The words were strange but the tune sounded familiar. I frowned.

Then Mill said, "Okay, okay," as Chuck came to sit on the chair beside him. "Now we're going to pick up the tempo." Mill banged the
keys, pointed to Chuck, who swung the noisemaker around several
times, then rang the cowbell as Mill beat on the tin drum and rattled a
tambourine.

I'd never heard such a sound in my life.

Wait a minute: yes, I had. Spike Jones.

Spike Jones and his crazy band playing "Cocktails for Two." That
was the song Mill had written new words to.

The cowbell clattered.

The tambourine shivered.

The Hummers hummed.

I walked out.

30

When I walked into the lobby, I thought I was back with Medea.

Mrs. Davidow was there, with a highball. I guess she needed forti-fication. Ree-Jane was there sulking.

A man and woman I didn't know were arguing, or at least the woman was. She was yelling at the man that they never should have gone out and left Bessie here.

I bet I knew who they were, and who Bessie was.

The man was looking pale and acting really milquetoasty. He kept patting her shoulder and muttering that Bessie had to be around.

My mother motioned me into the back office, and in a lowered voice, asked, "Have you seen Bessie Walls?"

"If she's who I think, she's up in the Big Garage."

"What?"

"Will's got her playing a Hummer."

It didn't make any difference whether she was playing a Hummer or a violin, my mother sucked in her breath and went stony cold. Re-ally when she goes silent all over, I think even her heart must stop beating. When her face looked ironclad like that, well, look out everybody. I was really pleased that Will was going to get it.

"Are you going to the garage? I could go with—"

"Stay here." She pointed at the floor with her finger, as if I might not be certain where "here" was.

She came back with Will and Bessie in tow ten minutes later.

Anyone who might think that Will would look hangdog or even scared by the prospect of facing wailing parents (with himself the cause of it) doesn't know my brother. He was wreathed in smiles.

He had the advantage, of course, of the mother's being so happy that Bessie was still alive, Will could have sold her into white slavery and Mrs. Walls would still be thankful. But that would only last a minute. Then the Wallses would have been really mad.

Still smiling as if he'd never stop, he reached out his hand to take Mr. Walls's. "It's nice to meet you; I'm really glad you're back. I was worried that Bessie here might have been forgotten—"

I couldn't believe he was saying this.

"—when we saw Bessie out on the croquet court and thought it would be a good idea to have her come to rehearsal, you know, so we could keep an eye on her." He gave Bessie his most smarmy smile. Bessie just stuck her fingers in her mouth. It didn't look like talent to me.

But the Wallses said they hadn't left Bessie alone; they'd paid Ree-Jane to babysit.

Everyone stared at Ree-Jane. Oh, how wonderful!

Ree-Jane made a move to leave, and Mrs. Davidow (to give her credit) gave her a black look and shook her head. So Ree-Jane just kept on sitting on the arm of the sofa, looking like she'd been served her last meal.

Will went on. "Bessie, in case you didn't know it, has a lot of talent. A lot of talent. I just put her in the chorus and she took to it right away. I just wanted to give her something to do and I was really surprised how she took to the stage like a duck to water." He went on, voicing concern for Bessie's welfare and managing to make this all the fault of the Wallses for going out and leaving Bessie alone and thanking God that he and Mill were around instead of, you know, some unseemly character.

Like who? I wanted to ask. The Woods? Walter? Will was so good he had even me wondering who was unseemly when I knew he was just turning the spotlight away from his savior-self onto some unidentified person. It's a good thing Mill hadn't come, too, or we'd all have been there till dawn while they fed each other lines that would weave into some sort of unbelievable tapestry.

Will kept on about Bessie's talent, her good looks, her way of handling herself—confidence that he would have expected from an adult, not one of Bessie's age. Every once in a while, Ree-Jane made another move to leave, and Mrs. Davidow stopped her.

As Will kept it up, the disbelieving looks of the Wallses turned to curious ones, then to almost pleased ones, and then to smiling ones.

My mother walked away before Will's performance was over, probably back to the kitchen to whip up a batch of Parker House rolls.

Lola Davidow made herself another drink.

Bessie just stood with her mouth open, looking dumb or having an asthma attack or something.

Will finally stopped talking and accepted the thanks of the Wallses for taking care of Bessie, and said that, of course, if Bessie wanted to, she could be in the production.

I figured the Wallses deserved whatever they got, if they were fools enough to take that in. I wanted to give Bessie my role so Paul could push her off the swing; then we'd see how pleased the Wallses were with Will.

The Wallses went off to bed and Will went off to the Big Garage. That left Mrs. Davidow and Ree-Jane and me, and I was content to stand around listening to Ree-Jane's getting raked over the coals around fifteen times. I figured that was the best I'd hear and went upstairs to Will's room to paw through his closet for the Spike Jones record.

In my room, I put the record on the Waitresses' phonograph and lay on my bed with my hands behind my head and listened to "Cocktails for Two."

> *"In some secluded rendevous"*
> *That overlooks the avenue . . ."*

Yep, that was the song, all right.

> *"As we enjoy a cigarette,*
> *To some exquisite chansonette . . ."*

Blah blah blah. Blah . . .

"My head may go reeling
But my heart will be obedient,
With intoxicating kisses
For the principal ingredient."

Spike went through the song once as if it were a romantic ballad, then switched over to his crazy instruments of washboards and chicken clucks and cowbells.

Before the cigarettes and cocktails there had been some introductory lines asking everyone if they wouldn't enjoy the right to be happy and carefree again.

"How would you like to enjoy the right to be carefree and gay once again?"

When had we all been carefree and gay the first time? When we were babies, maybe? But babies didn't know they were carefree, so how did that work? Did Bessie know she was carefree up there in the Big Garage? And what about Aurora? Maybe she was carefree when she was singing "Carry Me Back to Old Kentucky." I don't know. Maybe even I was carefree wandering around the Belle Ruin.

I think Will and Mill might be the only truly carefree ones, up there in the Big Garage, in Carefree City.

31

I figured if Reuben Stuck was in his sixties, he was probably retired from housepainting and would be home during the day, or if not home, hanging out someplace. That was pretty vague, but I didn't have any other way of finding him, so I caught the morning train for Cold Flat Junction.

On alighting, after giving a quick look up and down the platform and in the empty waiting room, I looked as I always did out over the field on the other side of the tracks at the far, dark trees and felt something pulling at me. No, not something, more nothing. It was almost as if emptiness was pulling at me, and you'd think a person would step back from this, would find it strange and fearful, but I didn't; I found it rather calming for some reason. Slowing down, almost comforting. That didn't last long because I started myself up again and walked, almost ran, along the path, brittle with stones and small sticks, to the Windy Run Diner. Yet I still took the time to turn halfway along and look back over my shoulder at the empty fields, farther off now, before picking up my pace again.

Again, I wondered about my methods. I wondered why I didn't simply go straight to the post office and ask the postmaster where Reuben Stuck lived. Yet I wondered if the postmaster would be much help. The times I had been in the post office intending to buy stamps and looking at the WANTED posters, nobody had been there, no cus-

tomers and no one at the counter. Then there was the church. I could
have asked the minister, only I was a little concerned he might try to
get me to join up; if I was to join a church, it certainly wouldn't be that
one. I rode on the church bus once the first time I came to Cold Flat
Junction and they were all praising the Lord whenever they got the
urge, and that was enough for me.

I went through the Windy Run Diner's louvered door, wondering,
as I had about the post office and the church, why I never just asked
directly for the information I wanted instead of going all the way
around Robin Hood's barn (as my mother liked to say). Again, I can
only cite my roundabout ways. It's as if an answer too easily gotten
isn't hardly worth the breath it takes to ask it.

"How's things, Emma?" asked Evren, much to Billy's annoyance as
Billy always wanted to be the one to get things going.

"Okay," I said.

"Hon, you want some pie or what?" asked Louise Snell. "There's
chocolate meringue today. It's real good."

"All your pies are good," I said. It was true. "Yes, chocolate
meringue." Then I spun around on the counter stool the way I used to
do when I was little, and I was only doing it now to see if I still liked
it. "Yes, everything's okay except we can't find anyone good to paint
the hotel." Now, I should have made it more specific to Reuben Stuck,
and before I could, they started in.

"Well, Don Joe here," said Evren, sitting on Don Joe's left, and
sounding excited about Don Joe's painting ability, "he used to paint
lots around Hebrides."

Don Joe waved that comment away, but his crimped little smile
showed he was glad Evren brought it up. "I never was real good at it."

The woman down the counter near me, the one in big glasses who
was always smoking, leaned forward to look down the line at Don Joe,
and said, "Oh, yes, you was. You painted city hall over there in
Cloverly."

"Well, now, Rita—"

I'd been wondering what her name was.

"—I had me a little help on that job." He chuckled, then turned to
me. "How long do you figure the job'll take?" He said this in a considering way.

It hadn't occurred to me that one of them might be a housepainter. I had to get him off that line of thought in a hurry. "You wouldn't want to do it, Don Joe. I'm telling you this frankly."

"Yeah?" He tipped back his blue cap and fixed me with a suspicious look. "And why's that?"

I twisted a strand of hair around my finger and looked pained with the thought. "Because the job's going to be run by one of the Simples." Don Joe would not want to get mixed up with a Simple, even if the Simples really existed. "I told you about them."

"Ones with the son that's a retard, you said."

Mervin, sitting in his usual booth with his wife, said, "Miller Simple, that's the boy."

How did they remember all this stuff? Even I couldn't remember it.

"No, he wasn't no *retard*," said Mervin's wife. "She never said that, she said he was 'touched.'"

Billy swung around on his stool, as the booth was behind him. "Depends on just what is the meaning of 'touched.' Now, it *could* mean 'retard.'" He swung back and lit up a cigarette.

I had my mouth slightly open as if words had gotten stuck in it and could not be spoken. What were we talking about? I shook myself a little. Oh, yes. The Simples. "I wouldn't say Miller's a retard, exactly."

"By God!" said Don Joe. "He ain't the one in charge, is he? He ain't overseein' this job, is he?"

"Don Joe," said Billy, "that's about the stupidest thing you ever did say, and you've come up with some whoppers. This Miller's only a kid, so how's he goin' to oversee painting a *hotel*?"

"I was only sayin', if it was Miller Simple, then I sure wouldn't want to do no painting."

It was too bad I'd made Miller a kid. "No, it's not him, but it's his uncle—"

"George," said Evren.

Mervin said, "George is the father."

Billy swung around again. "Mervin, what is it with you?" Billy's hands were fisted on his thighs. "All you want to do is argue."

"He don't mean nothin' by it, Billy," said the wife.

"Who's arguing?" objected Mervin. "All I said was—"

I broke in. "Mervin's right, though." Mervin usually was. "The uncle's name is Malcolm. Malcolm Simple and he is really hard to get along with."

Evren frowned. "Malcolm. Any of you ever heard of a Malcolm Simple? I ain't."

They all shook their heads.

Don Joe flicked ash from his Camel with his little finger and said, "Well, I guess there's one paintin' job I don't want."

To get off the Simples, I said, "My mother sent me to look for someone named Reuben Stuck. He's supposed to be a housepainter. A really good one." I ate my pie and watched them. It would take awhile as they considered. It would take them as long as they wanted to consider.

"There's lots of Stucks around," said Rita.

"Yeah. There's Elroy," said Don Joe. "Only I don't think he's a housepainter. Does Elroy paint?" he asked Evren.

I'd finished my chocolate pie in about five bites and was ready to go if only one of them could tell me where Reuben Stuck lived.

Mervin said, cutting into his custard pie, "She's not lookin' for Elroy. She said Reuben. Now, there's a Stuck they call Ben and I think they used to call him Ruby, lives out Hallelujah Road."

"Oh, thank you, Mervin." I had no idea what any of their last names were, except for Louise Snell.

Billy was fit to be tied; he looked like he could chew Mervin's ear off, and so did Mervin's wife, whose hand I saw spring across and hit Mervin's knuckles with a spoon as she told him not to rile people.

Disgusted, Billy said, "Mervin, how long you lived around here?"

"Fifteen years."

"Well, I been here all my damned life and nobody lives out Hallelujah Road no more."

Mervin had forked in another bit of pie and swallowed it. "Ben Stuck does."

That very nearly got Billy off his stool. I had to admire Mervin.

Louise Snell, who all the while had been leaning back against the glass shelves of cake and pie displays, broke in. "Billy, the fact you been living in Cold Flat Junction all your life does not make you an authority on everything about it. Here"—she reached under the counter—

"just you look in here." She slid a thin telephone directory toward Billy.

Billy just stove out his hands as if he was shoving the book back at her. "I don't need to."

Then all of us except Mervin, who kept on eating custard pie, were giving the flimsy book feisty looks as if we would be glad to do battle with it. With a sigh, Louise slid it back on the shelf.

"Anyway," said Don Joe, "people live on Hallelujah Road, they prob'ly ain't got phones anyway." His shoulders shook with laughter, as if this were the funniest idea.

Billy gave a saving-face laugh, too. "You got that right, Don Joe."

I slid off my own stool and asked Mervin, "Where's Hallelujah Road?" I wanted him to know I was on his side.

He said all I had to do was cross the tracks and take the first road on the right. It was a dirt road.

"What ain't?" said Billy, having to get his two cents in if it killed him.

I thanked them all and left.

Mervin was right; there were houses and people living in them along Hallelujah Road.

A boy probably not more than three stood on his sandy walk with his thumb in his mouth and a scrap of a blanket held to his ear like a phone. He watched me go by. I smiled and gave a little wave, but he did nothing back. I knew he was watching me all the way until the road curved a little and took me out of sight.

The road was dirt, and Billy was right; most of the roads were. I knew what was peculiar about Cold Flat Junction: it was like it was waiting around for whoever had started to come back and finish the job. Only they never did. I wondered if this was because the "junction" idea had never taken shape and the little town never achieved the glory it was made for. My mother said it was the automobile that had caused the railroads to founder and that all that planned-on glorification—a band playing while the passengers gaily alighted from the trains—had come to nothing. The gorgeous railroad station itself was proof that great things had been expected, and the fact that it was always empty now was proof that glory never came.

I scuffed along and tried to picture the station in that long-ago summer, with the women holding their train cases and looking terribly sophisticated, and men in their straw hats stepping down to the platform, little groups coming day in and day out, ladies holding on to their big hats so they wouldn't fly away in the wind stirred up by the engine.

I could picture all of this and it looked bright with happiness, but for some reason I preferred the station as it was now— empty, you might even say desolate. I stopped walking and thought about this as I watched someone's wash flapping on a line, blue work shirts, sheets printed with some tiny flowers of some kind.

Maybe I thought the station as it is now was more like me running on empty, as people say about a car with scant gas in its tank, so low on gas Dwayne said once when we drove in his truck, "It's running on fumes."

Only now I think it wasn't; it was running on Dwayne, running on hope.

A cat was sunning itself on a wicker bench on the porch of a house on the right, which was the one I took to be Reuben Stuck's because it looked freshly painted in a pale green color.

The man who came to the door was wearing an old wool shirt of dark blue and green squares, I think called a lumber jacket. His hair was thinning out and I could tell he was kind of conscious of that from the way he ran his hand over the top of his head. He wore rimless glasses and looked across the top of them, his forehead furrowed.

"Help you?"

He held the screen door open a little as if I were an adult whom he might ask in, which made me warm to him right away, although I'd told myself not to make judgments about people, but never seemed to listen to myself and went on snapping away.

"I was looking for Mr. Reuben Stuck."

"That'd be me." He still held open the screen door, but he didn't invite me in. I could certainly understand that, as you never know who might be standing on your porch. It could just as easily be someone with an ax behind his back. "You're the same Mr. Stuck as does house-painting? Professionally?" Here again I was being smooth, wanting him to know I knew the difference between him and a person who just slaps paint on the quickest way he can.

The corners of his mouth lit up a little in an almost-smile; he was still undecided, though. "Yeah, you could say that."

"My name's Emma Graham and my family's the Hotel Paradise Grahams?" Maybe I wasn't sure myself, if I put that like a question.

"Oh." Instead of asking me in, he stepped out onto the porch. Maybe I shouldn't have mentioned the Hotel Paradise. If we were going to just stand out here, it wouldn't be easy to work things around to reminiscing. "What I wondered—I mean what my mother wondered—is if you're still in the housepainting line of work?"

"Not so's you'd notice."

"She just wanted to get the hotel painted because it's looking kind of worn. . . . Look, my bad ankle's acting up something fierce"—I really liked the way I put this; it could have been any of them at the diner talking—"and I wonder if I could just sit down a spell?" I had turned my ankle out a little as I said this.

"Yeah, we can sit over there." He gestured toward the bench. The cat looked up, apparently having heard this, and it didn't look happy.

"Thank you very much." I limped over to the bench, where we sat down. The cat slunk away to another part of the porch in that dipped backbone way cats do when they can't wait to get away from you and your hands.

"How'd you hurt it?"

I almost said I didn't lay a gloved hand on the cat when I realized he was talking about my ankle. "It's just sprained. The doctor says it'll be okay in a few days."

"You oughta stay off it. Your mom could just have phoned up, instead of sending you all the way over here."

"Oh, but I was already here. Visiting. She said as long as I'm here to just stop by."

He looked doubtful, so I hurried on. "My mother says she thought of you because she remembered you painted that old hotel . . . what was the name?" I furrowed my brow.

"Belle Ruin, you mean? But shucks—"

(Did people really say that anymore?)

"—that's been more'n twenty years ago. Funny she'd recall that."

"But it was a famous hotel, wasn't it?"

He sighed. "Too bad it burned down. That was some place."

Good! He got into reminiscing without me even having to wheedle him around to it. "I would sure like to have seen it. Famous people stayed there, didn't they?"

He nodded. "A few, yeah. I don't recall who. Maybe they weren't so famous as all that." He smiled.

"I bet it was a beautiful place. I mean, after you got done painting." I was pleased with my diplomacy. "I bet a place like that has a lot of tragedies happen. I know the Hotel Paradise has had them." The only one I could think of offhand was Ree-Jane. "Somebody even told me about a kidnapping there."

Reuben Stuck leaned forward, elbows on knees, and gazed outward over the road. Or maybe inward. Maybe that's what we're doing when we seem to be looking at a landscape in the distance; maybe we're just looking at our own landscape. I would test this on myself some time when I wasn't so busy.

"That's right; there was. It was a baby that disappeared." He nodded, as if telling himself it was true.

I turned, wide eyed. "Oh, my goodness, a baby! How awful! Well, but what happened exactly?"

"Police came and never did much good. Back then La Porte had this no-account sheriff who couldn't find his own two feet."

"You weren't there when the baby was kidnapped?"

"Nope. But my tomfool ladder was, worse luck."

I could barely breathe, waiting for him to go on. It was like oxygen, someone else giving me information for a change, without me having to dig it up. "What did your ladder do?"

"It was leaning against those guests' window, or at least it was going past it—what was their name? Slade, I think. But the grandfather, his name was—Woodling? Woodacre—?"

"It doesn't matter, just go on."

"Does t'me, young lady. I pride myself on my memory. Pretty soon I'll be forgetting the whole incident. Woodlogger, maybe . . ."

"I remember! I just read it in the paper."

"You did? How? That was twenty-two or -three years ago."

"I know, it was an old newspaper Britten's used to wrap fish in."

"Fish? You mean Britten's over in Spirit Lake? He don't sell fish. What kind was it?"

"Spring trout. Now, what—?"

"What? There ain't no such a fish."

"Well, maybe it was pan-ready trout."

"That ain't the kind a fish. That's about the cooking of it."

I scrunched up my eyes. Why hadn't I stopped with 'old paper'? "Well, just ask Mr. Britten; he's the one sold it. Anyway, this paper mentioned the Woodruffs."

"That's it! Woodruff. Only you shoulda let me call it to mind."

"I'm sorry. Now what about the ladder? Did the police think somebody climbed it to take the baby?"

"Yeah, like me, you can believe that!" He hooked his two thumbs back toward his chest.

I gasped. "No! How terrible."

"Terrible and wrong. When I left off painting for the day, that ladder, it was farther along that side of the building. Two windows down from the Woodruffs or the Slades, whichever. Two windows farther along, that's where it was."

"Somebody moved it!"

He gave me a peculiar look, not that I blamed him. Why was this probably fourteen-year-old person (which is what most people took me for) who'd come about getting the hotel painted, why was she so interested in this old crime?

"The police didn't believe you?"

Reuben Stuck waved his hand, as if waving the police out of the picture. "They were just lookin' for somebody to blame. Those police was so shiftless, especially that idjit Mooma that couldn't find his finger if it was up his—s'cuse me—" He cleared his throat.

"But didn't they even find fingerprints? There must've been fingerprints on the rungs of that ladder. Maybe even footprints at the bottom."

"Oh, sure, mostly mine and around the other side, there was fingerprints of my two boys; they did some of the paintin'. But there were so many, it'd been hard to sort through them. I know what I think as far as the ones they couldn't match up—and it's a hotel, lots of people walking around—but what I think is that all of this was premeditated and like as not whoever done it, whoever climbed that ladder, well, he wore gloves and some of them hospital things that covers your feet. That's my thought on it, anyway."

"Or they could've put on somebody else's shoes, maybe."

"Now, that's good thinkin'. Maybe you should be a police instead of that damn fool Mooma back then."

"Somebody told me he was really stupid." I was happy to say this about any Mooma. "I think my mother said it."

"Your mom's right."

"What about the baby's parents? What did they do?"

"I can only tell you what I heard later. You can imagine it was the only topic of conversation for days. They said the mother set up an awful howl and she cussed out that babysitter for leaving the room. I think her name's Spiker. Lives round here now."

"It's all so strange."

He nodded. "Yeah, it is. And what's more strange is, they all packed their bags and went back to New York City. And that's the last we ever did hear, except for what the local newspaper ran still trying to keep up interest. And that damned fool reporter using any little speck of news coming his way from New York. Well, that don't make sense anyway. I mean the crime happened here, didn't it? And I can tell you, I followed the news real careful because they'd thought I had something to do with it, climbed the ladder and whisked that baby right out of its crib and down the ladder again. Well, that is the damnedest thing I ever did hear of."

He was looking out there across the fields. As his house was the last one on Hallelujah Road, nothing was between us and the lines of the trees I was always staring at from the railroad platform. I wanted to ask him, "What's out there?" But I figured he couldn't tell any more than I could. It was just something I needed to know and couldn't put my finger on, something like the Waitresses vanishing, something like the Girl, like the two deer at the stream's end. I did not know why the landscape was like them, it just was.

My heart felt pierced and I coughed to batten down the tears.

"Now what I can do," said Reuben Stuck, "is give an estimate."

I frowned. "What's that?" I didn't know what he was talking about.

"Painting. You tell your mom that I can come over sometime and write up an estimate for painting the hotel."

"Oh!" I really would have to watch myself. Forgetting why I came was not good. "I'll tell her. Okay." I tried to get back to the real topic, but I couldn't think of a way. "I'd best be getting back, I guess. Thanks for talking to me; it was really interesting."

"That's all right. I enjoyed it."

We both got out of our chairs and shook hands. I went down the steps and waved from the road. But he was gone.

It was nearly four o'clock, and I would be in time for the afternoon train if I headed for the station now, which is what I did. I passed the house on the right with the washing on the line and then the one where the boy still stood so that you'd think he was one of the plastic garden ornaments and not a real boy. I waved, wanting to scare some life into him, but he didn't move a muscle. Maybe he'd figured out the safest way to live was standing stock still and holding a blanket. Maybe he was right.

There was no one on the platform, but then there never was, and I sat on the green bench looking out over the fields as if I'd been hypnotized by that dark blue line of trees. There must be certain things that make us look at them, but we can't say what they mean because they don't have any words attached to them and sometimes not even a face, so it's like staring into vacancy, yet it's the most important thing of all. But since there aren't any words or pictures, we can't say what or why it is. I do not know what was so important about the Waitresses and the Girl. I may never know. But I do know I'll keep looking until I can put it all into words, as if it's my duty. I do know that.

32

The four o'clock train stopped at both La Porte and Spirit Lake, so I stayed on until Spirit Lake. It was convenient to have our own train station, even though it stopped only once a day.

Slaw's Garage was directly across the highway and since it wasn't yet time for me to be in the kitchen making salads, I would stop in at the garage and talk to Dwayne. Abel Slaw didn't want me in the garage in case there was an accident; he was afraid of lawsuits. I asked him did he really think I'd try suing him? And he said, well, maybe not you personally, but adults would sue him on my behalf. I asked did he really think anyone had enough interest in my behalf to sue a person? He just told me not to do it, not to go disturbing Dwayne and You-Boy.

I made sure Abel Slaw was busy on the phone before I went into the service area where You-Boy had a Chevy sedan on a lift and was looking at its underside but not doing anything.

Dwayne didn't care to use the lift even though it looked a lot more comfortable to be standing beneath the car instead of lying flat on your back under it. He said he liked to get up close; he could tell better what was wrong. I said I bet what he really liked was being hidden. He said, yeah, from certain people.

I said hello to You-Boy, who smiled in his lopsided way. Then I got down and tried to see under the car, but there wasn't enough space or light to see Dwayne's face clearly, as it was half in darkness. "Hi," I said.

He turned his head then. "You know, you shouldn't be looking under cars. Never tell what you might find." He followed this up with some banging with his wrench.

"Really? Well, now I think of it, I guess you're right." I rose and went to my usual seat, atop a stack of Goodyear tires.

"You want something? I got to get this car roadworthy by six P.M."

I kind of liked the voice coming out from under the car. It was like the good Lord talking. I looked at the big clock on the far wall. "You've got an hour and twenty minutes, then." I wished he'd come out. "I just wanted to tell you about this Reuben Stuck."

Clang. Bang. "Who's he?"

"He lives over in Cold Flat Junction. He was painting the Belle Ruin when the baby disappeared."

Dwayne slid out from underneath. "Where'd you meet him?"

"I just found out where he lived and went there."

Dwayne got up and wiped his hands on his oily rag. "You just went to a strange man's house? One day you're going to learn the hard way that you always take backup."

"No kidding?" I stretched my arms out and turned back and forth, taking in not only Slaw's but Spirit Lake and the whole wide world. "And just *where* am I supposed to get backup? Do you see any backup around here?"

He didn't answer that. He asked, "Which Stuck is he?"

"Reuben. I told you."

"My point being there are Stucks all over this county. When they have a reunion they have to advertise it in the *Conservative*. There are sane Stucks, and there are crazy Stucks, good Stucks and—"

"Oh, Dwayne, just stop, will you?" He got back down on the pallet and slid under the car. "Reuben Stuck said that when he came back the next day, he found the ladder two windows down from where he'd left it. Somebody had to have moved it."

A couple of soft *clunks* came from under the car. It didn't sound as if Dwayne had his heart in this car, a black Oldsmobile. He grunted; I didn't know why, so I just kept going. "The police were thinking maybe he did it himself. But then they stopped questioning because there wasn't a bit of evidence to show he did it. Can you imagine yourself being a suspect in something like this?"

"No, but I can imagine yourself being one."

I did not know whether he was laughing or not, not with all of the distorting sounds of pipes and wrench he started up when he made that comment. "I'll just ignore that."

"Okay."

It was so irritating. I could never get a reaction from him when I tried to insult him. He was better at this than me. "There were witnesses, or at least one, for the other would be *hearsay*." I was thinking of Ubub, to whom Ulub would have told anything he saw, or didn't see.

Dwayne came sliding out from under the car. "You sure do love that word, don't you?" He got up off the wooden pallet.

"No. It just happens to apply here because Ulub would tell Ubub and if Ubub tried to be a witness, he'd be told anything he'd heard from Ulub was hearsay."

"So how was it Ulub was outside of that hotel?"

"He was doing something on the grounds, and he was close to the ladder. He would have had to see if somebody went up it. Or came down it."

Dwayne wiped his hands, looking thoughtful. "He couldn't have been out there all the while the dance was on. What was he doing on the grounds at night?"

"Loading up wood for the fireplaces, I think he said. Woodpile was on—" I stopped suddenly, thinking about the Artist George tube and the Mr. Ree game.

"What's wrong?"

"Nothing. I was just thinking about that game, Mr. Ree."

"Uh-huh."

It irritated me that he was giving me a "meaningful" look, I guess you could say. "There's a woodshed on the game board. You could leave a weapon there—oh, nothing."

"Uh-huh. Did it ever strike you, Emma, there's an element of fantasy in all this?"

I sat up straight and glared. "No, it never has."

"Uh-huh."

"Oh, stop saying that! Anyway, what I was telling you about Ulub.

The thing is there was only a small amount of time between when the babysitter left to telephone and when Morris Slade went up to get Imogen a coat. When there was no one in the room. It was only twenty minutes. So Ulub didn't have to be there for very long."

"How do you know it was twenty minutes?"

The police report, but I didn't think I should admit to having taken it. "I just worked it out."

Dwayne shoved a stick of gum in his mouth and worked his jaw. "No, you didn't."

I got off the tires and put my hands on my hips. "Just how do you know that, Dwayne Hayden?"

"Easy. I know you." It was one of those almost-smiles he gave me, the ghost of a smile, a smile fled. There was that sadness again. As if this, and everything concerned with it, would some day be gone.

Carefully, Dwayne wiped each finger. As far as I could tell he wasn't doing much more than getting the oil back on. He pushed the rag into his pocket and said, "You think the ladder was put there to make it look like somebody on the outside did it? Like the Lindbergh baby."

"Well, that's what you think. You said so."

He shook his head. "What floor was the Slade party on?"

"Third."

"Ladder went up to the top, this Reuben Stuck said?"

"Uh-huh."

"If somebody crawled out the third-floor window and went up to the fourth floor, Ulub wouldn't have seen it or heard it, necessarily."

That had never occurred to me. "But somebody could hardly climb out, go up, and climb in again carrying a baby."

Dwayne shrugged. "I don't know. Maybe there were two people in on it."

I frowned. Mr. Gumbrel had said maybe it was Morris and Imogen together, but I had a hard time seeing one of them on that ladder with a baby.

Scuffing my way along the boardwalk and later up our gravel drive, I felt lackluster. Not that I was lustrous under any circumstances, but I felt especially dull right then. It didn't help that when I walked up the porch steps, I saw Ree-Jane sitting in a green rocker, her arm slung over the porch railing, practicing some model's pose. Since the Sheriff had told her off the day before, she'd been giving me the silent laugh treatment, I guess to imply that what I thought had happened in the Rainbow really hadn't.

She was like that. She could make herself believe anything. I thought she was crazy. We'd had a psychiatrist guest awhile back, and Mrs. Davidow had sicced her onto Ree-Jane. When the psychiatrist left, she didn't look too good herself.

Ree-Jane can appear to be looking at you, but she isn't, and it's obvious because she seems to be carrying on a mental conversation with an absent someone. Her mouth moves, she laughs. Not even Aurora Paradise does that. So here was Ree-Jane, laughing at no one or nothing, when she saw me coming up the steps.

"Having a good time?" I asked, innocently. "You were talking and laughing so hard I thought there must be other people here, maybe under the table." I bent over and peered beneath a table that wasn't big enough to hide the cat. "Nope. Nobody."

"You are *so* stupid. You think you're funny."

How boring this would be.

She went on doggedly. "You just don't have any imagination." She favored me with a lopsided, knowing smile.

I sat down for a while to see if I could drive her crazier than she already was. "I do, only my imagination knows it belongs to me." And I favored *her* with a lopsided smile.

"What's that supposed to mean?"

I had shoved my rocker around so I could drape my feet on the porch railing near her arm, which was quickly removed. "Only that you talk to yourself out loud; I only do that in my head."

There was a moment of silence while she tried to come up with a retort. "Maybe you just don't have anything to say that anyone would want to hear." She looked as if she'd won the Ping-Pong tournament. (I've seen her talking to herself even playing Ping-Pong.)

"Really? Mr. Gumbrel says circulation's up twenty-five percent since I started my story."

She waved her hand as if scattering smoke. All I needed was a mint julep and a cigarette. I could tap ash over the railing like Mrs. Davidow did. I liked watching that even though the bushes beneath the cigarette probably didn't. And sometimes she'd even flip her cigarette, still lit, out onto the gravel, which was probably dangerous, but I liked watching the fiery little arc it made before it landed.

"That old rag! Now if it was the *New York Times,* that'd be different. I guess you think you're going to be a famous reporter!"

"No, that's what you thought *you* were going to be until it turned out different." That got her. Past tense.

"I have more important things to do than write stupid stories." She was rocking in an agitated way.

I yawned and got up. It was time to get to the kitchen. "I know one thing you'd better not do again and that's follow me. I'll get a restraining order."

I left the rocker rocking behind me and didn't bother to turn at her. "You just wait!"

It was almost cheering these days being around Ree-Jane. Since I'd become famous writing the story of my near death and then had the Sheriff stand up for me and tell her off—well, Ree-Jane was just out of ammunition.

I was standing over the salad plates, putting rings of red pepper on them, thinking about the Slades. Two things happened twenty-odd years ago: one was that Fern Queen, Ben's daughter, left town and was gone many months. People in Cold Flat Junction said (not to me, of course) she left to have a baby. Number two: the Slade baby was kidnapped.

So if the Girl wasn't Ben's granddaughter, I'd bet a dollar to a doughnut with crinkles on it that she was the Slades' baby, little Fay, now twenty-two years old. And this is the reason she keeps turning up. I just wish somebody else had seen her besides me.

But I think I've learned a lesson and that is that you have to find your own answers to things. Even if they're the wrong answers. The point is the finding.

33

I was making Aurora's evening libation. The Alta Vista store must have been out of Gordon's gin, for there was Bombay Blue Sapphire Gin instead. There was also a blue liqueur called Blue Curaçao, which I thought very pretty. I added some Jim Beam, then ice and pineapple juice, stuck a miniature blue paper umbrella in it and got my tray. I would call it the Bombay Blues.

My imagination was frazzled. I don't know how Will and Mill did it, with every day requiring making things up. Maybe they were making up their lives. I don't know. Maybe they could do all of what they did because their contact with the real world was only coming in to eat or carrying the guests' bags. Even Will talking to Miss Bertha was Will running on imagination. I was kind of jealous, I have to admit. Will hardly ever got yelled at because he was both smooth and out of sight. Sometimes he was asked to take care of the front desk, but even that he and Mill managed to turn into a little production, for the front desk wasn't the busiest place in town. Mill would come limping up to the desk with his cane or gimpy leg and they'd put on "Guest with gimpy leg."

I stopped with my tray and thought: nothing fazes them; nothing stops them. Is that the way we should live, maybe?

Aurora took a smacking sip of her drink. "Well, *this* is different! Just let me taste it again. Now, *that* packs a wallop! What's it called?"

"Bombay Blues. It's one of those in-between-times drinks." That would be lost on Aurora, for there was never any in-between time for her unless it was in between the first drink and the second.

She took another sip and rolled it around in her mouth like a wine taster.

"I wondered if you remembered any more about the Belle Ruin and the night of the dance when the baby was stolen."

She stirred her drink with the little umbrella and said, "That was only a few years before those crazy Devereau sisters all went to hell."

To hell in a handbasket, as my mother liked to say. I wondered about the handbasket and what it meant. But then I wondered about everything. The thing was that Aurora was actually fixing the kidnapping in time, so I knew she was telling the truth. Well, as far as she knew it.

Slowly she shook her head, not in disagreement but in a wondering way. "Twenty-two, twenty-three years. To you that's a time you can't imagine it's so far back. To me it's nothing. It's yesterday."

I didn't want to stand there with my tray philosophizing. I wanted to know facts. Or at least, opinions. But I wanted to show her I sympathized, which I didn't. "I guess when you get older time kind of speeds up." I didn't guess this at all; it was just something to say.

"I was at that ball on the arm of Rufus Pyle. He was an adventurer!"

I wanted to say he'd have to be.

"My, but I did look beautiful in my yellow taffeta with the sweetheart neckline trimmed all around in little green satin leaves. My dance card was completely full."

I don't think they still had dance cards then.

"I danced with—let me see—Billy Martin and Eugene Spits and Thomas Rafferty and—"

Leaning first on one foot, then another, I let her go on. She named five or six more dancing partners, even Dr. McComb. Then I broke in. "What about the baby's mother and father?"

"Oh, you mean that Morris Slade and his wife? Why she was just a little fool and he had his eye on Daddy Woodruff's fortune."

I leaned against the wall. "The baby. Baby Fay. What happened? I mean the police came and what did they think?"

"If you're talking about that fool of a Carl Mooma, I don't think he ever had any real thoughts about anything. But whatever police were there knew it must have been a kidnapping. Here those Slades had hired that no-account, irresponsible Spiker girl. My Lord, she was the loopiest girl around. So I said to myself"—Aurora actually looked at me and in a serious vein—"why?"

I got off the wall. It's what I'd asked myself. "You mean why'd they get a babysitter who was known to be irresponsible?"

She nodded. "And the baby supposed to be sick. Why were they downstairs cavorting all around? Then there was the ladder. Then that Morris left and went upstairs after a couple of hours and that's when the shouting started." She raised her glass and shook an ice cube into her mouth. She said, "Poor thing was probably already dead and they put on about that kidnapping."

My mouth fell open. I dropped the tray, which clanged around my feet. I was trying to cram a dozen things into a question, picked up the tray and sputtered, "But did . . . I mean . . . did the police have any idea of *that*?"

"I told you once that sheriff never did anything without clearing it with Imogen's father. Woodruff pretty much owned the law around here."

She made it sound almost romantic. "You really think that baby was killed?"

"Smothered, I said to Doc McComb. But he just waved it off." She leaned toward me and said, in a very sinister tone, "I knew those two. As cold-blooded a pair as ever walked this earth."

I didn't say anything right away because I couldn't get the million words passing through my mind into a question. Finally, I asked, "But . . . why?"

She shrugged and rattled the one remaining ice cube in her glass. "With Morris Slade, it's always money."

This was something I couldn't get my mind around. "But then what did they do with the body?"

"Don't know."

I felt I really owed her a drink, so I took the glass and said I'd be right back. I left her humming and, as I walked down the stairs, heard her singing "My Old Kentucky Home." At least this time she got the state right.

34

I stood outside the Big Garage and tried to remember the code knock. This close to the performance, Will and Mill wanted to make sure nobody sneaked in, so we had this secret knock. I asked them why anyone would want to sneak into a Greek tragedy.

Will said, "It isn't a tragedy anymore, is it?"

"Only because you messed it up."

"I'm sorry," said Will, "if it offends your Greek sensibilities, but we want to attract a wide audience, including ones who don't read much."

"Can't read, you mean."

"You're such a snob. That's why we made it into a musical—to reach a wider audience. We felt we had to cut out some of the blood-shed. The Greeks were really into blood. There's no end of killing off mothers, fathers, sisters, kids, everything. Now that's not the way we live anymore. It's kind of dated."

"The only reason it's a musical is because you and Mill wanted to do a musical with your own songs in it."

Will said, "You're holding everybody up, you know that? I guess you'll never make it in the theater." He walked away. "You haven't even got your costume on."

That was another argument. It was promised that I would wear a tulle gown. But the only tulle gown we had, June Sikes would be wearing. I certainly would not take a chance with the Waitresses' midnight blue gown. So what I was wearing was a kind of cape covered with imitation chicken feathers. I tied it on with a bow at my neck. My role was nothing more than to come down on a swing, out of the clouds, supposedly as a deus ex machina, that only I troubled myself to pronounce correctly.

As I flounced up onto the stage, I wondered if maybe a deus ex machina is what Ben Queen was when he came rushing out of the darkness and saved my life. It was kind of miraculous, I had to admit. In another way, I'd saved *his* life because I'd never told the police (meaning the Sheriff) where he was. I knew I came to most people out of nowhere as a giant surprise.

I looked up at the crazy-grinning Paul, up there in the rafters, as I took my place on the swing.

"Hello, missus!" which was what Paul said to all women, little or big.

I believe I understood in that moment why Will and Mill liked to pick on Paul, with his pasty-looking moon-round face: he was just asking for it.

Will had acquired a baton (one of Chuck's drumsticks) and was tapping it on the stage. He was down where the audience would be sitting. "Okay, now, let's do the hardest scene first where Medea—" He looked at June, who was primping in front of a big mirror whose use I didn't know. I was now traveling in my swing by means of the pulley, operated by Mill, where I'd have to sit by Paul until I was lowered.

Then Will called up to me: "Oh, we made a change. You're to come down in this scene where Medea's chasing Chuck around to kill him."

"Why?" I was startled by any change that had to do with me.

He didn't answer.

Paul was playing one of the children. They would have to untie him for the performance and stick a ladder up against the rafter so he could get down after he tossed out the flour. It was also Chuck's job to operate the colored lights, so in the scenes he was in, there weren't any blobs of green or pink or blue wandering around the stage. I argued that they didn't have to have the flour in the script but Will said no. "You've got to descend in the right way."

"Right way? Right way? You have no idea what that is."

I said now, "Well, you don't have to have the flour in dress rehearsal, do you?"

Will looked at me—they both looked at me, Mill having come to join us—like I hadn't a clue about the theater. "What do you think 'dress rehearsal' *means*? Everything's got to be done as on opening night. You're never going to make it in the theater."

Mill shoved his glasses up on his thin nose with a finger and said, "You've got to apply yourself more."

They walked off, cocky as a couple of zombies in *Night of the Living Dead.*

What got me was that they paid no attention at all to my being famous and writing my ongoing story for the paper. People might just be coming to see *me,* after all. Will had even declined to be interviewed by the reporters swarming all over the hotel and asking him didn't he think it was wonderful about his brave little sister—

"No comment."

I was almost shot to death and he had no *comment*? He said to the reporters that he didn't want to intrude on my fame.

Mill gave the sign to Paul that I was coming up and then pulled the rope. I went swaying up to the rafters in my chicken-feather cape.

"Okay," said Will. "Medea, you come in from stage left when I call 'Action!' Chuck, you be playing with your train."

There had been a big argument when I'd seen the train. "This is Greece a long time ago. They didn't have toys like ours."

Will said they'd decided to update it to make it more "revelant" to our times.

"More what?"

"Revelant."

"Relevant," said Mill.

"Besides," said Will, "it saves on costumes."

I had pointed to Medea's white tulle and my chicken-feather cape. "Then why are June and I wearing this stuff?"

"To hearken back. Besides, June won't be in the play if she can't wear it. Action!"

June-Medea walked from the wings in her white tulle with enough eye shadow and lipstick on to keep Miss Isabel Barnett's kleptomania satisfied for a year. It was like sleepwalking. She had this huge cardboard knife hugged to her side.

Chuck (in his everyday clothes) had his back to her and was moving a wooden train around a track.

Will bellowed, "Make chugging noises!"

Chuck started *choo-chooing* as Medea crept up to him, raising the knife high, but Chuck seemed to sense "an unwelcome presence" (which is the direction written into the script) and he froze. When the knife started down in slow motion, so did I, in fast motion, swaying dangerously.

The knife missed because Chuck suddenly moved. Medea now was chasing him around the set (one of Will's masterpieces, I had to admit, of white columns, crumbling rocks and an old rusted wagon he'd found up near the Wood boys' house, spray-painted gold to look like a chariot). I was dumped on the stage with my trident (also gold). I yelled, "No more, no more, Medea!"

Medea froze, Chuck froze too and I walked over to take my place in the three-dancers chorus line. Mill came down thunderously hard on the piano and Will brought his hand down as if it held Medea's knife.

We sang:

> *"Ohhhhh Mahhh-deee-ah*
> *Mama mia!"*

"Start your kicks!"

With the next few words we threw up our legs in unison, something that Will said the New York Radio City Rockettes were masters of.

Will punched the air at every kick.

> *"Is this the last time that we're ever gonna see ya?"*

Kick. Kick.

> *"Oh, Medea! Don't you love us?"*

Kick. Kick.

By the time we'd rehearsed the whole play we were exhausted. Will wanted to go through it again, but I told him there'd be mutiny.

"We expect you here at seven sharp tomorrow night."

I said, just to annoy them, "Just remember the matinee for Miss Landis's orphans." This treat had been arranged—well, more *offered*—by me as an excuse to sit and talk with Miss Landis. My roundabout ways at times made work for others, but I didn't care.

"Maybe it'll make them feel better not having a mom and dad." Mill tittered, then looked at the rafters. "Should we let Paul down for dinner?"

"No, just keep him up there and throw him a banana."

They both laughed fit to kill.

35

It's strange that no one seems to remember, or at least doesn't speak of, Mr. LeClerc, the Frenchman from Rouen and the owner of the Belle Rouen. Yet he had been the one most affected, along with the family, by the kidnapping of Baby Fay.

There was a picture of Mr. LeClerc in one of the old *Conservatives,* but it was so bad an angle and he was squinting so, you really couldn't tell what he looked like. The squint I guessed was either from sun glare or from the pain of having this kidnapping happen in his hotel. That was too bad, I thought, that the hotel itself, innocent of any wrongdoing, had to suffer.

Now, if this event had taken place at the Hotel Paradise, Mrs. Davidow would be having a martini fest, handing out drinks and nuts hand over fist, going on to the press about the Morris Slades, how well she knew them, tale after tale for the reporters. *She* knew how publicity worked.

But Mr. LeClerc (whose first name was Jules, which I thought lovely) could only shake his head and sigh and make "pronouncements in his native tongue," to quote one of the reporters, things like *"Mon dieu, mon dieu,"* which I suppose most people knew meant "my God." But what got me about this was the reporters never even bothered to translate anything Mr. LeClerc said, as if they assumed people like Ubub and Ulub went around speaking fluent French.

Again sitting in the musty little room behind the *Conservative* front offices, I read every little bit about Mr. LeClerc as there was no one else I'd known like him and probably never would. (The Wood boys were the closest I got to a foreign tongue.) Mr. LeClerc sounded like a really nice man. And if a kidnapping wasn't enough bad luck, the Belle Ruin burned down several years later. Mr. LeClerc said that *"un malheur amens son frère,"* which I translated (with the help of a French dictionary beside the newspaper on the table) as "bad luck comes with his brother," which didn't make much sense, and I finally got it down to troubles coming in twos. One awful thing happens and that drags another awful thing along. The kidnapping and then the fire.

If the fire had happened right after the baby disappeared, I might have suspected there was a connection, like old Mr. Woodruff running amok and setting fire to the curtains. But three years separated the two events, and three years is just too long to seek revenge, except in the possible case of Ree-Jane and me. Mr. LeClerc could hardly have been blamed for what happened, although there were a lot of complaints about that ladder being left up against the hotel. *"Je ne sais pas, je ne sais pas."* He said that a lot: "I do not know." I got the impression from one of the newspapers—the *Cloverly Times* (which wasn't even as good as the *Conservative*)—they were hinting that Mr. LeClerc might be in on it. This was the trouble with reporters: they went around swatting flies, hoping at least one of them would stick to the wall. If you think everybody's guilty, you're right in the end about the one who is.

Poor Mr. LeClerc. Here was his whole life broken into bits, and then years later, the place burns down and his life lies about him in burned bits. There was nothing about where he went, only that he had gone. I wondered if he went back to Rouen. At least there people could understand him.

He said something about *"le bébé mal."* He was obviously referring to the baby. I looked up *"mal"* in my book. "Sick." The baby was sick. I hadn't seen this before in any of the accounts. It did not say what the baby was sick with.

Then I remembered what Gloria Spiker had said: *"They told me not to wake her up, but if she did wake and started crying to come and get them. That I should let her sleep, as that was the best medicine, they said. Well, she slept straight through, not a peep out of her. I was very quiet but*

I just had to make that phone call." And how she never dreamed she'd be out in the hall talking for twenty minutes. That's how long she was gone. With that ladder there, could someone have been watching through the window? she wondered. "That's what some people thought, you know."

But me, I was now back to thinking that's what someone *wanted* people to think—to think that the kidnapping was an outside job. The ladder being there, that could have been done by anyone in the hotel, anyone with strength enough to push it.

So now here was the second question: who would leave a sick baby just to go dancing? Then check on it only once in two hours or more? The first question was, who would leave *any* baby in the care of a girl like Gloria Spiker, who had a reputation for being undependable because she just wasn't very bright? Why had the Slades done these peculiar things? I went back to the newspaper and Mr. LeClerc. He had said (in English, I was glad to see) the Slades and Mr. Woodruff had arrived around dinnertime, had gone up to their room, their suite, with the baby all bundled up and Mrs. Slade carrying her. They had placed a dinner order with room service. Then they must have changed for the dance. One of the maids had described Mrs. Slade's dress as "just beautiful." It was dark green taffeta, she said; "it rustled." (My mind took off in that direction. I would like to have a dress that rustled.)

I sat fingering the page of newspaper that had darkened with age. It felt almost brittle, so I stopped; I did not want it damaged in case it might be "called into evidence," I believe was the way they put it on *Perry Mason.* I thought about that evening of the Slades' arrival. The Slades arriving at dinnertime, going up to their room with "le bébé." (It made me smile; the French word made the baby seem so much smaller.) Room service, Gloria Spiker, dance. I thought hard enough to start feeling hungry, so I stopped. I read the report again. I frowned. Who had seen the baby? Mr. LeClerc said it was bundled up. The room-service waiter hadn't seen her. Calling back to mind what Gloria Spiker had described, it sounded as if even Gloria hadn't seen the baby. The baby was sleeping in the other room and was not to be disturbed.

No one had seen the baby.

I looked at the cold cinder-block wall for a minute.

Maybe there was no baby.

I startled myself out of my chair like a sleeper suddenly waking.

Maybe the "fever" and the sleep were just a way of keeping others from asking to see the baby.

It was so strange an idea I think I stopped breathing. I think at that moment I understood the meaning of "breathtaking."

This was breathtaking news to be shared right away with the Sheriff.

I pounded up Alder Street, and up the courthouse stairs. I prayed: *Please let the Sheriff be there be there be there.*

He wasn't. The prayer went unanswered. I intended to point this out to Father Freeman as one among many. Maybe you can't pray when you're in a hurry. I pictured God saying, "If you can't even slow down for a minute . . ." I answered him, Well, maybe a person doesn't feel she needs to pray if she's out for a stroll or sitting in an armchair humming.

Donny Mooma was sitting at the Sheriff's desk when I burst into the room. Seeing me, he right away planted his feet upon the desk.

"Sam ain't here, so whyn't you just turn yourself around"—he made circles with his finger—"and hightail it outta here?"

"Where is he?"

Hands behind his head, Donny leaned back in the swivel chair. "I can't tell you that; it's po-lice business."

"Is he over at the Rainbow?" I could tell by Donny's annoyed look that that must be where he was.

I hightailed it out of there.

It surprised me to see Wanda sitting on the stool beside the cash register and not Shirl. Wanda was eating a rainbow-sprinkled doughnut. I said hello to her.

She said hello back and then, "This is part of my training, see, learning about taking money." Her voice dropped to a whisper. "Don't say nothing about me eating this doughnut. I'm not supposed to eat on the job, but I was just so hungry."

I assured her I wouldn't say a word, but I was still surprised that Shirl would let anyone except Maud, maybe, take her place at the cash register. Shirl didn't trust anyone when it came to the money end of the business.

"Shirl's gone off to the Prime Cut for her hair."

Shirl went to have her hair done every two weeks. I could never tell the difference between the before state and the after. Shirl could've spent a month at the Prime Cut getting all sorts of manicures and skin-pampering treatments and it wouldn't make one speck of difference. Some people's looks can just not be improved on and I was afraid I might be one of them.

I asked Wanda if the Sheriff was here and she pointed to the booths while she licked white icing off her fingers. "Back there. Ain't he sweet? He's just the sweetest man."

I smiled at this. Wanda was just the opposite of me, I think. Wanda was one who wore her heart on her sleeve. "He sure is," I said and hot-footed it back to our regular booth.

As I was sitting down across from him, I said, "I think I know what happened with the Slades!"

"The who?" said the Sheriff, looking puzzled over his coffee cup.

Couldn't adults focus their minds on anything? "The *Slades*. Who were at the Belle Ruin. The ones with the baby who was kidnapped!"

The Sheriff nodded then. "Yeah. Sorry. My brain's not working right today. What about the Slades? Have a doughnut."

Have a doughnut? I sighed, disappointed to realize the Sheriff didn't think this bygone crime was as important as I thought it was. It made me feel deflated. That was the right word, too; I felt the excitement slowly going out of me like air out of a balloon until I was flat. The leftover doughnut was just a plain one and I was too upset and disconsolate to eat it.

"Emma?" The Sheriff was looking concerned now. "What about the Slades?"

"Oh, nothing. It was just an idea." I also knew the Sheriff was such a stickler for evidence that my theory wouldn't get very far with him. I thought of Baby Fay and realized how flimsy the so-called evidence was. Well, there wasn't any, was there? And the Sheriff had to have evidence to back up what he did. He couldn't just go running around arresting people right and left without having evidence. And who was around to arrest, anyway? No one.

Just then Maud came along with a plate of fresh doughnuts. She shoved the plate toward me, saying, "You really should have one of these; they're just fresh made."

You could smell the warmth coming out of them. I thought I would have to take one just to show how grateful I was, so I did. I picked the one with chocolate sprinkles.

"Emma here's figured out something about the Slades."

Now Maud looked puzzled.

"Fay," I said, wanting to impress on him that at least I knew the details.

Maud said to me, "What about her?"

They were both just too casual for my taste. As I decided I could only eat half of one of the rainbow-sprinkled doughnuts, I said, "It's not anything. Just a theory about what happened. But I don't want to say more until I've given it more thought."

The Sheriff changed the subject. I guess it wasn't all that interesting to him. He said, "I saw a couple of flyers around town about the show. *Medea: The Musical.* That's going to bring in the customers; I've got to hand it to your brother and that friend of his—"

"Mill."

"The musician, right?"

"Yes. He's incredibly talented."

Maud said, "Well, it's going to be a big hit. I know over a dozen from town that plan on going tonight, and we'll—"

I sprang up. "Tonight! *Tonight.* I'm late! Thanks for the doughnuts." I charged down the aisle and behind the counter sitters. Shirl was back, looking as if she'd never gone.

36

Reba Sikes, another one of June's sisters, was taking tickets from those who had them and selling to those who were buying at the door. I wouldn't have trusted any of the Sikeses farther than I could throw them, but it didn't bother the producers.

The curtain was down and Will was peeking between the drapes and announcing every few minutes, "Good house!"

Will referred to the audience, present or absent, as the "house." I asked him if it was something he'd picked up from his Broadway days.

Mill was down in the "pit" (Broadway, again), warming things up with a really good rendition of what they said was Scott Joplin piano playing and I do think it set the mood, even though it was a Greek tragedy, for as Will said, "It's not a tragedy now."

"Who's out there?" I whispered. What I wanted to know was if the Sheriff was. And Maud, of course. Had they come together? And Dwayne, was he there?

Will just waved me back. He always acted as if I wore down his patience. I always told him I couldn't because he didn't have any.

Wearing my chicken-feather cape, I stuffed myself on the swing. Will came to stage right and worked the pulley. He did it faster than Mill (no patience) and it rocked too much, but I got up there and Paul said "Hi, missus," so I knew I was in the right place. Paul had a flashlight and I asked him what for. He didn't answer that, but said, "Ma's here, missus."

Was even the part-time help coming to our play?

I sat there, waiting. The swing was actually not uncomfortable by now and I was glad the action started without me. I could rest up. The dress rehearsal had been so strenuous I was still tired, too tired to kick, but I guessed I had to. From up here I could see a little over the top of the curtain and from what I saw and heard, the audience sounded pretty big. Maybe the Sheriff was right; maybe the flyers drew a lot of town people, maybe even Lake Noir people.

I started to get stage fright and reminded myself I only had one line to say besides the singing and kicking and decided stage fright would be wasted.

Paul was tied to a rafter with a bag of flour he was to toss out as I descended, making it look as if I was coming down through the clouds. If it hadn't been for Paul and the flour, I would have enjoyed sitting up there beyond all the busyness down on the stage.

The curtain opened onto the set of white pillars and rocks and it got a lot of applause. Will and Mill had even borrowed an armless statue from a dress shop and tossed a toga over her. I guess she was meant to represent Greece or the populace whenever the populace showed up, but, no, that was the Hummers, wasn't it? It was hard to keep things straight.

I sat up in my swing during the first act in which Medea kills the firstborn but which she does offstage. Well, she had to, didn't she? We couldn't find any kid to play the firstborn. (Who, I reminded Will, wasn't even in the original play, but a lot he cared.) So the audience *oohed* and *aahed* when June came in covered in blood. Most of it was on the apron that I insisted she wear because it was Ree-Jane's dress. I don't imagine a Greek woman would ordinarily wear an apron if she meant to do somebody in; but then if Ree-Jane had been Greek, they might have reconsidered. The apron was white and it kind of blended in, but not enough to keep Ree-Jane from standing up and yelling, "My dress! My sweet sixteen birthday dress!" She got *shushed!* all over the place and yanked back in her seat.

The audience really seemed to enjoy this story and there hadn't even been any singing yet. I told Paul that Will had said he wasn't supposed to throw so much flour on me, which made Paul stick his fist in the flour and toss it right then and there, which made me wonder, as I swept it from my face, if Paul was only pretending not to understand.

Suddenly, I was being lowered through a couple of handfuls of flour. *"The deux ex machina is lowered through clouds."* That's what it said on people's programs. And I must admit, it brought down the house. I almost felt as if a star was born at that very moment. It does something to you when you hear huge applause. It makes you feel as if you're slotted into life just right, as if you can't make any mistakes, as if everything you touch turns to gold. Spray-gold, anyway.

Medea came from the wings in her sleepwalking way with the knife and was stealing up on Chuck, who was *choo-choo*ing his wooden train around. I picked up my trident (also gold-sprayed) and yelled, "No more! No more, Medea!" That was my one line and I think I said it pretty well.

Medea froze, Chuck froze and I walked over to take my place in the three-dancers chorus line. Mill came down thunderously hard on the piano and Will brought his hand down as if it held Medea's knife.

We sang:

> *"Ohhhhh Mahhh-deee-ya*
> *Mama mia!"*

With the next words we threw up our legs in unison, like the New York Radio City Rockettes.

> *"What has happened to the way you used to be-ah?*

Kick. Kick.

> *"Don't you love us?*

Kick. Kick.

> *"Stab or club us"*

Kick. Kick.

> *"You would send us to the heavens up above us!"*

Kick. Kick.

"*Ohhhhh, Mahhh-deee-ya—*"

Kick. Kick.

"*Glad to see ya!*"

Kick. Kick.

"*But we're also glad that we don't have to BE ya!*"

Then slow kicks right and left as we sang

"*We think that life is fine
Here on the chorus line.
At the Hotel Par-a-diiiiii-ice.*"

Will had run up the stage steps and back to the wings during the standing applause for our number. We bowed and bowed. Will jerked on his armor (brown wrapping paper sprayed silver left over from the Tin Man's costume in *The Wizard of Oz*) and picked up his shield, the garbage can lid spray-painted gold, and came onstage while they were still applauding.

"*Quo vadis,* Medea?"

(I had argued heavily that this was a Roman expression, not a Greek one, and he'd just shrugged that off by claiming they were pretty much the same.)

But it didn't make any difference because the applause was so loud and enthusiastic, people standing and demanding an encore, that I could hardly believe it.

So the three of us ran through the song once again and I know our kicks were even more like the Rockettes' than before.

When the audience settled down not to silence but to a kind of electric murmur, Will did his "*Quo Vadis*" again, and Medea said, "Speak English, will you?" That broke the audience up again.

Chuck, being dead now, was free to go down to the pit, where Mill was rolling his fingers up and down, up and down the keys as if we were about to drown in a great wave of grief. Then I was surprised to see the Hummers step forward awkwardly, each holding a sheet of paper, which I guessed had words or something on it.

> *"Oh what delight*
>   *To be given the right*
>   *To be carefree and gay once again."*

Hummmm Hummm

Well, they didn't sing together and at least one was completely off key, and Bessie was looking at the others as if she didn't know why they were there, and Mill must have forgotten she wasn't old enough to read yet, still she did make an effort to sing a few of the words. Then they stepped back and Medea and Jason stepped center stage to sing their duet with the Hummers accompanying them.

> *"In some se-cluuu-ded arboretum"*

Hummmm Hummm

> *"That overlooks the Colosseum—"*

Hummmmmmmm.

> *"As we enjoy a cigarette"*

Hummmm Hummm

Like magic, Will produced two cigarettes and handed one to June, who put it in the corner of her mouth.

HumHumHumHum. . .

Will soloed:

> *"My head may go reeling"*

Hum hum

"After Creon hits the ceiling"

Hum hummmm

" 'Cause the kids are dead and gone
Still we've got to carry on
As long as this old world keeps wheeling"

Hum Hummmm

"I'll find the Fleece with my last breath"

HumHumHumHum

"I wish you would, I'm bored to death"

(June smoked.)

"Then we can carry out our dreadful plan
That all began
With cocktails—"

(kick)

"Cocktails"

(kick)

"Cocktails"

(kick)

"Cocktails for twooooo"

(kick, kick)

HumHumHumHum. . .

Then Mill and Chuck really speeded things up and let loose with drumsticks on a washboard, a cowbell, a car horn while Mill made goat noises.

It certainly didn't surprise me this demanded an encore. Half the "house" was on its feet clapping and whistling. So the finale, when it finally came, was not a finale, it was more a free-for-all.

We took our bows, all holding hands, except the Hummers got confused about where they were supposed to stand and what they were supposed to do, so they just *Hummed*.

37

There would be, of course, a nasty scene over what Ree-Jane called her sweet sixteen birthday gown. This birthday dinner dance had been held the summer before at the Silver Pear, and it must have been very expensive. Just to have dinner there was out of most people's price range, so to reserve the entire long porch that looked out over the lake (well, a sort of inlet) would have cost Mrs. Davidow a lot, for in addition to dinner, she had also hired a six-piece band from Cloverly.

There were sixteen guests. I had not been invited. The reason given was that I was too young. For two weeks before this big celebration, Ree-Jane delighted in talking about it and about me "not even being in your teens yet." She seemed to want to believe it was like not being vaccinated and walking around with smallpox.

Strangely, her mother told her to stop teasing me. Even stranger, since Mrs. Davidow was to attend as chaperone, she asked me to come along and have dinner with her. We'd be sitting someplace where we could see them without looking as though we were keeping an eye on them. I don't know if she felt bad for me or if she just wanted someone to sit with.

It was too bad that whenever Mrs. Davidow was out of the hotel, my mother had to stay. It was so unfair. Not that she would want to go to any celebration for Ree-Jane, but it might have been nice for her to have an expensive dinner she didn't have to cook herself.

The showdown after our performance that night over this white gown was major. I knew it would be, so I had to have time to stay hidden and think, and I thought best down in the Pink Elephant.

I could hear them upstairs, Ree-Jane mostly. She must have been yelling because I could hear her through the Pink Elephant's ceiling. There was a lot of pounding around up there; I could hear them make their way through the dining room to the kitchen, then to the front and back again. I sat listening and trying to figure out some plan of action while eating my 3 Musketeers bar (my favorite candy bar, for it had three layers, each a different flavor).

I was trying to think up a story. Maybe I could make somebody believe Ree-Jane had said I could borrow the gown and then gone into a coma and when she came out of it obviously she'd forgotten. Ree-Jane always looked like she was in a coma. No, that probably wouldn't work. Or maybe I could say the dress had been delivered to the wrong place . . . which made no sense at all. Or maybe someone had thought the gown could be—ah! Paul! Anyone could blame anything on Paul. Except Paul couldn't have gone into Mrs. Davidow's storage room (where the gown was kept near the whiskey crates), could he?

Feet kept pounding; Ree-Jane kept yelling; I kept thinking.

I heard my name being called from a distance and then the voices moved away.

I looked through my Whitman's candy box and found my money. Three fives, fifteen dollars. I had money stashed in a lot of different places around the hotel. It was getaway money. Money usually solved anybody's problems. I came up with a plan. I would write Ree-Jane a note. I took out my pad and ballpoint pen, dated it two days back and wrote:

> Dear Jane,
> You weren't in your room and we really need your white gown. I got it from the storage room. (The door was unlocked, and I went to close it and saw the dress hanging there.) Here's $15.00 for rent for

*it. If it gets bloody or dirty at all I'll of course have it cleaned at my
own expense.*
Thanks!!!
Your friend,
E. Graham

I went back and really crossed out "bloody." That wouldn't have
sounded very good for the dress. Now, I wondered how to get the note
up there.

Again, I heard my name, closer this time. Walter! Walter was the
only one who'd know where I might be except for Will and Mill, but
they'd never bother to help out Ree-Jane by searching for me. They,
naturally, were innocent of the crime.

I got up and went to the door. Soon there was a gentle tapping,
which was the way Walter announced his presence. I opened the door
and pulled him in.

"I just come to warn you—"

This was perfect! This was a godsend! (I might even mention it to
Father Freeman.)

Walter went on. "I never saw nobody as mad as that Ree-Jane
Davidow. You'd think you went and crashed her convertible. She's
fixin' to have a stroke."

"Walter, I have a mission for you." (Walter liked missions.) I
folded the note I'd written over three five-dollar bills and said, "Listen,
take this and if she's not in her room, put it someplace where she *could*
have missed seeing it, but also someplace she *might* have seen it if she
had a brain, which she doesn't. Like under the dresser scarf or her jewelry box. Understand?"

"Not the part after goin' to her room." He frowned.

I explained it all again and he said okay, he knew what I meant. He
said, "I know a good excuse for goin' to her room, case she catches me
there. I could just say I went to yours that's only just upstairs and I
thought I'd poke my head in hers to see if maybe you was there."

"That's brilliant!" Walter was nobody's fool. And it showed he understood his mission. "Is my mother really mad?"

"At first Miss Jen was, but what with Ree-Jane carryin' on like crazy now both of them are just tryin' to calm her down. Mrs. Davidow mixed up some cocktails."

"Okay. Good. Do this if the coast is clear."

"It's clear all right. They're in the Green Room now with their cocktails."

I looked at Walter's big wristwatch. "It's after ten." Since when did time matter? "Be sure you come right back and tell me when you've done it."

He said he sure would and left and walked up the road.

This was the first opportunity I'd had all day to think. I sat with my chin in my hands and thought about the Slades and Baby Fay. Was I right about there not being a baby? Or had they murdered her, as Aurora seemed to think? How was this possible? How could anybody murder a defenseless baby? Not just any baby, but your own? Why did this make me wonder, though? Hadn't I just spent nearly two hours in the presence of a mother who'd killed her children? Yes, but at least they weren't little babies. I tried to picture in my mind hands holding a pillow and slowly coming down over the face of a smiling, gurgling baby before the pillow stops all of that.

I could not even imagine Mrs. Davidow doing this to Baby Ree-Jane, and if that was so impossible, any baby being murdered was. Ree-Jane needed to be a Greek—not, of course, Medea, who had that queenliness about her and was a deep thinker, despite what she'd done. No, Ree-Jane would be one of the ordinary people who had the hardest of all lives. She didn't even have the brains to be a Hummer.

Aurora had to be wrong, and I might be right: they had done something to Baby Fay but they hadn't killed her.

I opened my Whitman's box again and took out the snapshot of Morris Slade and the one of Rose Queen and the Devereau sisters. I looked from Rose to Morris and back again many times. There was just no denying it: twenty-two years ago the Slades' baby either must have been abandoned, like Moses in the bulrushes (Father Freeman had helped out there), or else must have been given to a third party, maybe to adopt, maybe with a lot of old Mr. Woodruff's money.

Either way, she was back now. Was the Girl seeking revenge or just plain seeking?

Because she had been cast off, driven into the woods like an old scapegoat, with all the sins of others stuck to her or tied to her like a lot of jangling pots and pans.

But if she sought revenge, who was there now to revenge herself against? Maybe, in a way, that didn't matter. Just somebody would have to pay. Meanness. And for the meanness, payback; and for that payback, payback. Payback payback payback payback. The Greeks.

I was jostled out of this trance by a tapping at the door. Walter must be back.

"I done it," he said, looking pleased. "It was easy."

"Good! Where'd you put the note and money?"

"In one of them little drawers in her desk. I figured she hardly ever used her desk. I left it just pulled out a tiny bit."

I had forgotten the desk, probably because I couldn't picture Ree-Jane sitting there writing. Neither could Walter. "Walter, that's really smart! Let's go." I put my things back in the candy box and blew out the candles and we left. We walked back to the kitchen where we parted, Walter for home and me for the front of the hotel.

They were sitting there in the room just off the lobby, the Green Room we called it, a long beautiful room with pale green walls and white molding. There were two sofas and a lot of upholstered chairs. My mother sat on one sofa and Ree-Jane on the other. Lola Davidow was in a thronelike wing chair. They'd been watching *The Loretta Young Show* on television.

When she saw me, Ree-Jane jumped up quick as a jack-in-the-box. She pointed that long finger at me. "How dare you take my sweet sixteen gown? How *dare* you?"

Mrs. Davidow was trying to look really mad, but it was difficult after a couple of martinis. My mother just crimped her mouth in displeasure with me.

I stood there, mouth agape in astonishment. "But I wrote you a note and gave you rent money. You mean you didn't get it?" I tried to look totally startled.

This stopped her short as if she'd just had a flounder slapped across her face. Then she mumbled all sorts of puzzlements, ending with "You did not!"

"Maybe you didn't get it. Did you look in your desk drawer?"

"You *know* you didn't give me money or anything!"

I slowly shook my head. "Well, that's really too bad. I'll go up and get it."

She stood there, hands on hips and said, "No, you may not go into my room! I'll go myself!" She flounced out.

Mrs. Davidow was too interested in the television and Loretta Young's new gown to yell at me. (Loretta's show was on late that night because of some news program or national emergency I'm sure no one cared about.) I bet Loretta Young didn't wear this gown to her sweet sixteen birthday party. As a matter of fact, Loretta was sweeping into the room and down the wide shallow steps in just the way I bet Ree-Jane wishes she'd swept into the Silver Pear last summer, but didn't.

My mother gave me a sentence or two of rebuke, but I could see her eye was really on Loretta, too.

I stood humming beneath my breath as I heard the feet returning. This time the feet were going slowly, the way I think condemned prisoners walk to the chair or the gas chamber. She walked in with her head hanging, not in shame of course, but in uselessness. She had been boiling over and now all she could do was seethe. The note was clenched in her hand, and the money.

Poor Ree-Jane. She didn't stand a chance.

38

There were ten of them and they were definitely orphans. They looked askew, as if they hadn't been finished. Their faces were a little flat and their eyes held no secrets in the way of a nonorphan's eyes. That's probably because we who weren't orphans were always trying to hide things from our parents.

I believe I understood orphans in general because I was a sort of half or suborphan, having no father. I could imagine the orphans standing at the windows of the Bluebird Orphanage, watching for someone you were pretty sure would never come up the path. But you still watched.

Their clothes tended to be a little rumpled, as if they'd been packed away, with the intention of its being forever, and now had been unpacked and just shaken out. One girl wore a blue-and-white-checked pinafore that reminded me of Dorothy in *The Wizard of Oz*. A couple of the boys, maybe eight or nine years old, looked like Paul. Paul could easily pass for an orphan.

They were all gathered in the lobby. I whisked Aurora's drink up the stairs, only to be met by Ree-Jane in the long hall. When she saw me she laughed that phony caught-in-the-throat laugh as if she just couldn't contain herself. She pointed a long finger, wanting me to believe she just couldn't stop laughing, and said, "I guess I've never seen any worse play in my *life*. I felt sorry for you."

"What are you talking about? The audience really liked it."

That set her soundless laugh into action again. "My God, it was so *bad*, that's why people were laughing."

"I'll take my laughs any way I can get them. 'Bye." I literally scampered up the stairs to show her how lighthearted I was. I was around the bend before she could think of anything else to say.

"You were just making fools of yourselves!" yelled Ree-Jane, who wouldn't know if I was in hearing range or not.

I got to Aurora's room and was treated once again to her old Kentucky home.

> *"Weep no more, my laaaady,*
>   *Oh weep no more to-daaaaay."*

I plunked the drink down on the table beside her and she was too caught up in her song to do more than clasp her hand around the glass.

I ran down the stairs to the landing above the lobby. The orphans were acting jittery with expectation. Louise Landis stood among them, cool and calm. I really liked her. She was probably sixty or thereabouts (and she had once been Ben Queen's girl), but she never looked it at all. (Dwayne said she was really pretty, which irritated me, so I said, "Yes, pretty old. Ha ha.") She was the principal of the little school-house in Cold Flat Junction, a job I never would have imagined her doing, for she was too well educated and well read and smart for Cold Flat Junction. I think she might have kept on there because of Ben Queen.

"Hello, Emma. Here we are."

I greeted them. I wanted to give the impression I'd been thinking about them and planning this for days, when I'd never given it any thought at all until ten minutes ago. I raised my hands as if calling for order, though there wasn't any disorder. "We'll have lunch in a few minutes and then we'll all see a really good play about Medea." I wondered if I should give them a little lecture about the deus ex machina, but decided not to as it would be basically just showing off.

As I was giving them information that they already had anyway, Ree-Jane swept down the stairs, trying to look like Loretta Young, doing her model walk—toe down first, heel down second—which only gave her the gimpy look of Mill doing his bad leg performance. One or two orphans looked at her, but the others were attending to me.

Lola Davidow picked up the big brass bell at the desk and swung it. This was to announce lunch was ready. Mrs. Davidow thought the children would get a kick out of it. Mostly, it scared them, but Mrs. Davidow couldn't tell the difference and rang it again.

We had shoved three tables together with five on each side and at the top, a place for Miss Landis. I might have sat at the other end, but of course I had to serve along with Anna Paugh. Anna Paugh was so much nicer than Vera, I said she should be head waitress. (Actually, I thought I should be head waitress, given all my experience and my way with the guests, except for Miss Bertha. I was told that I didn't "inspire trust," whatever that meant.)

Lunch looked delicious. I had been in the kitchen watching my mother prepare it. At each place was a salad plate with a half-pear face (cloves for eyes, half a cherry for mouth, and thin strings of cheese for hair). The pear face rested on fruit cocktail and a small amount of cottage cheese in case the orphans didn't like cottage cheese.

"Why should they?" I had said. "Who does?" I myself didn't mind cottage cheese, but I didn't mind hardly anything. "The orphans have probably had to eat cottage cheese all their lives. Along with Jell-O." Here I was looking at a big copper mold of strawberry Jell-O.

"That's only the bottom layer that you're seeing."

"Really? Then what's on top?"

My mother exhaled and turned her cigarette around and put it down on the edge of the counter. "I guess you'll just have to wait and see, won't you?"

"I'd just as soon not." Now I was doing a little dance with my feet while I leaned with locked elbows on the counter. "Is it something whipped?"

"You could say that." She was counting out glass dessert plates. "There are three layers."

That sounded promising and I looked through the bottom of the shiny red Jell-O to see what was beneath it, but I couldn't.

We all trooped in, the orphans holding hands, so there were five sets of them. I thought it was pretty cute. They were all extremely spruced up for this outing, even if their clothes were a little wrinkled, for their faces and hair shone. And their eyes (the ones who weren't skewed a little) were very bright. I went before and Louise Landis brought up the rear.

I turned in the dining-room doorway and announced that this was the dining room and where we were sitting. They followed me to the table and Miss Landis figured out who was to sit where. The salads were already there, the plate on the left. The butter plate was above the fork where it was supposed to be, and the water glass above the knife. Immediately one boy named Mickey moved his butter plate in front of him and I had to move it back and he said, "But it's my plate!"

I just kind of rolled my eyes and told him "No, your *lunch* plate, which is much bigger, goes in *front* of you." I might not know much but I did know how to set a table.

One little girl started to wail, saying she couldn't eat her pear because it looked like somebody named Chrissie. Miss Landis tried to get her to stop, but she wouldn't; worse, a couple others were joining her, saying their pear faces looked like somebody, and I could see the trend was on and they'd all be doing it.

Now, a lot of people think waiting tables is the kind of job anybody could do, but I say just let them try. You've got to know people, you've got to be quick and, above all, you've got to be inventive. The rules—be quick, know people, be inventive—might apply pretty much just to Miss Bertha, but still they're good rules in general.

Pretty much the whole table was now in an uproar over their pear face, each one insisting it reminded them of someone—it was hardest on the several who swore the pear faces looked just like the mother who'd left them at the Bluebird Orphanage, and those orphans either flung the pear on the floor or stabbed it with a fork. Miss Landis was doing her best to shut them up, and I was, too. I shushed them (in no uncertain terms) and said, "Look! Here's what we do!" Then I picked up one of the salad plates and using a fork simply turned the pear over so the face disappeared. That satisfied most of them, but not, of course, the ones whose pears were on the floor.

What with the pear faces causing all that trouble, I was glad that the main course would be hamburgers on toasted buns and french fries. My mother made really good french fries. They were all happy with the main course. So happy that a few were throwing french fries at the others and whooping.

But wouldn't you know? I had forgotten all about Miss Bertha and Mrs. Fulbright, and here they came, trooping into the dining room at this moment. They stopped and stared, especially Miss Bertha, then sat down. Both of them were dressed like Victorian women in rustling black and gray material.

"Who are those children?" Miss Bertha demanded.

They were used to having the dining room to themselves at lunchtime.

"Orphans. We're giving them a special treat."

"*Orphans?* What are they doing here with us, then?" Miss Bertha shoved her place setting around just like Mickey had done. "They should be at home where they belong."

I felt like banging her over the head with my tray. "Miss Bertha, orphans don't have homes."

"Then where do they sleep? In the streets, probably."

Mrs. Fulbright, who had a generous heart, blushed—a rosebud dusting of pink came on her skin. "Bertha, the poor children need an outing once in a while."

Miss Bertha would have denied this, I'm sure, if she hadn't now focused on the food. A couple of them were still throwing french fries. "What's that they're eating?"

"Just hamburgers and french fried potatoes."

"Good. That's what I'll have."

Now, that would make my mother stand on her head. She was fixing macaroni and cheese for their lunch. "You don't want french fries. Fried food doesn't agree with you."

She picked up her spoon and began banging it against the edge of the table. "I want french fries!"

I noticed the orphans had stopped throwing them, finding Miss Bertha even more interesting.

"Bertha!" Mrs. Fulbright actually raised her voice, but Miss Bertha went right on babyishly banging away with her spoon.

Real willpower was all that kept me from picking her up and plunking her at the other end of the orphans' table.

Bangbangbangbang—

Mrs. Fulbright was mortified by her behavior and told me she would have whatever my mother had prepared for lunch.

I gave the orders to my mother, who stood, hands on hips, staring at me. "That old fool! She makes more noise than all of those children put together." Here she banged the frying pan back on the stove and told me to get another patty out of the refrigerator. I did, and one for myself, too, although I fully intended to eat some macaroni and cheese, too. I loved the crispy brown top my mother always got on it.

She put the hamburger patty on, tossed some more fries into the deep fryer. As the fries spit and sparked, it occurred to me that the way to shut up the orphans and make them stop throwing french fries was to distract them. My mother had taken a little tin of paprika from the lazy Susan she kept the spices on. She used it a lot to make a dish look more colorful sometimes. She sprinkled a little over the surface of Mrs. Fulbright's macaroni and cheese, which she was serving with peach relish made wonderfully aromatic with Marsala wine.

The hamburger was done and placed atop a warm bun; the french fries were degreased on paper towels and put beside the hamburger. When she turned to tell Walter what he was doing wrong with the dishes, my fingers nipped to the lazy Susan and took up a little can of cayenne pepper, a particularly hot kind called Devil Relish, which sported a little picture of a cartoon Satan, winking his eye. I tapped this onto the french fries with "a generous hand," as my mother sometimes said. It looked, of course, exactly like paprika.

I sailed in with my tray held high. I served them. The orphans were back to their old selves before they'd hushed up to watch Miss Bertha. When I saw her stuff the french fries in her mouth, I felt like yelling, as Will did, "Action!"

I was not disappointed.

There came an unholy yowl and Miss Bertha reared back so quickly she very nearly overturned her chair. Then she was up and doing a little dance as if movement would eliminate the heat of the pepper. I went to the table and reminded her that I had said fried food didn't agree with her and then it was time to serve the orphans dessert.

The middle layer of the Jell-O mold was Jell-O whipped with strawberry cream and the top layer was a smooth custard. The orphans loved this and sank into silence, still captivated by the old lady who was loudly complaining and offering to sue the Hotel Paradise for trying to kill her (again). I poured her more ice water, which, as most people know, just makes what's hot that much hotter.

Twenty minutes later, with the orphans completely calmed down and Miss Bertha in her loud deafness still talking about suing, we all trudged through a side door just outside of the dining room and went double file up to the Big Garage. It was just two o'clock, right on time.

I had Miss Landis seat them down in the front row and then ran backstage to sit in my swing. I was delighted to find that Paul was not in the rafters because Will had decided to dispense with the flour. "Why waste it?" he said. "This audience won't appreciate us anyway." Was he kidding? Ten kids out front and he thought throwing flour all over me wouldn't be appreciated?

"There's nothing in these kids' experience to prepare them for something as sophisticated and mind bending as *Medea.*"

I couldn't believe he really thought that. As far as sophistication and mind went, our production was right up there with throwing french fries. Sometimes my brother is so thickheaded . . .

The costumes were to be dispensed with also for this matinee, although if there's anyone who'd like chicken-feather capes and bejeweled gowns, ten of them were sitting right out there. And there was the problem of our second nighttime show. June Sikes refused to appear if she had to wear her own clothes. Before Will and Mill remembered the dark blue evening gown belonging to the Waitresses, I suggested that Medea wear my cape, which I would fix up for her. When Will frowned at this and asked me what I would then wear, I smiled and said, "Don't worry. I have my sources."

I would wear the Waitresses' blue evening gown. It wouldn't fit me, of course, but it would still be pretty. And it would remind me of the Waitresses and how colorful they'd been, how unlike my life now, which depended on me for whatever color I could get. I'd much rather it came from outside, from someone or other so I didn't have to work so hard.

The orphans loved the show, especially the swing coming down and Medea chasing Chuck with a knife. They also really liked the scene where Paul ran across the stage with no clothes on except his shoes, although that really wasn't part of it.

39

Next morning I served Miss Bertha and Mrs. Fulbright red flannel hash topped with a poached egg. It was a favorite breakfast of mine and of theirs—one of the very few occasions where our tastes meshed. I had been about to sprinkle some more Devil Pepper Relish in Miss Bertha's but decided against it as I wanted to go into town right after breakfast, and Miss Bertha would delay me, so I decided to forgo the pleasure of the pepper.

I found a big Heather Gay Struther shopping bag in the back office that I could use to transport the white gown to the cleaner's. I called Axel's Taxis to come pick me up around behind the hotel. I repeated this to the dispatcher—the drive *behind* the hotel, and to make sure Delbert understood that.

Then I strolled behind the hotel myself and up to the Big Garage— or "the theater" as Will was calling it now. The door was bolted and I knocked. What in the world did they have to keep secret now that the musical had been performed? It was ridiculous and really irritating.

The door opened a crack. "What?" said Will. I heard piano music. Mill was thumping the keys with real enthusiasm.

"What are you doing? What's so secret?"

"We're making a few changes. Never mind." He was pushing somebody away from the door.

"*Changes?* There's another performance tomorrow *night.*"

"It's nothing you need to know. We're just fooling around with the score."

"Oh, for heaven's sake." As he had taken to the garage's being "the theater," he had taken to calling the songs "the score."

"I want Ree-Jane's white gown. I promised to take it to the cleaner's."

Will didn't say anything. He just stared, as if he were trying to place me.

"Here." I had folded the shopping bag and pushed it through the opening. "Put it in this and put some newspaper over the top so you can't see the dress. That's only in case I run into her, which I probably will because of my bad luck."

"We don't have any newspapers."

I wished the crack was wide enough to reach my hands in and grab his throat. "For heaven's sake! You invent a whole play and you can't think of anything to put on top of a shopping bag?"

Will smiled his smile that always looked as if an ice pick would come right after. "I can put Paul's pants over it."

Suddenly, there was Paul, sticking his pie face up to the opening in the doorway. "Hello, missus!"

Will gave him a smack. Paul disappeared but not before I caught sight of the white tulle. *"What?* Why's he wearing Ree-Jane's gown?"

The only words Mill had got Paul to sing when he was featured as one of Medea's kids was what he said now: "I'm Medea!"

I threw myself against the door, but Will was too big to force away from it. Paul was probably shoving on it, too. "Are you *crazy!* Are you *insane?* Paul'll ruin that dress!"

"You're taking it to the cleaner's, you said."

I was so furious I could barely speak. My mouth opened and closed, opened and closed. Finally, I said, "I had enough trouble when there was only that little sprinkle of blood. And now stupid Paul's been dragging it all over the *garage!*"

"It only got a little dirt on it. He looks really funny. You just don't have any sense of humor." Then Will heaved a sigh. "Okay. Paul, take off the dress."

Paul's face appeared again. "I'm Medea!"

"No. *No,* Paul. *I'm* Medea and I'm going to *kill* you."

"Hello, missus."

"Take that dress off!" I was screaming as loud as Ree-Jane had done.

Finally, Will made him stand still long enough to yank off the dress. I thought I heard a sound I didn't like. "Don't *tear* it, my God . . . ! Did you tear it?"

"It's just a little rip in the tulle, that's all."

"Great! That's just *great*! How am I going to fix it? You should have to sew it; it's your fault."

"I don't sew. Here." Will opened the door wide enough to shove the shopping bag through it. "You can just tell her I did it. She won't get mad at me." He shut the door.

What was so infuriating was that he was right. Ree-Jane wouldn't get mad at him; she'd be able to get an apology out of him, and Will would love putting on that smarmy face and tone and just charming her all over the place. He'd even got her to let him drive her convertible.

In the cab, as Delbert drove me crazy with talk about the play (which at this point I'd rather forget all about), I was inspecting the gown. The bottom was so dirty it looked like it had been stepped on again and again—well, it had been, hadn't it? The dress was so long on Paul that of course he'd walked on it. I sank back and Delbert went on.

"There's lotsa folks talkin' about how good it was, even some sayin' they just might go back and see it again."

"I want to go to Jo-Leen's."

"The cleaner, you mean?"

"Do you know any other business call Jo-Leen's?"

"Well, no, I don't guess I do. You takin' that dress you been foolin' with to Jo-Leen?"

Fooling with. I didn't even answer. I checked my pocket to make sure I had the two tickets for the next performance in case I needed to bribe somebody for some reason.

Jo-Leen's was across from the library and next door to the historical society museum. Now that I knew so much about the Belle Ruin, I thought maybe I should go back.

I wasn't sure who exactly Jo-Leen was and the name might have been concocted as one name to stand for two people, a way of naming a business that I had always thought pretty dumb. It only made it harder to remember.

I knew Jo-Leen wasn't the thin, work-worn woman who was there behind the counter today as I pulled out the dress. "I hope you can clean this. A kid got hold of it and put it on and trailed it all over the floor. I could just kill him."

The woman laughed in a good-natured way. "Kids. I know what you mean. Got six of 'em myself and they're a handful, believe you me."

She was inspecting the dress as I stood with my mouth open. *Six* children to take care of! No wonder she looked work-worn. Six kids. I wondered why she didn't go to Lake Noir and rent a speedboat and zoom off and never come back. Or else kill a few of them, like Medea. What if there were *six* Pauls? But that was impossible. I could believe God made up the world in six days before I could ever believe He'd let six Pauls roam the earth.

"My, my," she said. "Well, it sure does look like he did."

At first I thought she was talking about God and the six Pauls, but she was talking about the dress.

"And there's this tulle been torn away from the waist. My, my." Sadly she shook her head.

"See that little spatter there on the top? That's ketchup-blood. Can you get that out?" For all I knew, it could've been real.

"My. Well, I expect so; we can get near anything out. But I'm afraid we can't do anything about this tear here. That's not a service we provide."

That was bad news. But I was sure I could deal with it. "When can I pick it up?" I was thinking maybe we could get away with using it again since Ree-Jane certainly wouldn't be back for another performance. I was a risk taker.

"Soonest, that'd be tomorrow afternoon."

"Thanks a lot. I appreciate your doing it."

"Oh, that's what we're here for!"

I wouldn't be here for anything if I had six kids. I'd be up in Alaska with the caribou and dogsleds.

I left Jo-Leen's feeling relieved and wondering if I could eat a doughnut, as I recently finished up a breakfast of red flannel hash and corn cakes with maple syrup. Lots of maple syrup. One thing I liked about corn cakes was that syrup just seeped right into them so you could keep putting it on. I had argued in a friendly way with my mother, saying that red flannel hash was the same as corned-beef hash. My mother said they were different. Since I had no idea at all about the difference, I sat looking at my corn cakes soaking up syrup and considered my argument.

Walter was eating his breakfast with me. "My mom used to say lots of people thought they was the same thing, but they wasn't."

I glared at him. Where was loyalty?

"See, Miss Smarty-pants," said my mother. "You don't know everything."

I didn't know anything, but I wasn't about to say it. "Well, Aurora told me they were different." She hadn't, but here was a person whose so-called opinions you could drag in any old time because she wasn't there to refute them. The last time Aurora Paradise had come downstairs was when we thought the place was burning down.

"*Aunt* Aurora to you. Don't call adults by their first names."

This was so boring. Why had I started it? Now I was sorry I hadn't put the peppercorns in Miss Bertha's hash. I wondered if when you were an adult whole days would go by with conversations like this.

I was remembering all this as I was walking from Jo-Leen's to the museum. Whenever I entered it, I could smell the past. Dwayne told me that William Faulkner had said the past wasn't dead, that "it isn't even past." That is one of the most comforting statements I have ever heard. It meant I could go back to when my dog was still alive, and my father. It meant the playhouse was still standing and that the Waitresses were still at the hotel. It meant that Rose Queen was still alive in Cold Flat Junction and Ben Queen wasn't hiding out.

I turned the pages of photographs of the Belle Rouen. It was so beautiful, with its luxurious lobby decorated with velvet drapes and crystal chandeliers; and the ballroom, with what looked like hundreds of people dancing, dancing, dancing. I could almost hear the band. And the dining rooms—there were three of them. For a few moments I imagined the hotel with three dining rooms and the effect it would have on Miss Bertha. She'd never be sure and would wander all over.

Here was the side of the hotel on which Reuben's ladder had been placed, though of course it wasn't in this photograph. I tried to picture someone going up that ladder and into the bedroom where the baby was supposedly sleeping, taking her out of her crib and then carrying her down the ladder. If this had happened (but I was pretty sure it hadn't) what would the baby have felt? I shut my eyes and tried to put myself in her place. But there was just no way to travel back to baby-hood and all of its sensations and colors.

And it was making me sad. I closed the book and left, heading for the Rainbow.

While I walked past McCrory's Five-and-Dime, I thought about re-pairing the white dress. My mother was a seamstress just as she was everything else. She made slipcovers, curtains and clothes. But I could hardly ask her to mend the dress, not after that big fight over it.

Then I recalled that there was someone I knew besides my mother who could sew: Miss Flagler. She had made beautiful dresses, espe-cially evening dresses, for local women. If I remembered correctly, she had even made dresses for the Devereau sisters. Now that she was in her seventies her eyes weren't as good as they used to be. "Actually," I recalled her saying, "I could probably whip up a dress blind." (I'd want to be blind, too, before I performed any service for Ree-Jane.) The job of sewing up the tulle would be a simple matter for Miss Flagler.

The Rainbow was just down the street from the Oak Tree Gift Shoppe, so I dashed in to get a doughnut. Donny Mooma was standing in front of the glassed-in pantry display, bending over and squinting his eyes so he could get right down with the lemon meringue pie. Of course, all he ever got was doughnuts, but I supposed he had to eye-ball every cake and pie in the process. Wanda was behind the counter and Shirl at the cash register.

Donny finally settled on what he wanted, pointing to the shelf of doughnuts. "No, not them kind, the new ones with colored bits on 'em, that's what I want."

"With the crinkles on? They're the best," said Wanda, as, smiling, she shook out a white bag and reached in for the doughnuts. I stood there waiting while Donny completed his most serious task of the day. He jerked back when he caught sight of me staring at him. "Whadda *you* want?"

"A doughnut," I said and smiled in a way meant to irritate, which it did.

Donny snatched the bag from Wanda and said, "I'm just gettin' these for Maureen and them." He handed over a dollar bill and Shirl rang up the sale. She took the cigarette out of the corner of her mouth long enough to give him back a dime.

Maureen was the secretary, but I had no idea who "them" might be. I still smiled and he glared and left. I thought it must be really awful to feel your life needed so much explaining you couldn't even buy a doughnut without finding an excuse for it. I would have felt almost sorry for him, except there were limits to my pity.

Wanda was telling me about the new doughnuts with the cherry bits inside them. She was always in a good humor. I didn't think anything in the world could make Wanda mad. Wanda was new and was only permitted three-minute breaks; anyone who could put up with that Shirl nonsense was pretty special, I thought. It was the opposite of Donny Mooma, who was always prepared to be mean even if it wasn't meanness that was coming at him. Then I thought who it was Wanda reminded me of: the Waitresses. I don't remember ever seeing them mad (although my memory of things when I was six probably wasn't all that reliable). I was truly taken aback by this.

I got three doughnuts because it was time for Miss Flagler's and Miss Flyte's tea or coffee break. I thought it would be only fair of me to supply the food for once. Anyway, Miss Flagler liked to bake things and always had some sort of delicious muffins or coffee cake, so my doughnuts would be second fiddles and they probably wouldn't eat them. All I hoped was that just to be polite they didn't take a bite out of them, like I'd do.

Miss Flagler was not in the narrow little shop. But since a bell above the door always tinkled, she would be there in a minute, I knew. Her own living quarters were right behind the one-room gift shop. Sometimes, I thought I would like to be her, not as old, of course, but just to have my life as neat and compact. I would probably stay in the shop more because I could look as long as I felt like looking at all of these small pieces nestled in small boxes or lying on the white satin that lined the bottom of the display shelves: silver bracelets, gemstones, little beaded purses, lace handkerchiefs—everything small. There wasn't anything as large as my Whitman's candy box.

Even the air seemed settled, as if nothing had disturbed it for years. It had always reminded me of something but I had never figured out what the something was. Such places seemed settled, undisturbed. Then I knew what the gift shop, and Miss Flyte's candle shop, and even Souder's old pharmacy reminded me of: the grounds of the Belle Ruin, where the air hung like old curtains, visited only by the deer that came to drink from the pool of water. It was complete, each of these places. It didn't need Miss Flyte to light her candles or Miss Flagler, her hands heavy with little gifts, or Mrs. Souder stirring a ribbed glass with a long spoon. These places didn't need any of us. I was beginning to fear some terrible loss until I realized it was a relief that these places didn't need me, either. A weight seemed to be lifting and then Miss Flagler came through the beaded curtain that separated her living space from the shop space.

"Why, Emma! Hello! Come on back and have some cocoa."

I followed Miss Flagler through her small dark living room to her white kitchen. It was so bright it throbbed. Miss Flyte was sitting at the porcelain-white kitchen table with a cup of tea. "Emma, we were just talking about you."

That pleased me, and I put my sack of doughnuts on the table.

"Doughnuts, how nice."

"We've been hearing about your brother's play from everyone."

"You have?" I was a little more interested in the three doughnuts I was putting on a plate Miss Flagler handed me than I was in Medea. She went back to heating up my cocoa.

Albertine had right away jumped up on her shelf and was sniffing my hair, and then chewing on it. I don't know why. Cats are just peculiar.

"People are saying it's so good they're going back tomorrow night."

"They are?" I watched Miss Flyte, who had taken up a knife and was cutting the doughnuts in half. That was not a good sign.

"Everyone who's been in the shop has said that," said Miss Flagler.

Since there were never more than two people in her shop at once, and often no one, I didn't see that would make much difference. I cornered the two halves of the doughnut covered with chocolate sprinkles.

Miss Flagler said as she poured out my cocoa, "My cousin in Hebrides called me. She said she was driving over to see it with several of her friends."

I frowned. News of the play was actually reaching beyond La

Porte? That was funny. I drank my cocoa as Albertine chewed a little patch of hair. "Really?"

"Helene Baum and her party called to reserve ten seats."

Reserve? I didn't know Will and Mill were taking reservations. "People are *reserving* seats?"

"Oh, my, yes. People who have seen it just loved your deus ex machina."

She had pronounced it correctly. Was the deus ex machina famous?

She continued. "A friend of mind is a professor of literature at the college over in Galista. He called me to see how he could get tickets and I told him I'd phone the hotel and get some."

"Galista? But that's over fifty miles away!"

Miss Flyte shrugged. "Apparently, he feels it's worth it. *Medea* is one of his favorites. He teaches it in one of his college classes."

My mouth was agape. I didn't even stuff the second half of the doughnut in it I was so surprised. Then I said, "But he's going to be really disappointed because it's so much different from the real play. A *lot* different. It's a musical, I hope you told him."

"Of course I did. That's part of the attraction. I must say your brother has a very original turn of mind!"

That was for sure. "Well, it's half his friend's doing. His name is Brownmiller but we call him Mill. He's responsible for the music. He's a great musician; he can play just about any instrument." Will didn't deserve all the credit.

Miss Flagler sighed. "I just hope we can squeeze in. By the time I called they only had one ticket left and weren't taking any more reservations after that. First come, first served is what the boy said. So I did manage to get a ticket for my friend."

I frowned. "Boy?"

"Yes."

Maybe it was Chuck taking calls. But they were just crazy enough to have Paul do it.

I smiled. "You'll get in." I took the other two tickets out of my pocket.

They were as pleased as if it'd been a flight to Paris. "My!" Miss Flyte opened her little purse.

I said, "No. They're on the house."

"How *nice*, Emma. Well, if there's ever anything we can do for you—"

Hopping right into that offer I told them about Ree-Jane's dress. I told them the whole story, including Paul galumphing around in it. They were in stitches.

When she finally stopped laughing, Miss Flagler said, "Of course I can mend the dress by tomorrow evening."

"Oh, good," I said. "I can get Axel's Taxis to pick it up from Jo-Leen's and bring it here, and then deliver it to the hotel."

Miss Flagler nodded, saying that would be fine, and that she would make sure Delbert understands exactly what he's supposed to do.

I said I hoped so.

Then Miss Flagler leaned closer and whispered, "No one will ever be able to tell it was torn." She patted my hand; it was as if she were involving herself in an especially attractive crime.

40

I went to Axel's Taxis, hoping to catch Axel, knowing I wouldn't. When I got there, Delbert was pulling up to the curb. I told him I wanted to go to Slaw's Garage.

"How come you want to go to Slaw's for?"

"Delbert, do you *have* to know?"

"'Course not. Just wonderin' why you don't want to be dropped at the hotel, is all."

I slid down in the seat so he couldn't trap my eyes in his rearview mirror. When we came to the outskirts of La Porte, I sat up to look at Arturo's neon sign, always anxious he might fill in the missing letters. But it was still blinking ART EAT. I hoped it would stay that way.

I sat up to tell Delbert that tomorrow I wanted him to pick up the white dress from the cleaner's and take it over to the gift shop. "Miss Flagler knows all about it." I knew I was probably weighing down his mind with more information than it could take in, but I still went on: "When she's done fixing it, she'll call you or me. I'm going to want you to bring the dress to the hotel, and make sure"—I leaned over the front seat to tell him right in his ear—"that you deliver it around *behind* the hotel, not the front. That's important, hear? Just give a honk and I'll come out and get it."

Naturally, Delbert did his best to make out that I just as well might ask him to play the part of Medea. He hemmed and hawed and twisted around, as if seeing me would make it all clearer. I guessed he did things like that to make himself feel more important than he was. He was certainly unimportant.

Ten minutes into his hemming and hawing, but nevertheless getting it straight what he was to do, Delbert was pulling onto the concrete skirt in front of Slaw's Garage. I got out and gave him the fare and a quarter tip. "You want me to wait, then take you to Hotel Paradise?"

I guessed the quarter tip so surprised him that he thought he should pay me back. "No thanks, Delbert. I can walk." I was being nice for once.

He nodded and pulled away.

Abel Slaw had come to his office door probably wondering if the sound of a car meant more business. I know he'd sooner see a head-on collision than me. "Hello, Mr. Slaw," I called out.

"Now, Emma, don't you go in where there's ve-*hic*-les being worked on."

Grumpiness was my reward for not falling out of the wreck and crawling in my own blood. "Okay, Mr. Slaw." I waved and went to stand just outside the garage door. He was always telling me that and I was always telling him okay. I stood out there until the telephone rang. If Abel Slaw spent half the time repairing ve-*hic*-les as he spent talking on the phone, he'd be a rich man.

I could see Dwayne's feet underneath a pickup truck and You-Boy under the hood of a classy-looking Cadillac. This was a mystery I could never figure out: Dwayne was a master mechanic, but he nearly always worked on these no-account vehicles, while You-Boy, who was only just competent, worked on the expensive fancy cars.

I hitched myself up on the same stack of new tires that seemed never called into use and said to Dwayne, "When do you get off?" He banged some tool against metal and didn't answer. "*Dwayne?*" My tone was more insistent.

"Yeah?"

"Are you going to the play tomorrow night? People really liked it."

"Wouldn't miss it for the world. Heard you stole the show." He whizzed out from under the car and smiled broadly.

I blushed. "No, I didn't." Though I wouldn't insist on this view if he wanted to believe it.

"Oh, I guess I must've heard wrong." He slid back under.

He was so irritating. "I didn't say I wasn't *good*. It's just the role is small."

The banging continued.

"I don't have much time. I have to get back and serve."

"Don't let me keep you."

He was always doing this to me. He'd say something nice, then take it back. Or maybe it was me who took it back, making a thing of being modest, which I wasn't. "I asked you before, what time do you get off work?"

"Depends how much there is to do. Six, six-thirty maybe. Then sometimes I go over to Jessie's."

Jessie's Restaurant was the other side of the railroad tracks, just about the only eating place down there. "Then you'd be done around seven, seven-thirty, which is perfect, since I don't get through serving and cleaning up until after seven. We only have the two dinner guests at the moment."

He pushed out from the truck and got to his feet, looking at me and wiping his hands on the oily rag. I wonder if mechanics ever changed rags.

"Yeah, well, our time schedules are the toast of Spirit Lake, I'm sure, but why do you want to know?"

"It's not important."

"No? Then why are you lining the two of us up?"

"I was just wondering if you wanted to drive over to the Belle Ruin when you get off, or after dinner. That's all. I thought maybe you'd like to hear my theory about the kidnapping."

"Oh, I would. But you can tell me that while you're sitting on that stack of tires."

I gave him a sidelong look that tried to say how silly that idea was. No, what I wanted to tell him was about the Belle Ruin and I wanted to be there when I told it. I don't know why. Then I saw out of the corner of my eye, Abel Slaw in the office about to replace the receiver, it looked like. I caught my breath and said, "I'll meet you at Jessie's Restaurant a little after seven." I hightailed it out of there before Abel came to the office to look in the garage. I said good-bye to You-Boy. I don't think he had many friends.

Anyway, if I left it like that, as a definite time and all, I knew Dwayne would go along with it; he was always being smart around me and teasing me, but he wouldn't disappoint me.

I got their dinner into them as quick as I could. Miss Bertha didn't make her usual one hundred complaints, maybe because there were still ones left over from breakfast and the complaint vault was sealed. Even when her baked potato rolled off her plate onto the floor she didn't raise the roof. I picked it up and set it on my empty tray and asked her if she'd like another one.

"Didn't want that one, did I? Skin's too tough. Why'd I want another?"

I went back to the kitchen, thinking Aurora Paradise was not going to get her fancy drink, and I said, "Walter can take her dinner up to her, can't he? I have to go to the Big Garage." A week ago this would have got me nowhere. But now, in the trail of our great success, it was a surefire excuse.

To that my mother agreed, and Walter said he'd be glad to do it. "Will give me a ticket for tomorrow night. That was awful nice of him."

"You deserve it," I said kindly.

"Where's Paul?" my mother asked. "His mother hasn't seen him in four days."

Lucky her. If that had been any other child the Sheriff would be combing the countryside. "He's up in the garage. Will and Mill had him sleep over."

"Couldn't they have let his mother know that's where he was?"

"I guess nobody thought to." And I also guessed nobody would think Paul would be missed.

My mother shook her head as if a great weariness had settled over her, but I knew that was kind of an act. She had a number of acts. She went back to decorating the macaroni and cheese with pimento for Aurora's dinner.

"Put on a double helping of that peach relish," I said. "She really likes it." Of course she did. "What's for dessert?"

"Snow Pudding."

"Yea!" I loved Snow Pudding. I think it was vanilla custard lightened and whitened with meringue.

When I took the two glass dishes of pudding, decorated with blue-berries, into the dining room, even Miss Bertha muttered approval. Then I had my own dinner, ending with two helpings of pudding. After that, I hiked up to the Big Garage. It was still early, a quarter to seven.

I knocked with the coded knock.

"Come on in," shouted Will. He must have been extremely busy if he couldn't come to the door and do his usual thing.

Mill was at the piano and it looked like he was making up some new piece of music. Will was spray-painting. I said, "Paul's mother wants to know where he is."

"Tell her he's okay. He's here."

I was sarcastic. "This is probably the last place he'd be okay. Anyway, I'm not telling her anything. I don't even know where they live."

"*Paul!*" Will yelled.

"Hello, missus!" came bouncing from the rafters.

"Do you have a phone at home?"

Paul didn't answer. He often didn't answer.

"Paul! Do you have a *telephone*?"

Silence. Then Paul yelled back, "It don't work!"

That's about as many words at a time I'd ever heard out of Paul's mouth.

"Where do you live?"

"That white house!"

I could barely make him out up there. He seemed to be gathering shadows, like Walter. "Look," I said to Will, "just get him down and send him home."

Mill had joined us by then and he and Will looked at me as if I'd gone insane.

Will said, "How can we let him leave? Tomorrow's a major performance. He's key."

"He's key? *Key?* What are you talking about? All he does is throw flour!"

"That's one of the changes. We're leaving out the flour. We decided it wasn't very realistic."

"Realistic? *Realistic? None* of this is realistic!" Still, I was delighted that they left out the flour.

"If we let him go," said Mill, "we'll never get him back again."

"Well, if he's not up there to throw the flour, what's he up there for?"

"Lightning bolts. It's much better."

Mill echoed that. "It's much better. I do drum rolls on the piano. You know, meaning thunder. It's fierce."

Will had picked up one of the things he'd been spray-painting silver and showed me. It was a long, jagged-edged piece of cardboard. "Paul's throwing these. Pretty good lightning bolts, right?"

My eyes narrowed. "Throwing them *where*?" As if I didn't know. "Not at me!"

Will gave one of his fed-up sighs. "What a coward. He's throwing them *around* you, not at you. Anyway, it's only cardboard."

They were both chewing Teaberry gum at the same speed and staring at me.

I had to remind myself they could always switch back to flour, and they would. It was blackmail. "That may be only *cardboard*, but *that*"— I pointed rafterward—"is *Paul*! Paul could drown me in a cupful of water."

They both snickered. The snickers were like the gum.

Mill shoved his glasses up his thin nose and said, "They'll probably just flutter around all over."

"Why are you doing lightning bolts?"

You could tell Will was searching for a reason. "It's more Greek."

Mill said that Chuck would run the yellow light around when the bolts came down. "We tried it. It's incredible!"

"The only thing that you want to be careful of," said Will, "is you don't throw your arms around as if you're trying to protect yourself. That wouldn't look good."

"Protecting myself is *exactly* what I'll be doing!"

Mill shrugged and said, "A deus ex machina wouldn't do that."

"Like I said," Will said again, "we just want it to be realistic."

My mouth had been agape an awful lot today and now it was agape again. There was no talking to them, nothing got through, so I just went physical and started pummeling Will. Of course, all he had to do was grab my arms.

Mill said, "Wait a minute—" He pulled Will over to the side where I couldn't hear.

They were back in a couple of minutes. Will said, "We got a new idea."

That was bad news. I groaned.

"We're thinking what if you go for Medea? You say 'Stop!' but she just keeps lowering the knife."

"In slow motion, see," said Mill.

"Right. In slow motion."

"So you start pummeling her."

"Pummeling."

They were chewing their gum in unison.

"No. That is a stupid idea. I know I can't reason with you because you're both crazy. I'm just saying no!"

"Hello, missus!" echoed from the rafters.

I walked out.

I ended up in the now-empty kitchen where I had another helping of Snow Pudding.

There are times when only food knows what you're talking about.

41

Jessie's Restaurant was across the highway from Abel Slaw's Garage, on the other side of the tracks. Jessie's would have been a diner except it didn't have booths. A diner has to have booths. Instead, Jessie had tables covered with oilcloth in very pretty patterns of flowers or vines. The food was okay but not brilliant; I had only been in it a few times and all I had had was a chocolate soda, and that was good.

There was always loud music coming from the jukebox, mostly country. But sometimes the Everly Brothers or Patience and Pru (Aurora's favorites) got played. Tonight it was Patience and Pru:

> *"I knoooow with the daw-ah-ah-ah-ahn*
> *That you-ou-ou-ou*
> *Will be go-ah-ah-ah-awn*
> *But to-niiight, you belon-ong to me."*

I loved that song.

It looked like Dwayne could learn a lesson from it, because he was leaning so far over the counter he could have reached down Jessie's dress. Oh, I saw as he leaned back up again, he'd just been taking a fork from a silverware holder under the counter. Jessie was really the one doing the leaning now, her arms folded on the countertop, talking while he forked up bites of his pie.

Boy, was she ever flirting. It was pretty silly of her; she had to be a lot older than Dwayne. Well, some older, anyway.

But Dwayne seemed to be concentrating on his pie more than on her, for all he did was to nod briefly, as if to suggest, yes, he was listening, when no, he wasn't. I recognized that nod; it was Will's nod and no one could pay less attention than Will.

I crossed the room and said hello as I sat down on the stool next to Dwayne.

"Well, doggone, look who's here."

"I could say the same for you." That I thought was quite a snappy rejoinder.

Jessie gave us an uncertain smile and plodded off in her rubber-soled working shoes that made a gentle sucking sound as she walked.

I turned back and forth on my stool, fingers on the counter for balance. "Is that pie good?"

Dwayne shrugged. "Pretty good. Not a ten by any means."

"You should taste my mother's apple pie."

"She a good cook?"

There was a question so pitifully understated I stopped turning to look at him. I realized I'd never said much to him about my mother's cooking. How did that happen, given it was most of what held me together? That's the trouble with food and why people get fat, probably, because they depended on it, maybe, to keep from blowing to bits. A gorgeous glue to hold them together.

"I never told you?"

"What?"

"My mother's the best cook around. *Far* around, like in the whole state. And maybe a few others. Why don't you come to the hotel for dinner? As long as you're eating out?"

He put the fork on the plate and picked up his coffee. "I'm too dirty and greasy when I finish work to eat in your dining room. The hotel's got to keep up its standards."

"*Standards?*" I thought that was really funny. "You should meet Miss Bertha, then."

"You want something?" He nodded toward the glass shelves—just like the Windy Run's—that housed the cakes and pies.

"No, thanks." Had I ever said that before when food was at hand?

Dwayne turned and looked out the window. "Still light, good." He took out his wallet, pulled out a ten-dollar bill for the food and a six-pack Jessie had set on the counter and left the bill, not asking for change. I knew that was way, way more than the check. Every once in a while I'd discover something about Dwayne that just contradicted the way he usually acted around me. His excellent manners when being introduced to people on the porch; reading William Faulkner all the time; being generous.

"Let's go," he said, sticking a cigarette in his mouth as we walked out. Inside the door was a drink machine where he put in a coin and a can of Coke dropped down. We headed to his truck.

Dwayne's old pickup truck had a hundred things wrong with it. You could hear pieces clanging and clinking around underneath. I just could not understand this. "You're a master mechanic. Why don't you fix this truck?"

"It's because I'm a mechanic that I don't have to. That noise you hear don't mean a thing." He exhaled a bushel of smoke.

"But you wouldn't put up with this in somebody else's car. You'd fix it."

"You don't listen much, do you? Of course I'd fix somebody else's car. That's what Abel Slaw pays me to do, doesn't he? Those people just must have these things fixed because they're not mechanics."

"Master mechanics."

He turned away. I think he smiled. "Anyway, it's the engine that counts. This is one sweet engine." He patted the dashboard as if to make sure the engine heard the compliment. "You're not hearing any dings comin' from the engine, now are you?"

"How could I? The rest of the truck's so loud it drowns everything out."

After we'd driven a little over a mile we turned off the highway onto an old dirt road that hardly anyone used now. But, then, why would they, as it only went as far as the Belle Ruin? Dusk was deepening and Dwayne switched on his headlights. The road went for about a half mile before we got to what was left of the old hotel.

I couldn't get over the fact that it still looked majestic, with those pillars of stone reaching up to the sky. Even mostly burned down, it was impressive. We pulled under—or would have been under—the porte cochere. The granite columns at the outside corners still stood there, but there was no roof to it, and the long wide stairs that would have gone up to the hotel's doors were gone except for the first one, which for some reason remained. The porte cochere had been big enough to shelter six or seven cars. Ours at the Hotel Paradise had room for two at the most.

We surveyed what was left of the hotel as if it were the site of some ancient ruin somewhere in Rome or maybe Greece. I guess I picked that up from Medea's surroundings.

Dwayne asked, "You know anything about archaeology?"

He set down the lantern from his truck and hunkered down, turning a rock in his hand. It was pretty, kind of fluorescent, depending on the slant you held it at.

"No. Do you?"

"Not one damned thing." He set the rock down carefully, as if some respect were owed these ruins.

I was just as glad he didn't know, so I wouldn't appear to have neglected my learning. But Dwayne was like that: he never seemed to mind not knowing.

We walked to the right and along to where it looked as if the turn would be to the east wing. I took out my map and the postcards, one of them showing the side of the hotel where the Slades' rooms were. I pointed to the spot where the ladder would have been. "Reuben Stuck says he never put the ladder there. You could say Reuben Stuck was the prime suspect." No, you couldn't; I just liked the feel of such words in my mouth. They meant business. "Reuben said he'd left the ladder two windows to the right of the baby's window. So somebody had to have moved it. I believe Reuben when he says it wasn't him."

Dwayne looked at me with a frown. "You spend fifty percent of your time over in Cold Flat Junction. You get on and off that train as often as the U.S. mail."

"No, I *don't*." I hated anyone knowing I was attached to a place—or a person, for that matter. They'd only laugh at you. "I have to go there because it's a big part of this whole story. It just seems everyone in it lives in Cold Flat Junction or Spirit Lake."

"Did it ever occur to you it might not be good for your health to go around asking questions of a prime suspect?"

"Well, but he's *not*, I mean not anymore. He was only a prime suspect (I loved that phrase) for a little while. Anyway, I've got a good reason. I'm interviewing people for my story."

Dwayne was kneeling down again looking at the foundation. "Yeah? I always thought the 'story' was about the Devereau sisters and Ben Queen pickin' one of 'em off. That, I must say, is one hell of a story."

"But that's what happens with stories; one story leads to another. Maybe life's just one long long long story."

Dwayne had risen again. "Just be careful. I don't like the idea of you poppin' up all over kingdom come askin' perfect strangers questions. Look what happened the last time."

There wasn't any "last time"; it was all still happening. "Morris Slade was from La Porte. He was a half brother of Rose Devereau. He's part of it and that makes his wife and the baby part of it."

"Where're they now?"

I hadn't really thought about it. It was as if Morris and Imogen and old Mr. Woodruff had ended with the kidnapping. "In New York, I guess, unless they took off for Paris, France or Mexico. Afraid the law might still find them out."

"Haven't got a dramatic bone in your body, have you?"

"Are you commenting on my acting?" I stopped, huffily.

He laughed. "Not a bit."

We were walking along to the next turning, which was the beautiful semicircle of the back part of the hotel. There were the kitchens, dining rooms and ballroom. I showed Dwayne my map, or Miss Llewelyn's, rather.

He looked upward. "I wish I'd seen it. God, but I wish I had."

This surprised me. Dwayne hardly ever gave his feelings away.

"Me, too. Around here is the ballroom." I walked ahead of him along what had been a stone path; weeds had grown up between the stones, and fallen leaves and thin branches nearly covered it. We supposed what had been the first dining room, which had burned to the ground, was next to the kitchen, where a huge range still stood. On the floor were charred pots and pans and broken crockery. "I look for plates and cups that have the name on them."

"Surprises me no one's hauled away that stove. People swarm around this sort of stuff like locusts."

We walked past the second dining room and then to the ballroom. Half the roof was gone and beneath it a wall burned halfway down. But aside from that, the ballroom was basically intact.

"It's still got furniture in it. Those velvet chairs against the walls and a settee. You'd think those things would go up in seconds."

Dwayne had stepped into the room and was looking down at the floor. "These planks look like that Chinese elm, one of the strongest woods, the best wood you can get outside of maybe bamboo. They haven't rotted; they haven't buckled. It's amazing." He had his lantern lit now and put it down on the floor, where it shed its light over the old gold of the settee's legs. He turned in a slow circle. I stepped onto the floor and turned as he did, looking up at the sky. Night was coming on slowly. I could see the evening star.

"Where did all the people come from who stayed here, or danced here? There must've been at least a hundred in here."

"Two hundred. I looked it up. As many as two hundred came for these balls and a lot of them stayed here in the hotel. It had nearly that many rooms. A hundred seventy-five is what the description in the paper said. The band"—I pointed to the far wall—"was down there. They were called The Royals. There were twelve of them, a good-sized band, from Camberwell."

Dwayne looked at me. "You sure did your homework on this place."

"Old newspaper stories. It's where I got the pictures, from the newspaper. And Miss Llewelyn, over at the museum, made this drawing, a kind of map that shows where the main rooms were downstairs and where the Slades' rooms were over there where the ladder was standing. They had two rooms, one just for the baby. Morris and Imogen were at the dance and the baby was in its crib back in the east wing." I pointed behind me, in case Dwayne had forgotten. "We're meant to think someone moved the ladder and climbed it and kidnapped the baby while the babysitter was on the phone down the hall.

No one came down it or went up it in the time the police said was the time the baby had to have been kidnapped. At least the babysitter was good for one thing: the timing. She admitted she was on the phone for twenty minutes. Morris Slade came upstairs from the dance. He asked how the baby had been and she said the baby hadn't woken up or anything. So between the time she left to telephone and Morris's coming upstairs—that was when Baby Fay was taken. He went in to look at her and discovered the baby was gone."

"You said no one went up or down the ladder."

"Ulub and Ubub were working on the grounds that night cleaning up dead branches and gathering wood for the fireplace. They were near the ladder. Or I guess they meant the ladder was in view, that no one could have used it without their seeing it."

Dwayne grew thoughtful. Another thing I liked about him was that he didn't say, "Can you depend on what *they* say?" I thought they were brave, sometimes putting themselves in a position where people could ignore them or disbelieve them or just laugh at them.

"So this Spiker girl—"

"Gloria Spiker Calhoun. I talked to her. She lives in Cold Flat Junction."

"She said the father—what was his name?—"

"Morris Slade."

"—that he was in the room when she got back from telephoning. How long had he been there?"

"What're you thinking?"

"I'm thinking it would probably only take a few minutes to take the baby downstairs and maybe put her in his car."

That had never occurred to me. "There were so many people around, though."

"Yeah, but that's an advantage in a way. People have their minds on dancing or cavorting around. Say the father slipped down some back stairs—"

I waited, but then he looked at the sky that was beginning to take on the purple of a bruise, and said, "I'm havin' a beer. Want one?"

"Ha ha ha. I know you got a Coke in Jessie's and brought it."

He started off. "You coming?"

"I'll wait here and think."

"God help us." He went off to his truck. Instead of cutting through, he walked the same way we had come. Out of respect, maybe.

I sat on the velvet chair and looked toward the pool, wishing the deer would come along to drink. I kept looking at the pool and the pines as if the looking would make them appear, as if I could conjure them up by the strength of my imagination. I wondered what it was that made that scene with the pool and the deer so right. As if we go through life blinded and "bugswirled" and "stumppocked," according to William Faulkner, that is, and just once in a while we're allowed to see truly.

I hadn't told Dwayne my theory. As usual I was holding back. Was it because it was an idea I didn't want to part with now, as if the telling of it would blow it away like sand? Holding back, like me wanting to be the last person to greet someone I really liked, thinking the last person is more easily remembered.

Why did I do this? Why did I not explode into his line of sight and blot out everything else? Why was I (as my mother would put it) so self-contained? Who would want to meet me if it meant to be met with indifference?

Sometimes I wished there were people who could see through this, like the Sheriff and Maud, like Dwayne. If they could, then I wouldn't have to work so hard at not showing my feelings. It was dangerous to do it; you could be laughed at, teased without mercy. You could be Ulub and Ubub.

I heard Dwayne coming back along the path. He didn't go "through" the hotel, but instead came back as he had gone.

It was as if the Belle Ruin still stood.

For some reason that heartened me. He seemed to have respect for things; it was second nature for him. He handed me the Coke and sat down on the dance floor near me. I said, "I'll tell you who I think the Slades' baby really is. It's someone I keep seeing."

He gave me a quizzical look and lit a cigarette. "Who?"

So I told him.

"She's a Fadeaway girl."

42

The next morning after breakfast I sat in my favorite spot on the front porch, a short section around the corner from the main part where no one would see me. It wasn't hidden in any way (as Ree-Jane always managed to find me) yet it was private. I liked to rock and look at the big tree that stood on its own little island of grass and milkweed. I could think here; there was something calming about the tree. The gravel driveway that led up from the highway split at the tree, one arm winding around to the front and the other running along the side and around to the back of the hotel where it circled again around the cocktail garden.

There was a lot of space, acres of it, so that it felt sometimes as if the hotel itself, and me in it, were floating on our own little island. It was very calming in spite of the shenanigans (as my mother put it) that went on there. The craziness and bad temper.

Dwayne had not agreed with Aurora's theory that the Slades could have killed their own baby; he said it was awful melodramatic, wasn't it? To which I had said, well, no more than your idea of Morris Slade doing the kidnapping. I didn't tell him that Mr. Gumbrel had said something of the same thing. He actually thought my own theory was more believable, which wasn't saying much (he added).

I guess it was just as well that he'd see what melodrama really *was* tonight.

Instead of going through the hotel to get to my room, I took the narrow path off the porch that looped around the side to the back entrance. That way I could avoid meeting up with people. I was in a mood not to talk but to ponder.

My room was on the third floor near the back. Ree-Jane's was on the second floor facing the front. Mrs. Davidow occupied two rooms, as close as the Hotel Paradise came to a suite. Sometimes she'd change it to the "suite" directly above on the second floor. My mother's room was at the top of the main staircase, and that might sound a good location, but the reason she was there was in case somebody came in at night she could wake up and go downstairs.

So you could tell pretty much who was considered valuable and who wasn't by the placement of the room. Mrs. Davidow and Ree-Jane had private baths. My mother and I had to travel down the hall to get to one. (So did Will, but I was never sure what room he was occupying because he was always switching it.)

I didn't mind my room, unluxurious as it was. I had painted the furniture pale blue. There were two dressers and a board that served as a dressing table between them. The bed was an iron one and the wardrobe was such a rich dark wood that I didn't want to cover it up with paint. I liked to lie on my bed and sometimes read and sometimes think. I thought about coming down in my swing amid bolts of lightning thrown by Paul. I decided it was better than the flour.

In my argument with them I had completely forgotten my reason for going to the garage in the first place: it was to get Paul to go home. It seemed to me Paul had as good a time as any of us, in spite of being tied up there to a rafter. Even his mother tied him to chairs to keep him from getting into my mother's elaborate cakes, which she'd leave to cool on the pastry table. I remember seeing him on the screened-in porch of the big kitchen and he seemed to think being tied to a chair was an adventure. In a way, it was, for he spent the time picking all of the threads out of his brand-new shoes. *"Paw! You want hit?"* She often had occasion to say this. Then she'd box his ear. His new shoes lay in pieces on the floor when his mother caught him that time. *"Paw! You want hit?"* Her own speech was a blur of words and "Paul" always came out "Paw."

I lay on my bed and looked at the long crack in the white paint on the ceiling. Where had Fay gone? Who stole her away? Who *gave* her away? (I couldn't stand the idea that someone had actually killed her on purpose.) Or could she have got sick of something or other and died, but for some reason her mother and father hadn't let anyone know it and had buried her? Why would anyone keep such a thing a secret? Maybe it had something to do with inheritance.

Whatever had happened, I could hardly stand thinking about it, unless, of course, she'd been handed over to some really nice couple, people who had been wanting a baby for a long time and it didn't look as if they ever would have one.

But all of these were old thoughts. I'd been running them through my mind for days. I had already decided, hadn't I? That no matter what had happened, she had come back, that what happened had happened at the Belle Ruin, and that she knew she wasn't the daughter of the ones who had taken her in. (And had they done it for money? For a lot of money?)

Maybe she'd seen an old newspaper the couple had saved about the kidnapping. I wonder what story they would have told her.

"We found you. What a stroke of luck that was! We found you on a park bench in the autumn. You were wrapped snugly in a blanket and the leaves were falling slowly and they were almost like another blanket. We should have gone to the police, but we didn't see what good it would do, trying to locate the parents who had left you there in the first place."

They would have shown her the newspaper.

"We didn't see this until you were eighteen. Eighteen. Imagine! You were grown up. It was hard to know what to do. A friend gave us this paper because of something we had said. What? We were simply, we were, we didn't know what to do or what to think. But finally we thought you had a right to know. Surely everybody at least deserves that. Everybody. This is where it apparently happened, here in this grand hotel."

Perhaps here there would be a photograph, perhaps even the same photograph as was in the *Conservative* of the fabulous Belle Rouen.

I lay for a while wondering how I would feel if my mother presented me with such a tale: *"Emma, you were kidnapped when you were four months old and—"*

I kind of liked the part about being snugly wrapped up and on a bench and the leaves drifting down. I could almost feel them if I kept my eyes closed.

And if these people who had found me showed me a newspaper clipping about this hotel I was kidnapped from and where it was, I'd find it and come here. Just as I was sure the Girl had done. She who looked not like Imogen Woodruff, but so much like Rose Devereau Queen.

I must've fallen asleep, for the next thing I knew I was jolted awake. I had been dreaming of Ree-Jane as a baby on a park bench and here she was in my room! She'd just walked in without knocking as she always did—that is, if she could deign to come into my room in the first place. Here she was, with her sarcastic smile, her hands on her hips and in a new dress.

"Wake up, Sleeping Beauty! Miss Jen is really storming around about you not being in the kitchen. It's lunchtime!" Her sneer was almost wired in.

"You should be on a park bench."

"What?" It annoyed her if I confused her.

The leaves fell, the snow fell, and in the spring, the rain fell as she lay there. No one came to pick her up—

Wait! A poor soul did come and took her from the bench—

She said, "What's that dumb smile for?"

—and a little bit later, took her back.

There was some kind of luncheon party today, people I didn't know, which was why Vera was there bustling around, unhappy because she had had to make the salads, a job that was beneath her dignity. Her black eyes snapped at me and her mouth was straight and thin as a ruler's edge. The stiff organdy cap that was part of her uniform seemed to quiver on her head.

My mother's eyes and mouth didn't look too happy, either. Only Walter was in a good mood and asked me if I'd been up in the Big Garage practicing the play.

I realized this would be a much better excuse than falling asleep, so I said, "Yes. Will and Mill made some changes." I lay my hand against my forehead. "It's *so* much more work!" The play had achieved a kind of reverence. Any bawling-out I might get would be forgotten or at least postponed.

My success, as part of it on top of my being famous for almost getting killed and "bringing a criminal to justice" (which I hadn't; Ben Queen had), made me wonder why I was still on the salad detail. I looked at the salads Vera had done; mine were much prettier.

I know I wasn't as good a waitress as Vera, but that would be like saying I wasn't as good a priest as Father Freeman. Actually, Vera could be said to be a high priest of waitressing. In that black uniform and stiff little cap she looked kind of priestly; the big tray raised on just her fingertips made it appear as if she carried something holy.

No, my own calling was more being famous. I was good at that.

I set these thoughts aside while I served Miss Bertha and Mrs. Fulbright. While they ate their soup I rushed over to the office, saw Mrs. Davidow was gone and poured about a cupful of Jack Daniel's into a small pitcher to save for the cocktail hour. I rushed this back to the icebox, where I put it down behind a block of ice. Then I drew Walter aside (though Walter was always "aside" in a way) and told him he'd be making Aurora's drink tonight. If there was one thing I did not want to do it was to get involved with Aurora this evening. I showed him where I'd put the cup of whiskey. "When it comes cocktail time, you just mix up the fruit and the juice, then pour this in. There should be enough for two drinks; you know she'll want a second one."

"Prob'ly."

After this, I took in ham pinwheels and peas to Miss Bertha and Mrs. Fulbright. My mother was so busy with the luncheon party that she'd forgotten about Miss Bertha and peas. Instead of removing them, I put a spoonful over Miss Bertha's cheese sauce.

I was nearly out the door when my mother said I should stay and help out Vera, and I said, in a kind of tortured way, "Dress rehearsal! The play, the play!" It was pleasantly surprising how "the play" was getting me out of just about everything. For once, it was true.

43

They had sold 135 tickets to the second performance.

I must say I was astonished not only that they'd sold that many seats, but that they could carry on as if nothing had happened, as if an audience of 135 was just all in a day's work. I mentioned this.

"Where will you get the chairs? What will they sit on?"

"We'll manage," he said. "Where were you this morning? We had stuff to go over."

"Where was I? You know I was *working*. Waiting tables. Waiting on Miss Bertha and a few others." That had been one other, actually. This was Mr. Muggs, who came a few times each year when he was on the road. He called himself a consultant, which meant traveling salesman, but I didn't make a point of this as he was a nice guest. He was also neat, so neat that when you went into his room to change the sheets, you thought, Oh, Mr. Muggs must've checked out. It was like he had erased any sign of himself and I wondered sometimes if someone was after him.

"So what did you go over?"

"The lightning bolts, for one thing."

"Okay, I know about the bolts."

"Then I told you there was new stuff. But it mostly doesn't have anything to do with your character, except your few lines."

"What few lines?"

"It's more of a solo."

"I'm supposed to *sing*? By myself? No. Not on your life."

Will was looking at me and chewing gum.

"*Listen,* for once!"

All he did was go over to a chair and come back with a coat. "You wear this."

I stared at it. "A *raincoat?* You're telling me to wear a raincoat that's too big for me?"

"Never mind that; it'll look swell." He was holding it by the shoulders, waiting for me to put it on. I did, knowing it was hopeless to refuse. The sleeves hung over my hands and the hem splashed around my feet. He smiled. "There. It's a great effect."

Now Mill was by us. He said, "We better practice a little till you get the words down."

"*What* words?"

They looked at each other and shrugged. *Hopeless me* was the heart of that shrug. They seemed to have forgotten that I had no idea what they were talking about. "Is this"—I held out one invisible hand—"this raincoat because of the storm? The lightning and all?"

Now Mill and Will were chewing gum in unison. Will said, "That's one reason, yeah."

I planted myself three inches from his nose. "That is the stupidest thing I ever heard. A deus ex machina in a raincoat! I'm a *god*! I don't wear clothes!"

Will let up on the gum long enough to grin. "We'd really like to try no clothes but I guess the audience isn't ready for that."

They both snickered as if that was the funniest thing.

Mill said, "It's the kind of raincoat called a mackintosh."

My eyes narrowed. I caught a glimpse.

"Mackintosh is what the English call it. Don't you know anything?"

"I know I'm not going to do this."

"Oh, come on. It's funny."

"No." I flung off the coat.

Mill was back at the piano, plundering the keys. There was the usual building up with a flourish at the end just before the song began. He sang in his nasal voice:

"I don't give a toss for a mack-in-tosh
'Cause I'm a deus ex machina.
No, not a machine, that's not what we mean
If you don't say it right we'll be HERE ALL NIGHT—"

I leaned against the stage, my head in my hands. "I don't believe it."

"It's a sing-along."

"Oh, that's just wonderful! A Greek sing-along."

Now they were making a big production of shrugging and sighing and looking defeated.

"Okay, then we'll have to replace you," said Will.

"With *who*? The show's *tonight*!"

I caught another glimpse.

"Ree-Jane. She said she'd be glad to do it. Especially the singing. She wants to be a famous singer with one of the big bands. Like Tommy Dorsey or someone."

"She wants to be a famous anything."

"Well, Ree-Jane wants to do it. She said she'd be really good in the swing because she's going to be a famous gymnast someday. She says she's graceful and all. She just wants flowers wrapped around the rope, and vines."

I grabbed up the coat and said to Mill. "I don't give a toss for a mackintosh."

"Great!" Mill came down on the keys like thunder, which was okay since I was dressed for stormy weather.

44

Not only did I have the pleasure of keeping Ree-Jane out of the show, I would also have the pleasure of telling her she was out, though I didn't think I would. I'd rather she found out when we both turned up to sit on the swing. (I bet they hadn't told her that Paul was in the rafters.)

I went to my favorite spot on the porch where the tree stood like a crossing guard. I was reading a movie magazine because that might get Ree-Jane started on her plan to go to Hollywood and become a star. Once she had told me that "film people" (as she called them) nearly always changed their names, and she would change hers to Ruby Jay Drew. That way, she could still use her matched luggage as the initials were the same. That is Ree-Jane's notion of being awfully clever.

She got out here even quicker than I expected. She fluted a hello to me and arranged herself, sidesaddle, on the porch railing. One of her career moves would involve riding and racing. She intended to become the first woman jockey in the United States. When I reminded her she was like a foot too tall, she didn't like it.

Today, she fanned out her skirt over the railing and told me the dress, a peach color, was new. I didn't respond. Then she flounced her hair around, letting one side of it drip over half her face. Someone had told her she looked a lot like Veronica Lake.

I didn't say anything.

"I hear that Will sold one hundred fifty tickets."

"One hundred thirty-five," I said.

"But that's *amazing*!"

"Yep. It's really popular. Mill said that some theater people were coming. Talent scouts, too." Will had said no such thing.

Again, she moved her head to get that wave in place over her eye and looked as if the photographers were already there, ganged up to take her picture. "You know, what I told Will was I'd be glad to let them use my sweet sixteen gown"—she paused for dramatic effect—"as long as I'm in it!"

Her laugh was so phony. She got off the railing, then back on it, re-arranging her dress. I thought *The Loretta Young Show* had come to Spirit Lake. I bet Will wouldn't tell her she wouldn't be in the play un-til she showed up at the Big Garage all ready to go. That was kind of cruel, and I savored it for a moment.

Now she was really trying to get my attention. She actually hummed the mackintosh song, waiting for me to react, which of course I didn't. I yawned. Sleepily I looked at her as if she'd turned up in the most bor-ing dream in the world.

"Do you recognize what I'm humming?"

"Um. Nope."

"You must not have gone to rehearsal, then."

"That's right."

She was getting really irritated because I wasn't asking her how she knew the song.

"When you didn't show up, Will came and got me."

More likely she was hanging around the Big Garage and they yanked her in just to have a warm body (well, a body, anyway) to point a bony finger at Medea and otherwise fill the deus ex machina role so the rehearsal could proceed. There had probably never been any intention of giving Ree-Jane the role; no, that was just Will's usual blackmail.

She fanned her skirt out a little more, probably a preview of the way she'd look coming down on the swing. "You said there'll be the-ater people there tonight."

I didn't even look up. "Probably come to shut it down."

"What? But it's a good show! It will be better tonight even."

"Oh, really?" I knew she meant because of her own beautiful side-saddle self.

She went on. "Anyway, that's not very loyal of you saying they'd shut it down, even if you were kidding. Will and Mill would be hurt."

She tried to look sad at the same time she tried to drape her hair over her right eye. It wasn't easy being Veronica Lake.

I laughed. "There's nothing they can't turn around to mean what they want it to mean."

Ree-Jane frowned her most squiggly brow frown. "I don't know what you mean."

I smiled my squiggliest smile. "Then you don't know Will and Mill."

Now she was getting really peeved and even crawled down from the porch railing to stand over me. "Well, I know them well enough to get a part in their play, how do you like *that*?"

I pretended great puzzlement. "Which part?"

"The Do-X-machine!"

My face was as expressionless as I could make it. "Oh, the under-study."

That pulled her up. "What understudy?"

"Mine."

That did it! "I'm one of the stars!"

"Well, you're one of the stars' understudies. You only go on if I go off. You know, if I get sick or lose my voice. But I don't think I will. First, though, if you're to be my understudy, you've got to learn how to pronounce 'deus ex machina.' As my understudy you'll really have to know that."

She opened and closed her mouth in that fishy way and then turned on her heel and marched off in the general direction of the Big Garage. If it hadn't been time for me to do the salads for dinner I would have liked nothing more than to follow her just to hear Will and Mill get rid of her. I closed my magazine as two cars pulled up. It was the Baums and their usual noisy crowd. Their dinner party was early this time, at six-thirty, to ensure they would all be sitting (or falling) down at seven. They would be seeing the show at eight. Vera, of course, would serve them and get the hefty tip. My mother had offered my services until I reminded her about the performance. The show, the play, the musical—all worked wonders.

Except for Miss Bertha, of course. I'd have time to serve them, but not enough time to put Tabasco sauce in the *jus* of her roast beef *au jus*. The time would then be wasted on slapping her on the back and getting her water and so forth. I wondered as I placed a thin circle of green pepper on top of the salad if maybe the Sheriff would turn up with somebody from the police lab, where they test all kinds of things, trying to identify the criminal, and run some tests on Miss Bertha's dinner.

"It's hot pepper sauce, as near as I can tell from this gravy . . ."

No.

". . . as near as I can tell from the stomach contents . . ."

That would mean Miss Bertha had to have her stomach pumped out. Although on *Perry Mason* they usually found the stomach contents after the person was dead, which wouldn't be a bad idea, either. Oh, what fun that would be!

"What are you doing? Are you practicing?"

I hadn't even heard my mother come up. She was making more Roquefort cheese salad dressing.

"Huh?"

"Well, you were sort of jerking around and laughing."

"I was? Oh, yes. The play has a lot of new stuff. It's hard to keep track."

"I'm sure all of you will be marvelous." The beater was going at a very slow speed to mash up the Roquefort cheese. She added olive oil a tiny bit at a time to keep the cheese from separating. That, of course, was the trick of it and what was left out if she gave the recipe to someone, like Helene Baum, who was always pestering for recipes. She'd just say "Blue cheese and oil, that's all it takes."

No, it wasn't. I've heard my mother respond to complaints about someone else not being able to get the dressing like hers. "I wonder if it's the altitude?" "I wonder if your oil was slightly rancid?" "Now, did you use real Roquefort? Or some other ordinary kind of blue cheese?"

You could use any kind of blue cheese. The secret was adding the oil practically drop by drop. So when my mother would accuse Will of "dissembling," I wanted to laugh, she being one of the world's master dissemblers. It occurred to me as I put a tiny piece of garlic under Miss Bertha's lettuce leaf that our lives were full of drama, even though they looked pretty dull.

Eagerly, I awaited the return of Ree-Jane. I figured she would come to the kitchen to complain to my mother, first because Will was her son, which made my mother responsible for his connivery; second, because it was the cocktail hour and Mrs. Davidow wasn't about to interrupt it with listening to any tale of woe from Ree-Jane. Or if she listened, she'd probably laugh and laugh. Not only that, tonight she'd be muscling in on the Baum party and unavailable.

As I hoped, Ree-Jane came clattering in; she was very heavy on her feet, which didn't add greatly to her model's walk. She was on the verge of tears, but at the same time she was acting the role of poor girl betrayed. I guess she wanted my mother to see how good she would have been and what the American theater scene would be cheated out of.

"Emma?" My mother dropped in oil and turned to me for an explanation.

I hear "Emma?" in this way all the time, as if I was answerable for any complaint, from the hot pepper in Miss Bertha's omelet to *Medea: The Musical*. I looked almost pitifully innocent. "You mean the understudy?" Now my smile was winning. "Maybe Will didn't explain it right, or maybe Ree-Jane didn't understand it right. Ree-Jane's my understudy. That's in case anything happens to me."

Now, that was worse than an out-and-out betrayal, a promise of something that evaporated as you watched. For "under" meant "beneath"—a copy, probably a bad one, an imitation. These words spun dizzily in my mind.

Ree-Jane stomped her foot (it surprised me that people really do this). "I'm not an understudy! But now I wouldn't be in that stupid play even if they paid me!"

"Ahhhhhhhhh—" I mock whined.

"Emma! Don't make things worse!"

And here I was thinking things had gotten a lot better.

On Mrs. Fulbright's salad I made a face out of chopped hard-boiled eggs and olives for eyes. A tiny length of pimento made the smile. But I had to pause when Miss Bertha ate her salad, fifteen minutes later, for she was shaking her head this way and that, like a dog that's got hold of something very unpleasant.

Then I was ready to tackle *Medea*.

45

We had more guests for dinner on the night of the performance than we'd had in I don't know how long. I couldn't have waited on all of them even if I weren't in the play. It made sense to have dinner at the hotel before going up to the Big Garage. Fortunately, Ann Paugh was there to take over this landslide of diners. There were about fifteen or sixteen, in addition to the Baum party (which included Mrs. Davidow as usual). I wondered if they would all be too drunk to sit and watch *Medea*, although I didn't think this would be much of a drawback. Considering all the screaming and bolts of lightning thrown, and the rushing around and blood, well, being sober might be a handicap.

Walking up to the Big Garage at seven-thirty, I was amazed by all of the theatergoers climbing out of their cars, many of which they'd drawn up on the grassy verge as other places were taken. A long time ago the Big Garage was a place for guests to park. There is also a Little Garage near it, but that wasn't used for anything but storage or working on some sort of project around the hotel. Paint, tools, boards, flowerpots were left here. And also gin and Wild Turkey, for I have seen Mrs. Davidow on rare occasions going into the Little Garage and coming out holding something that was not a flowerpot.

Will and Mill had made up tickets for this new crowd, squares with aluminum wrap on one side—very fancy—and ticket information on the other. The people were streaming toward the garage; that word—"streaming"—was an apt one for the tickets catching the late sun's rays looked like a silver river flashing by.

There were programs being sold at the door by Reba Sikes.

Will had reserved three rows of seats up front for those who had contributed to the Paradise Theater Fund ("in support of artistic culture in Spirit Lake"). I'd never even heard of this fund; I only knew it now because it was printed on the programs dropped on each of these seats.

Where had they come up with this theater fund stuff? The PTF, they called it, as if it had been around forever.

"When we were making the tickets. We can't be expected to foot all of the bills, can we?"

"Yes, because there *aren't* any bills. You two don't spend *money* on these plays."

We were up on the stage, where Will was fiddling with the rope on the swing. "That's what's holding us back. If we want to establish a repertory theater—"

"A *what*?"

He sighed his my-dumb-sister sigh. "One where the plays alternate; you know, you do one play for a couple of days or a whole week and then do another. Like that. The cast is always the same, see, so we don't have to audition other actors—"

"There *are* no other actors! *We're* not even actors!"

Will paid no attention to this criticism. Mill had come up onstage to talk about the opening number. Mill said, "You better go get your costume on."

I shrugged and it was then I noticed June/Medea. She was strutting around the stage, wearing the chicken-feather cape, and underneath it . . . I froze. "What's she got on underneath?"

"Underwear," said Mill with a snicker.

"It's Ree-Jane's *white gown*! The one I just got cleaned and mended. June's wearing that dress again! Where did you get it?"

"Delbert. He brought it to deliver. We happened to be out there, so we just took it off him."

I wanted to tear my hair out and grind my teeth down to my jawbone. "I'll kill him! I'll *kill* him! I told him to bring it around back here because I didn't want Ree-Jane or anyone to see it!"

"That was a good idea," said Will.

I tried getting right up in his face. "It's not much of an idea if June's going to strut around wearing it! Do you have any idea how big a lecture I got because we used that dress?"

"Well, June insisted."

"She wouldn't have if you hadn't hijacked it and brought it in here. I had to pay a lot to get it cleaned after you let Paul dress up in it."

"So we'll pay for it this time—I mean if it gets stained or anything."

Mill was tired of this argument. He said, "You want to run through your song?"

I just looked at him in an empty way. My mind was paralyzed by my discovery. "No."

Mill said, "I made these for you to hold up."

"Hold up—*what*?"

"Cue cards. To go along with the song. Along with not knowing how to say 'machina.' See, this has *mack-in-tosh* and then *mach-ine,* which is the wrong way to say it."

The "cards" were nearly poster size and written in huge letters.

"For the sing-along, like we discussed. You hold this up when you come to deus ex machina."

Now I leaned into his face: "This performance is starting in half an hour!" I looked at my watch. "You're crazy!"

"You don't have to practice holding them up. You just do it! And the sing-along is just getting them to—" Will paused and, thinking himself really funny, said, "—sing along." Then he and Mill both cracked up.

"We'll leave them up against the tree and you can just pick 'em up. Cinch."

Mill said, "We also got a couple more musicians. Betty Mooma plays the flute and Chuck's brother Joe plays trumpet. We don't have much leeway on numbers because they only know a few songs, but we're going to audition others."

"Wait. Audition for *what*?"

"*Medea: The Musical.* We're running through July."

My mouth really did drop open. I thought my jaw was going to land on the floor.

Will stood there warming his hands in his armpits, seeing no problem with anything. Maybe he should have ruled the world.

"You mean we've got to do *Medea* every week? Are you *kidding*?"

"We're writing another one to be run in repertory."

He really liked that word. "You mean now I've got to learn two plays?"

Will just chomped on his gum. "This isn't all about you, you know. As you seem to think." *Chomp, chomp.* "It's the demand. I had to turn away all kinds of people like you wouldn't believe. Listen, that summer playhouse over on Lake Noir is going to get a lot of competition. We'll be doing two plays, maybe even three, in repertory." He started to walk off, then turned. "Oh, yeah, I nearly forgot. You've got to be one of the kids tonight. Paul has stage fright."

"Stage fright? *Him?* I'd just like to see him with 'stage fright'!"

"Yeah, well, we kind of had to beat up on him a little for taking his clothes off and running across the stage."

They both snickered.

"He's already up in the rafters." Will called up.

"Hello, missus," cried Paul.

"That doesn't sound like stage fright to me."

Will walked away, popping up the fingers of one hand, meaning "five minutes."

Talk about stage fright! What was I supposed to do?

I went back into the dressing room—a couple of sheets hung over some poles—and got into my midnight blue gown. I looked at myself in the mirror and thanked the Waitresses. I can't remember ever seeing one of them at a time; there were three of them or none of them. They had appeared as one and disappeared. How could they have left, all together, so seamlessly? As if they had been erased. Though it had been only six years ago, it felt like a lifetime. Maybe it was.

They had dressed me up on the nights of the dances, and I was even smaller then. I think they must have pinned up the hem of this gown so I could dance without falling down. I would have to hold it up on the stage—oh, I still had these stupid shoes on, these light blue Keds. Well, the audience wouldn't notice them—

"Emma!" A loud whisper came from Will, who was motioning me to the other side of the stage as the music started.

June was tugging her cape closed. It hid Ree-Jane's gown pretty well, but only if she held it.

The music sounded like "The Marine's Hymn."

"What are they playing that for?"

"I told you, Betty and Joe only know a couple pieces. Now, all you have to do is walk on in the second scene or the one after Jason leaves. We added a song here—"

"What? You mean I've got another—"

"No, not *you*. Medea and Jason sing it. I'll hold out my hand toward you and you just come on. Chuck, too, but he'll be second because of the lights."

"The Marine's Hymn" was still going, but now only on trumpet and flute. The piano was weaving in "The Stars and Stripes Forever," and in a really jazzy way. I was stunned that the two played together made it sound as if some big band was out there. I had to admit Mill might be crazy but he knew music; he knew what would work.

When the piano stopped with a flourish, there was a lot of applause, even whistles and catcalls. It sounded like hundreds of people were out there.

Will pulled the curtain apart and there was even more frantic applause. Boy, they must have high expectations. I wondered if Sam and Maud and Dwayne were applauding. I hoped so.

Blue and green lights swept the stage as June kind of floated out as if she'd mastered Ree-Jane's model walk. She started talking about Jason "eyeing other women" and how miserable it was and that the Golden Fleece—

("Golden Fleece—*ha!*" she exclaimed.)

—was only an excuse to allow him to run off and meet his latest floozie.

Well, June was really (as Will had described it) "chewing the scenery," nothing but the white pillars and broken rocks, a couple of chairs and Chuck's model train. Chuck was still dancing the lights around, this time the pink and yellow. I had to admit the lighting was really effective. I was getting almost a good feeling about this production.

Will said, "I better get out there and shut her up." He was wearing a white sheet plastered to him with some narrow gold rope that looked like the belt of my mother's velvet robe. More applause for Jason.

"Medea!"

"You!" She flounced away.

"It's time for me to go in search of the Golden Fleece!" Then Will took a cigar from under the sheet and lit it up.

I was aghast.

The audience loved it. They loved everything. I think I could have gone out there and slapped them in the face with a wet fish and they'd still applaud.

Will could smoke a cigar in that Groucho Marx way of tapping ash and dancing his eyebrows. He was really funny.

"Don't think you can give me that old Fleece excuse! I know what you're up to!"

This banter went back and forth for what seemed like forever until there was a piano flourish and they moved to the front of the stage. Mill was playing what sounded like "Oh, How I Hate to Get Up in the Morning."

"We were a hap-pi-ly married coup-le."

They were doing the kicks like we did for "I'm Medea," first to one side, then to the other, arms around each other's waists, the audience laughing and clapping to beat the band, when suddenly there came a scream—not back in the wings, but from out there in the audience.

"That's my sweet sixteen gown again!"

I peeked out around the edge of the curtain and there was Ree-Jane yelling and pointing her bony finger at the stage like a deus ex machina. I certainly have to give Medea and Jason credit, for they didn't even interrupt their kicks. And the audience laughed and applauded, clearly thinking the outburst was just a stunt and all part of the play itself.

Ree-Jane sat down. Or, rather, Mrs. Davidow, who'd been sitting beside her, yanked her down.

Will and June continued their song. (Will can tune out anything he wants to.)

It was Medea's line:

"*Some day I'm going to mur-der the chil-dren,*
    Some day you're going to find them dead . . ."

It was time I figured for me to make an appearance and I adjusted my blue gown and fluffed my hair. Jason looked toward me and said, "Ah! Betsy!"

And I sauntered on to more applause, when I hadn't done anything at all. Then Chuck, hurrying from his lighting duties, came on when Will called, "And my good son, Jason Junior!"

More applause. Chuck said hi and immediately went to his model train, while I just stood there, wondering what to do.

Jason, leaving, announced, "I shall return!"

"I won't hold my breath," said Medea as the curtain closed on Act I to thunderous applause.

Act II began with me, deus ex machina, coming slowly down in the swing, bolts of cardboard lightning tossed down by Paul. I was having a hard time keeping from ducking and throwing up my arms, but I managed. I landed with a jolt. Mill started in with a jumpy little introduction to the mackintosh song, and I, with the posters at my side, sang: "I don't give a toss for a mackintosh, 'cause I'm a deus ex machina!" Then I held up the poster and yelled for everybody to sing! They all did. They seemed to love being included.

"*I'm not a machine,*
    That's not what I mean . . ."

Walter was still walking the aisle selling Angel Pie and Reba was pouring coffee into Styrofoam cups. No one seemed to think this a distraction, for some peculiar reason. The pie and coffee were going like, well, like my mother's Angel Pie usually goes. I guess it was pretty hard to get distracted from *Medea: The Musical*.

Chuck had set up the Ouija board on a broken pillar serving as a table. Betsy and Jason Junior sat down on a couple of big rocks.

My only line here was "Oh, great Ouija, father Jason has gone in search of the Golden Fleece. What is in store for us his children?"

There was a silence while the little cardboard triangle moved around—I mean, while we moved it—until the Ouija spelled out its message: D-E-A-T-H.

"Death!" we both exclaimed together. We did this without even having rehearsed it. I don't know, it all seemed so natural somehow. Which probably wasn't good.

Now it was time for Medea to come onstage with her knife, which she did, holding it up to her chest, probably in an attempt to show she cared, that the knife was where her heart was. Since Chuck had to stay there and nearly get murdered, it was really pretty eerie.

I was so scared—I mean, Betsy was—I rushed away. I had to rush because I had to go up and come down again. Will hauled away at the rope and I creaked up to the rafters.

"Hello, missus!" cried Paul, reaching his hand in a brown paper bag.

"Don't you dare throw that flour!"

Then I heard Chuck call out, "But Mother, dear, why do you carry that knife?"

As I came down on the swing with a thud, I could see Medea creeping toward him. I nearly fell off the swing as she raised the knife.

"Mother! Do not do this!" cried Chuck.

Swiftly I walked to the other part of the stage and held up my hand. "No! You cannot be so vile as to murder your son, Medea!"

Was June supposed to give me that dumb look?

"I don't see why not," she said a bit mildly, I thought.

"Because it is a most ghastly deed!"

She shrugged. "I've seen worse."

"Where did *that* line come from?

"No! No! It is a most ghastly deed! The ghastliest!"

Mill was settling in and attacking the piano again, whipping up a storm of introductory chords, then settling into what I guessed was our theme song, and we all came center stage, including the Hummers, who entered and stood behind us. The Hummers (I suspected) must have complained about their insignificant role in the drama for during "Oh, Medea," they started kicking along and adding to this move tossing their arms up in the air and waving their hands like members of the gospel mission. I could see this because the Hummers also had moved up from the rear to stand beside us. Bessie was right beside me and I think she was moving more than any of them, throwing up her arms, shaking her hands. The Wallses must have been really happy with this performance.

As we went on singing and kicking it occurred to me that there was no way of ruining our play. Anything that was wrong or bad with our performance was taken as something that *should* be wrong or bad. I had to give Will and Mill credit.

After we took our "Encore!" once again, Will came on with his *"Quo Vadis?"* quote and again the audience loved it. I wondered if the biggest round of applause came from Miss Flyte's friend from Galista College, though what someone like that could find in this "interpretation" (as Will put it) to applaud I couldn't understand.

The duet was coming up, so we all left the stage—all except for the Hummers, who stepped forward. They started singing—if you could call it that—and I wondered if Will wrote this into the play for the sake of Bessie's parents.

> *"Oh what delight*
> *To be given the right*
> *To be carefree and gay once again."*

Hummmm Hummm

Then they stepped back and Medea and Jason stepped forward to sing their duet with the Hummers accompanying them, this time staying in the background, for I noticed Will leaned down and ran his finger across his neck, razorlike, smiling all the while. Will (this I knew) was not going to be what I think they call "upstaged" by anyone. He was the biggest ham I'd ever seen.

He and June sang, June with her off-key raspy voice, which, like everything else in the play, was taken by the audience as intentional.

"In some se-clu-uu-ded arboretum"

Hummm Hummm

"That overlooks the Colosseum"

Hummmmmmm . . .

"As we enjoy a cigarette,"

Like magic, Will produced two cigarettes and handed one to June, who put it in the corner of her mouth but kept on singing.

> *"Two hands are sure to slyly meet beneath*
>   *The serviette with cock-tails for twoooo."*

HumHumHumHuuuummm

Here, to my surprise (for it hadn't been in the script before), two of the Hummers stepped forward with small trays, each holding a martini glass, served on one side to Will and the other side to June. I thought if this continued they'd have Lola Davidow up here, humming.

Will soloed:

> *"My head may go reeling"*

Hum hum

> *"After Creon hits the ceiling"*

Hum hum

> *"But we still will carry on,*
>   *Though the kids are dead and gone,*
>   *As long as this old world keeps wheeling."*

HumHumHumHuuuuum

"I'll find the Fleece with my last breath"

HumHumHumHum

"Well, hurry up, I'm bored to death."
(June smoked and sipped.)

HumHumHumHum . . .

Well, when they came to the end of "Cocktails for Two," with the "cocktails" (*kick*) "cocktails" (*kick*) "cocktails" (*kick kick*) all musical hell broke loose. Mill and Chuck and Joe came on with drumsticks on a washboard, cowbells and a car horn while Mill made goat noises and the trumpet just soared into "The Marine's Hymn." There was wild applause; the audience itself could have started a Spike Jones band just on the strength of this alone. It was rowdy. It was like some spring had been released and they could hardly control themselves. So the finale, when it finally came, was not a finale, it was more a free-for-all.

We took our bows, all holding hands, except the Hummers got confused about where they were supposed to stand and what they were supposed to do, so they just *hummed*.

46

I have never been one to rest, as they say, on my laurels. I would just have to congratulate myself as I was busy with something else.

So the next day, all morning, I worked on my installment of the Spirit Lake tragedy. The trouble was that now I mixed it up with the Belle Ruin tragedy. But then I thought, Why not make the Belle Ruin part of the first story?

There were certainly connections, the main one being that Morris Slade was Rose Devereau's half brother. That he looked just like her I would save for later. Another thing they had in common was that the Devereau sisters probably had attended dances at the Belle Ruin. At least Iris might have, and possibly Rose; I couldn't imagine the sour-mouthed Isabel doing it. I could just make the claim that "strong evidence suggests" they had. There wasn't any strong evidence.

I put my head in my hands. I couldn't think. Even though I was merely describing what had actually happened in the Spirit Lake part, I still couldn't get it down on paper. Maybe I really did have writer's block. (I wondered if there was "cook's block." I sincerely hoped not.) I thought about going down to the kitchen for a helping of bread pudding with vanilla sauce or maybe a rum roll. My mother made the best rum rolls in the whole world. Or maybe I should go up to the fourth floor and ask Aurora if she'd ever seen the Devereau sisters at the Belle Ruin balls.

I made a few spitballs from a strip of the blank paper and threw them at the hotel cat, who had joined me in the Pink Elephant and was curled up on top of the table. After a while I stopped that and wondered where Ben Queen was. I took up my freshly sharpened pencil and wrote across the top of the torn page:

WHERE HAS BEN QUEEN GONE?

I thought about this for a while and thought that I didn't have any more of an answer to this than I had a week ago.

I slumped in my chair and stared at myself in a broken piece of mirror I had propped against the sleeping cat, who never seemed to mind being used. Maybe I should change my hairstyle. What style? All it was was just the two sides pulled back behind my ears with four barrettes in it. I took them out and let my hair fall over one side of my face. I did not look any more like Veronica Lake than Ree-Jane did. I put the barrettes back in.

I wrote:

The Belle Ruin Tragedy

This could be just as good a story as the Spirit Lake one, except I didn't star in it as much, so I had to consider that. So I went back to my job du jour (as my mother was fond of saying) and wrote another line in the Devereaus-and-me story.

If you've ever been walked at night through a wood, and at gunpoint, you'll know how I felt.

But wait. How many people have walked at gunpoint in or out of the woods or anywhere else?

I erased "at gunpoint," but then the words that were left didn't say much. I put my head in my hands again. What about putting an owl in the story? And scrabblings under stones, and branches dropping? None of this had happened, of course, but it would add some details. Still, it wasn't just details I should be putting in, but the kinds of details. There was my kind and there was William Faulkner's kind. His were really good: "bugswirled" and "stumppocked."

Couldn't I tell how it had felt? But wasn't that the whole problem? That I couldn't describe how it made me feel. I looked at my sentence again, and thought for a moment, then I wrote,

The barneyed owl whoooing in the blinded dark.

I could always attach it to something later. I read it out loud. It had a definite Faulkner-like ring to it. I went on:

And then crashcold—

But crashcold what? What was I describing? Whatever could be described that way. The moon? No. It could look cold but how could it "crash"? Maybe a branch falling, an icy, snow-logged branch. But this was summer. Could a branch just be cold? Why not? Having to stick out there in all the rain and fog and so forth?

Then the crashcold branch splintered the air—

The trouble here was I couldn't figure out what the branch was about. What its point was. Noise? That was okay, but I was really going for silence in this walk.

And then I thought maybe I was supposed to get my knock-kneed fear into my surroundings. Maybe I should make the trees and stones seem afraid. My "knock-kneed fear." Well, there was a good word already made up. I erased the hyphen and made it one word, "knockkneed," so it sounded more like William Faulkner.

I was beginning to wonder if all this had really happened or if it was only just happening now. Did things happen only in writing about them?

I wondered how William Faulkner would have answered that question. I wondered how he'd written all those books.

I was so weary thinking of words that when lunchtime came it hardly registered that lunch today was again ham pinwheels with cheese sauce. I soon rallied.

It is all but impossible to convey the deliciousness of this dish. Begin with the ham: this is real ham, not Spam or anything like that; it is ground from the ham left over from last night's dinner of ham with raisin sauce. Then the pastry: this is rolled out very thin and then brushed with olive oil and then covered with the ground ham. It is then rolled up and cut into circular slices (from which it gets its name of "pinwheel"). Last, the cheese sauce: this is real melted cheddar, a bit of mustard added and a little milk. Cooked, of course, in a double boiler with added cream, which helps it along to its baby-skin smoothness. The ham is spicy, the pastry flaky, the cheese sauce satin. To tell the taste of this dish would require the words of William Faulkner. My mind was too tired to make up my own.

And this: Miss Bertha does not like this lunch. If there was no other reason to hate Miss Bertha—the hearing aid, the meanness, the hump—that she turns up her nose at ham pinwheels would do it.

I said to my mother, who was setting the plates on my tray, "Why waste the ham pinwheel on her?"

From the shadows around the dishwasher came Walter's voice, "If she don't eat it, I will." He was wiping a big platter.

"No, Walter. You should have a fresh one."

"Ain't no matter," he said.

But I was sure he appreciated my offer. Since it wouldn't mean me giving up my own, it was easy to be generous.

I whipped the tray into the dining room and served and stood there happily so lost in thought of my own lunch that I barely heard Miss Bertha bang her cane on the floor and yell that "Miss Jen" knew better than to give her this and she wanted an omelet.

I just smiled and sauntered away.

While I ate my ham pinwheel, I was led to think about Wanda Wayans and her doughnuts with sprinkles on them. Wanda was trying to lose weight and said she felt "real guilty" about eating a doughnut, but she just couldn't stand not. "I guess it's like a food tantrum," she said. I liked that. I tried to imagine a future completely without ham pinwheels and cheese sauce. I kind of shivered. Now, this is probably why diets don't work for most people. (I was glad I was too young to have to go on one.) They had food tantrums. It becomes not just this doughnut today, with its chocolate sprinkles, but all doughnuts and all sprinkles forever. It was like a person was being condemned to a life without any doughnuts with sprinkles, ever. This was so unthinkable that all you could do was to scream.

After my ham pinwheel (and a half) I felt so restored from my morning's word trials I decided to go to the Belle Ruin. I set out with my map and photos, hoping I would find something, some evidence that would tell me my solution to the fate of Baby Fay was correct.

I knew it was unreasonable to expect to find a clue after twenty-two years, and I had looked before—hadn't I?—and found nothing. But reason was not always right, and how would I know but there might be something far-flung from the hotel itself, like a doll or a little shoe that landed outside of the fire ringing the structure. I had before been thinking of something that would say she had been there and had been taken down the ladder; now I was looking for something that showed she had not. It is much harder looking for evidence of an event that never happened.

But my purpose wasn't only to find proof of what I thought. I liked going to the Belle Ruin for its own sake. I thought it was awful that such a gorgeous place had burned down, and that no one came here anymore. I think I wanted to keep it company. It was another of those places that drew me, just as the old Devereau house and its dark wall-paper, or Crystal Spring with its cold tin cup for drinking, or that line of dark trees way out from the Cold Flat Junction station whose presence urged me to stop and look.

I was like a fern, pressing my face against these places and leaving the dimmest imprint. Not deep enough to prove I'd been there, but enough to raise the question: "Could it be that Emma came this way?"

The walk seemed shorter now that I'd done it several times, and it also seemed familiar, like one of those places you feel right in being there, as if you were a little puzzle piece that snapped right in. As if your footsteps had been there before you, and you could fit your feet into their faint outlines. You belonged, I guess is what people say. I belonged.

The day was cold and glassy and everything in it clear-cut. Most of us most of the time had to live in fuzz, not being sure where we were or what we were looking at. Dwayne and I had driven up from the highway to the front of the hotel, or what once was the front. Today I had come to it from another direction and therefore ended up in the back where the ballroom had been.

I went into the ballroom where another hunk of rafter had given way and fallen on the charred floorboards. I kept away from that part, the end where the band would have been playing dance music; even so, most people would think I was endangering life and limb.

By my phonograph was the dance book and I studied the waltz steps that looked easy enough in the book but weren't all that easy to do. I slid my right foot on the count of one, then brought my other foot up on two and then a third step. It felt clumsy; I didn't think I was doing it right. Music would probably help. At least the space wouldn't be empty. I wound up the record player and put a Nelson Eddy–Jeanette MacDonald on: "Sweethearts."

I slid around for a little while, wondering if it was easier if you had a partner. Like in my days at the Rony Plaza. When my waltzing feet took me past the glassless window where I could see the little pond, I'd look, not wanting to miss the two deer that drank from it, wondering if it was always the same two deer. I suppose I would not know the difference. When the record came to an end and the arm scraped along it, I went to change the record. I passed the window and my eye registered movement out there. I stopped and looked, but it wasn't the deer, it was the Girl, wearing the same milk blue dress she'd worn the first time I'd seen her.

I know what it means to stand transfixed and I stood there, afraid to look away for fear she'd vanish. She was kneeling on the ground by the pool, her hands cupped, drinking.

Why didn't I call? Why didn't I run to the pool? I thought, She has so much to tell you. Then I realized she had nothing to tell. She could talk about her past only from whatever time she could remember.

This was the sixth time I'd seen her: two times on the railroad platform in Cold Flat Junction; once in La Porte; twice more at the Devereau house. Now at the Belle Ruin.

I knew now, probably should have known before, what she was doing in these parts, especially here: looking for a way back. It was from here she'd disappeared, from the Belle Ruin.

How had she found out? Was it, as I'd imagined before, from seeing an old newspaper clipping that the people who had found her had foolishly kept? You'd think they'd hide it away in some locked desk or drawer like a gun that must be kept from children. Yes, you'd think they'd keep it out of sight. Or had she come across some old friend who'd heard about the Belle Ruin and how a baby had been stolen from there "with pale hair and quiet eyes, gray eyes like yours."

If where we are is home and always has been, or if unknown to us we have another, home.

The next time I looked up she was gone.

47

It amazes me sometimes how a crucial piece of information can come to you from the least likely source, in this case from Miss Isabel Barnett.

The next morning I was in McCrory's Five-and-Dime looking for buttons my mother was going to sew onto one of Ree-Jane's hand-me-downs to make it look like something new I was getting. It was a Heather Gay Struther last year's dress and it would take more than new buttons to make it one I'd want to wear. A stick of dynamite in each big pocket lit, and quickly handed back to Ree-Jane, now *that* would be a dress.

Smiling as I watched Ree-Jane blown to bits in my mind, I sifted through some more buttons. There were some for children, like the ones with six different birds painted on them and another with Disney characters. Naturally, these would be unsuitable (one of my mother's favorite words) for me. They were kind of cute, though, for a younger child.

I was comparing those two button cards when I looked across the aisle at the cosmetics counter and saw Miss Isabel Barnett. She was dressed, as always, spanking clean and bright. She must have spent a lot of time washing herself and her clothes, for I have never seen Miss Isabel anything but bandbox fresh. Today it was a yellow seersucker, a crisp little white hat and a white purse. It was that purse she dropped a tube of lipstick into, after looking right and left.

I was fascinated. I had never actually seen a person shoplift before. I gave her a minute to move on to the powder and rouge so she wouldn't think I'd witnessed the lipstick theft. She was a person you just couldn't stand to embarrass. I wondered what a career in shoplifting would be like as I moved to the cosmetics counter and said, "Good morning, Miss Barnett."

She flinched just a bit. "Oh, Emma." She breathed easier. "Why, how are you?"

I said I was fine, thank you. "I like that color rouge." I nodded toward the Angel Face coral rouge in its tidy little container which she was holding.

"You don't think it's too bright for me?"

"No. Your skin is so young looking it would take any color."

That made her blush and look surprised. I guess compliments of any kind were few and far between in a kleptomaniac climate. But so far as I was concerned, Miss Isabel's flaws were out in the open, a thing you couldn't say for most of the people in town.

"Why, thank you, Emma. That's a very sweet thing to say." Doubtfully, she looked at the Tangee lipstick she had picked up. "I just don't know about this color, either."

I turned away and put the button card down to examine the lipsticks. I wondered what it would be like to apply all this makeup—eye shadow, mascara, eye liner—those looked especially hard. And hardly worth it, if Ree-Jane's face was any example. I thought of other faces, rouged and powdered, and wondered how much difference it made. If you wore it for a long enough time you'd start to believe you wouldn't look good without it. A little wave of sadness washed over me that I didn't need.

"I like those buttons," she said.

I had put down the cards to pick up the lipstick. I honestly don't know why I was carrying the buttons around. They were much too childish. "Oh. They're cute, but—"

"I expect you don't wear makeup, do you?"

"No. I'm not old enough."

She sighed and picked up a compact of pressed powder. "Sometimes I think life is all rules and regulations and nothing else. There has to be a time for everything—to eat to sleep to go to stay. At least my upbringing seemed like that. You know, when I saw the advertisement for *Medea,* I was struck by how free your lives—your brother's and yours—must be."

Free? Maybe Will's was with all of his time spent on another planet. "I have to wait on tables myself," came out grumpily.

"Yes, but what you do *with* such forced servitude—that's the important thing."

Forced servitude! My eyes flew open. How wonderful! I imagined my poor self dragging around in chains. I knew here was a phrase I'd find useful.

Miss Isabel was opening another powder compact. "I mean that your mind can be elsewhere. Not waiting on tables." She looked out over the counters. "Hamlet said something about being counted a king of infinite space even if he was in a nutshell. 'I would count myself a king of infinite space.' It's all imagination, you see, that makes you a king of infinite space."

All I wanted was to be king of the kitchen and tell Vera where to go.

"Imagination, that's the ticket." She snapped the compact closed, then picked up a box of loose powder that looked too big to go into the purse. "I can only wish I had more."

And all of a sudden I thought, was that the thing that made her steal lipsticks and jewelry and handkerchiefs? But I only knew faintly what I meant, what I was reaching for, and it vanished in the next breath.

"Well! Time for lunch. Why don't you join me, Emma?"

I of course intended to go to the Rainbow anyway, so I said, "I only have to stop in Souder's Pharmacy on the way."

It was probably useless to ask the Souders about a day twenty-two years ago. But it wouldn't hurt. There was a slim chance one or the other of them would recall the Slades stopping in the pharmacy. Morris Slade had been so handsome and popular that his marrying had been a big thing for La Porte.

Hardly anyone had prescriptions filled by old Mr. Souder anymore as his palsy was so bad people were afraid of his mixing things together. Cough syrup could be dangerous, someone had said. And shaking out pills wasn't very safe, either.

I remarked to Miss Isabel as we were walking up Alder how I always had liked Souder's Pharmacy because it was so cool and dark. She agreed it had none of the harsh brightness of Whalen's across the street with its aisles and aisles of crowded shelves as big as the A&P. I thought it would be a good place for shoplifting, but I didn't say this.

Whalen's had two druggists, the one who owned the store (who was a little too smiley for me) and a girl he was training. Before Whalen's opened, prescription drugs were pretty much filled at Souder's. Now, Whalen's was taking nearly all of the business.

So into Souder's we went, into its cavelike coolness. Miss Isabel had remarked on its old-timey feeling—the dark wood, the marble-topped counter and the tables on cast-iron legs. The two overhead fans, turning too slowly to stir up much air, but I thought their very slowness was a comfort. And it was the only place in town (she said) where she could buy Evening in Paris cologne, which was her favorite.

I said hello to Mrs. Souder, who nodded, but I couldn't tell if it was a hello nod or just her Parkinson's acting up. A lot of the time she was either nodding or shaking her head. Her hands weren't all that sure of themselves, either, but as she operated the soda-sundae end of the business, shaking hands only meant an extra dab of ice cream or splash of fizzy water and chocolate.

Miss Isabel and I went to the rear of the store where prescriptions were given to Mr. Souder and where the perfumes and toilet waters were displayed. Mr. Souder worked in the room behind a beaded curtain that I loved to hear clink when he came through it. To the left of this open door was an oblong through which he could look, though I didn't see him do it much and Mrs. Souder always took prescriptions and handed them through this little window and took the blue bottles and amber vials and handed them back to the customer. Mr. Souder would, of course, tend to all this if Mrs. Souder was out.

We stood in the rear, Miss Isabel bending down to look at the perfume display. I *ping*'d the little bell for service, which brought Mrs. Souder, nodding along.

"Prescription?" she asked.

"No, ma'am. I just wanted to ask you and Mr. Souder a question about something a long time ago. Twenty-two years ago."

It surprised me that this seemed to interest both of them. He came through the beaded curtain and I listened to the *chink chink* before continuing. "Do you remember the old Belle Rouen (trying to pronounce it correctly, but not succeeding)?"

Right away, Mr. Souder said, "Burned to the ground, didn't it?"

Mrs. Souder nodded away, so I couldn't be sure if she agreed.

"Yes, sir, it did. Do you recall the *day* it burned down?" I didn't want to put words in his mouth, or hers.

Mrs. Souder looked at Mr. Souder, wondering, I guess, if they did remember.

Mr. Souder scratched his jaw, covered with a fine white stubble. "I do." He snapped his fingers and looked at Mrs. Souder. "You recall that, don't you, Dora? Why, Morris Slade got you to make him a root-beer float!"

She looked at us with filmy eyes and then up at the ceiling fans, shaking her head as if memory of a root-beer float was uncertain.

So I prompted both of them. "Didn't Morris get something else?" *Medicine? Prescription?*

Mrs. Souder said, "Black cow's what he got."

The difference between the two drinks being nothing more than root beer and Coca-Cola, I had to give her credit. "No, no. I don't mean a fountain drink."

Mr. Souder, whose mouth had a tendency to hang open as if words might come along to fill it and save him the trouble of thought, said, "Well, I don't think they got any perfume or anything. I mean besides the prescription filled."

I could hardly keep from jumping up and down with excitement. But here came the tricky part: "Do you recall who it was for?"

"Oh, the baby, yes. Morris said the baby was colicky, I think."

"Did they have the baby with them?" I held my breath.

They nodded. "Baby carriage," said Mrs. Souder. "Said the baby had to be bundled up 'cause of this fever. Something like that."

"They didn't take the baby out and show her to you?" Breath held again.

"No, indeed. Always thought of her—that Imogen—as a jumped-up little girl, too good for us La Porte people. And then that baby goes and gets herself kidnapped!" As if this were a consequence of being jumped up.

"So you didn't actually *see* the baby?"

Miss Isabel opened her mouth to say something, but then stopped.

Mrs. Souder frowned as if none of this was her fault after all. "Like I said, that baby was all bundled up. But they sure talked and talked about her." She squinted. "Out-of-town prescription, I recall. Wasn't one of our doctors. I guess some only trust those big city specialists."

Mr. Souder scratched his bristly jaw again. "New York City, I think it was."

"Well, thanks very much. You both have really good memories."

They seemed pleased to hear it and Mr. Souder went back through the beaded curtain.

Miss Isabel put the dark blue bottle of Evening in Paris on the counter by the cash register. "I'll just have this, Mrs. Souder, if you don't mind."

Mrs. Souder rang it up and slipped it in a little bag and almost smiled when she said, "Thank you."

Then the two of us went out into a day so bright after the darkness of the pharmacy that it seemed to graze our faces.

48

I know I was much too old to skip, but I was skipping on the sidewalk away from and back to Miss Isabel Barnett, who laughed and
said, "Why, Emma! What's put you in such a good mood?"

I just smiled. I knew what the Souders had said didn't prove the
baby *wasn't* in the carriage, but it also didn't prove that she *was*, since
neither of the Souders had seen her. I was more and more sure of this:
there was no baby, whatever they'd meant to do with Baby Fay they'd
already done—most likely handed her over to some nice people who'd
always wanted a baby. Handed over the baby and a lot of money with
her. And all of the talk about the baby's illness and getting the prescription filled was simply meant to make sure people like the Souders
would say, oh, yes, they brought their baby in for medicine. The baby
was with them. It was to make sure the pharmacist remembered this.

We went into the Rainbow, Shirl obviously surprised I was with
Miss Isabel Barnett, as if she couldn't imagine me being of interest to
an adult, except for Maud. And the Sheriff, of course. I waved to Maud,
who was setting down cups of coffee for Dodge Haines and Bubby
Dubois.

We took a booth in the back, Miss Barnett's regular booth, she being the only person Shirl permitted to occupy a booth by herself. There
were signs in the booths telling customers there had to be at least two
people sitting there, otherwise to take one of the tables up front or sit

at the counter. The booth at the back was exempt from this rule, for it was the waitresses' break booth. That's the one I always sat in, though Shirl sometimes strolled back and asked me if I was looking for a waitress job, and I said, no, I already had one.

Right off, I looked at the menu, even though I knew I'd order chili. I just enjoyed reading menus; it was comforting to know there was all of this food around. It wasn't nearly as comfortable as the food around our own kitchen, but I liked to think of all of these warm things being cooked or baked up.

Wanda Wayans came to take our order. Miss Barnett asked after Wanda's family and so forth. All I ever asked after with Wanda was those new doughnuts. She liked to talk about them and so did I. Miss Barnett ordered a toasted cheese sandwich with pickles and french fries (which is what she nearly always had for lunch) and I ordered my chili.

As she unstuck the hat pin in her white straw hat, Miss Barnett said, "You know, you were asking old Mr. Souder about the Slades' baby?"

"Yes. You probably remember the baby was kidnapped. I guess you must remember that." I realized that Miss Barnett could very easily have attended those dances at the Belle Ruin, and I meant to ask her about that particular night.

"Well, I was going to say something but I didn't want to interrupt your conversation with the Souders. You see, I met up with Morris and Imogen as they came out of Souder's."

I felt something—my stomach, maybe—throw a switch. News was coming down the track that I wouldn't like, not one bit. I could feel it and all I could think of was throwing the switch back again to stop her. But of course I didn't.

"We chatted for a bit and I looked at the poor little thing, and—"

"You *saw* the baby?"

"Why, yes. The thing is, though, that they clearly didn't want me to see her, and I thought how terrible, what a terrible shame it was."

I wanted to shut my ears, put my hands over them and press hard enough to keep her voice away. But I just sat stock-still; it's the way I always do, with a blank face so no one will know how hard I'm feeling.

"That parents could be so ashamed of their child. I never could understand about that description in the paper, you know, after the poor little tyke was kidnapped, why in the description, nothing was said about the Down syndrome, which would be surely the most noticeable thing as far as the description was concerned. "Oh, thank you, Wanda." Wanda had just put down our lunches.

"What do you mean? What's this Down thing?"

"Oh, I thought you knew. Down syndrome? A lot of people call it mongoloidism, which is too bad because it's always thought of as retarded. You know, the rather flatness of the face and slanted eyes. Like that poor little Jamie Switzer."

Oh, no. Oh, *no*. If it was possible to fall through my seat, the floor the earth underneath, I would have done it. But all I did was to fall back against the booth.

I was wrong. For the *second* time, I was wrong. Two solutions, and both wrong. Twice I had thought I had discovered who the Girl was, and twice now been wrong. First thinking she was Ben Queen's granddaughter and now thinking she was Morris Slade's daughter. She was not Fay Slade. For even if I didn't know anything else, I certainly knew that her face, so much like Rose's, had never had even a passing acquaintance with anything like Jamie Switzer's.

I had thought so hard and done so much investigating and was as sure now as I had been the first time. I hung my head and was afraid I was going to cry. Miss Barnett was still talking but I wasn't listening anymore. I was too overcome; I was so overcome I hadn't even noticed the Sheriff had come in and was in the usual booth across from us. I only half heard Miss Barnett saying hello to him and he to her.

Everything had fit; each little piece of the puzzle and now here it was blown to bits. It was like watching as, piece by piece, the charred remains of the Belle Ruin fell to the ground. I had made it all up.

I sat silent for a while poking the little bite-size crackers around the top of my chili, not remembering putting them on and wondering if life from now on was to be like this, doing things without really knowing I was doing them: hearing someone talk without really hearing; seeing the Sheriff without really seeing. Everything was to be so muted, it would almost disappear like a one-note song from Patsy Cline.

See? I must have eaten a few spoonfuls of chili without noticing for a third was gone. I sighed. It was like that.

"Is something wrong, dear? You don't seem to be enjoying your chili much."

But I guess part of me was, the undead part. I saw her glance at her little circle of wristwatch. "I'm afraid I have to go; I have an appointment with Dr. Baum."

"Oh. Okay, and thanks for the lunch, Miss Barnett."

She had her hat on again and was sticking the pin in to hold it. She had such a nice, old-fashioned look. "I've enjoyed it, Emma." Then she picked up the check Wanda had left and slid across the booth and said good-bye.

With my elbow on the table and my head propped in my hand, I stirred my spoon around in what was left of my chili. I looked up to see the Sheriff standing beside the booth with his coffee and little plate of doughnuts.

"Mind?"

I just nodded my head for him to sit down and he slid across the other seat. He didn't say anything. I guess he was waiting for me to. That really irritated me. After all, I was the one who was already here. I felt anger stirring in me. My mind teetered, as if it just didn't know which direction to go.

And I felt as if I were sitting on that dock at Maud's house on Lake Noir, with the black water lapping my feet in the wake of a speedboat gone by. The Sheriff was a tiny figure on the other side of the lake, yet no farther apart than the table between us. I did not know where to put this thought, into what box of feelings. Loneliness, fear, misery, the blue devils. So I just blinked at him.

"Want a doughnut? I don't think I can polish off another one." He shoved the small plate closer to me and said, "Wanda's favorite—rainbow crinkles."

I almost smiled before I caught my mouth turning up. Most people wouldn't even have heard what Wanda called them, or else they'd just correct her. "Thank you. I might be able to eat half of it." I broke the doughnut in two; one half was a little bigger than the other. After a brief argument with myself about good manners and selfishness, I picked up the smaller half and pushed the plate to the middle of the table.

The Sheriff said, "I imagine Isabel Barnett was glad for your company. She seemed to be enjoying herself."

"She took a Tangee lipstick from the five-and-dime." I was surprised at myself. Why was I telling on her? Well, the Sheriff knew, of course, and even had this arrangement with her. "Why's she a kleptomaniac?" I came down a little hard on the "maniac" part of the word.

The Sheriff drank his coffee and shook his head. "Don't know. Maybe she feels . . . deprived or empty."

"Then I should be one. I'm pretty empty." As proof of this I picked up the other doughnut half.

"Really? Why's that?"

I didn't answer, for I didn't know what to say.

"You looked like you'd lost your best friend."

I *did*. I started picking the pink and white sprinkles off the doughnut just so I could keep my eyes down. Traitorous tears were readying themselves to spring to my eyes. Why? Why did I feel that way about someone I'd never even spoken to?

"The Belle Ruin," I said and stopped.

He nodded.

"Remember I was talking about the kidnapping?"

Again, he nodded.

I was not sure how to go on. I picked the last couple of sprinkles off the doughnut. "You remember I told you about the Girl I kept seeing?"

The Sheriff scratched beneath his uniform collar, looking as if he were concentrating on this. "You asked me if I'd seen her. You bumped into me on Second Street, said she'd come that way. And you said you'd seen her several times."

What a memory, I thought, awed. "I did. In Cold Flat Junction and out at the Devereau place, and the lake."

"Did you find out who she was?"

"No. Who I *thought* she was." I was shredding a paper napkin from the chrome napkin holder. "I thought she was the baby. Baby Fay, the one belonging to the Slades, the one that was kidnapped."

"What?" The Sheriff gave a surprised laugh.

I told him what I thought was the whole story and he was silent during the telling, as if he were carefully digesting it. When I finished, he said, "You think it was staged?"

He was more interested in the kidnapping than in who the Girl was. I could hardly blame him; he was a policeman, after all. "See, Miss

Barnett was going by Souder's when Morris and Imogen and the baby came out that day—"

"What day was this?" He took out a small notebook from his shirt pocket and was taking notes.

"Well, it was the same day the baby was kidnapped. They were in La Porte getting medicine for her. She had a cold or a fever or something. Miss Barnett saw the baby, though, and this is what's so important. She said their baby had something called Down disease."

"Down syndrome?"

I nodded. "It's like being mongoloid, or something. Like the way Jamie Switzer looks. I mean I've always felt sorry for Jamie." I'd never felt for Jamie at all except to think I was glad I didn't look like that. "So if that's true, the Girl could hardly have grown up to look like she does. She's beautiful, as pretty as Rose Devereau ever was."

He said, "I'm looking into this. I'll talk to Ulub and Ubub and this Stuck fellow. What's his first name?"

"Reuben." I told the Sheriff where he lived. "And there's Gloria Spiker—Calhoun's her married name—who lives in the blue house."

"I'll talk to her also."

"You mean you're going to *investigate*?"

"Of course. It sounds as if there never was an investigation. We won't be able to indict anybody since the only thing the Slades might have done was to impede or obstruct justice. That could be the reason there was never any ransom demand, that and the fact that the FBI wouldn't get involved. Without a ransom demand, who can really demonstrate there's been a kidnapping? It could all be some sort of domestic dispute."

"But where would you ever look for her? It could be anybody around that age. Anywhere."

"No. It would have to have happened around here. Remember, Isabel Barnett saw that baby that same evening, just hours before this alleged kidnapping."

"That still leaves hundreds of girls that age."

"Not really. Down syndrome, remember?"

I'd forgotten that.

"The Slade child can't be the girl you've kept tabs on, then."

"I haven't kept tabs on her. I wish I *could*. She just comes and goes, appears and then—disappears."

"And the last time was at the Belle Ruin."

I nodded.

"What's the closest you've been to her?"

I thought about it. "The closest was at the Cold Flat Junction train station, on the platform. At the Belle Ruin, she was by a pool of water that deer like to come and drink from. I think it's the end of a stream or a creek maybe."

"Bitterroot River. A tributary flows near to the Belle Ruin. How far away was she then?"

He seemed to be taking this seriously, I was pleased to see. His elbows on the table, he rested his chin atop his folded hands. He looked intent.

"Maybe . . . well . . . as far as the distance back to front of the Rainbow here. Why? Are you saying maybe she was too far away for me to be sure it was the same person?"

"No."

"She looks like Rose Devereau and like Morris Slade. He was Rose's half brother. I never knew before they had the same mother. Do you see?"

"That's pretty complicated."

"I guess you mean it doesn't make sense." I slumped.

"It makes perfect sense."

I was surprised. "But you still think she's just a ghost. (There it was again, "just" a ghost. As if being a ghost didn't count for anything.) Well, it's true that nobody else I know has ever seen her."

"I don't mean that, either. Maybe I'll go over there with you, Maud, too." He thought for a moment. "We could even go tonight, if you want to. When Maud's finished here."

I was so astonished by this offer I couldn't answer right away. Then I said, "Can Dwayne go, too? He can drive me in his truck; we went there before." It was almost as if I were recommending vacation spots.

"Sure." He returned his notebook to his pocket. "You could still be right about the bogus kidnapping. Nobody came up with a theory like that, not even the police. You're pretty clever."

My mind just went blank at the compliment from the Sheriff, after all of that hearsay evidence business. It was so blank I even spoke the truth. "Maybe they didn't care."

He looked at me. "Why do you, Emma?"

"I don't know."

Two truths inside of one minute.

A record.

The Sheriff had to go back to the courthouse then and so he left.

As I walked toward the door, Maud beckoned me over to the counter where she was making a chocolate soda.

"That show was absolutely wonderful, Emma. *Wonderful.* Sam thinks you all should put it on in a regular theater, like the summer theater out at the lake. *Medea* is better than anything they've ever done." She plopped another scoop of chocolate ice cream into the soda glass. "But I said, no, where it's at—I mean in that garage—that's part of it, part of the charm. All that helter-skelter running around." She smiled at the chocolate soda she was now fizzing up with a couple yanks of the handle of the seltzer machine.

"They're writing another one," I said, only half seeing her squirt a bunch of whipped cream on the top.

"Another? I can hardly wait." She forked out a maraschino cherry and dropped it on top of the whipped cream.

"Yes. It's to be a mystery." She slipped a straw in the glass. "Who's that for? That soda?"

Maud slid it across the marble counter. "You. I thought you looked a little down earlier on."

That was so nice (although I don't know I liked people reading my feelings). I thanked her, deciding I would drink a little of it just to be polite. I hardly tasted it, though, except to note the Reddi-wip wasn't quite as good as whatever Mrs. Souder used. I managed to avoid talking to Bubby Dubois, who sat on the stool next to me. Bubby. What a name for a grown man. Though he didn't act like one. He had Reddi-wip white hair that went in folds and waves, and pink skin the color of a baby's. He was always dressed in seersucker in the warmer months. Right now, he squeezed my shoulder in a way I didn't like, and I shook his hand away. Ulub and Ubub were sitting on the other side of Bubby and leaning forward to give me little waves and salutes, as if they just couldn't get enough of a saying hello. That made me smile.

I licked the long soda spoon and let it plink back in the ribbed glass. I circled round a couple of times on the stool and then jumped down. Since I was going to the *Conservative* offices, I stopped at the pastry shelves and told Wanda I'd like two doughnuts with rainbow sprinkles and she said, "Yes, ma'am," and shook a white bag out and put them in. "Them's my favorite, too." I paid for them, Shirl inspecting the coins I handed her like they might be counterfeit or maybe left over from the Civil War. I walked out.

49

As I walked toward the office of the *Conservative*, I scuffed along the pavement, kicking whatever lay in my pathway. I was exerting poor-me energy. Poor-me energy was lackadaisical and glum and didn't much care if you used it or not. It didn't bounce at all. There was still (I reminded myself) the mystery of just what had happened to Baby Fay. And what Miss Isabel Barnett had told me was even more evidence that they had gotten rid of her. Now I knew there was more of a reason (at least for them) to give the baby up: they were ashamed of her. Really ashamed. That was why the description said nothing about this Down syndrome.

I stopped to look at one of the ads for our production taped onto a street lamp. Words had been heavily inked in with what might have been Magic Marker: MORE PERFORMANCES TO BE GIVEN: WATCH THIS SPACE. Will and Mill probably paid someone to make the changes, probably to change it on all of the lampposts. They certainly wouldn't have come into La Porte to do it. They only stirred themselves from the Big Garage to go to Spirit Lake to fish off the little bridge.

"It's where I get my best ideas," Will had said.

"On Mars, that's where you get them." I said. "Or maybe from aliens. They're always good for ideas."

He had sighed and shaken his head. Hopeless. "You just don't get it, do you?"

"What? Get what? You mean like when you suspended Paul by ropes and wires over a bed of coals?"

Will rolled his eyes. "The coals weren't burning, for God's sakes. Have some fucking sense."

I didn't say anything as I wanted the sound of "fucking" to hang in the air.

I continued past Whalen's and the toothy pharmacist, the one who smiled so much you'd think his face would break.

The dark stairs up to the newspaper offices always gave off an air of menace, which I liked. It seemed in keeping with the story I was writing. Mr. Gumbrel was just coming out of his small office, the one with glass on three sides, halfway down. He liked to see what was going on.

"Emma!" he called, waving me over and into his office. "We need something on *Medea.*"

"Like what?"

Mr. Gumbrel seemed actually excited about this. "Background. Your brother, what he's been up to in his life. And that musician friend of his—Brownmill? That his name?"

My mouth did a lot of dropping open these days. "My brother? You want an article on him and Brownmiller?"

"Interesting name." Mr. Gumbrel had furrows in his brow deep as our rows of beans.

"No, it isn't. It's just a stupid name he got stuck with. There's nothing interesting about it. Or them." I hoped that closed the matter. Good grief, with all the mysteries to be solved, was I supposed to give my precious time over to thinking up stuff to say about Will and Mill?

Mr. Gumbrel's eyes narrowed. "I guess you know his mother?"

"Mrs. Conroy? I know she baits hooks for him."

Mr. Gumbrel gave a sneezy sort of laugh. "Thing is, have you ever thought how interesting your past is?"

My past, maybe. Not theirs.

Mr. Gumbrel had put a shredded-up cigar in his mouth and was kind of moving it around as if for exercise. "You could interview them, see where all this talent comes from, see what they're going to do next—"

"I know what they're doing next: a mystery. It's nothing at all like *Medea: The Musical.*"

"Now, I can see it might be hard to interview your own brother . . ."

Hard? Impossible's more like it. "They wouldn't do an interview."

"Really? Why not?" He blew out a bale of smoke. "If nothing else, it's publicity. Free publicity."

I shrugged. "Will doesn't care about publicity. Neither does Mill. Reporters from all those papers, even from Camberwell, tried to get them to answer questions after I nearly got murdered"—in case he'd forgotten the Tragedies—"but neither one of them had a thing to say to the press. ("The press"—I loved newspaper jargon.) I flapped my head in a "be gone" gesture. "They just couldn't be bothered."

"That is even more interesting! A true artistic temperament. Kind of 'theater-is-my-life' stuff. That would be your approach."

Theater being Will's life was probably true in a crazy way. If you count burying yourself in the Big Garage and making things up as you go along, and tying Paul up on the rafters—yes, I guess it was.

Mr. Gumbrel was ruffing up the little hair he had that encircled his bald head. "Okay, if you don't think you . . . okay, we can put Suzie Whitelaw on it. She could just follow Will and Brownmill around."

"Brown*miller.* Even if they didn't kill her right away, it makes no difference because they never go anyplace except sometimes to fish, or up to Greg's for Orange Crush and the pinball machine. They'd never let her follow them." It was just so laughable.

Mr. Gumbrel rocked his swivel chair, arms crossed over his chest. He nodded and *hmm*'d a few times, then started curling his tie up from the bottom. He wasn't convinced, of course, that I knew these two. Didn't I have enough trouble? For I knew they'd find a way to shake off Suzie and she'd just end up being my problem. I clapped my hand on my forehead—a dramatic gesture, yes, but I felt I had the right to a little drama.

"I thought you wanted to see me about my piece on the Spirit Lake Tragedy." But since when did what really happened ever take precedence over what didn't but we wish would have? Good grief! Was *Medea* going to overshadow everything? The search for Ben Queen?

The shooting of Fern Queen? The kidnapping of Fay Slade? The dreadful Devereau sisters? My own near murder?

And then I suddenly realized that's just what *Medea* was about: bloody murder, revenge and lunacy.

You could say it was a play for all of us.

50

This thinking about lunatics reminded me of Miss Bertha and Aurora and that I'd better be getting back to the Hotel Paradise to do the salads and Aurora's drink.

"Back to the *ho*-tel, right?" said Delbert, gunning the gas.

"No. Stop by the graveyard to see if Dracula made it back before dawn." I sat directly behind the driver's seat so he couldn't see me.

"You've always got some smart-ass answer, you know that?"

"I'm telling Axel you called me a smart-ass." How could I? I could never find him.

"Well," Delbert fumed. But at least he shut up and we got to the *ho*-tel in silence for once.

First, I made tracks to the Big Garage to warn Will and Mill about Suzie Whitelaw. As long as she didn't bother me, I didn't care if she hung around till hell froze over. I just wanted to get inside and see what they were doing.

There was so much noise I wondered how they could hear themselves think: hammering, screeching (from Paul, probably), a phonograph playing Spike Jones's "My Old Flame" to kettles and washboards and cowbells.

I knocked and it all stopped. Stopped. This never ceased to amaze me. Everything shut down and went dead silent. How did they do that? I bet Sherman would have liked to know so no one in Atlanta, including Scarlett O'Hara, would ever have heard the army coming.

The door opened the usual crack and Will said, "What?"

"It's me. I'm part of the whole repertory theater, if you recall. And I've got something to tell you."

"Okay. Tell me."

"Well, let me in and I will."

Will heaved a big sigh and then unlatched the door.

Mill was hammering on one end of a structure they'd built that I had to admit looked exactly like the inside of an airplane with its side toward the audience removed. There were pairs of what looked like old theater seats which were meant for passengers.

"Where'd you get those?"

"From the Orion. Mr. McComas was going to junk them."

There was somebody wearing a brown leather helmet sitting in the cockpit in front of the controls. The helmet hid most of his (or her) face. I walked over there.

"Hello, missus!" hollered Paul.

"What's Paul doing piloting your plane? Are you crazy?"

Will gave me a withering look. "The plane doesn't take off, for God's sakes!"

"With Paul at the controls, how can you be sure?"

"So what do you want to tell us? We're busy."

Mill had moved from hammering the plane over to the piano, where he was trilling keys and mouthing some song.

"Is this going to be another musical? *Murder in the Sky: The Musical?*"

"We haven't decided yet. So go on, tell me whatever it is."

"Mr. Gumbrel's siccing Suzie Whitelaw on you, you know, his reporter? One of them. Mr. Gumbrel seems to think you're worth interviewing, the both of you."

"Well, we're not."

"Aren't you even interested why?"

He was rummaging in a pile of wood and metal pieces, some of which were bands of metal in weird shapes. Where did they get this stuff? Did it grow in here? Will was flinging first one piece, then another out of the pile. "I know why. Because we've got a hit on our hands." He picked up a steering wheel that looked like it came from a kiddie cart that he then took over to the cockpit and fixed to something already there. Paul grabbed it right away.

"Anyway, I'm just telling you. I thought you'd like to be warned."

Will was studying the wheel. "Yeah."

Now Mill was singing:

> *"Today we'll fly fly fly*
> *Up in the sky sky sky."*

"Is there really a murder in this play?"

Will gave me a look. "It's called *Murder in the Sky*, isn't it?"

"Yeah, but . . . who do I play?"

He smiled. "The victim."

That figured.

It was quiet in the kitchen as it was only a little after four and not even time to start on the salads. Everything else seemed to be under control— vegetables steaming, pies baking, bread dough rising beneath its tea towel.

Despite my disappointment in hearing about the Down sickness, I was really looking forward to tonight, so I set about making Aurora's drink in a better frame of mind. I decided on something simple, as there was still a half bottle of rum behind the ice. A couple of shots of that, together with a little brandy and banana liqueur, which I'd found tucked away on a shelf in the back office behind shoe boxes full of tax stuff. Pineapple juice and half a banana went into the blender with ice and I watched it jitter away while possible names ticker-taped through my head. Rum banana pine rum apple rum ba. That was it! "Rumba!"

I got out my small tray, set the glass on it and went through the dining room, hoping I wouldn't run into Ree-Jane. Then I recalled she'd said this morning—she'd actually been up at nine o'clock—she was going with her friend Pat someplace that was supposed to impress me, but didn't since I couldn't remember what it was.

Sailing up the lobby stairs, I sang softly, "Ree-Jane will fly fly fly, up in the sky sky sky, and then she'll die die die" until I reached the fourth floor.

"You got my drink, miss?" Aurora called even before she saw me.

I turned into her room. "It's not even cocktail hour yet; I'm early; I interrupted what I was doing just to make your drink. Here—" I held it out. It was quite a lovely pale yellow. "It's called a Rumba."

Her fingers in her fingerless silvery crocheted gloves grasped the glass. "Ha ha! Oh, I could do a mean rumba in my day. Tango, too." She sipped the drink.

Tango. I made a mental note to use tangerine juice sometime, maybe with Blue Sapphire Vodka and ran the ticker tape again: Sapphire Glo tango tanga blue.

"What the devil are you doing? Your lips are moving. You're getting crazy as a coot. This is a very good drink. Ask me, you missed your calling."

"Missed it? I haven't been called to anything yet."

"Sure you have. You wait tables here at the Hotel Paradise."

"I don't think waiting tables here in Castle Coot is exactly a calling. Father Freeman has a calling; my mother has a calling; Mr. Gumbrel has a calling; even Will has a calling—"

"I'm determined to see that show. Heard it's a humdinger. Hard to believe, but everybody's talking about it."

I frowned. "How would you know? You never leave Castle Coot, either."

She adjusted her gloves, pushing the little pearl button that closed the glove around her wrist into the tiny hole that held it. "Plenty of time for another." She raised her glass, half empty, giving me time, I guess, to prepare to run downstairs again.

"I want some information first."

"Again? My Lord, girlie, it's all you ever think about! Diggin' stuff up. Don't you have enough trouble in the present you don't need to go scrabbling about in the past? What? What d'ya want to know?"

"Did you ever see the Slade baby?"

She narrowed her eyes and pushed her glasses more firmly on her nose as if that might make her hear better. "You mean Morris Slade's and that sappy Imogen Woodruff's?"

"That's right. Fay's what they called her, at least I'm pretty sure."

"I never recalled her name, but, yes, I did see her. Why?"

"Did she look like she had Down disease?"

Now, Aurora actually cupped her ear, not because of any deafness but because she thought the question was crazy. "What in hell are you talking about? Down what?"

"It's a person who's kind of mongolian—"

Now it was clear. "Oh, you mean mongolian idiots."

"They're not idiots," I insisted, forgetting my own earlier attempt to remember that word.

"Retards, then."

I rolled my eyes and shook my head. "The point here is was the Slade baby one of them?"

Aurora actually seemed to be thinking. She turned her head to gaze out the window, which was open and had been screened. There was a nice breeze carrying a scent I didn't recognize, nor could I imagine its source, for the garden was four floors down. But I closed my eyes and tried to hold on to it, one of those happenings you want to stick in your memory.

She turned, "I don't recall and that's the truth." She jiggled her glass and sucked out a piece of ice.

"But wouldn't there have been talk?" I hadn't thought of talk in a general way, I mean beyond specific people like Aurora and Miss Flagler and so forth. There would surely have been others in La Porte and around, recalling how, twenty-two years ago, a baby had been kidnapped. They would certainly then have tried to fix in their minds what the baby looked like. The trouble was how much one baby looked like another.

"Where'd you get this foolish idea anyway?"

"From Miss Isabel Barnett."

Aurora looked pained. "That woman? Don't be daft. She's the biggest liar in three counties and a kleptomaniac to boot."

Now I took a step back, breathless. Was Aurora right or was she just contradicting Miss Barnett's account for the sake of contradiction? Weren't things hard enough on my brain that now I'd have to consider this: that Miss Barnett was just saying what she did about Down syndrome to be more interesting or something like that? Maybe that was the reason she was a kleptomaniac—to be more interesting. Though I certainly wondered about any old person with all her money lying just for the attention. But if Aurora knew Miss Barnett was a kleptomaniac, then why not that Miss Barnett was a liar? Yet I'd never heard anyone say about her that she was less than truthful. Everyone respected Miss Barnett. I reminded myself there'd just be no reason to lie about the baby. Oh, it was too, too much.

"Prob'ly," Aurora added, "it was a foundling."

"What's that?"

"Little bitty baby gets stolen and another put in her place."

This was getting so complicated, I felt as if I'd just drunk three Rumbas.

She went on, "Maybe that Morris Slade took her himself."

"I thought that, too. But why would he?"

"Why? He was a no-good, thieving, drinking, conceited boy. And a ladies' man. He had a crush on me, remember, but I was on to him, miss! Why, he'd've never stuck me in a corner and gone on about his merry ways like he did with Imogen Woodruff. Morris Slade wouldn't've wanted to be bothered with a baby, not him."

"But nobody went in or out of that room by way of that ladder. I think it was just put there to make it look like the baby was kidnapped."

"That's pretty smart." She shoved her glass toward me and this time I took it. "Better hop it; it's near dinnertime."

In the kitchen again, I asked Walter to take Aurora her drink along with her dinner. My mother asked me why I couldn't do it myself; she needed Walter to get through those dishes because we didn't have enough ruby goblets for a dinner party that night. I said because I was supposed to do the salads and all the rest, wasn't I? And she knew how Great-aunt Aurora could talk the leg off a table.

I fixed the boring little salad plates, not even bothering to arrange their contents prettily, but just tossing on the onion and pepper rings and sliced black olives all anyhow.

I did not want to wonder if Aurora was right and Isabel Barnett was just making it up about the Down disease or syndrome or whatever. How could anything be so complicated that the minute you heard what you thought was the truth, the next minute you heard it was a big lie. Back and forth, back and forth like Ping-Pong.

I didn't even add the hot pepper I'd chopped up that morning to put in Miss Bertha's salad. Things were that bad. I sighed and wondered if this dull feeling was what growing up was all about.

And age thirteen was coming. Thirteen was coming down the tracks right at me. And after thirteen came, there'd be no stopping it. There'd be high school and thinking about my hair, and makeup and boys and being catty, and college and more boys and on and on and on. But even so, it wasn't what was coming fast at me that was so upsetting, it was what was left behind. That was frightening.

Look at what growing up usually meant: becoming more mature (whatever that was) and being, I suppose, more tolerant. It might even mean understanding Ree-Jane, maybe sympathizing. Oh, Lord. That wouldn't happen until I was forty or fifty (at the earliest), but even so . . . Sprinkling hard-boiled egg on the salads I gave it a try. Me, age forty, watching Ree-Jane, still in her sweet sixteen gown moving around the dance floor like a lump and me thinking, "Ah, poor thing, dear Ree-Jane, she can't help herself . . ."

I shuddered. Could life actually come to that? Could it make such a liar of you you couldn't tell anymore what was hateful and what wasn't? In that later life I imagined Miss Bertha, who'd be around at a hundred and twenty, stubbing around, her hump bent over so far her nose was nearly touching her shoe, and me patting her and saying, "Oh, Miss Bertha, let me help you with that, let me pick it up for you, dear woman." Mrs. Fulbright would be there, too, only she would just be withering away, looking like a pile of brown leaves and nice as ever.

I squinched my eyes shut. Thirteen. Fourteen. Eighteen. Twenty-three.

I hightailed it to the icebox and grabbed out the plate with the hot pepper and nearly ran back to plant the bits through Miss Bertha's salad, carefully, evenly throughout, so she couldn't miss them. I stepped back and smiled.

That was what they called being childish. It was what I called being twelve.

The salad having had its desired effect—Miss Bertha yelling for the worst antidote, water, and me, of course, happily supplying it (wouldn't she ever *learn*?)—and dinner over, I decided to walk the boardwalk to Slaw's Garage and see if Dwayne was still working and if not, go on over to Jessie's Restaurant where he ate his dinner. I didn't even have a piece of Angel Pie for my dessert.

"You mean you're eschewing Angel Pie?" asked my mother.

I noted down that word "eschew" and said only that for some reason I just didn't feel like dessert. My mother asked me was I sick? Briefly I considered saying something wan and sickly, thinking it might get me out of waiting tables at breakfast for once, but decided not to, as it might mean I'd have to go straight to bed to be convincing.

My real reason for not having dessert was because I wanted to eat it at Jessie's and I didn't think the boardwalk walk would be enough to work off the feeling of fullness I'd have. Anyway, I could always come to the kitchen that night and cut myself a slice of pie.

I was not a person who believed life was a sacrifice.

Dwayne was sitting on his same stool and as I looked around, I saw several familiar faces, familiar from just my last visit. The same people there at the same tables or in the same booths and I thought how much like the Windy Run Diner it was. Maybe every town had a place like this.

That, I thought, was what life was meant to be: full of sameness. Even when it appeared to be doing something different—say, me in a fur-lined coat being attacked by a grizzly bear in Alaska—it really wasn't different. I could not work out why it wasn't, but it just wasn't.

Dwayne was talking to Jessie again, and that too was the same. I climbed up on the same empty stool beside him and said hello to him and to Jessie and asked, "What kind of pie do you have tonight?"

"Same as every night—"

(See?)

"—there's apple, blackberry, lemon chiffon, coconut cream—"

"Coconut cream, please."

"You want that à la mode?"

What? A cream pie à la mode? "No, I think I'll eschew that."

Dwayne made a noise into his coffee cup and I looked at him. His face was perfectly straight. "Is that pecan pie you're eating?" I asked.

"It is. Good, too."

I wanted to advise him the only person who wasn't a Georgia native but who could make pecan pie was my mother. She claimed if you make it too sweet and with too much molasses, you ruin it. But I didn't tell him, thinking that might destroy his pleasure in eating it. I would tell him later. The more you knew what was superb food and what merely pretty good, the better off you were.

"Get tired of your mom's cooking?" he said.

I looked at him. I'd heard some insane things in the past days, but that might have been the insanest. I didn't bother answering.

Jessie was back setting down my pie with a fork and then refilling Dwayne's coffee cup. "You said you'd go. If you're not too busy," I said.

He held his cup in both hands and blew gently on the surface so that the steam curled away from him. "Well, there's that Olympic ice-skating competition I'm down for, but I guess I can eschew that."

I almost said you think you're so smart, but caught myself just in time. "Thanks," I said.

"What are we looking for this time? Why's Sam DeGheyn going? Maud?"

"They're just interested in this story—"

Dwayne grinned. "Oh, it's a story all right."

I frowned. "The Sheriff's going to investigate the kidnapping—that is, if there *was* one. If that's what it was."

He turned to look at me, his cup still between his hands. "Now you think it was something else?" He shook his head. "I swear to heaven, girl, but you do have a complicated mind."

"It's not *me*. It's just that one thing comes and cancels out the thing before. Like finding out from someone today that the Slade baby had this thing called Down's disease."

"Down's?" Sadly, he shook his head. "She had it, did she? That's a shame." He frowned. "Who told you that?"

"It was Miss Barnett—Isabel Barnett in La Porte who saw her—the Slade baby—on the very day of the kidnapping. Only Aurora Paradise says she's an awful liar."

"From what I heard about Aurora Paradise, she should talk."

"So you think I should believe Miss Barnett instead of Aurora?" This was disappointing.

"I don't rightly know what you should believe. Only you know that. You're the one sifting the evidence."

Again, I frowned. "What evidence?"

He laughed. "Good question. Then I guess there goes your theory about this young lady you keep seeing, right?"

I nodded and pushed my plate away, pie half eaten. I really didn't want any more.

Dwayne picked up his check and slid mine over to him, too. "Let's go out to the truck."

"Wait! I really didn't mean for you to pay for my pie." I made a try at grabbing it back.

"Uh-huh!" He kept it out of my reach and put down money for both. "I'm glad for the company."

As we got up I said, in one of the truly heartfelt utterances of the last days, maybe of the last years, "Thank you, Dwayne."

"My pleasure."

51

Dwayne's truck bumped along the driveway, which appeared even more littered with leaves, sticks and fallen branches than before.

"William Faulkner would call this 'sticklittered,'" I said, as we pulled up where the porte cochere had been.

"Yeah, probably. Actually Billy Faulkner would've liked this place. Any writer would." We both got out. "I guess they're already here." He nodded toward the tan police car. "I mean, unless the place is being raided." He stood looking up at the darkening sky, then got his lantern out of the truck bed. He had brought another six-pack and a Coke.

I took a deep breath. Everything smelled of rain, clean and fresh. I could hear voices, and in another minute, Maud and the Sheriff came up to us.

We all said hello and it was like we were four people marooned out here and glad of one another's company. We all had something in common, only I wasn't sure what, even though I was twelve and they were grown up, or maybe that was it, that they hadn't lost being twelve the way most adults did.

The Sheriff had a flashlight stuck in his belt in back, the way criminals in movies carried guns sometimes. I had my map and postcards and walked him around to the spot where the ladder had been. Dwayne and Maud followed. I liked being in charge. It didn't happen often. It didn't happen at all, to tell the truth.

The Sheriff looked up to where the third floor might possibly have been, and to where the ladder had been propped. He *hmm'd* a few times.

"What are you looking at?" asked Maud. "What was there?"

I told her. "Dwayne thinks maybe it was more than one person and the kidnapper took the baby out the window to the ladder and instead of going down, went up."

All of us stood around looking up. I noticed that looking at empty air didn't bother them. I folded my arms across my chest and was scratching my elbows as I often did when I was thinking. Maybe we all had to be able to look at empty air this way if we would ever stand a chance of figuring things out. I was going deeper into this thought and losing my way. Half the time I didn't know what I meant.

"I don't think so."

At first, I thought the Sheriff was reading my mind. But then I realized he was speaking about Dwayne's theory.

"It's one thing to move from a ladder into a room. It's another thing, and a thing that's lots harder, to move the other way. It would be awkward if it was only you moving. But if you were carrying a baby, it'd be damned hard."

Maud said, "Not if you were in the circus doing a high-wire act, or if you were a gymnast."

The Sheriff just looked at her. "Maud, do you see any gymnasts around here? Do you see any circus performers?" He swept the area with his arms.

Dwayne laughed.

Maud said, "Well, we don't know who there was *then*."

"Did I ever tell you you'd make a lousy cop? You go for the most impossible answer right off and without thinking about the problem."

Dwayne said, "Let's have a beer before Emma drinks it all." He turned and walked off to his truck.

The two of them didn't even seem to notice, they were so wrapped up in bickering.

"Morris Slade," said the Sheriff, "never joined the circus as far as we know."

Maud was lighting a cigarette. "No, but who says it was Morris Slade? He was the father, for God's sakes."

I saw the lesson that *Medea* should have taught her hadn't been learned.

"Because I think Emma's on the right track," answered the Sheriff.

"First time for everything," said Dwayne, handing each of them a can of Rolling Rock and me a Coke.

They thanked him.

"Ha ha ha," I said, reserving my thanks.

Dwayne said, "Let's go around back. It's kind of spooky."

"Spooky? What's spooky about it?" I said as we crunched through leaves and sticks and broken glass, now and then stepping over fallen limbs. *"Dwayne?"* I hated when people didn't answer me.

"Your girl, your Fadeaway girl. Which I think is really a neat idea." He stopped and took a swig of beer. Two swigs.

"What are you talking about? Are you drunk or something?" I stopped, hands on hips. "Stop talking as if you know her." I was really irritated.

"Okay," he said, and walked on.

I chased after. Why couldn't I remember that Dwayne took things literally when it suited his purpose? If he had a purpose.

The Sheriff asked, "That the stream you were talking about?"

"Yes." I hoped *he* wasn't going to bring up the Girl, too.

"End of the Bitterroot River," he said, that was all.

Maud had walked on ahead and now stopped outside the ball-room. "Look at this," she said, shaking her head in a wondering way. "However did this escape the fire? How did it manage not to burn?"

"It's a wonder," said the Sheriff. "Even some furniture's left."

Maud was looking at a chair, smoothing her hand over its velvet surface. "Somebody had to have brought these pieces here."

I took a step back. That had never occurred to me.

"Come on, Maud. Who'd do that? A couple of velvet upholstered chairs? If it was a cot, maybe."

"I don't know, I kind of like the idea," Dwayne said.

Now they were all looking at me. "Well, it wasn't *me*, for heaven's sake! Can you see me lugging those chairs a mile through the woods?"

"Yeah, I can," said Dwayne, staring up at the sky, as if wondering if I'd stuck a few stars in place. He reached down and lit the lantern, which flared out and cast our thin shadows along the floor.

"Well, here's a phonograph. Don't tell me someone didn't bring that. Records, too." She cranked it up.

Embarrassed, I said, "It's mine."

"Good. I love this song." The needle weaved into "Moonlight Serenade."

She took a couple of turns to the music until the Sheriff set down his beer and went over and put his arm around her.

I watched them dance, jealous, I'm sure.

"I guess you don't know how," said Dwayne.

"Oh, don't be dumb. Of course, I do."

"Okay, then—" He pulled me onto the floor.

"You're too tall. How can I reach that far?" I took a few galumphing steps.

"Listen, anyone who can get through those *Medea* numbers can dance standing on her head. Just put your hand on my arm . . . there you go."

And there we went. Glenn Miller and his slide trombone went with us. The four of us went around and around and I was once again back with the Waitresses, those flighty, colorful Birds of Paradise.

It was as good as dancing at the Rony Plaza, maybe even better.

I led.